SONGBIRD
OF THE
SORROWS

ISBN: 978 1 7635393 0 3 (paperback)
ISBN: 978 1 7635393 2 7 (hardcover)
ASIN: B0D2WDL9HF (kindle)

First edition, June 2024

Cover art by Catrina Barquist
(@catrina_paints)
Map and chapter illustrations by Virginia Allyn
(@virginiaallyn)
Editing by Claire Bradshaw and Rae Moody
(@rmoodyauthor)
Proofreading by Emma Hatton, Starlit Edit Services
(@thestarlitnook)
Character art by Alexandra Filippova
(@avocatt_art)

Songbird
of the
Sorrows

Braidee Otto

To anyone trapped in a cage.
Break free, spread your wings.
May your flight be long.

TRIGGER WARNINGS

Songbird of the Sorrows is a thrilling and adventurous, romantic fantasy set in a realm on the cusp of war. Readers who may be sensitive to the following elements, please take note, and prepare to enter the Empyrieos.

Abandonment
Abduction of an adult (implied)
Battle
Blood and gore
Death and violence
Emotional abuse/manipulation
Explicit sex/sexual activities
Graphic language
Hallucinations
Mental health/PTSD
Non-consensual sex/sexual assault (non-graphic)
Poisoning
Stillbirth (mentioned on page)
Substance abuse
Torture

PRONUNCIATIONS

Some of the words and names in this book are inspired by or derived from the Greek language. They have been translated into the Roman alphabet to make them easier to read.

CHARACTERS
Aella Sotiría: ay-el-lah so-ti-ree-uh
Calliope: cal-i-oh-pee
Cynna: sin-uh
Daedalus: day-dal-us
Hestion: hest-ee-on
Kallias: kal-lee-us
Keres Selmonious: care-es sel-moh-nee-us
Lyxander: lie-zan-der (**Xan:** zan)
Melantha: mel-ann-tha
Nyssa: nis-sah
Skiepo: ski-yep-oh
Titaia: tie-tay-uh
Yiannis: yah-nis

LOCATIONS
Arkhadia: ark-hay-dee-ah
Corinth: core-inth
Cretia: cree-sha
Elotia: el-oh-sha
Empyrieos: em-peer-e-os
Eretria: air-eh-tree-uh
Maricious: mar-rish-us
Reveza: rev-ee-zuh
Sarathros: sa-ra-th-ross
Solorai Sea: sol-or-i sea

THE GODS
Anemoi: an-ee-moy
Boreas: bore-ee-us
Eurus: your-us
Notos: note-us
Zephyrus: zeph-ee-rus

RACES
Harpaurai: harp-or-i
Tycheroi: ty-share-oi
Nymphai: nim-ph-i

OTHER
Calda: call-duh
Drachma: druk-muh
Goiteia: goy-ti-yah
Goiteian: goy-ti-yen

Kalokairi: kal-oak-yeah-ree
Kylix: ky-lix
Theïkós: they-kos
Thíasos ton Theíon: thee-us-os ton the-on

GLOSSARY

THE GODS
The Anemoi: the four gods who founded the realm of the Empyrieos.
Boreas: God of the North and Winter Wind.
Eurus: God of the East and Autumn Wind.
Notos: God of the South and Summer Wind.
Zephyrus: God of the West and Spring Wind.

RACES
Harpaurai: a mythical avian race believed to have been created by Boreas.
Tycheroi: fortunate ones—the common race in the Empyrieos. They are long-lived and blessed with soul magic by the gods.
Nymphai: offspring from the union of a nymph and tycheroi. They have minor elemental affinities and physical attributes depending on their nymph heritage.
Nymph: an elemental spirit that prefers to dwell amongst nature, but can take a physical form.
Sphinx: a mythical creature with the torso of a woman, the body of a feline, and wings.

LOCATIONS

Arkhadia: the northern, winter kingdom that honors the god Boreas.

Eretria: the eastern, autumn kingdom that honors the god Eurus.

Isle of the Winds: a large isle in the center of the Sarathros where acolytes of the Anemoi live in worship. The isle is neutral ground.

The Empyrieos: the realm of the four kingdoms.

The Sorrows: the southern, summer kingdom that honors the god Notos. Sixty-four isles and islands form the Sorrows.

Reveza: the western, spring kingdom that honors the god Zephyrus.

Rithean Range: the mountain range encompassing the north-eastern border of Eretria.

The Sarathros: the passage of water dividing the Arkhadia, Eretria, and Reveza. A result of the God War.

Solorai Sea: the southern ocean.

THE AVIARY

Aviary: the secret order of the Sorrows with a trained network of spies and assassins embedded throughout the Empyrieos.

Book of Names: a book containing the identities of each member inducted into the Aviary.

Eagle: the leader of the Aviary and advisor to the Crown of the Sorrows.

Fledgling: an Aviary trainee.

Flight: a cohort of Aviary members sent on regular missions.

Owl: a knowledge-keeper and member of the advisory council within the Aviary.

Naming: an Aviary ceremony where a Fledgling receives their codename and becomes a Songbird.

Nightwing: an Aviary assassin.

Songbird: an Aviary spy.

Song: the term for information of interest or a code to identify a fellow undercover Aviary member.

OTHER:

Acolytes of the Anemoi: a religious people that live on the Isle of the Winds and devote their lives to worship of the Anemoi.

Aether: the atmosphere and force that attracts a body or object toward the ground.

Calda: a popular warm beverage of watered down wine, seasoned with herbs and spices.

Drachma: the currency used within the Empyrieos.

Goiteía: an alphabet of marks used to harness the soul magic each tycheroi is born with. The more one uses *goiteía,* the shorter their lifespan.

Goiteían: a person who sells the service of mark carving, or is in servitude to carve *goiteía* for another.

Graver: an etching tool used to carve *goiteía* marks.

Kalokairi: the summer festival celebrated once a year in the Sorrows.

Kylix: a wide and shallow drinking cup, often used for ceremonial purposes.

Somniseed: a small black seed with narcotic properties. Often used for by those with insomnia and nightmares.

Soul magic: the magic woven into the souls of tycheroi by the gods. It can only be harnessed by carving *goiteía,* but is depleted with every use.

Sýmvolo: a religious symbol of one or all of the Anemoi.

The God War: a war that occurred centuries ago. Prior to the war, the Empyrieos was one solid land mass, but the final stand between the Anemoi tore the land apart.

Theïkós: the magic that runs through the royal bloodlines, granting control over the seasons and some elements.

Thíasos ton Theíon: Troupe of the Divine—a renowned performance troupe that travels across the four kingdoms.

If you love listening to music as you read, you can find the curated *Songbird of the Sorrows* playlist by scanning the QR code below:

ONE

I WAS BORN DEAD.

Before the gods saw fit to grant me life. Before my mother surrendered her soul to save mine.

Perhaps it was my first dance with death that made me so reckless. Maybe it choreographed my perception of life itself. Propelling me toward choices others—in their sanity—would avoid.

But even *I* had to admit, this was a terrible idea. It may be the worst idea I've ever conjured up.

My arms tremble from the strain of the aether trying to force my body back toward solid ground, and my fingers ache as I dig them deeper into the crevices between the stones and mortar. A trickle of sweat trails down my spine, pooling at the base of my back, another tickling its way down my heated forehead.

I ignore it all, straining as I pull myself higher.

One hand over the other.

One steadying breath after the last.

The wind caresses my body as I cling to the side of the tower. Not a threat to make me fall, but a promise to catch me if I do. The sensation is reassuring, but as the toe of my sandal slips from my newest foothold, my heart still jumps to my throat.

I draw in a deep breath, tightening my grip on the wall. With every ounce of determination, I bring my body closer, my foot frantically seeking another dent in the surface. The rush of my blood thunders through my ears with each drawn-out moment, until my sandal notches into place. Cautiously, I lean into it, testing the crack with my weight to be sure it will hold. When it does, I breathe a sigh of relief, leaning my forehead against the sun-warmed stone.

It's not the height that scares me. It's not even the risk of falling. It's the fact I'm running out of time.

Do not be seen.

That was the order.

Scaling one of the tallest towers in the Sorrows may not be the most effective strategy—unless you know its secrets as well as I do.

Every day as the sun sets and the afternoon light hits this same wall, its white-painted bricks light up like a beacon. If you try looking at it too hard—or too long—your eyes water, and your vision will blur. It's almost impossible to watch, and even more unlikely to see a lone figure clinging to its side. The white linen clothing I wear only adds to my camouflage.

But neither of those things will prove to be helpful if

this takes too long. The sun will soon set, and with it, my opportunity.

With that sobering thought, I turn my gaze up toward the seventh-floor window a short distance above me. The arched shutters are thrown open, inviting the evening breeze inside. I fight the victorious smile attempting to break free and assess the cracks that stand out like blackened scars against stone, mapping the rest of my upward journey.

And then I move.

It takes a few moments to reach the window ledge, and the white glow of the tower fades with each fervent beat of my heart. Still, I pause, closing my eyes and listening for any sounds within.

Beautiful silence.

Exhaling, I clutch the ledge with one hand, and then the other. My stomach flutters as my feet come away from the wall, and I hoist myself up to get a visual.

The soft glow of the sun shining over my shoulder bathes the room, causing the sparse furniture within to mask the corners in darkness. Three men in the center cast the longest shadows, their focus on the door in front of them.

I recognize the man in the middle. With his close-cropped hair, lean form standing tall, and arms clasped behind his back, Master Bittern looks like a soldier standing at attention. I'm unfamiliar with the other two. But the white robes they wear tell me it's because they spend most of their time hiding away in the archives.

They have laid out an assortment of bags and satchels in front of them, with their contents spilling across the polished surface of a heavy cypress desk. A quick count of the satchels confirms I'm not the last one to arrive.

Thank Notos.

Arms trembling, I haul myself up, biting my lip to suppress a grunt of exertion as it tries to push past my throat. With a quick swipe of my sleeve, I wipe the sweat from my face and settle into position on the windowsill. One leg bent while the other dangles over the edge as I lean my back against the stone wall.

A perfect picture of nonchalance.

It's not until I untie the bag from my belt, making the items within clink together, the three men whirl around. I refrain from rolling my eyes at the astonished stares of the two in white robes, keeping them trained on the authority in the room instead.

"Nice of you to join us, Fledgling." The words rasp from his throat, sending a familiar shiver up my spine, and my eyes dip toward the jagged seam of pale skin around his neck.

Master Bittern is a legend within the order. The story of his near capture in the North is the most popular tale whispered about in the safety of the shadows. Rumors say he faced off against a group of ten Arkhadian soldiers on his own and, during the skirmish, he received his vicious neck wound. While it had failed to take his life, the struggle had damaged his vocal cords beyond repair, and when he finally made it back to the Sorrows, he took up the mantle of training new recruits instead.

The spy master strolls forward, leaning past me to gaze out the window. His brows raise as he looks down—so subtly I question whether I witnessed it—but his face remains otherwise impassive.

"One might think you have a death wish, Aella." He says my name so softly, I doubt the others hear it. Still, my eyes flick nervously toward them.

My true name is known by only a select few individuals within the Aviary. So few, in fact, I can count the number of people trusted with the truth on one hand.

Once I'm satisfied the other men hadn't overheard, I reply, "It's not the first time I've heard it, Master."

I doubt it will be the last.

Master Bittern hums under his breath, and I don't have a chance to consider the dimming glow in my chest before he swipes the pouch from my hand, upending the contents into his waiting palm.

Out falls a gold-tipped black quill, a heavy golden chain with a circular pendant, and a sharp throwing knife. Master Bittern selects the knife first, holding it up for everyone in the room to see. Somewhere behind me, a quill scratches against parchment, but I keep my eyes fixed on the man in front of me.

"One of Master Hawk's throwing blades," I say, tilting my head toward the serrated strokes carved into the steel handle.

M.H.

The weapons master values his blades above all else. I'd heard of at least three others who had attempted to steal one during their final trials over the past few years. My success today was more thanks to Master Hawk being distracted by preparations for an assignment, rather than a testament to my skill.

Master Bittern inclines his head, passing the knife to the white-robed man hovering behind him. When he turns back, he selects the pendant, letting the thick chain dangle from his fingertips.

The circular amulet twirls, catching the rays of sunlight streaming through the window and casting it around the room. It spins back toward me, revealing the four-pointed star sitting above a downward-pointing triangle etched into its surface.

"The *sýmvolo* of the High Priest of Notos," I offer, a hint of smugness staining my words.

I can't help it. The man rarely takes it off, and it had taken weeks of observation to mark the times he did so. Another week to have a perfect replica forged.

Master Bittern raises a brow at me. The movement on his usually stoic face tells me he also knows the precise moments the High Priest removes his *sýmvolo*. I wince as images of the temple's bathhouse crash through my mind—steam curling from the water, failing to conceal miles of aging flesh.

My wince morphs into a shudder.

As he did with the throwing knife, the spy master passes the pendant and chain to his offsider without a word, and then only one object remains.

The quill.

Master Bittern's expression doesn't change. But his eyes pierce mine with an intensity that makes my heart pound, and my palms grow slick with sweat. My throat dries up along with my earlier bravado, and I swallow a few times before I can coax words past my lips.

"A quill," I start, steeling myself before I go on, "from the Eagle's office."

Parchment tears, the sound stark against the now-thick silence of the room. On the edge of my vision, the other man's eyes widen, followed by an owlish blink. In the distant recesses of my mind, I note how apt the small motion is.

The three men step away from me, their heads bending close as they speak in harsh whispers. I worry my bottom lip as I watch them.

Steal three items of significance and return to the Aviary. Do not get caught. Do not be seen.

That was the order. My one ultimate test.

And I followed it perfectly…but maybe I took this too far.

Like anywhere else, there's a hierarchy in the Aviary.

Fledgling is the term used for the students of the order, those undergoing training before the Naming ceremony, where they become a Songbird and can take on missions across the Empyrieos. The Songbirds are the scouts, spies, and occasional thieves. The order embedded a network within the Sorrows and the lands beyond the Solorai Sea. They observe and listen to the composition of songs throughout the kingdoms, reporting everything they discover. Next are the Nightwings; like the Songbirds, they're also tasked with un-veiling the secrets of the Empyrieos, only they have a deadlier skill set at their disposal. The Owls are our knowledge-keep-ers, recording all the information the Aviary receives from far and wide while serving as advisors. At the pinnacle of the order, the Eagle reigns supreme.

In the wake of the God War, my great-grandfather established the Aviary. As new kingdoms rose from the chaos and destruction, he believed—for our cluster of islands to prosper—we needed to hold an advantage.

That advantage was knowledge.

The order was born from this belief; the idea taking flight from the significance of the sky's feathered creatures in those early years. They became a necessity of life in the Sorrows. From correspondence between the kingdoms, tracking incoming storms, and hunting schools of fish, they played a vital role in our people's survival. According to our beliefs, Notos, God of the South and Summer Wind, sent his winged companions as a blessing.

A gift.

Perhaps if the gods were so concerned about our survival, they wouldn't have started a fucking war.

I blink away the thought in time to spot the miniscule upward twitch at the corner of Master Bittern's lips as he turns to face me. Relief washes over me like the first cooling rain after a long dry season.

"That will be all, Fledgling," he says as he places the quill on the desk. "Your acquisitions are impressive, to say the least."

I jump from my perch, bowing my head, even as the other two men avoid looking at me. As though being associated with me could risk the Eagle's wrath.

In all fairness, it might.

With quick strides, I cross the room and reach for the door handle. But before I can take hold, it flies open.

I pull up short as a young girl darts in, her dusty cheeks

flushed and eyes sparkling with unguarded excitement. The patched linens she wears, the bare feet, and tangled hair all make her appear like nothing more than a street urchin.

But, of course, that's the point.

No one suspects a scrappy child to be eavesdropping on their conversations. And it isn't hard to teach one to act like an orphan—not when most are before the Aviary brings them into the fold.

Urchins, orphans, or those like me.

Unwanted.

My chest tightens along with my grasp on the handle of the door. I force myself to ignore the feeling, relinquishing my hold one unfurled finger at a time.

Those emotions serve no purpose to me now. They belong to the ghost of a girl I once was. The one whose father refuses to acknowledge her. The one he blames for the skeletal remnants of a soul stolen too soon. Not the woman I am today.

Those emotions only weaken me—I cannot afford to be *weak.*

I keep my body as still as possible, observing as the girl stands on the tips of her toes and Master Bittern leans in close.

As her lips part, a gust of wind rushes through the open window, carrying snatches of her whispered words to my waiting ears.

"*The Nightingale* docked…Alpha Flight has returned…"

Without a sound, I slip out the door and into the shadows.

TWO

I LEAN AGAINST THE golden eagle statue on the domed roof, the hot metal talons digging into my back. It wasn't long after my father handed me over to the order that I found my favorite perch. The zenith of the Aviary—right above the nest where the messenger birds rest.

I don't know what possessed me to climb through the arched windows and hoist myself onto the roof all those years ago, but the view stole the breath from my lungs. Maybe I took it to heart when my new masters told me my purpose—to be the eyes and ears of my kingdom. Or maybe I felt the same inspiration that compelled me to climb the tower today.

Whatever the reason, after several years of living here, it's become something of a habit.

The sun warms my face as it burns its descent over the horizon, casting a golden veil across the ocean and gilding the isles below.

The smell of brine drifts toward me on a dry summer wind, filling me with a clashing sense of both freedom and restriction.

From this height, I can see the endless stretch of ocean around the isles, reaching out in almost every direction.

Every direction, but one.

North.

Reveza and Eretria, and Arkhadia beyond them.

Those sprawling lands stretch along the horizon. A shattered coastline hinting at adventures waiting to unfold. Stories waiting to be told.

Just the sight of it—close enough to glimpse but too far to grasp—manifests a subtle ache in my chest. The sensation lingers, feeling both heavy and hollow at once.

Sighing, I drop my gaze below.

Home.

The Sorrows.

Sixty-four scattered isles that once formed the southern peninsula of the Empyrieos, cast adrift in the Solorai Sea. Of course, all four kingdoms were part of the once-great land.

But that was before the God War.

My eyes drift closed as the wind tugs at my clothing, tangling with the tresses of hair that have escaped my braid. A breeze catches in the fabric of my hooded wrap, and I wonder what it would be like to be one of the birds the Sorrows held in such high regard. What it would feel like to spread my feathered wings and bound along the air's teasing current.

Soaring and gliding.

Farther and farther away.

The sharp prick of metal at my back wrenches me back to reality.

I huff out a breath and open my eyes, pushing aside the rich brown locks of hair the wind had tugged free. I trace the passage of the Grand Canal as it carves its way through the rugged parcels of land until my gaze arrives at the harbor.

The world dims at the edges of my vision.

Vivid hues of whitewashed stone and turquoise fade to the palest shades of gray as I stare intently at the ship docked in the port. A gust of wind makes the sails billow, and I can no longer hear past the rapid beating of my heart at the sight of a nightingale emblazoned on the faded fabric.

Because I had watched the same ship set out a year ago, and I've been waiting for it to return ever since.

Foolish little butterflies take flight in my stomach, beating their wings in time with the sails fluttering in the sea breeze.

I smother them—holding my breath captive as I hunt down and extinguish each flicker from existence. Once it's done, my chest aches with the new emptiness.

Much better.

With an ease that only comes from years of practice, I slide down the slope of the roof—grabbing onto the eave before the weightlessness that comes with falling—and swing through the open window.

I land lightly on the balls of my feet, but my sudden appearance still startles the birds in the nest.

I cast an apologetic glance their way before striding toward the stairwell.

Today is about to get interesting.

News of Alpha Flight's arrival has spread like a storm surge. Although, that's not surprising when you're part of the biggest intelligence network in all the four kingdoms.

The entrance hall below is the busiest I've seen in seven years. Everyone is eager to glimpse the Aviary's elite return or hear a whisper of the latest mission across the sea.

I lean against the railing of the second-floor landing, a small smirk itching at the corner of my mouth as I watch the crowd.

Fledglings mill about; some are familiar faces from my cohort, but most are the younger initiates. They hide in shadowed alcoves or pretend to admire the portraits lining the walls with feigned fascination. At first glance, they seem casual, but every so often their eyes drift toward the arched wooden doors at the front of the hall before darting away.

Not only are their intentions obvious, but they're foolish to think Alpha Flight wouldn't plan for this kind of reception. When the most skilled members of the order are together in a unit, you can't expect them to swoop through the front door.

No doubt they've already been sequestered away in the Eagle's office to deliver their official mission report.

A brief laugh huffs out of me as I tug the hood of my wrap over my forehead and steal down the stairs, taking a sharp left at the bottom. I weave my way through the room, slipping into the hallway behind the staircase before picking up my pace.

When I push through the kitchen door at the end of the hall, a genuine smile blooms across my face as Maria looks up from the giant dishes of moussaka she's placing in the oven. My mouth waters at the sight, and I eye a bowl of apricots and grapes on the central table.

The kitchen is one of the only things I like about the Aviary. Pots and pans hang from frames suspended from the ceiling, shelves gorged with jars of herbs and spices line the walls, and an oven sits over a large fireplace burning hungrily to the left. The far wall is lined with windows, open now to let in the evening breeze, and a wooden door leading to a small herb garden and laneway. A long table swallows up the center of the kitchen, the baked wood of its surface dusted in flour where Sophie and Eva—two of the kitchen girls—are shaping dough into flatbread.

It's chaos.

Beautiful, comfortable chaos.

But my absolute favorite thing about the kitchen is Maria. Partly because she's an excellent cook, and partly because of the look she's giving me now. Hands on her round hips with a wooden spoon in her grip, wild brunette curls pinned haphazardly on the top of her head, brows almost disappearing into her hairline.

Maria's age is a mystery to me.

Every time I ask, she refuses to say, telling me to mind my own gods-damned business. But the faint lines crinkling the tawny skin around her eyes suggest she's lived for at least a few centuries, or that she's used a fair bit of *goiteía* throughout her life.

Magic isn't uncommon amongst our kind.

Tycheroi.

The *fortunate ones*.

When the Anemoi discovered the Empyrieos and created us, they gifted our people with long life, enduring bodies, and exceptional sight and hearing.

The four gods used threads of their own power in our creation, weaving it into our souls. I'm not certain if it feels the same for everyone else, but I've always imagined it like a glowing presence nestled beside my heart.

To tap into this magic, we have *goiteía*, symbols that can harness the power and turn it into something tangible. To create something permanent or imbue an object with power, the symbols can be carved or etched into a surface. For something temporary, the marks only need to be drawn.

Yet not everyone is willing to pay the price *goiteía* demands.

With each use, your soul magic is drained, and the glowing energy starts to dwindle—taking a little of your life force with it. A few days out of hundreds of years isn't significant, but extensive use of *goiteía* could cut a lifespan in half.

The other form is *theïkós*, intrinsic magic running through bloodlines, granting control over the seasons and their elements. This is the magic of nymphs, their descendants, and the gods themselves. But when the new kingdoms rose in the aftermath of the God War, the Anemoi gifted *theïkós* to the new monarchies. They bequeathed the power of the seasons to any with the right blood flowing through their veins.

Summer for the south, autumn for the east, spring for the west, and winter for the north.

The power of the wind and skies, they kept to themselves. *Their* divine domain.

As a daughter of the Sotiría bloodline—the royal line of the Sorrows—my affinity should be for the fire and heat of Summer. But the sun's flame has never sung to me. Never beckoned me with the allure of its fiery power. Never whispered its secrets in my ear.

Another condemning mark against my name in the eyes of my father.

"Well?" Maria barks out, the tone of her voice and the arch of her brows telling me it's not the first time she's spoken.

"Oh, hello, Mimi," I say, my voice sweet enough to rot my teeth. "It's nice to see you, too."

"Drop the act," she says, waving her spoon at me. "The day I fall for it is the day the Eagle asks for my hand in marriage."

"Today might be your *lucky* day," I say, sarcasm dripping from my words as I perch on a stool at the table. I sneak a glance to where the two young girls are throwing shy looks in my direction. "What do you both think?"

Sophie looks like she's doing her best to keep a straight face when Eva chimes in, "I think she's more interested in fish than poultry."

My jaw just about hits the floor as Maria's face flushes a deep ochre. "Mimi, you gods-damned minx! It's Petra, isn't it? I always thought our fish deliveries were a little too regular."

She swings her wooden spoon at me, but I lean aside in time to dodge the blow.

"I'll hear not one more word out of you, or you won't be eating my food for a week!" Maria points her weapon at the other girls, making it clear the threat is for all of us.

I arch a brow at her but can't help feeling a little impressed as Sophie and Eva hastily bend back over the dough. They're both new here—assigned to the kitchen since they were too old to become Fledglings—so they don't realize she's full of shit.

The woman *lives* to fill stomachs.

Even now, when I'm twenty-three years old, she still takes every opportunity to feed me. Still perceives me as the spectral waif who drifted in years ago, longing for more than nourishment.

Ravenous for some small kindness to sustain me.

Maria only reinforces the belief when she turns back to me, a hopeful lilt to her voice. "Hungry?"

I consider it—the tantalizing aroma from the oven wafting toward me—but shake my head. "I've got errands to take care of, and I'm covering the last few hours of an Elotia shift today."

"Again?" Maria frowns, her lips pursing with disapproval. A perfect image of what I imagine a concerned grandmother might look like. "It *is* okay to rest sometimes."

I shrug. "I was offered a new pair of sandals."

"You know you get an allowance, right?" The exasperation in her voice is as clear as the azure waters surrounding the Sorrows. "And when you become a Songbird, there's this thing called a *wage*."

"I'm saving," I say, plucking an apricot from the bowl on the table as I slide off the stool. I bite into the ripe flesh and close my eyes, savoring the sweet nectar as it bursts across my tongue.

"For what? A palace to swan around in?"

The apricot loses its sweetness, souring in my mouth. I let my arm drop, forcing myself to swallow the fruit's flesh as the juice drips onto the stone floor and bleeds into the cracks.

One might think being raised in a palace with all my needs taken care of would have made me frivolous with money, but there's nothing quite like being ousted from your life and cast into the unknown to make you cautious. I would be the first to admit I hoard *drachma* like the mythical dragons of stories. I wish I could say it's only coins, but these days my hoarding extends to almost anything.

Anything that could help buy my way out of this Anemoi-cursed life.

But Maria doesn't know my past—isn't aware of the way her words needle into my mind. So, I force a smile as I head toward the back door. "Just so you know," I say, tossing the uneaten apricot into a scrap bin. "I won't forget this conversation when you're banging down my palace doors and asking to run my kitchen."

Maria scoffs. "If it ever happens, I expect you to have someone do the cooking for *me*," she shouts at my retreating back.

"Maybe you should try being nicer to me, then."

The door swings shut behind me, cutting off her retort as I step out into the lingering light.

THREE

I TILT MY CHIN down, letting my hood cast a shadow over my face, veiling it from the swarm of people around me.

Elotia is one of the largest islands in the Sorrows. Formed in the shape of a waning crescent moon, it cradles the kingdom's busiest harbor in its embrace. Wooden docks extend into turquoise waters like the jagged teeth of a great sea beast, with merchant ships and fishermen's vessels tethered to their posts.

Amidst sun-bleached warehouses and workshops, the Seiros Lighthouse looms on the eastern end, while on the northern tip, the clustered buildings give way to a market-place.

No matter when I visit the island it's always bustling with activity.

Despite it being well into the evening, dockworkers unload luggage from vessels, fishermen haul their day's catch, craftsmen boast from shopfronts, and merchants prowl the

19

cobblestoned streets as they hawk their wares.

There's an energy to the island; a thrill lingering in the air.

I wish I could grasp it. Capture it in one of the many empty jars lining the shelves in my bedroom and never let it go. As if a simple memento sitting on my shelf could make a moment—a feeling—last forever.

The harbor disappears as I round a corner, replaced with the view of a narrow alley, the tall walls on either side blocking out what little sunlight still lingers. My feet move along the cobbled path of their own accord, leading me to a door so unobtrusive—if not for the flickering lantern hanging above, illuminating the sign nailed into its aged wood—you might miss it.

Skiepo's Gravery and other Curiosities.

I push through the creaking door, a cascade of tiny bells tinkling overhead, announcing my arrival to what I am convinced is a hoarder's den disguised as a shop.

Overflowing shelves climb the walls from floor to ceiling, the thick wood bowing from the weight of their burdens. A weary wooden counter crouches in front of a curtain sagging against the back wall. Its surface scarred and weathered, like it's been on a journey around all the four kingdoms, and finally found a quiet place to rest. Small tables laden with pots of gravers and etchers for carving *goiteía,* clay bowls piled high with sticks of chalk, and an abundance of quills crowd the rest of the space, leaving just enough room for patrons to inspect them.

With every visit, I swear the shop feels even more congested than the last. One of these days, I'm sure I'll come in and find the shelves falling from the walls.

"Just a moment!" a muffled voice calls from behind the curtain.

I weave my way around the cluttered tables, taking extra care not to bump into any of the displays. Skiepo knows the precise locations of everything amidst his organized chaos. Once, I brushed against a giant seashell, shifting it a hairsbreadth out of place, and he huffed and puffed like I had beseeched Notos to set a storm loose in his shop.

When I reach the counter, I ring the dusty bell on its surface, grinning at the disgruntled mumbling from the back room.

"I said a *moment*," Skiepo shouts, "impatient bloody—"

The words cut off as the drab curtain swings aside, revealing the man himself. He scowls, dumping a basket of what looks to be hundreds of woven bracelets on the counter.

I arch an expectant brow in return, plucking one to inspect. The coarse yarn scratches against my fingertips, and my brows inch higher at the small mark carved into the bronze disk at its center. An eight-pointed star above a small circular symbol reminiscent of a wheel.

The *goiteía* for luck.

I drop the bracelet like it's burned me, my eyes lingering on the countless others.

Strength, bravery, love, protection.

The sight of years wasted on mere luck churns my stomach. Someone selling pieces of their soul for another to wear it as a trinket on their wrist.

My disdain for the soul magic isn't common amongst other

tycheroi. For me it is deeply personal. It was how my mother had saved my life the day I was born—by carving an ancient symbol into our chests and begging the Anemoi to accept her sacrifice. The symbols faded as my mother did, and the only evidence it occurred is long since buried. But the warm glow of the magic in my chest doesn't feel like it belongs to me, and the thought of burning through something so precious makes my stomach revolt.

"Oh, wipe the tragic look off your face," Skiepo says. "People have to make money somehow, don't they?"

I fix him with a narrow-eyed stare, but he meets it with one of his own. Deep brown eyes peering at me through thin slits. "Did you make all of those?"

"Don't be daft, girl. I lack years for carving *goiteía*."

I don't doubt it.

Since I've known Skiepo, his hair has faded to the same shade as the dust coating his untouched curiosities. Wisps curl around a face etched with so many lines it resembles the intricate grain of the well-worn counter he now leans against.

It's as though he's transforming into one of his oddities. Someday, I'll visit and likely find him sitting atop a shelf, another object gathering dust in some forgotten corner.

Somewhere deep in my mind, a dissonant chord strikes at the thought, the sound resonating through me, leaving a lingering sense of unease in its wake. I rub my chest, trying to shift the sensation. "I thought we agreed you wouldn't call me *girl* anymore."

"We agreed to no such thing. I'm almost five centuries old, and you're essentially an infant," he huffs. "Besides, I've got nothing else to call you."

I let my hand fall, rolling my eyes so hard I thank the gods they don't get stuck in the back of my head. Skiepo *hates* not knowing my name. Especially since I've been coming to his shop every couple of months for the past few years. "Alright then, *old man*."

He huffs again, but the small uptick to his lips is smug this time, probably chalking this conversation up as his win. "What can I do for you? Need a new graver to carve away your problems? Perfume to make men swoon, perhaps? I got a fresh batch, straight from the flower fields of Reveza."

He wriggles his wiry brows at me, and I bite my tongue, forcing back the laugh that pushes up my throat at the absurdity of it. "When have I given the impression of wanting to make men swoon?"

Undeterred, he shrugs. "There's a time for everything. I once knew a girl—"

"I need more somniseed," I say, cutting off another enthralling tale about the *good old days*. I've endured my fair share of those, and I have places to be.

The old man's brow knits into a frown, his wizened lips wrinkling as they press together in a firm line. "What happened to the last vial? You only picked it up last month."

"A friend needed some." The lie tastes bitter on my tongue, but the words come easy. "So, if you have a spare vial, I'll take two."

Skiepo worries his bottom lip, his eyes raking over my face as if he might read the truth written there.

He won't.

With a slump of his shoulders, he shuffles behind the curtain, reappearing with two small, corked vials in his hand. The small seeds inside shimmer like tiny black pearls. The dim light in the store shifts over their surface as he places the vials on the counter.

My arm snakes out to snatch them, but his hand closes over mine. Our eyes clash, and my next breath catches in my throat at the concern I see shining in his. For a man who peddles black market items, he sure is reluctant to hand them over.

"Tell your friend to be careful," he says, relinquishing his grip. "Only one seed every three nights."

Breathe.

The reminder echoes through my mind—presses on my lungs.

With a rushed exhale, I pull two silver *drachma* from the purse tied to my waist belt. Tossing them to the counter and pocketing the vials, I offer him a smirk. "Don't worry, old man. I know the rules."

I'm just not very good at following them sometimes.

The tension in my lower back becomes too hard to ignore. I shift to ease it, being careful not to move beyond the shadows concealing me on the rooftop.

My gaze catches on a group of tycheroi waiting beside a ship at a nearby dock. Broad smiles stretch their faces and eyes sparkle as they talk amongst themselves. Hands dance with each word, orchestrating a symphony of gestures—no doubt reminiscing about a grand adventure across the seas.

Gentle waves lap against the hull of the boat, the rhythmic beat beckoning me closer.

How would it feel to abandon reason and board a ship? To sail toward the unknown, guided only by the stars and my own restless heart?

Freedom.

The word is a whisper. One echoing on the wind in this stolen moment, stirring memories not quite formed but aching to be. Yet another foolish dream.

With effort, I force my gaze back to the lantern-lit markets.

Despite the moon having crested the sky, the heat is oppressive. My skin prickles as a pearl of sweat beads down my back, trailing the curve of my spine. My lower back twitches, as though reminding me of its discomfort, and I finally give in.

Scooting to the edge of the rooftop, I dangle my legs over the shadowed alley below. The noise from the market fades into the background as I brace myself for the descent. With a surge of adrenaline coursing through my veins, I let myself fall; the wind rushing past my ears. Time slows as I twist my body and touch down with a perfect crouch, absorbing the impact with the precision of a well-trained acrobat.

I adjust the hood of my wrap as I stand and step out to the crowded street, letting myself merge with the crowd. While I drift through the press of bodies, taking in the sights and sounds of those around me, my eyes stay alert, and my ears strain to catch anything of note.

A gentle smile tugs at the corner of my mouth as a group of children rush by. Their laughter rings with a joy reserved for those unbound by constraints.

When I first joined the Aviary, being amongst the people was a mesmerizing experience. Since I spent my childhood behind the walls of the palace, the life that unfolded on the scattered isles and winding waterways captivated me.

The citizens of the Sorrows all know they have a princess—they've just never seen me. Never known I walk amongst them or watch on from the shadows. I've heard some interesting rumors about myself over the years. Some say I'm so hideous my father had no choice but to send me away, while others argue it's the opposite.

When the Eagle sunk his talons into me, the official story was I had journeyed to the Isle of the Winds to learn from the Acolytes of the Anemoi. For the past seven years, my decoy has lived there, upholding the illusion in case anyone became too intrigued.

My lip curls, resentment burning in my gut. I blow out a frustrated breath and pivot toward the docks. The last few hours were uneventful—though I'll need to let Nyssa know that not only is Lord Arsenio having an affair with a courtesan but has also gotten a local seamstress pregnant. For months now, she's been following the scandal, persuading me to place bets on when his life will come crumbling down around him.

I think talking about others' dramas gives her a sense of normalcy. I'd love to tell the asshole's wife myself—I can't stand that sort of betrayal—but if the Eagle ever caught wind of it, I would be caned or collared for bringing notice to myself.

I reach the edge of the harbor and my eyes land on a familiar ship. The crew mills about on the deck, the barnacle-dotted hull silhouetted against the moonlight and its white script cast in shadow.

The Nightingale.

The name is obvious to me, but knowing the order is necessary for the connection. Outsiders believe the Aviary building is a home and institute funded by the Crown for displaced and orphaned children. Only a select few know its true purpose.

My eyes track the darkened outlines of the crew.

Curiosity killed the canary.

The thought trickles through my mind as I hover on the edge of indecision.

"Curse it."

I head down the dock, keeping my gait casual and relaxed. As I'm standing beside the ship, I kneel and unbuckle a strap on my sandal, closing my eyes and taking a calming breath. The rest of the isle's noise fades into the background and the wind settles, allowing me to focus.

An insidious feeling rears its head, gnawing at my edges. I shouldn't be doing this—spying on order business. If I'm caught, the price might be more than I'm willing to pay.

But as quickly as the feeling comes on, it disappears, and the voices of the crew reach my ears.

"A whole bloody year," a rough voice says. "I'll be a gods-damned lucky bastard if my woman hasn't up and left me for some other prick!"

The rest of the crew chuckle and jeer at him.

"If she hasn't left you by now, she'll be packing her bags when she learns you'll be setting sail again in a week's time."

"If I have to spend days at sea with you again, you sorry bastard, I'll throw myself overboard."

"Better fill your pockets with stones now. Same crew, same trip."

"Notos' balls." The first man's curse sends up a chorus of rumbling laughter before an authoritative bark cuts off the noise.

I buckle my sandal and stand, trusting my feet to guide me home as unease curls in my gut.

It's rare for a Flight to be sent on a mission so soon after they've returned—unheard of to be sent to the same location. To do so, chanced someone remembering you.

And being remembered could be your downfall.

So, what task is crucial enough to be worth the risk?

FOUR

I GENTLY PUSH THE door of my bedroom shut, feeling a sense
of peace wash over me as it closes with a comforting *snick*.
I slump against the door, looking down with a frown at the
whisper of parchment against the rough, wooden floor.

I eye the folded note beneath my foot with no small amount
of suspicion. The dainty flower scrawled on its ivory surface
tells me it's from Nyssa, but the knowledge only makes me
more suspicious.

With a sigh, I bend down and snatch it up, walking further
into the room as I unfold the parchment.

Dear Not-quite-royal Pain in My Ass,

*I can only assume since I returned to Master Bittern
with my items before you that you were too ambitious
with your acquisitions.*

I hope you didn't come and find me right away because you are getting laid in celebration or took on another shift, and not because you were being corrected for insubordination.

I groan, running a hand down my face.

She's likely been stressed the entire evening, wondering where I've been and if I passed the last test. I should have gone to see her instead of climbing to the rooftop. I'm surprised she isn't pounding down my door right now.

If it's the former, good on you! It's about time you let your kitty out to play. If it's the latter, you need to learn how to live a little.

Regardless of which reason is true, the others are going to The Muse tonight to celebrate our last moments as Fledglings. Please come! I don't want you there, I need you there.

Faithfully,

The Best and Probably Only Friend You'll Ever Have.

"Absolutely not." I tear the top of the note off and pop it in my mouth, chewing vigorously before I swallow. Not the most pleasant experience, but the easiest way to make potentially condemning information disappear.

Nyssa is one of the few people I had chosen to trust with my story. I smooth the note out and—with one of the many pins stuck in the wall—add it to my collection before stepping back to admire it.

Over the past seven years, I have covered every wall in my room, pinning up maps, sketches, and sheets of Nyssa's discarded poetry. A growing collection that makes it feel more like a home.

My gaze drifts around the room, taking in the shelves overflowing with books and mementos, the cluttered desk under a small window, and the bed draped in linens, a single nightstand at its side. Above my bed hangs a framed map of the Empyrieos, its aged parchment studded with a collection of pearl pins, marking all the places my brother and I dreamed of seeing one day.

In a few quick strides, I'm climbing on my bed and pulling the map from the wall. My fingers tracing the jagged lines of the Sarathros—the passage of water dividing the northern kingdoms.

A scar from the God War no amount of magic in the realm could heal.

History says the war started because of greed and jealousy amongst the Anemoi—the same thing they left their first world to escape. They fought over which season would have precedence, and which bloodline should rule the land. During the ultimate battle, the gods used magic so powerful it tore the kingdom apart.

Afterwards, they retreated to their corners of the world and—from the shattered shards of the Empyrieos—they created new kingdoms and royal bloodlines in its stead.

The east claimed the name Eretria, the former capital of the old kingdom. There they live in perpetual autumn, a plentiful land forever on the cusp of change, where the countryside is tinted in shades of ochre and leaves carry on Eurus' cool winds. To the west, Reveza fell into a state of endless spring, a kingdom of blissful sunshine, blooming flowers, and Zephyrus' light breezes. The north became Arkhadia, a wintery land of frost, snow-capped mountains, and Boreas' icy gales.

The south suffered most.

Isolated from the other lands, with its enduring heat and the dry summer wind of Notos, the Sorrows' new name was apt in the beginning.

Against my will, my eyes drift toward my window.

I always wonder if a cruel twist of fate or the petty machinations of the Eagle ensured I have a perfect view of the palace from my bedroom. The white palace glows under the moon, the light catching and reflecting off its many arched windows. White flags emblazoned with golden sea eagles flutter from the tops of the cerulean-domed towers as they pierce the black velvet sky.

My chest constricts at the sight. Those walls sheltered me throughout my childhood. I doubt a day will come when it's not strange to gaze at them from afar.

With a groan, I place the map aside before unbuckling my sandals and kicking them off, letting them fall unceremoniously to the floor. With deft fingers, I remove the belt from my waist, the dagger and purse coming away with it, and set them on the nightstand. After a moment's hesitation, I unclip the earring from the middle of my right ear, the *goiteía* marks engraved on its surface are cast in shadow as I place it amongst the other items.

A shiver trembles though me at the sensation of cobwebs falling from my skin. I pull the heavy braid of my hair over my shoulder, watching as it brightens from the deep brown shade to ashen blonde.

I rarely take the earring off—I never know if I'll be woken in the middle of the night—but I just want to feel like myself. Even if it's only for a moment.

I frown, looking down at the simple golden ring on my finger, and then fall back amongst the pillows with a sigh. I close my eyes, trying to shut the world out, but it's still too loud.

Too chaotic.

Thoughts clamor in my mind, each of them slaying the other to take precedence. Only for the slain thoughts to revive, avenge themselves, and begin the vicious cycle anew.

My hand drifts to the pocket of my pants, feeling the smooth texture of glass, and my fingers curl around the vials. I pull them free, setting one aside on the nightstand while I grip the other in a tight fist.

Just one. Every third night.

The promise echoes in my mind, pushing all other thoughts away as a solid weight settles on my chest. I pop the cork and pinch a seed between the tips of my fingers—ignoring the slight tremor I see in them—and place it in my mouth.

Biting down, I cringe at the bitterness, and then let it settle underneath my tongue.

The change is instant.

A haze of calm envelopes me and warmth tingles in my lips. My chest.

The tips of my fingers and toes.

My eyes drift shut, darkness cocooning me as I slip into the welcoming embrace of a dreamless sleep.

I jolt awake to pounding on my bedroom door.

"You better not be hiding under the covers from me," a teasing voice shouts from the hall, and the frantic beating of my heart calms.

Nyssa.

With a groan, I burrow deeper into my bed, dragging a pillow over my head to drown her out, but my feather-stuffed shield proves to be useless against incessant hammering.

"Open this door right now, or I'll shout your name at the top of my lungs."

A cringe rattles through me at her threat, and I curse under my breath. I throw my pillow across the room as I drag myself out of bed, and then stomp my way to the door.

"Ae—"

I wrench the door open and pull her in before she gets a chance to finish. With a quick glance to check the corridor is clear, I close the door and turn to her.

Nyssa stands beside me, an innocent expression on her face I do not trust for a moment.

"It was unlocked," I snarl at her.

"I know," she says with a smirk. Her hazel eyes twinkling as she pushes past me—as easily as she shoved her way into my life so many years ago—and calls over her shoulder, "This was a more effective way to get your sorry ass out of bed."

She saunters across the room and begins rummaging through my wardrobe. Nyssa is a maelstrom. She tears into your life like a raging wind, churning up the ocean with enough force to make the sea-floor tremble. A storm of chaos that fills you with equal parts fear and excitement, both terrifying and beautiful to behold.

I wouldn't have her any other way.

"What are you doing?" I ask, amusement tugging my lips into a smile despite the annoyance I try to clutch on to. As she guts my wardrobe like it's her greatest adversary, the last threads slip through my fingers and dissipate.

"Emergency intervention. If I left these decisions up to you, you'd never leave this room."

"Don't be so dramatic," I scoff.

"If I'm so wrong…" Nyssa pauses her perusal of my clothing and quirks a brow at me over her shoulder. She's already dressed for the night. Her curves are draped with a burgundy dress—the rich color a perfect complement to the soft russet of her skin. Gold bangles wrap around her wrists, and chains are artfully threaded through the dark, cinnamon curls cascading down her back. "Then tell me you didn't finish your test, take on a shift, and pass out upon returning to this little, comfortable cave of yours."

I stare at her blankly, before dropping my gaze to the dusty linen pants and undershirt I collapsed in earlier. My hooded wrap lies in a tangled mess on the bed next to the discarded map, having fallen off as I slept.

At least I took my sandals and belt off.

"That's what I thought." She pulls out a powder-blue dress and holds it up against my body.

I glance down at it and frown.

"This one," Nyssa states, draping it over my bed and pushing me toward the bathing chamber. "You have two minutes to wash the day's dirt off. Don't get your hair wet."

"Nyssa, I really don't—"

"Come on, just one drink and then you can leave," she pleads. "I know the others will be so happy if you do. The shock on their faces will be worth it."

The others.

My traitorous eyes drift back to the window—to the luminous stone walls of the palace. Walls separating me and the people I once cared for. After being sent to the Aviary, I felt each one of those losses like they were physical cracks in my heart.

A spider's web of fractures.

It made me build my own walls. Brick by brick, surrounding myself to keep others out. It's simpler that way.

But my mortar must be weak because it disintegrates before Nyssa.

I stifle what would be my hundredth groan of the day and strip my clothes, dropping them to the floor and creating a trail all the way to my bathing chamber. Two minutes is nowhere near enough time to even fill the tub, so I wet a cloth in the basin and scrub over every inch of my body. When I head back out to my room, Nyssa has my clothing, accessories, and sandals all selected and laid out for me.

"Have I told you lately how much you annoy me?" I ask.

"At least thirteen times this week." Nyssa throws a towel and I snatch it from the air before it hits me in the face.

"I heard a song today," I say, drying myself off. The phrase was a significant one amongst Aviary members. It could either mean you have learned a piece of information you need to share, or it could confirm the other person you were speaking with was a member of the order.

"Oh! Any news of the Lord Arsenio drama?"

"No—well, *yes*. He got a seamstress pregnant, so it won't be long before his wife finds out he's an unfaithful bastard."

"I hope she castrates him for it," Nyssa sighs wistfully. "What else did you hear?"

"The crew on *The Nightingale* were singing an interesting tune."

"The ship Alpha Flight was aboard?"

"The same." I worry my bottom lip, hesitating before my next words. "Apparently, they're going back again. Soon."

A small frown creases the space between her elegant brows. I hate seeing it there. *Putting* it there. "Luc—*Lark* mentioned nothing."

I smile at the way she fumbles over her brother's name. Lucaz went through his Naming a year ago and the order assigned him to Alpha Flight before they were sent on their mission across the sea. The past year has been challenging for her since it's the first time they have been apart all their lives.

My breath stutters when what she said sinks in, and I peer up at her, my fingers curling around the rough fibers of the towel. "You've seen him?"

"I saw him briefly this afternoon. They've all been in and out of briefings since they returned, but…" she pauses, frown deepening before she shakes her head, "I'm sure it's nothing to be concerned about. Lark will tell me if it is."

"Of course he will," I agree, shoving off the unease that has been lingering since this evening. I trail my fingers over the soft fabric of the dress Nyssa picked out, smiling at the silken texture beneath my fingertips.

Over the years, I've developed a deep appreciation for pants while training with the order, but I miss having a reason to dress up. To be soft and feminine.

The Aviary is no place for soft things.

Being soft leads to a watery grave at the bottom of the Solorai Sea.

"Lark is coming tonight," Nyssa says behind me, and the back of my neck prickles at her sly tone.

"Oh?" I drop the towel on the end of my bed and pick up the dress, but her next words freeze me mid-motion.

"Raven will probably come too."

My eyes narrow and I turn my glare on her, contemplating giving her the evil eye. Apparently, it's nowhere near as threatening as it feels, since the only response it elicits is a laugh.

"Notos, save me from annoying brats and their meddlesome ways," I mutter as I pull the dress over my head. The silk glides against my skin as it slides down my body, the pleated fabric falling to my ankles. I pick up the embroidered navy-and-gold girdle belt and tie it around my waist, cinching the fabric so only a glimpse of my legs will show when I walk. Two matching golden cuffs sit on the end of my bed, and I slip them on my wrists as Nyssa undoes my thick braid and brushes out my hair.

"My work here is done!" she announces, throwing her arms wide and flinging my brush across the room in the same motion. It hits the wall and lands on the wooden floor with a clatter. I eye it with an arched eyebrow, but then shrug. I'm used to her antics.

I turn to face her but pause as I glimpse myself in the mirror leaning against the wall.

Ashen hair falls in glossy waves past my waist. Against the tawny shade of my skin, the contrast only makes it appear lighter. It's rare to see tycheroi with light hair in the Sorrows—shades of brown and black being most common. When I first came to the Aviary, I thought they would make me color it with dye to keep my identity hidden. But the Eagle had given me an earring engraved with *goiteía* instead and instructed me to wear it whenever I wasn't alone.

Pure relief filled that moment.

I inherited my hair from my mother—a foreigner from the winter kingdom, Arkhadia—and it's always felt like one of my only connections to her. My stormy blue eyes are hers, too—another uncommon trait in the south.

Sometimes I wonder how much I resemble her. Perhaps

that's the reason my father couldn't stand to keep me around. He never spoke of her when I was young, and all I know is where she came from and her name.

After my birth, my father forbade everyone from speaking of her.

I blink away the stinging in my eyes as Nyssa appears in the reflection behind me. Her rosebud lips purse as she hands me the small golden earring.

Exhaling through my nose, I fasten it on my right ear among the collection of hoops and other jewelry. I turn back to the mirror, watching as my reflection transforms. Ashen hair darkens to rich brown, and my eyes deepen to the color of wet clay.

"It might help if you try not to glare so much." She says the words like she's attempting to placate a wild animal. I scowl at her, and then wipe the expression from my face when I realize I'm only proving her right.

I stride over to my nightstand and pick up my dagger, pulling it free from the belt holster. I stroke my thumb over the intricate blade, like a large feather dipped in molten metal, before being honed to lethal sharpness at the point. The handle is just as unique, carved from a shimmering ivory stone and adorned with a silver scale etched in foreign markings.

It's my most prized possession.

Besides my own features, it's the only tangible thing I have from my mother.

Biting my lip, I pull a garter sheath from the drawer and buckle it to my right thigh. As the warmth of the polished handle seeps into my skin, the comforting heat inches through my body. A subtle tension I didn't notice before melts away, and my next breath comes easier.

When I glance up, Nyssa is watching me, exasperation clear on her face. The corner of my mouth twitches with the urge to laugh. "You know I love to accessorize."

"They're going to promote you to a Nightwing in no time," she says, grabbing my wrist and towing me toward the door. "Now come on, we're missing the fun."

FIVE

Excitement perfumes the air as Nyssa and I step off our ferry and onto the crowded streets of Maricious. The Muse looms before us—people queued at the door, hoping to join those silhouetted against stained glass windows within.

As the most popular establishment in the Sorrows, tycheroi from every isle visit, drawn in by the allure of its owner, Lady Calliope, and the entertainment she has to offer.

No one knows much about her past, only that when she was young, Lady Calliope moved here from Reveza with a small fortune in gold and a wealth of talent. The mystery she cultivates, along with her rich eastern accent, tumbling bronze hair, and sultry features, only adds to the success of her business.

A curated blend of tavern, music hall, and pleasure house, The Muse is packed out most nights. When Lady Calliope holds her infamous parties, people line up on the street hoping they'll make it inside.

Tonight is such a night, but—fortunately for us—Calliope is a longstanding colleague of the Aviary. Nyssa and I have both worked closely with her over the years, learning the arts of dance, seduction, and crafting personas.

Those lessons are among my favorites from my time as a Fledgling.

I've always loved to dance. When I was living in the palace, I had the best instructors to be found in the Sorrows. I was relieved when my masters told me I could continue, since the increased mastery over our physical movements dancing fosters is valuable in our line of work.

We stroll past the line to the front door. I don't recognize the door guard who is here tonight, but Nyssa and I both ad-just our hair behind our ears, flashing the small gold piercings we wear. A golden eagle in flight with a ruby-encrusted eye, dangling from a small hoop through the top of each of our left ears.

The only visible sign of the order we belong to.

It's common for our people to wear jewelry, so—while the guard knows to grant access to anyone wearing them—he won't understand the true significance of ours.

The guard opens the door without hesitation and ushers us through, no flicker of emotion crossing his stoic face. A chorus of groans and protests follows, cut off as the door shuts behind us as quickly as it opened.

When you enter The Muse, it's like you're stepping into another world.

A bar stretches along the right wall, workers juggling clay

bottles and cups as they serve their guests. Sheer mauve fabric drapes across the space and hundreds of candles flicker in their sconces. On the far wall, every bit of stone is covered with hanging mirrors in different shapes and sizes, their ornate frames painted gold. Patrons lounge on velvet chaises in varying shades of crimson and indigo, admiring the performer who croons along to the heady beat of the musicians, her sapphire hair tumbling around her shoulders like a waterfall. Others lean against a mezzanine above, laughing and watching the swell of activity beneath them.

Nyssa links her fingers through mine, and we weave toward the back of the hall where draped curtains conceal a raised section. We climb the few stairs and part the fabric, finding the rest of our cohort reclining in a circle of lounges and armchairs, a low table in the middle filled with meze. The sight of dolmades, grilled octopus, tzatziki, olives, and fresh vegetables makes my stomach growl, reminding me all I've eaten today was a bite of the apricot I swiped from the kitchens earlier.

The group cheers when they see us, scooting over in their seats to make room. Nyssa flops down between Mateo and Calix, who both turn to smirk at her, and I perch on the edge of a chaise next to Syrus, who offers me a shy smile.

"Glad to see you managed to drag the bookworm out of her den, Nys," Calix says as he rests his arm on the lounge behind her.

"It's funny how accurate that imagery is," Nyssa says with a laugh.

I pull a cushion from behind my back and throw it so fast

she doesn't have time to react. She squeals as it hits her square in the face, and I settle back with a smug smile.

"I can't help that I'm so dedicated to learning," I say.

"What exactly is it you *learn* in your dirty romance novels, El?" Nyssa asks with faux innocence, using the name the others know me by.

When new recruits first arrive at the Aviary, they're supposed to give up their former name and life. Up until the ceremony, we're expected to only respond to the title 'Fledgling'. However, on a night quite like this one, our cohort decided to break the rule. I couldn't tell them my real name, and 'El' was the first thing that came to mind.

I narrow my eyes at her, but follow the thought and steer the conversation in a different direction. "How's everyone feeling about the Naming?"

"I can't wait!" Mateo crows, downing the contents of his cup. Nyssa elbows him in the ribs and he adds in a hushed voice, "I hope I get sent to Reveza."

His words ignite a familiar debate, as everyone argues which kingdom would be the ideal destination. A palpable sense of excitement simmers beneath the surface, mingled with a growing tension as the ceremony draws near.

The Naming is a graduation of sorts, although instead of leaving to pursue our own lives afterwards, we take a vow to serve their agenda and undertake the missions they assign us. It's a perfect scenario for those like Nyssa and Lark, who didn't have families or homes and were taken in, educated, clothed, fed, and given a stable future.

For me, it's different.

Before my father handed me over to the Aviary, I had a home at the Palace of Sorrows. The royal tutors educated me, and I never wore the same clothes twice.

But most importantly, I had Kallias.

Thinking about my brother makes my heart ache. The burning, throbbing pain of a wound allowed to fester too long. Despite being born to different mothers; we grew up as close as siblings could. He is the only thing I truly miss from my old life. I could take or leave the rest.

"I'm feeling nervous." Syrus' gentle voice beside me pulls me back from the edge of yet another turbulent mood. "About the change and facing the unknown."

Syrus will make a perfect Songbird—an even better Owl with how quiet and observant he is. He tucks a brunette curl behind his ear and offers a chagrined smile. I reach out and give his hand a comforting squeeze, pulling it away just as quickly when I notice Luci glaring at me from his other side.

"Does anyone know what actually happens at the ceremony?" Mateo asks, and I turn back to the group.

"They pray to Notos for divine guidance and then carve your name into your skin," says a voice from behind me.

I watch as the faces of my cohort pale at the words, but a smile teases at the edge of my lips.

Because *that* particular voice is only good for speaking one thing.

Bullshit.

Nyssa chokes on a laugh as she launches off the lounge, throwing herself into her brother's waiting arms. The two of them could be twins for how similar they appear. All cinnamon curls, russet skin, and hazel eyes sparkling with mirth. He's almost ten years older than her, not that you can tell by the way he behaves.

"I missed you so much," Nyssa exclaims.

"I guess I missed you a little," Lark jokes, but the gentle warmth in his gaze as he looks down at her speaks the truth for him. He pins me with those eyes and pouts. "Didn't you miss me too, trouble?"

I huff a laugh at his antics but stand to embrace him anyway. Lark wraps an arm around me, taking care not to spill the wine in his hand while still holding Nyssa with the other. "I'm rather disappointed you didn't fall overboard on the journey back," I mutter, causing him to squeeze me even harder before letting go.

"Can we circle back to the skin carving for a moment?" Mateo asks in a tight voice.

I drop back to my seat and Nyssa returns to hers. Lark pulls up a chair next to me and sits on it backwards, a sly grin curling across his face before he opens his mouth, but Nyssa launches the pillow I threw earlier toward him. He blocks it with a laugh, shielding the cup in his hand like it holds all the years of his life.

As I'm about to reassure the others he's only joking, another voice joins in, its deep melody swirling through the air and pebbling my skin.

"You're scaring the Fledglings, Lark."

I suck in a breath as my stomach swoops and my heart flutters like the frantic wings of a hummingbird.

Raven.

When I finally turn around, it's hard to reconcile the fact it's been a year since I last saw him. He looks the same as I remember. Deep, brown hair—wild and windswept—falls around the strong, angular planes of his face. Short stubble dusts his jawline, softening some of its sharpness and framing wide lips that are set in a firm line. The honey-brown of his eyes is piercing against his bronze skin, a shade lighter than it usually is after a year away from the sun-drenched islands of the Sorrows.

Time itself must have paused and woven its way into his orbit. Every minute he spent away felt like an eternity, and yet, his presence now makes the past year seem like a blurred, distant dream. I'm tempted to reach out and touch him—to confirm he's truly here, not a figment of my imagination.

I pull back from the urge, tangling my fingers in the fabric of my dress as a strange mix of awareness and trepidation weave a fragile shield around me.

"El," he says, and the way his deep, smooth voice caresses my false name effectively shatters the shield, sending a shiver rolling down my spine. I know he sees it when a shadow of a smile ghosts his lips.

I wasn't even aware I was holding my breath until it escapes me, trembling through my lips as a shuddering exhale. "Raven," I say, clearing my throat when it comes out as a barely audible rasp. "Welcome back."

I tear my gaze away from him, facing Nyssa instead. My eyes narrow on my traitorous friend when I see she's fanning herself with her hand, eyes darting back and forth.

Raven's attention is a fiery brand, scorching my skin as it

lingers on me a moment longer. I only relax when he greets the others and pulls up a seat next to Lark, sighing in relief when the position blocks him from view.

I take advantage of the moment to scrape all my feelings off the floor and shove them back into the locked box in my mind where they belong.

"The Naming is not as dramatic as Lark would have you believe," Raven finally answers Mateo's question. "The Eagle will lead a ceremony, where each of you will be called to pledge yourselves to the Aviary and you'll be given your new name."

"And then you'll all be sent away to creep and crawl through the shadows of the kingdoms, stealing the songs of all tycheroi-kind," Lark adds with a dramatic flourish, taking a deep drink of his wine.

I roll my eyes at him but can't deny the anxiety creeping through my mind. Everyone has gone silent, each lost in their own thoughts as nerves start to outweigh the earlier excitement.

I study the faces of everyone around me, wondering if we'll be together for more than a few moments after this. A part of me hopes we will, yet another part hopes I cross the Solorai Sea and never return.

Guilt flares, a fiery ember sparking in my gut as my gaze lands on Nyssa, and Kal's smiling face flashes through my mind.

Suddenly, the room feels stifling.

I stand, causing Nyssa to raise her brows in question, but I give a small shake of my head. "I'll be back," I mouth.

She nods and turns back to Mateo, a flirtatious smile on her lips as she leans toward him.

I draw in a deep breath and release it slowly, stepping through the curtains to the crowded main hall. I've barely taken three steps toward the entrance when a muscular arm snakes around my waist, holding me in place.

"Fucking Notos!" I curse, jolting as I'm pulled back against a firm body.

"Now, darling, is that any way to talk about our beloved God?"

I push down the disappointment that swells at the sultry voice and the scent of the ocean filling the air around me.

"I'm sure he would feel honored." I spin until I'm looking up at the man holding me in place.

Hair, such a dark blue it's almost black in the dim lighting, falls in silken waves past his shoulders, framing a face no doubt carved in the likeness of the gods. Turquoise eyes fringed by lashes that have every woman in the Sorrows envious, and plump lips that smirk down at me.

"I know I'd certainly be honored if you spoke about me in such a way," he says with a grin. Light lands on his sharp cheekbones from the movement, shimmering across the sapphire scales speckling his skin like freckles.

Kashton is an incorrigible flirt. I've never been certain if it's because of his upbringing or part of his nature. He's a nymphai, and was born from the union of a water nymph—a nature spirit with an affinity for the rivers and seas—and a tycheroi.

He's been at The Muse for as long as I can recall, likely

before my birth, and climbed his way from courtesan to Calliope's right hand. As part of my Aviary education, he had helped train me in the arts of seduction and temptation and—once I was older—he tried his hardest to tempt me into his bedroom. After being denied at every turn, we settled into something akin to friendship.

Now, my thoughts are preoccupied with a different shade of hair and a pair of honey-colored eyes.

"Why the long face, darling?" he teases. "Am I not the man you were hoping I'd be? Perhaps you would prefer it if I was taller, darker, and named after a bird?"

I ignore his questions, and the small voice in my head that quietly agrees with him. "Is there a purpose for this ambush, Kash? Or are you here to seduce me?"

"The night I have you writhing in pleasure on my bed will be a joyous one indeed. Unfortunately, it may not be tonight. The Lady wants to see you."

I worry my lip and cast my eyes back toward the curtain hiding my friends, hesitating a moment longer. "Alright, take me to her."

Kashton throws me a grin that transforms his face from beautiful to breathtaking. He grabs my hand and pulls me toward the wall of mirrors. When we reach the largest mirror, he reaches out with his other hand and presses on the part of the painted golden frame where I know a latch is hidden. With a sharp click, the mirror swings forward a crack, and he pulls it open, bowing at the waist and ushering me through.

I step into the dim room, my gaze passing over the familiar cedar and crushed velvet décor dappled by the lantern light shining through the stained glass windows along the back wall. Calliope sits at a heavy wooden desk beyond a pair of chaise lounges in the center, quill in hand, scratching at parchment.

The door closes behind me and I glance over my shoulder, eyes lingering on the wall that now separates me from the main hall.

The mirrors on this side of the wall have always fascinated me. Though they appear as a decorative feature in the hall, they act as a one way looking glass on the inside, providing a clear view for Calliope to keep an eye on her guests. Between them and the loyal courtesans whispering in her ear, she would have known the moment I set foot within The Muse.

"Take a seat, sweet anemone. I won't be a moment," Calliope says, the use of the endearment confirms she knows it's me even without looking up from the parchment in front of her. She names each of the Aviary girls when they first come to train with her after a flower. A tradition she keeps to remind us of our grace and delicacy, but also the strength and resilience we possess.

I smile as I sit on the chaise closest to me, unlacing my sandals and slipping them off before curling my legs up beneath me, watching the merriment through the mirrors while I wait.

A moment passes before Calliope settles on the couch beside me, and I turn to face her. Her bronze curls a waterfall around her heart-shaped face, and her rich russet skin glimmering in the flickering lantern light. She pulls my hand between hers and looks me over before her warm ochre eyes settle on my own. "How is my favorite flower?"

I huff a laugh, but a smile creeps across my face, nonetheless. "I bet you say the same to every one of us."

"Only the prettiest ones."

"I'm flattered," I deadpan.

"As you should be," she says matter-of-factly, releasing my hand and leaning back against the cushions. "You're also avoiding the question."

"I'm fine."

"Fine…" Calliope muses, her eyes turning distant. "A duplicitous word. You say it often. But you know if you ever need me, all you must do is ask."

"Kash sent me in," I say, choosing to ignore her meaning. It's no simple matter to be open with people when you have been trained to keep secrets. To stay hidden. Although Calliope is one of the few I trust, some truths are best kept locked away.

She watches me a moment longer before inclining her head. "I heard a Flight landed this morning, but they'll be taking off again soon."

I go still. "Where did you hear that?"

"A little bird told me." She offers the words with a casual shrug, as though being privy to the secrets of the Aviary is of little consequence to her.

"And why would you tell me?"

"To warn you, dear girl. You'll be taking off with them. It's almost time for you to leave this rusting cage of yours. To finally spread those glorious wings."

"You can't be certain of that," I say, but my heart skips a beat, my breathing growing shallow. "We haven't been given our names or missions yet."

Calliope watches me silently, her eyes taking every inch of me in. As though, if she looks close enough, she'll be able to penetrate past the layers of skin and tissue to where my heart and soul hide beneath. Eventually, she shrugs her graceful shoulders. "I have seen it."

The unsteady beat of my heart takes off in a flutter of frantic wings. "You're an oracle?"

There hasn't been an oracle in the Empyrieos since the God War—not one who has stepped forward, at least. During those days, the warring armies conscripted them and forced them to use their gift in the pursuit of victory. In the centuries that followed, it was unclear whether the Anemoi stripped the power of foresight from the realm, or if anyone who found themselves in possession of the gift had kept it hidden.

I'd always suspected Calliope was blessed with the sight. Or cursed, depending on how you look at it. Often, things she has said foreshadowed events, but they were little things. Inconsequential. Never enough to confirm one way or the other. Yet here she is now, confiding a truth she holds close to her heart and shattering any doubt as surely as a tempest obliterates silence.

"Not quite," she laughs, a rich, smoky sound. "At least, not in the way you're thinking."

"Why?" I ask, barely more than a whisper. A single word, holding so many questions I struggle to voice. Why was she trusting me with her secret? Why was Alpha Flight being sent away again? Why was I being sent with them?

Calliope stands and glides toward her desk, pouring two

cups of wine from the clay decanter waiting there. Silently, she walks back toward me and holds out a cup. I take it between numb fingers, and she retreats again, leaning against the wooden surface as she faces me with a contemplative look.

"Do you remember what you said to me when we first met?"

I shake my head as I bring the cup to my lips. The sweet wine spills over my tongue, but I barely register the taste.

"You put your hands on your hips and, with this adorable little scowl on your face, you announced, 'nobody tells me how to behave'."

I choke on my next sip of wine.

"I saw myself in you. In fact, I still do. Headstrong, wilful, passionate." Calliope looks down into her wine cup and lifts her shoulders with an elegant shrug. "I suppose you could say I've grown attached over the years."

Warmth blooms in my chest, and I glance away to hide how it creeps across my cheeks, not entirely sure how to respond to her confession.

"So, the reason I'm telling you this," she continues, "is because I care. And because I care, I fear. I mostly see fleeting flashes and fragments within my mind. Impressions. However, a feeling always accompanies those impressions, and they are considerably more telling."

"And what did you feel?" I ask, uncertain I want to know, but also knowing I need to.

"Nothing good, sweet anemone. Nothing good."

SIX

I PUSH THROUGH THE back door of The Muse and lean against the rough stone wall, the warm night air heating my lungs as I draw in a deep breath. The moon hangs high in the sky, casting a soft glow over the canal that edges the isle. I can still hear music and laughter from inside, but out here, it's muted. Peaceful.

Letting out a sigh, I attempt to shake off Calliope's words as they relentlessly echo in my mind. She has always had a way of getting under my skin, of knowing me better than I know myself. Like I am the very flower she calls me, and with a few simple words she could peel away my petals and see right into the pistil of my being. Only this time, her words have left a heavy weight on my chest.

The coarse rasp of a sandal on cobblestone slices through the silence. My heart jolts as I instinctively draw back into the shadows, plastering myself against the wooden door. My fingers brush over the worn texture of the wood, seeking purchase as the darkness envelopes me. I steady my breaths and strain my senses, tuning out the muffled merriment within The Muse and the sound of my blood rushing in my ears.

Damn Calliope and her ability to crawl under my skin.

Cursing myself for being so on edge, I peer into the dimly lit alley, eyes narrowing when I spot a familiar figure step into the path of the moon's light. The pale glow illuminates the sharp lines of Raven's face as it angles toward my hiding spot, and I pull my body deeper into the shadowed doorway.

The tense set to his broad shoulders awakens my curiosity. The insistent creature unfurls from its slumber in the pit of my stomach, stretching languidly and clawing for attention. Ravenous for the secrets hidden behind the man's clenched jaw and guarded eyes.

His movements are too purposeful. Too poised.

Familiar.

I imagine I look much the same on my clandestine visits to see my brother at the palace. My eyes narrow at the realization, curiosity gouging its claws in deep.

After a moment, Raven raises the hood of his cowl, veering onto the narrow street behind the neighboring building. The inky tendrils of shadows eagerly reach out to embrace him as he walks further into their depths.

I hesitate, listening to the sound of his footsteps echoing through the night, steadily growing fainter. I shouldn't follow him. I should go back to the Aviary, curl up in my bed, and get a good night's rest before the Naming ceremony tomorrow.

Despite myself, I hover on the knife's edge of indecision,

wondering which way I fall will cut the least.

Fuck it.

With an absent wish that my clothing was more appropriate for tracking, I slip from the doorway, syncing my footsteps with the distant echo of his. Easily falling into the stealth I have developed through my training, I stalk through the sinewy maze of alleyways, dodging the pools of light that spill from the windows of cramped buildings. Raven's path is irregular, weaving through the labyrinthine back streets of Maricious toward the southern side of the isle.

When he abruptly rounds a corner, a subtle tingle hums through my veins, steadily growing stronger until a surge of energy floods my body. My heart rate quickens, pounding in my chest like a drum in time with each calculated step. Every sensation becomes heightened, and the starlit night around me takes on more vibrant hues.

Shadows turn violet.

Puddles of light gain an incandescent glow.

And that's when I hear it, or rather, the *lack* of it.

Footsteps no longer sound in front of me.

I pause at the edge of the building—muscles tense, ready to spring into action at a moment's notice—and peer around the corner.

The alley is empty.

He's just...gone.

"Always so curious," a deep, velvety voice whispers in my ear, right before I'm pushed up against the wall. "I'm glad to see some things never change."

Raven's lips curl into a taunting smirk as he uses his forearm to pin my body to the unforgiving stone at my back. I'm forced to look up to meet his gaze so I can glare at him. "How did you know?"

"I've been playing this game much longer than you."

"Boasting doesn't suit you, Raven."

His laughter, low and infectious, dances in the cool night air. "Still as feisty too," he murmurs, his gaze softening as it returns to mine.

"And you're still as arrogant as I remember," I retort, though the teasing lilt in my voice contradicts the harshness of my words.

"Ah, but you wouldn't have me any other way, would you?"

My breath falters and I become painfully aware of how dangerously close his face is to mine. So close that if I leaned forward an inch our lips would be touching.

Too close.

Raven must realize it at the same time as I do. A frown creases his brow, and he steps back, letting his arm fall to his side.

I wince as the light-heartedness between us evaporates, remembering the last time a moment like this unfolded.

We'd be breaking the rules.

My throat tightens as the words clang through my mind, landing in the hollowed-out space in my chest.

The rules.

Don't ask questions. Obey your orders. Respect your masters. But most of all, love no one.

The Aviary drills them into us the moment our feet first pass the threshold. To ask questions was to question the Aviary itself. To disobey orders showed a lack of duty. To disrespect your masters was insubordination.

But to love someone was worst of all. It was a shift in allegiance, altering priorities and eclipsing purpose. If you loved someone, you could never put the needs of the Aviary before them. You would move the sun, the moon, and all the stars in the night sky to ensure they were safe.

Or, at least, I would.

But I also wasn't a fool.

I knew nothing could happen between us, and Raven had known the same. Which is exactly why—when we recognized how far those feelings had gone—we put an end to it ourselves.

It had felt like crushing the sweetest smelling flower before it ever had a chance to bloom. Sometimes it was better to crush a bud than let it grow, only to watch it die when it couldn't survive the soil it was rooted in.

"Come with me?" His unexpected question cuts through my thoughts, jarring me back to the dimly lit alley.

I let it linger in the air between us, unsure of what my answer should be. Those three little words could have so much meaning hidden beneath the surface. A simple invitation, or a siren's call to a more perilous path.

One woven with mutual destruction.

My eyes roam over the moonlit planes of his face, like the silver beams of light might reveal the answer there.

When it proves hopeless, I finally relent. "Where?"

"Just trust me."

And even after all this time, I do.
So much for not being a fool.

I frown as the ferryman pulls up at the small dock of Ioa. An undercurrent of confusion stirs within me, timing itself with the gentle lapping of waves against the vessel as we dismount. I glance around as Raven pays for our passage, taking in the humble collection of stone and wood houses scattered around the isle, a warm glow emanating from a few windows despite the late hour. The tang of seaweed battles with the stinging scent of fresh fish in the air, and I wrinkle my nose.

"Too strong for your fragile sensitivities, princess?" Raven teases, and I fight the visceral reaction my body wants to have at the sound of his old nickname for me falling so casually from his lips.

I toss a glare his way. "I don't come out to the Southern Isles often."

He chuckles, a low rumble vibrating through the still night, as he takes the lead, navigating the meandering paths of the isle with the ease of familiarity. I fall into step behind him—too curious not to.

As we pass through a muddled maze of small stone houses, I glance at Raven from the corner of my eye, still not quite believing he's right here next to me. Like no time had passed at all.

But it did.

As if sensing my gaze, he turns to me, a shadow of a smile playing on his lips that doesn't quite reach his eyes. "Are you ready?"

I blanch at his question. "Ready for what?"

He flashes me another smile, before picking up his pace, turning down a small laneway to a house set subtly apart from the others. Even in the dim light, I can see its stones have less weathering, and someone has carved *goiteía* symbols on the door for luck and protection. He lifts a hand, hesitating for a mere heartbeat before his knuckles rap against the wood in a rhythmic pattern: two quick taps, a pause, then three more.

"Raven—"

The door swings open, cutting off my words and revealing an older woman whose eyes carry all the warmth of a Sorrows summer. Raven's face mirrors the same affection, raw and revealing in ways he would never allow under the scrutiny of the Aviary.

In ways I've never seen before.

The thought pulls a thread in my stomach, making it tighten to a knot. I frown, picking at it and pulling it loose before I ball it up and toss it into the shadows of my mind.

"My boy," she says, swooping in and wrapping her arms around him. It's not until she pulls away, her eyes shift to me, widening with an intrigue that quickens my pulse. "And who might this be?"

"El," Raven easily supplies, and I plaster an amiable smile on my face. "A friend. El, this is Areti."

"Well, it's lovely to meet you, dear," Areti says. "Now, come inside, both of you."

Raven follows her in without hesitation, while I linger in the doorway, a spirit tethered to the threshold. But as a flurry of tiny bodies suddenly ambush him, I drift inside, entranced by the display of warmth and life. Five little boys, each one a cacophony of giggles and shouts, scramble to claim his attention. Small, darting hands and feet tangle in a squall of chaos and affection that has my eyes growing wider by the second.

Raven, the stoic sentinel I know, becomes swept away in their youthful tempest as his laughter merges with theirs. It's a sight so stark against the Raven of my mind, I'm torn between fascination and confusion.

He meets my gaze over the tops of their disheveled heads, and there's an unspoken conversation in his stare. A confession.

An olive branch.

I turn away, taking in my surroundings instead. A worn wooden table anchors the room, its surface grooved with memories of countless meals and gatherings. In the far corner, flames dance playfully in a modest hearth, casting a golden hue on the well-loved furniture and lacing the air with woodsmoke and sage. I smile at the netting, trinkets, and scribbled drawings adorning the stone walls. They remind me of my own room. Although, where I have tried to make my small sanctuary at the Aviary something it's not, this place is truly a home.

The last part makes my eyes drift back to the man still roughhousing with the group of young boys.

I met Raven not long after I had been sent to the Aviary.

From the start, a palpable tension existed between us. He greeted me with a sarcastic remark, calling me a spoiled princess—since I apparently acted like one—and without hesitation, I fired back, telling him he was an uptight ass. In the months that followed, we were at war with one another. But when he'd caught another boy pushing me around, everything had changed, and animosity had given way to friendship. Over time, our friendship grew into something deeper, and I eventually confided in him.

It made his chosen nickname for me even more amusing to him.

But even after all those years spent together in the Aviary's halls, I had never learned a thing about Raven's past that wasn't broadly known within the order. It never crossed my mind he could have a place like this.

And he never told me.

Something sharper weaves its way through the confusion, curling tight around my ribs and pinching. My gaze catches on the eagle piercing through the lobe of his ear and lingers there, only breaking when Areti's chastising voice carries across the room.

"Alright, boys, that's enough! All of you were supposed to be in bed."

"Please, one story," a little boy with hair as dark as Raven's begs.

"We haven't seen him for ages," whines another.

Areti huffs, folding her arms over her chest and looks at Raven in question.

"You heard them," he says, "they haven't seen me in ages."

Raven sits down in the old armchair and the boys kneel at his feet, watching him with childlike awe. I subtly touch my face, making sure I'm not watching him with the same expression, causing Areti to chuckle under her breath as she slips a clay cup into my hands. The warmth seeps into my palms and I peer down at the contents, closing my eyes as I savor the aroma of spiced *calda*.

I take a seat at the small table as Raven begins, his voice weaving a tale as old as the Empyrieos itself, about a brave nymph who defied the odds. The room falls into a hushed silence, hanging onto every word. Her story isn't filled with grandiose battles or wondrous magic; it's a subtle saga about resilience, a lone soul traversing the treacherous kingdoms to find her home.

An ache builds in the hollow of my chest as both the story and scene play out before me. I know what it's like to be lost, to wander through a world that seems both familiar and foreign at the same time. But unlike the nymph in Raven's story, I didn't have the freedom to go searching.

The Aviary sinks its talons in—sharp claws scraping to the bone—until the two fuse together. Until you can no longer find the difference between the essence that is yours and that which is not.

The echoes of the nymph's journey linger in my mind after the story ends, and Areti announces it's the boys' bedtime. Raven rises, his frame silhouetted against the hearth's glow, and folds into the empty chair beside me.

"I didn't know you had family," I say quietly, watching as the boys play out one of the scenes while Areti ushers them through a door at the back of the room.

"I don't," he says, and I frown, waiting for him to continue. "But Areti is as close to family as I'll come."

"How did you meet her?"

"She found me washed up on the banks of Ioa. She tried to take care of me for a time, always taking in strays." Raven shakes his head, an affectionate smile hovering at the edge of his mouth. I've seen him smile more tonight than I have in all the years I've known him. "But I think she realized I needed more than she could give, so she brought me to the Aviary."

"You didn't have to bring me here," I say, feeling like I've intruded on something private. Something sacred.

"Oh, I know." His smile turns teasing. "I could have lost you in seconds back on Maricious."

"If you're so talented," I say, my voice dripping with sarcasm, "then why didn't you?"

"Because tomorrow, I want you to remember why we do what we do." His tone sobers, losing its taunting lilt. "I want you to remember that it's not about us, it's about our people. *Your people.*"

My gaze drifts back toward the door Areti and the boys disappeared through. The weight of his words settles like a mantle on my shoulders, and as the fire dwindles to embers, I wonder if I'll ever be ready to bear it.

SEVEN

SUNLIGHT SPILLS THROUGH THE window of my bedroom, dripping over my face and heralding the arrival of Naming Day all too soon.

After last night's revelations, I tossed and turned in my bed, consumed by the prospect of finally crossing the Solorai Sea like I have always dreamed. But the warning in both Calliope's and Raven's words added a sharp edge to the excitement, twisting it into the bitter sting of anticipation.

I ended up returning home afterwards, and I know an interrogation from Nyssa will be on my agenda for the day. Groaning at the thought, I kick my sheets down and force myself from the bed, shuffling over to my wardrobe.

When I got back last night, my ceremonial garb was hanging from the door, washed and pressed by one of the Aviary's silent staff. The outfit is made of the finest cloth in the purest white, and in the traditional style of our kind. A floor-length chiton with an intricate pattern of filigree and little songbirds stitched in gold and silver thread along the hem and the cuff clasps around the neck. Over the gown is a matching hooded robe, the same pattern of birds stitched along the border. It lacks the delicacy of the modern clothing styles that came about after the God War, but is beautiful, nonetheless.

As I examine the embroidery, the growing unease from the past few days rears its head again. Calliope's words of warning warp through my mind, making me question how prepared I am to take flight and leave the safety of the Sorrows behind.

A sharp tapping at my window pulls me from my thoughts and a genuine smile curves my mouth at the sight of fluttering white wings beyond the glass. I hurry to the window, throwing it open with a soft laugh as Cinder flies through like a feathered arrow finally released from a bow. He circles my room once before landing lightly on my desk, ruffling his black-spotted feathers and cocking his head to the side, fixing me with one beady eye.

Kal and I discovered Cinder as a young hatchling. We didn't recognize him as a hawk until he grew, and his plumage came in. He fell from his nest and into a palace chimney, his tiny white body tinted charcoal with soot from the burnt-out fireplace. Hence, Cinder was a fitting name for our new feathery friend.

At first, we tried to find his nest and return him to his family, but when Kal nearly fell from one of the palace turrets, we kept him instead. Together, we hand-reared him and trained him to carry our secret messages back and forth, but—much to Kal's dismay—Cinder preferred to spend most of his time with me.

Cinder holds out the leg and I spot a strip of curled parchment tied with twine. I remove the note and gently stroke the feathers on his back, scratching the spot between his wings.

"Clever boy," I croon, grabbing a small jar and sprinkling some flakes of dried fish, eliciting a satisfied squawk in response.

I unfurl the parchment and trace my finger along the looping letters. Warmth sparks in my chest at the swirling strokes of Kal's quill.

Eastern gardens. Half an hour.

I drop the note and hurry to my wardrobe, quickly pulling on a pair of white linen pants and a matching shirt. I tame my hair into a braid—still a shade of brown since I rarely remove my *goiteía* earring—and throw my hooded wrap around my shoulders. After a moment's hesitation, I strap my dagger to my waist as well, hiding it beneath the draping fabric of my wrap.

Once I'm done, I glance over to Cinder as he pecks at the last scraps of fish. He cocks his head again, blinking slowly.

"Want to be my second set of eyes?"

He gives a shrill caw in response, and I swear the tone of it says, *obviously*. If birds could roll their eyes, Cinder would do it, and often. I grin and tilt my head to the side as he launches in a flurry of wings to land on my shoulder. His talons dig through the fabric, but rather than making me flinch, a sense of comfort settles inside of me.

Despite the early hour, I sneak from my room, skulking my way through the Aviary. In a building full of spies, you can never be too careful.

Instinct carries me on light feet through the shadowed alleyways to the edge of Vinta, the small isle where the Aviary stands. I slip around the last corner of a building and Santora comes into view.

This close to the royal isle, I must be cautious. Despite being the daughter of the king, the Eagle has made it clear I'm not to have any contact with my old life while I'm still in training, claiming it would compromise my ability as a Songbird. Plus, there's the tiny detail of everyone believing I'm on the Isle of the Winds. On the surface, I obey his rules, but Kal and I have a shared love for breaking them.

I crouch in the early morning shadows, eyeing the path ahead. At a click of my tongue, Cinder takes flight, gliding over the cobbled street to land on the bridge arching over the water. He cocks his head from side to side before giving a single squawk.

The coast is clear.

I stand from my hiding place, darting across the street and over the bridge. Cinder swoops past me, taking the lead and scouting ahead.

The moment I set foot on the island, the changes are obvious. Rows of pristine white villas belonging to the upper society of the Sorrows line the meticulously cobbled streets, and small manicured courtyards bloom with bougainvillea and citrus trees. I dart from row to row, steadily making my way toward the looming palace walls. When the eastern gatehouse comes into view, I crouch behind a potted apricot tree, squinting at the guards stationed on either side.

As I watch, a third guard joins them. His tall, broad form is clad in the same official garb as the others, but the cerulean himation clasped at his shoulder marks him as one of the royal guards. The other two offer him a swift salute before turning and marching inside, and the royal guard takes his post. Assuming this is part of Kal's plan, I rise from my crouch and rush forward. The guard doesn't move at my approach, and I take the slight quirk of his lips as a good sign.

Probably thinks I'm here for a very *different reason.*

I wince at the thought, shaking it free from my mind as I slip through the gatehouse.

Like every time before, my feet stall when I step beyond the archway, breath catching in my throat at the sight before me.

The Palace of Sorrows.

A paved pathway cuts through the surrounding immaculate gardens, leading to an arcade of intricately carved stone columns. The palace glows in the morning light, its white towers rising against a backdrop of soft blue and lilac streaking through the dawn sky, cerulean flags fluttering in a sea breeze. Hundreds of windows glimmer with the reflection of the rising sun.

The memory of attempting to count them with Kal when we were children rises from the depths of my mind, drawing forth a soft, nostalgic smile.

Cinder swoops past me once again, and I tear my gaze away, following him through the tall hedges and ornate topiary shrubs that have kept my clandestine visits hidden from prying eyes for the past seven years.

A hand clamps down on my wrist and tugs me around a bend, pulling me down into the shadows of a hedge sculpted into the likeness of my great-grandfather, King Cadmus. With barely a thought, I unsheathe my dagger and swing it toward my attacker's throat. My stomach bottoms out and I only just manage to pull it back when I come face-to-face with my brother's sparkling ochre eyes.

"Are you trying to get us caught?" I hiss, punching him in the shoulder as I slam the blade back into its sheath at my waist. "Or get yourself *killed*?"

"Come on, Aella," Kallias taunts, "I didn't take you as the type to scare easily."

I huff out a breath of mock annoyance, but as usual, Kal sees right through me, offering a teasing grin as he pulls me into a hug.

"I heard the Naming is today. I wanted to see how you were feeling."

I shrug myself out of his arms with a grimace.

He chuckles. "That bad, huh?"

"I feel like there's so much happening around me, and I'm in the dark." The confession falls easily from my lips, giving voice to the concern that has been lingering within me since last night. "Everyone always seems to know things concerning me before I know them myself. I hate not knowing what to expect."

Kal runs a hand through the waves of his dark hair and sighs. His eyes drift back toward the palace as he replies.

"There's a lot of that happening around here."

His words peck at my apprehension, like birds of prey pulling scraps from a carcass. A frown creases my brow as I add concern for my brother to my worries.

"Something's bothering you. What is it?"

"I'm unsure. Father has been absent a lot, cooped up in his study and meeting with that vulture of a man who stole you away. Even though I'll be ruling in his stead one day, he won't confide in me. I've tried to get him to talk to me, but he brushes me off and tells me it's nothing to concern myself with. But I *feel* it, Aella. There's this…tension you can sense when you're around him, like he's a serpent coiled and waiting to strike. The servants are also aware—I can only imagine what gossip is spreading amongst them."

My heart fractures in my chest. I lean back and watch Cinder as he perches within the leafy crown of the King Cadmus hedge, his feathered head twitching in each direction while he keeps a lookout. A wave of emotions floods through me. Grief, guilt, and anger.

So much anger.

Before our father sent me away with the Eagle, Kal and I believed we would always be there for one another. From the moment I could crawl, we were inseparable. As thick as thieves, running around the palace and its grounds. But it was all a fantasy, the ignorance of childhood, shattered too soon by a reality much bleaker.

"Do you remember the time we thought he was planning to propose to that gods-awful Lady Cynthia?" I ask, the specter of an idea taking shape in my mind.

The lines on Kal's forehead deepen. "And we broke into his study to find the proof?"

I nod. "Maybe it's time for a repeat?"

A smile blooms across his face and the cracks in my heart stitch back together again. Not all the way, but close enough.

Cinder lets out a shrill squawk from above.

Our time is up.

"I should go." As soon as I speak the words, I regret them. I hate not being able to offer the support Kal desperately needs, but we have both been cursed to navigate this world alone.

"I know, but we'll meet again soon. After the ceremony?" He phrases it as a question, but the casualness of his tone cannot hide his concern that this may be the last time we see each other.

I pull him into an embrace this time, holding on tight as he wraps me in his arms.

"After the ceremony," I whisper.

Walking away from him doesn't hurt any less with time. Especially when I'm uncertain about what I'm walking toward.

We stand in lines of pairs before the ornate arched doors of the hall, all of us cloaked in the same white ceremonial garb that I found hanging in my room earlier this morning.

The air is so thick with tension you could cut it with a fine blade.

We were given strict instructions of what order our procession was to be in for the ceremony. I stand at the back, with Nyssa to my right. I can sense her throwing me furtive glances, but I keep my eyes straight ahead, glued to the intricate carvings etched into the wood.

The heavy doors swing open, a screeching groan of hinges shattering the silence. The sound scrapes its way up my spine, prickling my skin with unease. As our cohort moves, I draw in a deep breath, steeling myself as I step forward with them.

In all my years at the Aviary, this is my first time entering the ceremonial hall. Stone columns line the walls of the large, square chamber, stretching up to a ceiling that has been transformed into an artful canvas, its paintings portraying the history of the Sorrows and the rise of our order. The history of a kingdom and its secrets on display, all captured by a masterful hand.

Several Owls stand along the far wall, dressed in white ceremonial robes like our own, their faces hidden beneath deep hoods. The last light of day shines through the arched windows of the western wall, setting dust motes alight and pooling in amber puddles on the polished marble floor. In the center of the hall is a circular dais, adorned with a golden pedestal in the shape of an eagle in flight. The eagle's wings spread to support the weight of the ancient tome resting on its back.

The Book of Names.

The book holding the identities of every single person to ever be inducted into the order. Including mine, after today.

I tear my eyes away from the book and turn my attention

to the man standing beside it.

Lord Amon Malis. *The Eagle.*

I breathe through my nose, fighting the urge to fist my hands as bitterness rises like bile in my throat.

His features are sharp like cut glass. Fathomless eyes the color of a soulless night sky, sleek black hair braided down the back of his golden ceremonial robes. Those barren eyes flick toward me and a shiver travels unbidden down my spine.

Like a well-orchestrated dance, our two lines split, the twelve of us forming up around the circular dais before standing to attention. When I first came to the Aviary, our number was eighteen, but over the years a third of our group has gone missing. After no answers and countless punishments, we became all too acquainted with the first rule.

Ask no questions.

As one, we wait with bated breath. My heart thumps painfully against my ribcage as I fight to keep my expression neutral and my posture straight. The tension in the room hones to a lethal sharpness as endless moments pass.

Finally, the Eagle cuts through the silence.

"You have been chosen for this day, each of you." His steely voice echoes around the chamber like the metallic song of blades clashing in battle. "From Fledglings you have been reared, guided, and trained in our order—now it is time to spread your wings. Today is not only an acknowledgement of your accomplishments, but also the ultimate test of your dedication and loyalty to our kingdom. You will each drink from the Eagle's Kylix, and—if the great god Notos deems you worthy—you will be recorded in *The Book of Names.* From this day forth, under the watchful eyes of the Aviary, you will shed your past self and begin your life anew."

The dissident part of me is tempted to ask what will happen if Notos doesn't deem us worthy. To question how he will judge us, considering he disappeared centuries ago. Fortunately, I manage enough self-restraint to hold my tongue.

"Fledgling," Lord Malis says, his eyes fixed to my right. "Make your vow."

My body tenses as Mateo steps forward, head held high and voice clear as he speaks.

"From this time forward, under the eyes of Notos, God of the Southern Land and Wind, Bringer of Summer, I pledge my life and allegiance to the Aviary and the Sorrows. I vow to be the eyes of the Eagle and the wind beneath the wings of our order. From this day until my last day."

An Owl steps into the circle and approaches Mateo, gripping a large *kylix* by its handles. My eyes narrow on the vessel as a thrum of power emanates from it. A trickle of unease runs through me at the unfamiliar markings carved into its golden surface—they're unlike any *goiteía* I've seen before.

After a brief hesitation, Mateo reaches out to grasp the handles, bringing the vessel to his lips. He closes his eyes, throat bobbing as he swallows. The rest of us hold our breath. Not a whisper of air escapes us as we watch the scene unfold.

Up on the dais, Lord Malis raises his eyes from the pages of the book, the shadow of a smile on his face. "Welcome to the Aviary, Petrel. May your flight be long."

Matteo steps back to his place in the circle, a broad grin breaking out on his face when our eyes connect. I return it, relief soaking into my bones, easing away some of the tension I've been carrying.

I watch on in stoic silence while Lord Malis carries on with the ceremony. As each of my cohort makes their vow and receives their name, I vaguely wonder how many bird breeds there are in the kingdoms.

The thought shatters apart as a shrill scream pierces the air.

The Owl snatches the *kylix* out of Luci's hands, and she viciously claws at her throat, carving red welts into her skin. She chokes on another scream, blood dripping from her mouth, before she collapses with a wet, rasping gasp.

We all watch in horrified silence, shock freezing our feet to the marble floor beneath us as Luci finally falls still.

"Such a shame." The Eagle's vicious words slash through the room—carving a hole through my chest and tearing the air from my lungs. My gaze rips from Luci to his to find his black stare boring into me as the next word leaves his lips. "Continue."

To my right, Nyssa trembles beside Luci's unmoving body. Her usually warm skin a pallid shade as she speaks her oath, accepting the vessel with shaky hands. I hold my breath as she brings the *kylix* to her lips, only releasing it once she hands it back and appears unaffected—the air escapes my burning lungs in a tenuous sigh of relief.

She's safe. Nyssa is safe.

And then the Owl stands before me.

"Fledgling." Lord Malis' cold voice forces my eyes back toward where he stands on the dais. There's something more in his tone, like he's daring me to refuse my fate. Daring me to give him any excuse to punish me and put me in my place.

I despise the way he watches me, like he's always waiting for something. I push my shoulders back and lift my chin, meeting his bottomless stare as he continues.

"Make your vow."

The words flow from my lips and pride burns within me at the strength in my voice. With the final word, I accept the *kylix*, drinking the very last drops of liquid.

Thoughts race through my mind as magic crawls through me. It forces itself down my throat and claws through my bloodstream, attempting to scent every secret and every shadowed corner of my soul.

Perhaps I'll be the next to drop dead. Maybe whatever *goiteía* is carved into the kylix will deem me unworthy and claim my life as penance.

I smother a gasp when power surges within me, cresting like a wave rolling into shore, cascading through my entire being. It crashes over the crawling sensation with such force the magic from the *kylix* disintegrates.

Moments of tense silence pass, and throughout them all, I refuse to drop the Eagle's gaze. Refuse to let even a sliver of the confusion whirling inside me slip past my defenses.

Eventually, the lingering sensations fade entirely, and Lord Malis drops his eyes from me. I inhale sharply with relief as the sound of a quill scratching against parchment penetrates the pounding of my heart in my ears.

"Welcome to the Aviary, Starling. May your flight be long."

EIGHT

STARLING.

I pass the name back and forth in my mind as I lie in my bed, staring sightlessly up at the canopy.

I savor it.

Despise it.

Twist it back and forth to examine each letter and syllable, uncertain whether the thrill it evokes outweighs the sorrow.

How is one meant to react when told to leave behind the life they have always known? To abandon it like an old, ragged garment for a shiny new one?

Most likely, I should be filled with pride and anticipation. But I've always seen this new garment for what it is—made from the finest fabric, but with a clasp of broken glass waiting to be wrapped around my throat.

The image of Luci's prone body on the marble floor flashes through my mind once again. The sound of her choking sobs reverberates through my skull, and the cold, unfeeling words that followed echo endlessly.

Such a shame.

I'm more than accustomed to the brutality of the Aviary. I've been on the receiving end of Lord Malis' ire more times than I care to remember. I've spent days locked in cells without food or water as punishment and been manacled with *goiteía* cuffs that burned my skin and left me feeling sick and hollow. I've endured all of this and more in the name of building resilience and instilling obedience.

Over the years, the shock of it has waned, replaced with simmering fury.

A soft tap comes from my door, and I drag myself out of bed with a sigh. I trudge over and pull it open, freezing in place when a pair of striking honey-brown eyes meet mine.

"Raven." I pull my nightgown closer around my body, suppressing a shiver at the way he tracks the movement closely. "What are you doing here?"

"I need you to come with me."

I peer over his shoulder, frowning when I see Nyssa hovering in the hall behind him, also dressed in nothing more than her nightclothes. I arch a brow at her in question and she returns it with a shrug, no more enlightened than I am.

"Can I get dressed?" I ask.

"There's no need," Raven calls over his shoulder, already striding down the hall.

I pull my door shut and fall into step beside my friend. "Any idea what this is about, *Sparrow*?" It's strange to call her by her new name. In my heart and mind, she will always be Nyssa to me, regardless of what the Aviary commands.

She groans under her breath. "Of all the birds in the realm, I get named after the plainest one. Why couldn't *I* be called Starling? Or Falcon?"

"I think it's cute."

From the corner of my eye, I see Nyssa turn her head slowly to glare at me. "No red-blooded woman wants to be thought of as *cute*, Aella."

I bite my lip to hold in a laugh. "It could be worse," I offer with a shrug.

"Yeah, like what?"

"I hear there's a species of bird common in Reveza called a dickcissel."

Nyssa makes a choking sound and slams a palm over her mouth, smothering her laughter. "Okay, you're right. I'll take Sparrow over *that* any day."

Raven leads us up the stairs and we trail behind him. With his back turned, My gaze wanders over him, taking in the loose black linen shirt that does nothing to hide his broad shoulders and tapered waist. My eyes drift lower, noting the way the muscles of his ass flex with each step through the black leather of his pants. Nyssa chuckles knowingly beside me and I shoot her a warning glare, shoving my elbow into her ribcage for good measure.

Finally, Raven comes to a stop outside a single door emblazoned with an eagle, and any amusement I felt swiftly sours.

As though he can sense the change in my mood, he cuts me a warning glance, and then raps his knuckles sharply on the door. After a brief pause, he pushes it open and leads us inside.

The scent of old books and parchment permeates Lord Malis' dimly lit study. Candles flicker on wooden bookcases, casting shadows across the walls. Ancient relics and manuscripts line the shelves, each one carrying the weight of centuries of history within its worn and tattered pages, making me question how so many rarities have made their way to this one room in our broken kingdom.

My gaze lands on Lord Malis as he looks up from his desk. The edges of his mouth curl sardonically as he gestures at the four chairs facing him. Lark already reclines in one, and he wiggles his eyebrows at me as I take the seat beside him. When Raven and Nyssa settle into the others, Lord Malis looks at each of us intently—a silent warning that any disobedience will result in swift punishment.

"Sparrow. Starling." His fathomless eyes lock onto me, making my skin crawl. "Thank you for coming at such a late hour, but I am sure you will appreciate the gravity of this situation once I give you your assignments."

Nyssa and I sit in silence as we wait for him to continue. Calliope's warning from the night before rears up in my mind and I grip the edges of my seat, trying my best to smother the rising sense of foreboding.

"As you are aware, both Raven and Lark recently returned from an assignment in Eretria. What is *not* commonly known amongst the order is the purpose of their mission. Over a year ago, we received word from one of our Songbirds that the King of Eretria had come into possession of a weapon. A weapon so lethal, it could mean the end of our world as we know it. After that first missive, we lost contact with our

Songbird and can only assume he was caught."

Lord Malis stands from his desk and walks to the window, staring out into the abyss of darkness beyond as he continues.

"Few in our kingdom will remember what it was like during the God War. Destruction and bloodshed devastated the lands, and—while we are no longer at war—the divides in our kingdoms have only become more pronounced over time. Tensions are rising across the Empyrieos, and the songs we have heard suggest war may no longer remain in the history books. King Daedalus is poisoned by greed, parading as a visionary with claims to reunite the kingdoms under one crown. With this weapon in their hands, Eretria holds an advantage over the rest of the kingdoms. We cannot allow his vision of one kingdom with one king to come to pass."

Lord Malis turns back to face us.

"The two of you will accompany Raven and Lark to Eretria in a week's time. Alpha Flight will travel to the capital, Vilea, with the aim to infiltrate the court and seize the weapon. I cannot stress the importance of success. The fate of our kingdom—*our realm*—depends on it."

I keep my expression clear despite the urge to frown. What type of weapon could be powerful enough to tip the scales in a war?

"What is the weapon, my lord?" Nyssa asks, echoing my thoughts.

"That remains to be seen. Alpha Flight was able to narrow down its location but could not get close enough to determine exactly what it is they are hiding. While you and Starling will mainly be focused on infiltration and distraction, the rest of the Flight will be responsible for finding the weapon and seizing it."

"And once we have this weapon," I ask, all the potential risks running through my mind, "what will be the extraction plan?"

"Raven and Lark will fill you in on the details. That will be all."

The four of us bow our heads respectfully and stand to leave. As we reach the door, Lord Malis calls out behind us. "Starling, a word."

Nyssa shoots me a worried look but follows Raven and her brother out into the hall as I turn back. I'm given no indication to sit this time, so I remain standing, hands clasped behind my back.

Unfeeling eyes survey me as Lord Malis leans back in his chair. He picks up a small dagger from his desk, tapping it against the palm of his hand. I steel myself to not so much as twitch under the brutal intensity of his surveillance. The seconds drag by before he finally speaks. "Do you know why I took you into the Aviary?"

The question catches me off guard.

It's rhetorical—both he and I know the answer. Not only is the Eagle the authority of the Aviary, but the position also makes him an advisor to the Crown.

"Because my father wanted me gone, Eagle." I force myself to remain still as he rises from his chair and approaches me, splitting my attention between his face and the dagger he still holds.

"Yes, and when he consulted me on the matter, I could not

let such an opportunity pass me by. To have the royal blood of the Sorrows here, within my control. The possibilities, what I could accomplish with you. Endless." My pulse spikes as he circles me, pumping adrenaline into my body when I lose sight of him. Cold metal presses against my neck before he whispers his next words in my ear, dripping with something hungry. *Greedy.* "I wonder, if I slit your throat open now, what else might bleed out of you?"

As if in response to his question, a tempest roils inside of me.

Destructive and stained with fury.

With effort, I force the sensation down—silently thanking all four of the Anemoi that he's standing behind me and can't see the strain that must show on my face. I school my expression to one of acceptance as the cold steel falls from my throat and Lord Malis steps in front of me.

"You will play a very particular role in this assignment, and I need you to be prepared," he says.

Sharp words build on the tip of my tongue. Jagged and cutting, like shards of broken glass. But I swallow them down, wincing as they slice and scrape my throat on the way down. "I will do whatever the Aviary requires of me, Eagle," I say instead.

A cruel smirk curls his pale lips. He's satisfied with the response, like he thinks he's finally broken me. Decimated the person I once was.

He couldn't be more wrong.

"You will play the role of..." he pauses, dragging out the moment like a viper before it strikes. "Princess Aella Sotiría of the Sorrows."

I blink slowly.

I was expecting this.

Joining the Aviary, being told by my masters not to dye my hair, the decoy—*my decoy*—acting out a false life amongst the acolytes. I *knew* there was a reason.

Despite my efforts to reassure myself, his words land like a physical blow. My nails bite into the palms of my hands so hard I'm sure I've drawn blood. All I know is I can't breathe, and I want to *scream*. But while pure chaos takes over my mind, I maintain my forged expression of passive acceptance.

I won't let him see beneath the facade. I won't let him have more power over me.

"As the Eagle commands," I say with an incline of my head.

I don't miss the flash of disappointment in his black eyes. Of course, the sick bastard wanted it to hurt.

I refuse to give him the satisfaction.

"Tomorrow night, the king will hold a celebration in honor of your return to the Sorrows." He chuckles under his breath before he continues. "He is hosting a dignitary from Eretria—a lord of high standing in their royal court—and you are to make an impression on him. This will give your stance credence when you eventually arrive."

"Why?" The question slips past my lips before I can catch it, but—fortunately—he's all too eager to explain.

"Because you will compete in Eretria's Royal Trials, to win the position of the Prince's bride."

My throat constricts at the smugness of his tone. I try to swallow, but my mouth is dry as sand. I'm seized by the sudden desire to lunge at him, snatch his blade, and shred the satisfied expression from his face. To paint the manuscript-lined wall with the crimson of his blood.

I breathe deeply and blink the violent vision away.

"What of my decoy?" I ask.

"She is being dealt with." Something sinister gleams in his gaze, and I shiver. "Now, have I made myself clear?"

"Of course, Eagle. I'll do my best."

"You will not *do your best*. You will win."

The edges of my vision blur before slamming back into sharp focus; just to watch any hope of a future crumble in the wake of his expectations. Winning would not only mean I would be trapped in a life at the side of a foreign prince. It would mean being the Eagle's puppet on a set of long strings.

A fate there would be no escape from.

"You won't disappoint me, Aella." His cold voice cuts through my racing thoughts, but it's the next words that shred through my mental defenses. "You remember what happens when you disappoint me, don't you?"

Images invade my mind before I can strengthen my defenses.

Shattered planks of a boat…bubbles floating to the surface of a dark, hungry canal…a too-small hand reaching…and then gone.

The air leaves my lungs in a shuddering exhale. I blink rapidly to clear my vision, nervously twisting the ring on my finger to help center myself.

"I'm glad you are still clear on what's at stake. I would hate to lose Nyssa. She is a promising Songbird, after all." His smile is as malicious as his words, sharp teeth glinting in the candlelight. "If you succeed, I will allow her to stay there—you will need a handmaiden or two."

"That is most gracious, Eagle."

"Dismissed."

I lower my head once more, forcing myself to turn and walk from the room with a measured stride. All I want is to run. To scream my rage at the lonely moon in the sky.

But I won't.

I can't.

The Eagle's message is clear. If I fail, Nyssa will pay the price.

If she is the cage he chooses to trap me with, I will gladly stay prisoner for the rest of my existence. Anything to keep her safe.

I push the fury to the back of my mind, bury it in the shadows that linger there, and lock it away where no one else will ever find it.

Hopefully, not even me.

I find myself on the roof of the Aviary tower. With my thoughts a maelstrom and my eyes unseeing, my feet led the way here. Following the same path I have walked countless times before, to where it's now deeply rooted in my subconscious.

The night sky is an endless stretch of black velvet, the stars shrouded by an incoming storm. The moon peeks out from behind a cloud, its light casting an eerie glow over the Sorrows, silver dripping across the shifting waters of the Solorai Sea below.

"No wonder they all left," I whisper to the moon, thinking of the Anemoi and their descendants who all but vanished after the God War ended all those centuries ago. I suppose I wouldn't be all too surprised if the Anemoi chose to leave this world behind rather than walk among us as they once did. Tycheroi can be fickle and cruel; I wonder whether our kind was a disappointment to our creators. Perhaps they left after the war because they were too ashamed to see their great kingdom torn apart, the race they had created slaughtering one another.

Ashamed of us.

Of *themselves*.

I can only imagine we have grown worse over the centuries. Only now, instead of openly waging war, we do it in secret, with subterfuge and trickery.

Then again, if we were made in the gods' image as the histories claim, maybe this is exactly what they intended. Maybe they observe us from afar, laughing and eagerly awaiting the next turn of events. The God War started with them, after all.

I shake the treacherous thought off as the soft scuff of a footstep sounds below. Everyone in the Aviary moves in complete silence, so I appreciate the fact that whoever is approaching is giving me the courtesy of announcing themselves.

A moment passes before Raven pulls himself over the edge of the rooftop and settles beside me. He says nothing, only stares into the distance while we sit in silence.

Did he know? I wouldn't be surprised if he did. Maybe this was the reason for his vague warning last night. The Eagle has always favored Raven. Some in the Aviary even refer to him as the Eagle's adopted son—insisting that favor was the reason he flew through the ranks to become the commander of Alpha Flight.

I don't know how long we've been sitting in silence. It could be seconds, minutes, hours—eventually my thoughts grow too loud, roaring in my ears like the rush of a storm at sea.

"Is nothing sacred anymore?" The words burst free before I can stop them, and I close my eyes, quietly berating myself.

"I wasn't aware you had laid claim to the rooftop."

"Well, I have. I staked my claim seven years ago."

"My sincerest apologies, princess."

I fix him with a furious glare, absently taking pleasure in the way he winces.

"He told you, then?" Raven asks softly.

I hum in response, neither confirming nor denying it, but glance at him from the corner of my eyes.

He's breathtaking in the moonlight, staring out at sea with a forlorn look that tempers my anger. Silver highlights the rich brown of his hair, almost black in the night. It paints the angles of his face, caressing the sharpness of his jaw and the softness of his lips. I trace each detail with my eyes, like I've done countless times before. This may be one of the last quiet moments I will get to see him like this.

When my gaze finally travels up to his eyes, they burn back at me—fiery pools of amber that sear my soul. Raven reaches up with a large hand that belies the gentleness of his fingertips brushing across my cheekbone.

"This is not the life I had hoped for," I admit. How often had I perched on this rooftop, dreaming of the land across the sea? How frequently had I yearned for adventure, for something beyond the mere semblance of a life I lived? Yet now, as the opportunity arises, it feels as though I am being trapped with another bar in my cage.

Raven presses his palm more firmly to my cheek and I lean into the warmth of his touch. "You are strong, Aella of the Sorrows," he breathes the words, like a prayer. "You are strong enough for this."

I close my eyes and breathe in deep, savoring his scent of woodsmoke and cinnamon, the warmth of his hand on my face. Falling into this gentle moment, so unlike the Raven I know, and praying it will last. But when I open my eyes, I finally see the shutters fall in his, sealing away the tenderness from a heartbeat ago. He drops his hand and stands. I miss the warmth as surely as I would miss a limb from my body.

"Come. There's much to do before we leave, and you need your rest." He pulls me up, hands dropping to my waist and steadying me. They linger there for a moment, before he lets them fall away and grabs my hand instead.

I let him lead me from the roof in silence, pushing aside the ache in my chest and hoping I can find the strength he claims to see.

NINE

OUR NARROW BOAT GLIDES along the Grand Canal. The deep blue of the water below glimmers in the morning light, contrasting with the colorful buildings lining the docks and banks.

Almost a year ago, citizens from all over the Sorrows gathered along the canal and stained the facades in an array of rainbow colors as part of *Kalokairi*, the summer festival. After a few months in the southern heat, the colors faded, giving the buildings a more rustic charm.

The air is heavy with change, the dry heat of summer reluctantly releasing its hold as the wet season approaches. Where my hand hangs over the side of the vessel, the wind slips through my fingers, dancing along to a secret song I imagine I can hear.

"There's a storm coming."

Nyssa snorts a laugh. "Thank you for that premonition. I

never would have guessed."

"Oh, shut up." I spin toward her and smack her playfully on the arm, but she only grins back at me.

"Why would you want to talk about the weather when there are much more interesting things to discuss?"

My eyes flick to where the skipper stands at the bow, his long paddle steering us toward Inkora, the artisan isle of craftworkers and boutiques. As well as keen eyesight and exceptional speed, our kind has incredibly sharp hearing. There's no way we can discuss Aviary business without him being privy to our words.

I incline my head toward the man and arch a brow at Nyssa, lowering my voice to a conspiratorial whisper. "You mean that scandal with Lord Arsenio and the fisherman's daughter?" I study the skipper's movements as he subtly angles his head toward us.

Eavesdropping bastard.

"Exactly," Nyssa says in an equally hushed voice, catching on. "Someone really ought to tell his poor wife."

We continue the rest of the trip in silence, watching the color-stained facades slip by until the boat docks. As we disembark, I slip a copper drachma into the skipper's hand, and he pointedly avoids my eyes. No doubt word of Lord Arsenio's infidelity will have reached every isle in the Sorrows by the end of the day. It serves the disloyal prick right, but a soft pang hits my heart as I think of his wife learning about his betrayal.

Nyssa and I head down the cobbled street toward Maker's Square, a plaza full of the finest craftworkers and seamstresses the Sorrows has to offer. The tall cypress trees grow in uniformly placed rows, trimmed perfectly to the same height. All the plants in the Sorrows are the same. Manicured gardens, blooming bougainvillea, orchards, and crawling wisteria.

"What do you think a forest will look like?" I ask, turning toward Nyssa.

A slow smile takes over her face. "I've heard they're wild. Apparently, the forests in the other kingdoms are so big they take up nearly half of the land."

"Have you ever even looked at a map, Nyssa?"

"Only when Master Kestrel made us study the kingdoms in geography, but his classes were so dull," she says with a shrug. "I suppose we'll be finding out for ourselves soon enough."

"Did Lark and Raven tell you anything else after you left last night?"

From the corner of my eye, I see her grimace. It's more of a full body cringe, actually.

"Only that you'll be required to play the part of the princess. Which is ridiculous, really. How does someone pretend to be themselves?"

"It's more of a *return*, I suppose." I keep my tone light, playing it off like it doesn't bother me at all. "Just another of the Eagle's convoluted plans."

"Let's not worry about the plan for now, Your Highness," Nyssa says with a wicked grin, linking her arm through mine. "We need to find you a dress that will piss off your father."

She pulls me forward as the street opens to a grand square. A small crowd gathers around a young man playing a lute on the edge of a circular stone fountain. Water streams from the top, cascading down the scantily carved forms of nymphs before

95

collecting in the pool below. His melodious voice rises above the chatter, merging with the notes from his instrument and the sound of trickling water.

The shopfronts lining the square, with windows displaying wares and doors flung wide in invitation, are stained in a similar fashion to the buildings along the Grand Canal. We slip seamlessly through the other shoppers until we find our destination. The limestone is stained salmon pink, the door a rich cedar painted with little vines and red roses along its edges. Three beautiful dresses are displayed in the shop window, each more extravagant and revealing than the last, and golden-painted script curls across the windowpane.

Miss Daphne's Dressmakers.

I wrinkle my nose and glance at Nyssa beseechingly. "Couldn't I wear one of the gowns I already have?"

She scoffs and pushes through the door, calling over her shoulder, "You need a dress fit for a princess, not for a tavern."

Reluctantly, I follow her in, wincing at the tinkle of the shop bell announcing our arrival. The interior is lined with shelves of fabrics in vibrant colors and immaculate creations of silk and chiffon. Plush velvet chairs fill the center of the room around a low table adorned with a vase of slightly wilted roses. At the back of the shop, a counter is stacked high with wrapped parcels and boxes, and a simple wooden door leads through to the sewing and dressing rooms.

In a flurry of silks, ribbons, and brunette curls, Daphne herself bursts through the door, a falsely sweet smile on her angular face. Yet another on the Aviary's payroll, Daphne uses her business to loosen the tongues of upper society who don't have access to the kingdom's royal tailor. I could have gone to the tailor myself now that the rumors are spreading of my supposed return to the isles, but I'd take Daphne over a chance encounter with my father any day.

"Little Fledglings! Take a seat, my dears," she says, her high-pitched tone grating on my nerves.

"It's Starling and Sparrow now," I say, hiding a smirk as Nyssa rolls her eyes and we both settle into the chairs.

"La! Yes, the Naming." Daphne takes the seat across from us, a curious light in her hazel eyes. "You have received assignments, yes?"

"And where did you hear that?" Nyssa asks.

"A little bird told me," she says, a smug smile blooming across her face.

I force back another cringe. I'm certain that little bird was none other than Lord Malis himself.

I'm also certain they're fucking.

Despite my efforts, the shudder I was trying to suppress rolls up my spine at that thought.

Nyssa must notice I'm struggling and takes pity on me, directing the conversation toward safer waters. "With that in mind, Aella needs a gown for tonight."

"La! But of course." Daphne claps her hands together and stands. "I have a few creations that will be perfect for the occasion."

She rushes to the back room, and I turn an accusatory glare on Nyssa when Daphne calls for me to join her. My traitorous friend grins at me and wiggles her fingers in a small wave. I continue to glare at her, but—seeing no other options—trudge through to the dressing room. My eyebrows climb up my forehead at the sight of the dresses Daphne already has waiting for me. The bell rings from the front room and she leaves with a final word to call for her if I need.

Alone, I eye the dresses, doubt creeping into my mind. I love getting dressed up and, aside from last night, it's been so long since I could. Yet, there are too many frills and bows in this selection for my liking—the styles more typical of those popular in the western kingdom, Reveza, than the Sorrows. One is even the same color as the squash Mimi grows in her garden outside the Aviary's kitchen. I narrow my eyes at it, certain Daphne has chosen her worst dresses to spite me.

A faint shimmer of the palest gray catches my eye between a mess of peach and pink, and I pull it from the rack. Tiny pearls scatter across the bust and waist of the gown, dripping down the fine pleats of the fabric. Its halter ties are longer than the dress itself, leaving the impression of a cape.

I strip off my clothes and slip on the dress, making a mess of the neckline as I attempt to tie it in the right way. I wrinkle my nose at the large knot I end up with.

"Daphne!" I call. The door opens and footsteps approach. "I think this is the one. Can you help me tie the back?"

Nothing but silence greets me.

I turn with a frown and freeze, barely concealing the shock from my face.

Raven stands in the middle of the room, his usual confident expression replaced with something that makes my heart bleed into my chest cavity. He works his jaw as his eyes rake over every inch of skin exposed by the dress. I feel that gaze as surely as I would feel his hands upon my flesh, and it *burns*. When he looks back up, the color of his eyes is darker in the dim light of the dressing room, and I get lost in their heated amber depths.

"I think you're right," he says, his deep voice smooth and rich like honey.

"What?" I ask, blinking myself back into reality.

His smile is heartbreaking as he nods his head at the dress I'm wearing. "Turn around."

I narrow my eyes at him, but slowly spin. My neck prickles with awareness, body taut with a tension that melts away when warm fingers sweep my hair over my shoulder.

Dangerous.

This is dangerous.

But as he ties the knot at the base of my neck and smooths the material over my shoulders, my waist, those thoughts melt away too.

I allow it for a moment, closing my eyes and savoring the sensation. The warmth pooling in my stomach, the fine hairs on my body rising—and then I douse it with an icy shower of reality. Clearing my throat, I open my eyes and step around him, moving to the mirror and doing my best to ignore the way he looms like a shadow behind me.

"Is there a reason you're stalking me?" I ask, running my hands down the slight flare of my hips where the fabric clings before draping to the floor like a waterfall. As I thought, the long ties of the halter flow over my back, falling to the floor where it pools in a short train.

"I don't think you're in the position to talk about stalking."

"*I* had a reason." My eyes find Raven's in the reflection. "You looked suspicious."

"I have my reasons too, princess."

I press my lips into a firm line, trying to ignore how the nickname needles its way past my defenses. "And they are?"

"I came to confirm the arrangements are all made for this evening. You need to be ready and waiting before the sun starts to set." Raven's eyes sweep down the length of my body before meeting mine again. "You look beautiful."

His words trap the air in my lungs and a burning pressure builds in my chest.

Those molten honey eyes linger on my reflection a moment longer before he spins on his heel and leaves.

It's not until the door closes behind him that I'm finally able to breathe again.

Despite the still-warm night, the chamber I wait in is cold. The air presses in on me, and the distant footsteps and muffled voices echoing through the stone walls only add to the suffocating weight of this moment.

After Nyssa and I left Daphne's, the day was consumed with ensuring I appeared like the princess the people were expecting to see, followed by an exceptionally detailed staging of my return to the Sorrows. Despite it all, my arrival at the palace had been anticlimactic.

The opulent halls and grandeur of the surroundings—entirely familiar, yet strangely foreign—only heighten my anticipation as I await my father's introduction to the upper echelons of southern society.

A heavy sigh escapes me, and I absentmindedly run my fingers through the intricate pleats of my dress. A futile attempt to distract myself from the weight of the gilded crown of laurel leaves and carnations upon my head.

I smooth my expression as the heavy oak door behind me creaks open, and my father enters the room.

King Costa.

His figure is equal parts imposing and familiar, not unlike the palace we stand within. I drop to a curtsy, only rising when he says so, and then hesitantly take him in.

With our long lifespans, tycheroi age slowly once they reach maturity, so it's a shock to see my father looking so much older than I remember. He looks so much like Kal; both have ochre eyes and wavy mahogany hair. Only our father's is now streaked with silver at his temples beneath the simple golden circlet he wears, and fine wrinkles of time have started to mar his tawny skin.

He watches me back as closely, and I wonder what he sees in me. Does he only see what I look like on the surface, or does he see beyond that? Does he only see my mother's eyes when he stares into mine, or does he see the scarred soul peering back at him?

As if in answer, his mouth firms, and our eyes connect again. I almost flinch at the disdain I see writhing in their depths.

"Come," he says, his voice deep and commanding as he

holds his crooked arm out. I tentatively take it, the connection searing my palm, and let him lead me. He pauses before the doorway, and I breathe deep, bracing myself. "Prove to me you're not a waste of your mother's life."

The air flees my lungs, a whisper-thin escape, as his words strike deep. A lethal blade to my heart. The metallic tang of bile coats my tongue, but I swallow it down, refusing to let it surface. Instead, I steel my spine and lift my chin. I know what he really wants is to see me beaten down. To see me broken.

Breathe.

I take a steadying breath and plaster a serene smile on my face as he raps his knuckles against the door, and they swing open at the signal. We step out to the crowded dining hall, my arm still locked within his. The enormity of the chamber is a crushing weight, vaulted ceilings lost in shadow, vast tapestries depicting the storied history of the Sorrows dancing in the flicker of candlelight. Spectral scents of roasted delicacies intermingle with the heavy perfume of nobility.

Heads adorned with glittering jewels and eyes full of curiosity turn toward us. The rabble of conversation cascades into silence, only broken by the scrape of chairs against polished stone as the gathered tycheroi rise from the long table.

I am strong enough for this.

I chant Raven's words in my mind, hoping if I think them enough, they will eventually be true.

Still, my skin crawls with the sensation of their eyes on me. Probing, judging, seeking the vulnerabilities beneath my smiling mask. We come to a stop at the head of the table and my father's grip tightens, a silent warning to maintain my facade.

"Honored guests," his voice echoes through the cavernous space, "it is my pleasure to introduce you all to my daughter, Princess Aella Sotiría, who has returned from her education on the Isle of the Winds. Please sit with us, dine with us, and help us celebrate this momentous occasion."

We take our seats to a chorus of cheers, and it's only then I allow my gaze to land on my brother. Kal sits across from me in the chair to our father's right. The haunted look in his eyes contradicts the smile on his face.

He knows.

Maybe not the full extent of what's taking place here, but he knows this isn't a case of our father having a change of heart.

"Aella, my dear," Father says, as though he didn't tell me I wasn't worth the air I breathe a moment earlier. "I'd like to introduce you to Lord Yiannis. He traveled all this way from Eretria to meet you."

I pull my eyes away from Kal and turn my attention to the man beside me, offering him a sweet smile. His brown hair is tied back from his face, highlighting a square jaw and dull brown eyes.

"A pleasure, Princess." He takes my hand and plants a chaste kiss on my fingers.

"The pleasure is mine, Lord Yiannis."

"It must be nice to return home after all this time. How did you find your education?"

I know all the plants that can poison, and the plants that can heal. I know how to pick locks and scale walls in the dead of night.

I know the lethal points on a body where even the slightest cut from a blade can be fatal. From a distance, I can throw a blade accurately enough to hit all of them.

"It was very interesting," I say. "I learned a great deal."

Lord Yiannis' polite smile grows into a more genuine one. "A studious woman, then?"

"I suppose one might say so," I offer, reaching for a cup of wine.

Kal coughs from across the table and my eyes dart to him, narrowing slightly as I see him hiding a smirk behind his own cup. "Apologies, my wine went down the wrong way."

"I have devoured every book I can get my hands on about your kingdom, my lord," I say, drawing Yiannis' attention away from my foolish brother. "It sounds like such a beautiful place."

"I think you would be quite at home in our court's library. We have some rare and interesting texts. Perhaps I can show them to you when you're in Eretria for the trials?"

I fight the urge to laugh. To tell him that for me to *be quite at home* anywhere, I would first need to be familiar with the concept.

Kal places his cup loudly on the table. He looks to me, and then to the lord at my side, his brows tightening into a frown. "The trials—"

"Enough, Kallias." Our father's words could freeze the Sorrows over even in the peak of dry season. They settle over our end of the table, sending a chill down my spine.

Fortunately, the palace staff arriving with food overshadows the tension, and I give my foolish brother a warning glare while Lord Yiannis is distracted. Polite chatter takes over our group throughout the meal, but as the sweet refrain of a lute strikes up and guests get up to dance, I slip away from the table.

I head straight to the eastern side of the hall, pushing through the doors and stepping out onto the terrace. A shuddering sigh escapes me as the cool night air wraps around my body like a welcoming embrace. Tilting my head back, I close my eyes, listening intently to the sound of the ocean in the distance, savoring the comforting caress of the breeze across my cheeks.

I don't move at the sound of the door opening and closing behind me. Keeping my eyes shut even as I feel the warmth of a body settle at my side.

"Care to enlighten me on what tonight's little performance is about?"

With a sigh, I open my eyes and angle my face toward Kal. The moon isn't hiding tonight; her full body casts a silver crown of light on his hair, highlighting sharp cheekbones and deepening the shadows of his creased brow.

I memorize every detail, burning my brother's image into my mind. This could be the last time I see him. My eyes burn at the realization, so I turn away.

I will be strong. If not for me, then for him.

"I leave for Eretria tomorrow," I say, clearing my throat when the words come out strained. "I'm going to be playing the role of *Princess Aella Sotiría*. The touching family reunion tonight was the start of my act."

Kal curses, running a hand through his hair. "The Naming

was yesterday and they're sending you off so soon?"

"You're just jealous you can't come with me." I keep my tone light, teasing, so as not to alert him of my own misgivings.

He snorts a laugh, but then a distant expression takes hold of his features as he turns to face the night. "We were meant to see the world together."

The image of an old map flashes before my eyes, cities marked with shiny pearl pins. Childish plans made in furtive whispers and silent prayers sent to the gods echo through my mind.

Maybe they were listening all along.

Or maybe this is the next scene of their grand play, and they're watching in silence, waiting for it to unfold.

TEN

I TILT MY FACE toward the sun as it crests on the horizon, casting rose pink streaks against the blooming dawn. The sky is almost clear of clouds, save for a few fluffy forms that drift in the distance over the Solorai Sea.

I'll miss the summer sun—the feel of it warming my skin. All those times I cursed Notos for making our kingdom so gods-damned hot, and now I wish I hadn't taken it for granted.

With a bitter laugh under my breath, I turn away.

The docks of Elotia are bustling this morning. Early fishermen are bringing in their catch of the day, horse-drawn carts line the harbor, and deckhands rush back and forth, hauling cargo and preparing ships to set sail.

Beside me, Nyssa vibrates with excitement as we sit on a pair of barrels at the northern tip of the harbor, watching the crew of *The Nightingale* jump at the captain's barked orders.

The hull of the ship has been scraped clean of barnacles, its wooden boards freshly tarred, and even the script has been re-painted. The lowered sails flutter in a strengthening morning wind, hinting at a successful day ahead.

A flash of darkness appears in the corner of my vision, and I glance toward it, catching sight of Raven as he moves seamlessly through the crowd. Unable to help myself, my eyes take in every detail with the hunger of a starving beast. Black pants hug his muscular thighs and sturdy boots are laced up to his calves. A loose, black linen shirt hangs from his shoulders, unlaced at the throat, revealing the carved bronze skin of his chest.

"I think they should try looking less serious," Nyssa muses. Her words widen my view and I take in the full scene before me.

Lark walks alongside Raven, an unfamiliar trio trailing in their wake. All of them have the same sharp focus in their eyes as they prowl through the crowded docks. Despite their inconspicuous attire—and the mischievous smile hovering at the corner of Lark's mouth—an unmistakable aura of danger surrounds them.

We jump off the barrels, hefting up our packs, as Lark comes up between us, slinging his arms over our shoulders and dragging us down the docks.

"Ah, my little Fledglings," he says wistfully. "I remember when I was in your shoes. Fresh from the nest, admiring all the pretty Nightwings and their shiny feathers."

"First, we're Songbirds now." Nyssa rolls her eyes dramatically on his other side. "Second, I really hope the delusions of grandeur aren't hereditary."

"It's no delusion, little sister. I've been told by many ladies and gentlemen how *grand* I can be."

Nyssa and I both make gagging noises and I follow up with a sharp elbow to Lark's ribs. He groans in pain, releasing me from his hold. Walking backwards, I point a threatening finger at him. "You keep that shit to yourself, Lark. I have enough nightmares as it is."

He mock-glares at me and I grin back, before spinning around and looking up at the ship. A heavy plank of wood acts as a bridge between the dock and the vessel. I eye the plank as it bobs and sways, and the same unease from the past few days surges with the swell of the tide.

"Scared, princess?"

I glance up as Raven passes, throwing me a teasing smile and heading up the gangway with predatory grace. I tilt my head as he climbs, silently praising the Anemoi for giving me such a perfect view.

A throat clears behind me, and I turn to see Nyssa and Lark standing there with twin expressions: cocked brows and knowing smiles.

"Not a word," I growl.

Throwing my concerns to the wind, I walk up the narrow gangway. As I go to step on board, the ship lurches and I stumble. I'm about to right myself when a firm arm wraps around my waist, halting the progress of my fall and pulling me into a hard, warm body.

My *thank you* dies on my lips as I look up and see who that arm belongs to.

"Don't tell me you were slacking off while I was gone, Starling?" Raven's eyes dance with amusement.

"I've been getting plenty of practice," I snark back, attempting to push out of his arms.

He doesn't let go.

I become intensely aware of every inch of our bodies, the places we touch burning through my clothes. His eyes leave a scorching path in their wake as they roam over my face, and the way they linger on my lips sends heat racing through my bloodstream.

A soft thud sounds behind me, and Raven's arm tightens briefly before he lets go and takes a few steps back.

"Oh gods," Nyssa groans as the ship lurches again. "If I don't find these sea legs everyone talks about immediately, this is going to be a painful experience for us all."

"I'm putting a silver *drachma* on my little sister puking her guts up within the hour," Lark states. "Any takers?"

"That is a bet I'm not willing to take," I say, tearing my eyes away from Raven to scan the ship.

The main deck is broader than it first appeared from the docks. It's vastly different to the triremes that once required hundreds of tycheroi sitting at oars to move through the seas. Three tall masts support heavy sails, draped in shrouds of rope netting. The main mast in the center is the tallest, piercing the sky, with a crossbeam and crow's nest at the top. The deck is flat, with only the raised helm at the rear. Crew members stomp across the wooden boards, calling out to one another as they secure crates and tighten knots. The ropes fixing the ship to the dock creak and strain as the water rocks the vessel from below.

"Come on," Raven says. "I'll introduce you to the captain."

The three of us follow him up to the stern, while the rest of the Flight hovers on the main deck. A burly man stands at the helm, one hand on his hip and the other shielding his eyes from the rising sun as he watches his crew climb the rigging.

"Captain Nikolas," Raven calls as we approach.

The man turns, a broad smile taking over his roguishly handsome face as he clasps hands with Raven. Nyssa hums thoughtfully behind me and I bite my lip to hold back a smile.

"Lark you've met, but this is Starling and Sparrow." Raven indicates each of us in turn.

My chest tightens at the sound of my new name, but I offer a smile as I take in the captain's features. His black hair is tied back from his face, a few shorter strands falling forward. He's shorter than Raven's six-foot frame, but significantly broader. A strong jaw, slightly broad nose, deep umber eyes, and dazzling smile all come together to form a handsome face.

In short, he's *exactly* Nyssa's type.

"It's a pleasure to meet you, Captain," the woman herself purrs.

Laughter bubbles up through my chest, and I bite my lip so hard I taste blood.

"And you, sweet Sparrow. But, please, call me Nikolas." He flashes her that roguish smile and I prepare to catch her if she swoons. Fortunately, she doesn't. It's a close call, though.

"How long until we leave port?" I ask.

"The crew has everything in order, so we'll push off now that you're all on board."

The captain's eyes linger on my face as he responds, a glimmer of amusement creeping into them when Raven clears his throat.

"Same quarters as last time?" Raven asks. His tone has cooled slightly from the earlier warmth.

Captain Nikolas gives a nod, the corner of his mouth twitching like he's trying to hide yet another smile. "I trust you'll get your Flight settled?"

Raven nods before gesturing for us to follow, and we fall into step behind him.

"I'm hot," Nyssa says, fanning herself as she blows out a breath. "Is anyone else hot?"

"Careful, Lark," I tease. "I think your sister may be feeling a bit faint."

He groans in response, nudging her hurriedly down the stairs to put distance between her and the captain.

"In my defense," Nyssa says, "did you see those muscles? If you didn't, I would recommend visiting a healer to check your sight. Because there were *a lot* of them."

The laugh I'd been trying so hard to suppress earlier bursts out of me. Raven cuts me a look over his shoulder and I fall silent, offering him my most innocent smile.

The rest of our companions join us as we head through the doors under the forecastle and into the belly of the ship. On the second level, we step into a narrow corridor lined with slim doors, each opening to a small room with a set of bunk beds and a small porthole window. Nyssa and I quickly slip into a room together. The space not taken up by the bunks is just big enough that we could stand on opposite sides and touch the tips of our fingers together.

I peer at her from the corner of my eye before quickly shouldering off my pack and flinging it onto the bottom bunk. "Mine."

She curses and glares at the top bunk like it's hiding a nest of poisonous snakes. "How long are we at sea again?"

"Five days, depending on the weather."

At that moment, the ship gives a sudden lurch and we both fall forward onto my bunk.

"Notos' balls! What was that?"

I push back the hair that's escaped my braid, amused at the fact she's already adopted the sailor's curse I taught her the other day. "I think the crew pushed off from the dock."

"So, we're not about to be buried in a watery grave?"

"Not yet." I grin at her wickedly and she groans.

"I hate this endless rocking motion already."

I eye her skeptically. "We travel on ferries all the time."

"This is different," she pouts.

"Let's go get some fresh air. We can watch the Sorrows fade into the distance."

"Ugh. I'm going to lie here for a while and pray to the Anemoi for swift winds."

"That's the spirit," I say cheerfully.

She salutes me with her middle finger as I close the door and head above deck, climbing the stairs up to the forecastle. I lean against the railing and watch the harbor as the ship sails away. The sun has risen further, casting the southern sky in vibrant hues of pink and gold, silhouetting the Sorrows in an incandescent glow.

My eyes drift toward the palace, morning light glinting off its windows. As the distance between me and the familiarity of those white-stained towers stretches, the hollow space in my chest yawns wider, a yearning ache spilling into the void.

"You're facing the wrong way." The deep, smooth voice wraps around me, a warm whisper of breath on the arch of my ear, pebbling my skin and pulling me from my melancholy thoughts.

I turn to regard Raven, noting the way the wind tousles those dark waves of his, tangling them over his forehead. My eyes track down his beautiful face, drifting to his lips before flicking back up to his eyes. They turn molten at my obvious perusal.

I clear my throat. "Why do you say that?"

He grabs my waist and I battle back the shiver his touch ignites as he spins me around, angling my body toward the front of the ship.

"Never focus on what's behind you, Starling. The future holds too much promise to be ignored."

Our Flight gathers in the captain's cabin that evening.

Heavy clouds formed throughout the day, angry gray bruises blooming across the sky. A light rain now falls beyond the cabin windows, the flickering lantern light within highlighting the tracks of heavier drops as they trace delicate lines down the glass surface.

All seven of us sit around a large oak table, a map of the Empyrieos carved into its surface with painstaking detail. As Flight Commander, Raven sits at the head of the table, with Lark taking the seat to his right. Both scrutinize the nicks and grooves in the wood like they hold all the secrets of the realm.

On Raven's left is Myna, leaning back in her chair with arms crossed and midnight hair tumbling around her shoulders. She notices me looking, and smiles, the motion drawing my attention to the small scar on her lower lip—the only imperfection on her bronze skin. Nyssa and I had both been struck by awe when we met her. Myna was renowned in the Aviary as one of the most skilled Songbirds. She had a talent for sneaking into even the most guarded of places.

Beside Myna, Heron sits stiffly. He's a regal-looking man with long chestnut hair, golden skin, and cheekbones and a tongue sharp enough to cut stone. When I introduced myself earlier, he dashed the hopes I had briefly entertained of having sleepovers and braiding each other's hair.

Then there's Lory—the youngest of our group, save for Nyssa and me. He reminds me of Lark, only with tousled, light brown curls and a smattering of freckles on his faun skin that suggest he wasn't born in the Sorrows.

Raven clears his throat, ending my scrutiny of the others.

"We all know the aim of our assignment, but I'll go over it once again for the benefit of our new members."

Eyes from all around the table flick toward Nyssa and me. Heron rubs at his temple and leans back in his seat.

"Our orders are to infiltrate the Royal Court of Eretria and seize the weapon they have found. On our last trip, we narrowed down a list of potential locations where it could be hidden. On that list are the dungeons below the castle and the vaults hidden within the mountain." Raven pauses and casts his eyes around the table. When everyone nods, he goes on. "We have extensive logs of the guard detail and schedules throughout the palace, including these specific locations. Additionally, we managed to bring some assets on board, mainly servants and a few lower-tier guards. This time around, our presence will be public. Starling is to provide a distraction for the royal family. Sparrow and Myna will support her in the roles of handmaidens, while the rest of us will pose as a guard retinue."

"Remind us why the Fledglings needed to come," Heron says, his tone suggesting this isn't the first time this conversation has taken place. "Myna knows the etiquette and protocols. She could easily have played the part."

Myna snorts and shakes her head.

"That could have worked," Raven says slowly, "except Myna is more valuable if she can disappear and help with the search. Besides, the amount of *goiteía* it would have required to alter her appearance so drastically would have required too great a cost."

"Starling doesn't look like the princess either."

I bite my lip to hold back my smirk, but it's an effort to maintain a straight face. Since I haven't removed my *goiteía* earring, and my true identity is a secret even from the Flight, only Nyssa and Raven would know why Heron's statement is so amusing.

"She has a charm to change her hair and eye color and will

start wearing it when we get close to Vilea." Raven's tone brooks no arguments and Heron narrows his eyes at me from across the table.

I offer him a cheerful smile in return.

That's a definite no on the hair braiding.

Lory tries—and fails—to smother a laugh, his hazel eyes sparkling with mirth in the lantern light.

"Rather than heading to Port Serre on Eretria's southern coast and traveling overland," Raven continues, "we'll be taking the route along the eastern seaboard and traveling through the Sarathros before docking at Corinth. It will add a few days to our journey at sea, but it's much easier for the crew to control the vessel in the passage if we work with the current rather than against it. Being the largest port city in the eastern kingdom, it will also mean we can arrive unnoticed. That will be our last stop before we meet the other order members and assume our aliases. We will stay at an Aviary safehouse while we gather the necessary items to make our cover viable. From there, it's only two days on the road to the court."

My heart pounds harder with each detail, and it dawns on me how long this plan has been in place. These aren't the kind of details that can be arranged with a week's notice. Nyssa catches my eye, brows lifting in a way that tells me she's thinking the same.

"The king is expecting our arrival?" Myna asks.

"We sent a bird two weeks ago, expressing our intention for Princess Aella to visit. The king responded with an extension of his hospitality from his ambassador, Lord Yiannis."

"Do we have an exit strategy in place?" Heron asks.

"There will be a ball held at the court in a month's time. We need to locate the weapon before then. It will be our best chance for extraction considering the entire palace will be in attendance in some capacity."

Heads all around the table nod in agreement, but I tense when I see Nyssa's brow creasing with confusion.

"What is the ball in celebration of?" She asks, leaning forward in her seat.

Fuck.

Lark and I lock eyes across the table, and his are as wide as my own must be. I'd been so preoccupied over the past few days; I'd assumed he would tell her. Apparently, he'd thought the same of me.

I should have told her. Should have gone to her the moment I left the Eagle's office. I'd been too blinded by my own emotions to consider how she might react to this. Because the reality is, my life will not be the only one altered by this. If I win—*when* I win—I won't be returning home to the Sorrows. I'll be staying in Eretria.

And she'll be staying with me.

"Prince Keres Selmonious is holding trials to find his bride in two weeks' time. It's a tradition the eastern court has followed since their rise after the God War." His shoulders stiffen as he says the words. I try to catch his gaze, but he avoids looking at me. "Starling will compete in them to ensure he is preoccupied."

I watch in silence, all too aware of the eyes on me, waiting to see my reaction. I don't give them one, my gaze fixed to Nyssa's face as it pales slightly beneath the lantern light.

"If Starling wins, then it will hopefully lesson any suspicion cast on the Sorrows." Lark adds, his jaw clenches before he forges on, "but it also means she'll remain there. So will Myna, Heron, and you."

Nyssa's eyes widen and flick to me.

"Are there any other questions?" Raven asks, the words coming out clipped. When everyone shakes their head, he rises from his seat. "We'll discuss the finer details when we settle in Corinth."

With a final nod, Raven leaves the room, his presence lingering in the air like a fading whisper. The others steadily filter out behind him, their footsteps echoing softly against the walls until silence envelops the space.

Until Nyssa and I are the last at the table.

I worry my lip, suffocating under the pressing weight of guilt, while she sits lost in thought.

After long, drawn-out minutes, she finally breaks the silence. But instead of the anger or hurt I was expecting, Nyssa's laughter bounces off the walls of the cabin.

"*You* have to compete for a prince," she finally gets out between breaths.

My confusion dies a swift and brutal death, and I hit her with my most murderous glare. "Nyssa."

"Yeah?" she asks with a watery smile. I watch as she tries and fails to wrangle it under some semblance of control.

"Shut the fuck up."

She doesn't.

And we talk until the early hours of the morning.

ELEVEN

WHEN I WAKE ON our fifth and final day at sea, it's to the warm rays of mid-morning sun shining through the cabin porthole. Overhead, footsteps echo as the crew crosses the deck, and shouted commands seep through the floorboards.

We've been lucky on the journey so far. The weather has remained mostly clear and free of storms, gifting us with brilliant blue skies during the day and starlit ones during the night. The seas have been calm, the boat steady on the deep waters, and the initial nausea I felt when we first pushed off from port has long since faded. Unfortunately, the same can't be said for Nyssa. She spent most of the time coalescing in our cabin.

I've barely seen Raven since our meeting on the first night. Something that should not be possible in such close quarters, but I think he's been avoiding me as much as I have him.

For the past five days of our journey, Myna has been

running through the etiquette of Vilea and its court. Although Nyssa and I learned of all the different cultural and societal expectations of the four kingdoms at the Aviary, we jumped on the offer to make sure the protocols were fresh in our minds.

The ship bucks beneath me, jolting me from my thoughts as I stretch my cramped body and rub the sleep from my eyes. I crawl out of my small bunk, ducking under one of Nyssa's feet where it hangs over the side of hers, and peer outside. Not too far off in the distance, the ocean crashes against jagged cliffs, and my old excitement reignites, like the sun emerging after a storm.

Turning in the small space, I shake Nyssa's foot to wake her. She groans, pulling her blankets further over her head.

"Go away. You're not a queen yet." The words come out muffled from within her burrow.

"It looks like we're heading into the Sarathros. You know you'll regret it if you don't come and see."

She throws her blankets off and fixes me with a glare that would freeze a lesser woman in place. Instead, I simply offer her a dazzling smile before pulling on my clothing and braiding my hair back from my face. Nyssa finally climbs down from her bunk and gets ready, grumbling under her breath the whole time.

When we emerge from the deck below, the view we're greeted with takes my breath away.

Jagged cliffs loom above us like two ancient sentinels guarding the kingdoms. The serrated rocks rise from the depths of the ocean, black and menacing against the pale blue sky. Wind howls through the crevices, creating an eerie symphony that carries to where we stand, as insignificant as ants before great earthen deities.

To the left, the cliffs of Eretria steadily decline into the distance, giving way to rocky beaches. Twisting paths and shadowy caves mar the black stone, tempting me with the many secrets they promise to hide. In contrast, the cliffs of Arkhadia continue to climb, rising into a majestic range of mountains, some of which are so tall their peaks are hidden beneath a blanket of clouds. Right down the center, the ocean flows through the mouth of the Sarathros.

From the maps I've seen of the kingdoms, I know this is the narrowest part of the passage; the easternmost points of the land on either side of the break stretch toward one another. There is an almost melancholy feel to it, like two star-crossed lovers torn apart and doomed to watch the other for the rest of time. Forever reaching out, but never able to close the distance.

"Morning, ladies!"

Nyssa and I tear our eyes away from the view and turn to where Captain Nikolas stands at the helm.

"Captain," Nyssa greets him with a flutter of lashes and coy smile, and I work hard not to roll my eyes. Despite spending most of the time on the ship with her head buried in a bucket or hanging overboard while she hurls her guts up, she's still managed to find the energy to flirt. My friend is relentless.

"You'll want to find something to hold on to!" Nikolas calls. "It's a bit of a wild ride heading into the Sarathros."

Rather than risk being tossed overboard, we head up the

stairs to join him at the helm. The water has grown rough and choppy, making it difficult to keep my footing, but I take hold of the railing on the upper deck and plant my feet wide. Nikolas flashes us one of his trademark smiles before giving his full attention back to the wheel.

Facing forward again, I catch sight of the remnants of a building far in the distance, nestled in the mountains lining the cliffs of Arkhadia. Even in its state of ruin, there is something so profoundly captivating about its forgotten beauty I'm unable to look away. From this distance I can make out the crumbled black stone walls, glimmering in the light that manages to pierce through the veil of clouds. If it weren't for my enhanced eyesight, I wouldn't be able to see it at all, the stone blending almost completely with the dark mountains.

"What's that?" I call out to the captain over the sound of the waves. I don't recall seeing the ruins marked on my map back in the Sorrows. Sadness overwhelms me, realizing this place was deemed too insignificant to be recorded. How many of these forgotten landmarks were disregarded after the war? What else is out there, waiting to be rediscovered?

Nikolas grimaces as he follows my line of sight, his shoulders tensing as he strains against the pull of the ocean.

"A remnant of the Empyrieos, before the God War tore the world apart."

I frown. "What happened to the people who lived there?"

"Legends say it was home to a people favored by Boreas himself, but they died during the war," Nikolas muses, his gaze drifting back toward Arkhadia. "I suppose there's no one remaining to call it home now."

"And it's been left to fall to ruin?" Nyssa asks, her eyes wide with astonishment.

"Few are brave enough to live so deep in the Thalkans."

I open my mouth to respond, but the ship lurches, flinging my body into the railing. I grip the wood tight while the captain's words hang heavy in the air, mixing with the tension amongst the crew as we draw nearer to the cliffs.

Beneath us, the ship creaks and groans as it battles against the waves and I turn my attention to the sailors shouting orders and pulling on ropes below, straining to keep *The Nightingale* firmly on its course. We start to enter the mouth of the Sarathros and the ship shudders as waves crash against its hull like blows from a blacksmith's hammer. The wind howls, tearing at the sails and ripping my hair free from its braid. Saltwater sprays my skin, stinging my eyes and leaving my lips parched.

"Hold on," Nikolas warns, his voice tight. I eye him sidelong as he grunts at the helm, rolled up sleeves revealing the straining muscles of his forearms as he holds the wheel steady.

"We'll make it through?" I ask, trying to keep my tone light, despite the sliver of apprehension slowly widening within me. Regardless of my effort, the words come out strained through gritted teeth. The air gets trapped in my lungs, my body unwilling to release it in case I end up overboard.

"My lady and I have ridden the Sarathros countless times before. The trick is all in keeping her steady."

The confidence in his tone, lacking its usual playboy charm, eases my concerns, and I slowly release my pent-up breath, easing the burn in my chest.

Regardless, I maintain my death grip on the railing.

Tense moments crawl past while Nyssa and I battle to stay upright. My heart beats in my throat and I remain silent, not willing to risk distracting the captain from his task with nervous chatter. The ship lurches again, and the prow rises, angling toward the lightning bolt of blue sky between the craggy clifftops above us. My stomach bottoms out as we crest a rough wave and the ship slams back down. Seawater crashes over the deck, drenching us all in its salty spray.

Nyssa gasps as her hold on the railing slips, and I grab hold of her before she topples over. Her face has lost its usual warmth, taking on the pallid green I've become more familiar with over the past few days.

She starts to thank me, but then fixes me with a narrow-eyed glare. "I knew I should have stayed in bed."

A slightly manic laugh bubbles up from my chest, sharpened by the roiling mix of fear and exhilaration.

Finally, the narrow passage broadens, the cliffs lining the channel curl apart as they drop off toward sea level. The sea calms and the ship settles back into a steady flow, gliding through the gentle rise and fall of tamer waters. A cheer goes up amongst the crew and the tension in my body falls away as a thrill of adrenaline surges through me. The triumph in the air is so tangible I can't help but break into a smile.

"Are you okay?" I ask Nyssa, giving her wrist a gentle squeeze.

"I feel like Notos chewed me up and spat me out."

"So, the usual, then?"

Her eyes narrow on my smirk, and she plants her hands on her hips like she's about to give me a lecture. The wet hair plastered across her forehead and the gray tinge to her russet skin diminishes the effect. "I'm going to go lie down before I add last night's dinner to the seawater drenching your clothes." She turns with her nose in the air, wobbling down the steps and back belowdecks.

Nikolas chuckles as we watch her go, much more relaxed than he was moments ago. "Not one for the sea, is she?"

"Apparently, the waterways of the Sorrows are vastly different to the ocean."

The adrenaline seeps out of my body and a chill trembles up my spine as normal sensation steadily returns. I rub my hands up and down my arms, trying to achieve some semblance of warmth. It doesn't help much, considering I look like I've taken a bath fully clothed.

Before my eyes, the water drains from the fabric, slowly pooling at my feet before snaking along the deck and over the side of the ship.

I watch, slack-jawed, before turning to the captain, now bone-dry and completely baffled.

"How..."

He inclines his head toward the deck beneath my feet, and the grin he flashes at me is downright devious. My eyes lower, and it's only then I spot the small *goiteía* marks etched into the wooden planks of the vessel. A few familiar markings stand out. The one for water, three rows of jagged wave lines, and the mark to drain, a chevron with a single line bisecting the middle, are the most common. Another is also repeated: two

126

parallel lines bisected by a wavy line. The mark for strength.

"Why didn't you carve any to control the ship?" I ask distractedly, while my mind tallies the various markings around the deck. There's easily a hundred of them notched into the boards beneath my feet, the railings, the masts, and even the stern itself. I can't hold back a wince as I realize how much magic the ship has been infused with. It must have taken years off the life of the carver.

If they're even still breathing at all.

"Now, where would be the fun in that?"

I'm struck speechless, torn between frustration and amusement.

Nikolas booms a laugh and I hear the chuckles echoing around the deck, drawing my gaze to the rest of the crew, who throw us surreptitious glances. I narrow my eyes back at them.

"Tell me, Starling, did you feel the fear of the unknown? The rush of excitement flooding your body? The thrill of triumph?"

I push my annoyance aside and think over his words for a moment—not that I really need to. If I am truly honest with myself, I felt all those things and more. There's no denying it, so I nod in response.

"Exactly. Magic is a wonderful thing. A gift from the gods. But *feeling* is also magical. If we used *goiteía* for everything, nothing would be worth living for."

"A captain and a wise man," I chuckle, shaking my head. "Who would have thought?"

Nikolas flashes his dazzling grin again, and this time I

return it.

"Obviously you won't see it from here, but Vilea is on the other side of those mountains." He nods behind me, and I turn.

The cliff still rises from the water, but about three feet up, it gives way to a towering mountain range—not as tall as those we passed on Arkhadia, but magnificent, nonetheless. The peaks reach for the sky, piercing the low-lying clouds like the sharp teeth of a dragon. Under the golden rays of sunlight seeping through the white veil, the mountains have an ethereal quality, light shimmering off thick white veins running through their rocky sides.

"That's the Rithean Range?"

"It is." Nikolas gives me an appraising look. "Have you traveled to Eretria before?"

"Only through books."

"Ah, so you're a scholar, then?"

"No," I scoff. "A dreamer, I suppose."

"Now *that* makes more sense."

Since the waters have calmed, I loosen my death grip on the railing and angle my face toward him. "What makes you say that?"

"You can always tell when a person has adventure in their blood and dreams in their soul," the captain says, a glimmer of respect in his eyes bringing a small blush to my cheeks. "They're the ones who stand at the helm when the oceans are rough. Even if there's no promise of making it through the storm."

A soft smile curves my lips before a commotion draws my attention. The rest of the Flight is emerging from belowdecks.

I watch Raven glance around before he turns and sees me, his eyes catching the light and making my heart race for the second time this morning.

"How long until we reach Corinth?" I ask, pushing off from the railing and heading toward the stairs.

"We're about three hours away, and it's a smooth journey from here."

"See you in a few hours, then," I call over my shoulder. With the feeling of eyes tracking my every move, I scurry down the steps and make my way below deck.

Through sheer force of will and stubbornness, I resist the urge to turn. Knowing if I do, I'll find warm amber eyes staring back at me.

And that's a pull I won't be able to resist.

TWELVE

THE DOCKS OF CORINTH are a city all on their own. A maze of double-story piers and decks, wooden bridges, and staircases. Hundreds of boats, both large and small, are tethered along every length, making me wonder how their owners navigate them into place.

Nikolas and his crew docked our ship at one of the quieter outer piers so we could disembark without too much notice. Even then, the area was crawling with tycheroi and nymphai alike. Our Flight had to move swiftly as we disembarked, slipping away into the shadows and alleys to avoid curious gazes.

Now, with the hoods of our cloaks drawn up, we weave our way through the city, navigating between abandoned alleyways and crowded streets. After half an hour of matching the Flight's furious pace, we come to a stop outside a nondescript building: gray stone stacked at least six stories high with small windows set back in the surface. There's a single pockmarked wooden door at its center, an aged sign hanging overhead with the symbol of a bird in flight burned into the wood above engraved script.

The Rook's Nest.

My nose wrinkles at the sight. I glance at Nyssa from the corner of my eye, and she returns it with a dubious look of her own. But we silently follow the others inside, nevertheless.

As far as safe houses go, I suppose it's safe to assume this place doesn't get many patrons. Fortunately, the inside of the building isn't as bad as I thought it would be. An aged bar lines the back wall, shelves of alcohol stocked precariously high and a curtained-off doorway behind it. A lit fireplace warms the room, casting golden light and making shadows dance around the walls. Cozy furniture fills the rest of the space, a few other tycheroi scattered amongst the cushions. A couple of them eye us briefly, curious expressions on their faces, but most avert their gazes.

We approach the bar and Raven rings a bell. Quicker than I can draw my next breath, a man emerges from behind the curtain. He doesn't seem like a typical innkeeper. With his broad build, dark hair cropped short, and a scar bisecting his right eye, he looks more like a mercenary.

"Raven," he drawls, his dark eyes tracking over each member of our group. "Back so soon?"

"You know what they say, Jax." Lark waltzes up and leans against the bar. "No rest for the wicked."

The man—Jax—rolls his eyes and cocks a brow at Raven, though amusement is written clearly on his face. "Did you really have to bring this one back with you?"

"He's like a severe case of bedbugs. I can't seem to get rid of him," Raven replies.

Lark scoffs, holding a hand to his heart in mock hurt. "If you ever found me in your bed, Raven, you wouldn't want to get rid of me. Isn't that right, Jax?"

The man's eyes heat as they linger on Lark.

My brows rise to my hairline and Nyssa gags beside me. "I did not need to hear that," she mutters under her breath.

Jax clears his throat, turning back to Raven. "I'll grab your keys."

"If you would be so kind."

Jax lifts a wooden case from beneath the bar. It jingles as he places it on the bench. He pulls a small silver key from around his neck to unlock it before lifting the lid. He rummages around for a moment, muttering under his breath, and then hands over a ring of identical brass keys.

Raven accepts them, throwing a purse into Jax's waiting hand with a metallic thud. The man finally cracks a smile. "Pleasure doing business with you, as usual. You know the house rules."

With a final heated glance at Lark, Jax retreats behind the curtain.

"Really?" Raven asks dryly.

Lark gives a winning smile. "There's something about a man with scars."

Raven shakes his head before turning back to our group and nodding toward the stairs.

We climb all six flights until we reach the top floor. The

landing is big enough for us as Raven unlocks the single door on this level. When he opens it, we step into a large rectangular room, its walls are lined with doors and a cramped common area in the middle. Six doors line the room, three on each side, presumably leading to the bedrooms, with—hopefully—a bathroom. Nyssa and I exchange a quick glance before taking the first door to the right.

The bedroom is barely bigger than our cabin on *The Nightingale.* A shuttered window keeps the night at bay, while fine cracks form a spiderweb pattern on the plaster walls.

The beds push against opposite walls, leaving a small space in between them and—as Nyssa lights a lantern—I frown at the lumpy blankets piled on top. I deposit my bag on the misshapen surface and head out to the common room, falling onto a faded lounge.

"Thank the fucking gods for solid ground," Myna groans, as she and Heron collapse into a pair of armchairs.

"I never want to even see a ship again," Nyssa agrees, running her fingers through her knotted curls. I move my legs from the lounge so she can sit beside me.

"Not even if they're captained by dashing, *muscular* men?" I tease.

She scowls back at me but then shrugs, failing to hide her smile.

"I've arranged for Captain Nikolas to meet us in Port Serre," Raven says when he joins us. "When we leave the court, we'll head overland, and then it's only a day at sea from there."

"So, what's the plan now, boss?" Lory asks, lying upside down in his armchair and dangling his legs over the backrest.

"For now, you can do what you want, so long as you don't draw any notice to yourselves. Tomorrow, we'll be waking early to meet the other Crows on the outskirts of the city."

"So, you're saying we have a night off?" Lark grins slyly, casting a look around at the rest of us.

"That's right," Raven says, straight-faced, though there's a glimmer of amusement in his eyes.

"Well," Lory flips around, leaning forward eagerly. "Shall we give our lovely Songbirds a taste of a night away?"

I draw in a deep breath and exhale while I toy with the *goiteía* cuff clasped in my ear.

The others are all waiting downstairs, ready to head out for a night in Corinth. When Lory first raised the idea, I couldn't think of anything worse after almost a week at sea, but then the excitement seized me. My body came alive with renewed energy and the thrill of getting lost in a new city.

The only thing standing between me and fully embracing the night is a single challenge I need to confront.

Raven.

We've traded only a few tense glances and words since our first night on the ship, and it's been driving me mad. Even though it was partially self-imposed; anxiety and frustration have been my two constant companions this past week. I need it to stop. I need a clear mind to focus on this mission.

But I can't do either of those if I'm trying to avoid him.

To avoid the feelings which should have been dead and buried.

Straightening my spine and strengthening my resolve, I force myself to lift a hand and knock gently on the closed door before me. It opens, revealing a shirtless Raven within.

As quickly as my resolve is built, it crumbles, and every thought running through my mind eddies out.

His body is a work of art, all golden, toned muscle that looks to be carved by the gods themselves. I curl my hands at my sides, resisting the temptation to trace the dips and valleys of his torso for myself.

"Starling?"

My eyes dart back to his, and I almost lose myself in their molten depths. I glance away, clearing my throat and fighting to regain some semblance of composure. When I finally get the words past my lips, the accusation dies, sounding breathless instead.

"You've been avoiding me."

"I've been busy." His tone is short, but when I look up, I see his eyes drift to my lips.

His words add fuel to my earlier frustration, rekindling my ire. "What might have kept you busy on a ship in the middle of the ocean?"

Raven runs an irritated hand through his hair, upsetting the brown waves, a muscle ticking in his jaw. "What do you want me to say, Starling?"

"How about the truth? Do you not think I'm capable of carrying out this mission?"

He laughs, but it's a bitter sound. Self-deprecating.

"No, I'm not worried you're *not* capable."

"Then what is it?" I demand, frowning at him.

He braces his hands on either side of the doorframe, his eyes burning into mine with an intensity that sends my heart racing as he towers over me. I take a step back, hoping the small distance will lessen the heat of his gaze.

"You want the truth, princess?"

"Always," I bite back.

"The truth is, I can't stand the thought of watching you flirt your way into the good graces of some prick, just for the sake of this mission. The idea of standing by while you parade around in some gods-damned trial for another—"

He shakes his head, leaving the rest unsaid. The roughness of his voice and the possession lining his words has heat pooling low in my stomach.

He drops his hands from the doorframe and prowls closer, until we're barely inches apart. For a moment we stare at each other, our eyes wide, and breathing ragged. It's like we're standing on a precipice. One move could push us off the edge and the other could as easily drag us back to safer ground.

I don't think I want safety.

I don't want to be pushed, either.

I want to *jump*.

"Why?" I ask.

"Because for an entire year *this* was all I could think about."

He barely says the words before he's tilting my jaw further and pressing his lips to mine. He tastes like honey, and cinnamon, and all the things I'm not supposed to have. His hands cup the back of my neck, tangling in my hair, and I slide mine up his chest, the texture like silk and stone beneath my palms. A moan slips from my lips, dragging a responding growl from his. I can't count the number of times I have relived the memory of his lips on mine.

But no memory compares to this.

Hands slip down the arch of my back and over the curve of my ass, gripping the backs of my thighs as he drags me up his body. I part my legs and wrap them around his waist as my back hits the wall, and he grinds his hips against mine.

I gasp as pleasure thrums through me and he swallows the sound greedily, devouring it like a dying man desperate for air. My hands roam every inch of his body they can find. Mapping the sharp angles of his face, running through his hair, scoring marks down the curve of his back.

It isn't enough.

I want more. *Need* more.

Steps sound in the hall—a slow ascent on the stairs, dashing out the smoldering flames with the cold, harsh waters of reality.

"Put me down." My words are a whisper, but the command in them is clear.

Raven stiffens, but does as I ask, lowering me slowly down the length of his body until I'm standing on my own two feet.

"Star—"

"No," I cut him off, combing my fingers through my hair as I battle my own desires for some semblance of self-control. I watch him retreat into his room and pull on a shirt and put on his shoes. I breathe in a deep, trembling breath, and my next words taste bitter as I force them past my lips. "We need to leave the past where it belongs, Raven. This will be easier on us both if we do."

He fixes the last buckle, and those honeyed eyes meet mine, their heat finally tempered. "If that's what you want."

Without another word, he turns, and storms from the room.

In the Sorrows, the isle of Maricious is the place everyone goes for a night out in town. Its banks and alleys are lined with bars and courtesan houses catering to every desire.

Corinth reminds me of Maricious. In the way a raindrop reminds me of a thunderstorm.

Despite the late hour—or maybe because of it—the streets are still bustling with activity, as vibrant as they were when we first arrived earlier in the day. Music and laughter spills from balconies and windows, carrying through the air and blending into a melody of contagious joy.

"Where are we going?" I ask the group. They walk with a familiarity that makes me wonder how much of their first year on assignment was spent exploring the nighttime streets of this city.

"The Winged Serpent," Lory says, a boyish grin taking over his face.

"Imagine The Muse," Lark chimes in, "only bigger."

"And then imagine if it was completely different," Lory adds, Lark nodding along like he's said something incredibly wise.

Nyssa and I lock eyes, mirroring each other's confusion.

"There it is!"

The eagerness in Lark's voice drags my attention away and I focus on where he's pointing. Up ahead, the street forks, splitting off into two smaller lanes that continue to twist and turn, leading deeper into the labyrinth of the city. Where the two lanes merge, a building rises, four stories tall and painted in a deep hue reminiscent of black grape wine. Its windows glow with a captivating light, pulsing from deep indigo to mauve in time with the throbbing music flowing within. The sign above the double doors at its center has no words, but is instead emblazoned with a silver serpent, feathered wings on either side, spread out in flight.

I don't notice the burly man standing in front of the doors until we get closer. His huge arms cross over his chest and his steely eyes flick over us as we approach. Apparently, we pass some sort of test, because he steps aside and jerks his head in permission to enter.

As soon as we do, Lark's and Lory's earlier words make complete and total sense. It reminds me so much of The Muse, but at the same time, it's entirely different.

The floor we walk onto forms a wide balcony that wraps around the room. A bar to our left is crowded with patrons, while others sit in groups at the tables and chairs dotted around the space. In the middle of the building is an open void, and when I lift my gaze, I can see the balconies of all four floors. Silky material drapes from the high ceiling; along the lengths of those silks, scantily clad performers twist and bend in a seductive aerial dance, the fabric wrapping and slipping around their lithe bodies.

Our group heads toward a staircase to the right. It leads to another level below, and here the silken drapes end, brushing the ground floor beneath, where people weave and dance between the fabric along to the hypnotic symphony filling the air.

"Dear gods," Nyssa breathes beside me, transfixed by the aerial dancers. "When I die, I want to return as a piece of silk."

"Same," Lark agrees with a dreamy sigh.

My eyes move to Myna on the other side of them, both my eyebrows no doubt disappearing into my hairline.

"You grew up with these two?"

"Not entirely," I say, "but seven years is a *long* time.

"I'm so sorry," she says solemnly.

"Hey!" Lark and Nyssa shout at the same time, both wearing the same affronted expression.

"I'll have you know," Lark says, taking Nyssa's arm and folding it through his. "We are excellent company."

"Excellent," Nyssa concurs, and the two of them strut down the stairs.

"I thought one version of Lark was too much to handle." Myna shakes her head, but a small, affectionate smile lifts her lips as we follow the pair.

"The two of them together are a whole other level of chaos."

"May the Anemoi have mercy on us all."

A laugh bubbles out of me, slowly simmering away as we reach the lower level. My smile remains. The atmosphere is contagious.

We weave through the dancing bodies, finding the rest of our group scattered across a set of velvet lounges, bottles of wine and goblets already set out on a low table. Raven looks up as we approach, and I let my eyes graze past the empty spot next to him before taking a seat beside Lory. He offers me wine along with a broad grin, and I gratefully accept both. I drink deep, closing my eyes and humming as the rich flavor explodes on my tongue.

For a while we drink and talk amongst ourselves, until Nyssa grabs my hand and—with a mischievous grin—pulls me toward the dancefloor. Myna joins us, and the three of us move in perfect sync with the hypnotic music filling the air. The pulsating beat guides our bodies, and we surrender ourselves to its rhythm, letting it carry us away. Allowing ourselves to enjoy this one last moment. A wide smile spreads across my face as I give in to the intoxicating ambiance, the wine in my system making my movements fluid and my mood euphoric.

My neck prickles with awareness, the intensity of it sending shivers down my spine. I turn around to find Raven's piercing eyes locked on me. Time slows as my body instinctively responds. The memory of his lips on mine floods my mind, until it's all I can think about. As if my body has a mind of its own, my movements slow, becoming sensual and seductive. Silk slips against my shoulder, reminding me of the feel of him beneath my palms, and my heart beats harder.

For this moment, I dance for him.

For what could have been.

And for the remainder of the night, his gaze never leaves me.

THIRTEEN

THE CARRIAGE ROCKS BACK and forth as it makes its way through the winding roads of the Eretrian countryside. The seats inside are luxurious, lined with soft, crimson velvet and smelling of lavender and cedarwood. The windows are made from delicate stained glass that casts a colorful, mosaic-like pattern across my lap as the afternoon sun shines through.

It's my first experience riding in a carriage. The narrow lanes and waterways of the Sorrows don't make them popular back home, with small boats and ferries being the preferred mode of transport.

I'm not sure if it's the unfamiliar and incessant rocking causing the queasy sensation lingering in my stomach, or our impending arrival in Vilea. Either way, the feeling has crept into every limb, holding me captive in a state of unease.

We met the other order members at the eastern edge of the city early this morning, our disguises, and personas firmly in place. It was strange to see so many Songbirds and Nightwings gathered in one place outside the Aviary. Even stranger to see them all wearing the garb of the Palace of Sorrows. Once introductions were made, we were ready to move.

But before our group had set off, another joined us.

I didn't need to feign my delight at the sight that greeted us: a convoy of caravans trundling up the road, brightly painted wagons and carriages glimmering like a trail of precious jewels in the morning light. Adorned with intricate carvings and paintings, each wagon has its own story to tell, and the horses pulling them are just as colorful, their manes and tails braided with ribbons and their coats glistening.

The *Thíasos ton Theíon*.

The most renowned performance troupe across all the kingdoms of the Empyrieos and—much to Raven's dismay—are also on their way to Vilea.

I wish I could be out there with the rest of them.

Although I haven't been on a horse in months, I crave the sense of adventure. The sensation of the wind in my hair and the sight of a new land unfurling before me. Instead, I'm stuck in this carriage for the entire trip with less-than-ideal company.

I turn to take in my companions. Nyssa is fast asleep beside me, her face pressed against the window, little puffs of fog clouding the glass with each breath from her parted lips. She passed out not long after we set off, and I envy her for it. The closer we get to Eretria, the more restless I become.

I haven't slept properly since before the Naming, and I'm

all too aware of the somniseed stashed in my new luggage trunk. Despite having two full vials from Skiepo, I've been trying to stop taking the little seeds. It's proving to be more of a challenge than I'd thought, and the idea of a dreamless sleep is all too tempting.

Across from me, Myna stretches across another velvet bench, reading a book like each word is a morsel of food and she's been starving for weeks on end. Not a word has been shared between us for hours. The only sound is of horse hooves and carriage wheels grinding over the dusty road. A staccato rhythm that seeps through the wood.

As though she can sense my scrutiny, Myna glances up from her book and returns it in kind.

"It won't be easy, you realize," she says.

"The trials?" I scoff. "I doubt the search for a prince's bride will be harder than what the Aviary puts us through."

"No. *Pretending* they're difficult is what won't be easy. You'll need to struggle through them. Or, at the very least, make a show of it."

I hum non-committedly under my breath, my eyes trailing back toward the carriage window as I desperately try to ignore the chill that skitters down my spine. It's sound advice, particularly coming from someone such as her. But she doesn't understand all the stakes—wasn't present for the Eagle's threats.

I'd need to find some kind of balance. One that sets me apart, but doesn't give rise to suspicion. I'm meant to be a princess after all, not a discarded daughter raised within the Aviary.

I turn back, narrowing my gaze on Myna when I find her attention so easily returned to the book cradled in her hands. She has a habit of this, I'd noticed. Of making little statements that make my mind spin, or testing Nyssa and I on different facets of our cover story.

I relinquish a tenuous breath and turn my thoughts to the most frequent topic of our impromptu tests.

Names.

As if we didn't have enough of *those* to remember already. Each of our Flight has chosen a slight variation of their Aviary-given name in case they need to provide one on the mission.

Draven, Lars, Lyna, Cheron, Lorenzo, Sarra.

I lean back in my seat and close my eyes, chanting those names over and over, until they're more engrained in my mind than my own. Eventually, I must fall asleep, because after what seems like a few moments, the sharp rap of knuckles on our carriage door jolts me awake. Nyssa sits bolt upright beside me, confusion lining her face and red imprints on her cheek. I glance out the window, but can only make out the faint outline of bodies moving in the dark.

"We've stopped to camp for the night." Myna's voice draws my gaze as she closes her book and shoves it into her bag. "That was Lory letting us know we can head out."

"Thank the Anemoi," I say, shielding a yawn with my hand as I move toward the door. "I need a break from this carriage."

I self-consciously run my hand over my hair, nerves fluttering at the silken texture. I took my earring out this morning, and the thought of my real appearance being on display twists my stomach into a tight knot.

"It suits you," Myna offers with a smile.

I let my hands fall. "Thank you."

"Now, game face on, *Princess*."

I grumble at the snark in Myna's tone but follow her advice, regardless. By the time my feet touch the grassy ground, I have my mask in place. Nyssa and Myna both follow me, and the three of us stand frozen before the scene that greets us, awe suspending my body mid-stride.

The troupe has guided their caravans into a circular wall, creating a sheltered space around an enormous bonfire. Against the dark and cloudy night, strings of tiny lanterns shine, as if the stars have been plucked from the sky above and captured in little glass prisons. Larger colored lanterns bob between them, spilling rainbow-hued pools of light across the soft grass.

Dozens of people move around the area, some setting up rugs, tables, and chairs pulled from the backs of their wagons, while others set to work on preparing an evening meal over the fire. As I examine them further, I notice more than half of them have the unique features of the nymphai: hair in shades of blue, green, and red, shimmering patches of scales blending with skin, and small horns curling from their foreheads. The atmosphere is thick with the scent of woodsmoke and with laughter, their camaraderie, and carefree spirits palpable in the air.

Out here, in the middle of nowhere, this troupe has created an entire world of their own. A place with its own rules and customs. Their own way of life.

Beneath my admiration, something bittersweet brews. A part of me craves what they have—the freedom, the closeness between them. It's not something I'm familiar with. Aside from the few constants in my life, the list of people I hold dear to me is limited. Even the time spent with our Flight over the past week and a half has been tense, lacking the sense of fellowship I always pictured in my mind.

My eyes seek the familiar faces of our group, finding them preparing tents for the night and tending to the horses. Unbidden, my gaze drifts to Raven, watching as he runs his hands through his hair, pushing away the locks that have fallen across his forehead. As though he can sense the heat of my perusal, he looks up. Amber eyes collide with mine, making my heart stutter in my chest as I remember the other night.

Hands slip down the arch of my back, over the curve of my ass, gripping the backs of my thighs as he—

"Princess," a smoky voice calls out to me, pulling my attention toward the tall, dark figure approaching. "What do you think?"

The Troupe Master's features are still partially hidden in shadow, the light from above catching only on the angles of his face. He has a lean, muscled physique and is dressed in a coal-black tailored suit. His dark hair is like a sheet of silk, falling to the middle of his back. There is an effeminacy to the way he moves through the night. He's elegant, show-stopping, but I have the sense that—if he truly wanted to—he could simply slip away, fading into the shadows. My intuition tells me he has at least some nymph blood in his veins, but I can't determine which. He has no defining features that hint at a specific element, but there's something in the way he moves that tells me he's more than your average tycheroi.

"It's beautiful, Leto," I say with a genuine smile. "I've seen nothing quite like it."

"I'm glad you think so." His dark eyes dance as he considers me before extending an elbow. "Would you and your ladies care to join us for dinner? We usually trade stories around the campfire in the evenings."

"Of course, we'd love to," I answer, taking his offered arm and allowing him to lead me toward the warmth of the fire, Nyssa and Myna trailing a few steps behind.

As we move through the campsite, smiles greet us from all directions. Some of the troupe shyly drop their eyes when they meet my gaze, while others make more flamboyant displays with bows and courtly greetings.

We come to a stop in the warm glow of the fire, and my eyes widen at the embroidered rugs and plush pillows waiting for us on the grass. A low wooden table overflows with cured meats, dried fruits, steaming bread rolls, and hard cheeses. The sight makes my mouth water.

"Your head guard tells me you're heading to the Palace of Vilea to take part in the Royal Trials," the Troupe Master says, slicing into the juicy flesh of an apple with a small knife.

"Yes, that's right," I reply, piling items onto my plate.

"Have you heard much about the trials?"

"I've read about them a little, but it's not a custom we practice in the Sorrows. Although, I haven't heard of them taking place in the other kingdoms, either."

"I wouldn't imagine so. They directly result from Eretria's

perception of its own superiority. From what I've heard, they are closely linked to our land's history."

"How so?"

"Oh, that's a good story!" a man says as he collapses onto a rug beside Leto. His lithe body reclines against the pillows, and he flashes us a rakish smile. Even with his dark, wavy hair cut shorter, the similarities between him and the Troupe Master are many. "Tell that one."

"A bit of decorum doesn't go astray, Pan," Leto says dryly to the newcomer.

"Surely the princess knew what she was signing up for when she decided to travel with *Thíasos ton Theíon*," Pan replies, stealing the half-eaten apple from Leto's hand and taking a bite.

A snort of laughter entirely inappropriate for a princess escapes me, but fortunately, it's covered by another new voice.

"Sorry, Master Leto." A willowy nymphai with long, silvery hair and delicate features sits on Pan's other side. "You should know by now, there's no reining him in."

Leto releases a breath slowly through his nose before turning to us, a sardonic smile curling his lips. "I apologize for these two. This is my younger brother, Pan, and one of our more talented dancers, Eleni."

"No need to apologize," I say with a wave of my hand. "I *would* love to hear that story, though."

"In our troupe, we don't simply tell stories, Princess. We show them."

A twinkle dances in Leto's eyes as he raises his hands, a shimmering swirl of shadow seeps from his skin and forms between his fingers, coalescing in the middle of our group.

My jaw drops as a scene takes shape, the shadows taking on the form of four winged men inside a windowless room.

My earlier suspicions were right. Leto has nymph blood in his veins—*shadow nymph blood*. Which should be impossible since everyone believed they died out during the God War.

I bite my tongue, holding back the questions forcing their way up my throat, and watch in awe as the shadows move, playing out the story as Leto's magnetic voice tells the tale.

The histories say the Anemoi came from a land far away. They were lesser gods amongst their kind, held captive by another who sought to use them for their powers. They were kept in an enchanted tower with no windows, so they could not fly away. Until one day, their captor left the tower door unlocked.

But getting out of their tower was only the first trial they faced. The Anemoi hurried down the stairs until they reached the bottom, only to realize that the tower was concealed within a labyrinth. A maze of madness, which could easily lead them astray if they were not quick-witted and clever.

As they raced through the labyrinth, the Anemoi used an age-old trick, keeping their palms on the left wall to ensure they didn't get lost. Until they came upon another door. One that refused to open.

They pulled and heaved, twisting the handle this way and that. They tried blasting it with wind, freezing it with the ice of winter, burning it with the fire of the summer sun, and rumbling the earth. All to no avail.

The Anemoi argued amongst themselves, each blaming the other for their situation, but an echoing voice silenced them. "That will not do."

The Anemoi jumped apart, looking around but seeing no one at all. Until out of the shadows, a creature emerged, with a face and upper body of a beautiful woman, the body of a feline, and wings not unlike their own.

"Who are you?" Eurus, the East Wind, demanded.

"I am many things," the creature replied, her cat-like eyes tracking their every move. "A keeper of secrets, and answers, and doors. But you may call me Sphinx."

"And will you open this door for us?" Boreas asked. He was the North Wind, the oldest and wisest of the four.

"Not yet."

"Why not?" Notos growled, the heat of the South Wind simmering in his voice.

"You must answer my riddle first."

"Well, go on then," said Zephyrus, the West Wind and calmest of the brothers. "Ask it."

Sphinx emitted an echoing growl, almost like it was clearing its throat. "What goes through it, but never goes in and never comes out?"

The Anemoi all paused, then their argument resumed, all proclaiming they knew the answer. Only Boreas, the oldest and wisest of the brothers, watched on in silence.

"Quickly now, but remember, you can only answer once," Sphinx taunted, pacing back and forth before them.

"I know it," Boreas stated, locking eyes with each of his brothers. They watched him back, before nodding acceptance.

"Let us hear it, then."

"A keyhole."

Sphinx went silent, and the Anemoi held their collective breath as they awaited its judgment. From the air itself, a key appeared in the keyhole. A sharp click broke the silence as it turned, and the door swung open. They wasted no time running through, but Sphinx's voice stopped them.

"This door has not opened for centuries, and I have been stuck here until my riddle was answered. I would escape with you if you would allow it."

The Anemoi took pity on the creature and all agreed.

"Better run as swift as yourselves, young winds. He will know the door has been opened."

Heeding the warning, they ran as fast as they could. They used their wings to propel them forward as they weaved and turned through the maze, but as another door came into view, music stopped them in their tracks. The song of a harp wrapped around them, tempting and seducing them to turn around, to head back. But they knew this was yet another trap, and they summoned all their strength to move forward.

Each step was a struggle, each note of the harp begging them to turn. To look.

Eurus was the first to fall, the temptation taking him to the ground. Even so, he did not turn. Zephyrus fell next, and the creature growled, urging them to keep moving.

Another sound joined the music: the heavy pounding of footfalls steadily drawing closer. With fear in their minds, but determination in their hearts, the Anemoi continued toward the door. They fought tooth and nail, clawing their way forward, and finally they made it.

The moment they passed the threshold, the music fell away, and the open air greeted them. It rejoiced, welcoming its old friends. They wasted no time celebrating, the five of them spreading their wings and flying off into the distance.

The Anemoi all agreed that they could never return to their homeland. So, they continued to fly north. Hours turned into days, days turned into weeks, and weeks turned into months. Until finally they came across a land untouched by their kind. It was here they finally decided to rest, and, as years passed without discovery, it was here they created the Empyrieos.

The image of the Anemoi exploring the new land dissipates before my eyes, shadows dissolving into the air.

Silence falls over our group, and it's only then I notice Leto holds the rapt attention of everyone in the camp. Even his own troupe is captivated by his ability as a storyteller.

Eventually, Pan's lilting voice breaks the spell. "I bet you've never seen a story told like that, have you, Princess?"

"No." The word comes out in a whisper, and I clear my throat. "It was beautiful."

"Thank you, Your Highness," Leto says, inclining his head as his dark eyes track over my face. "We should probably pack up. It's another long day tomorrow, and we all need our rest."

As our Flight turns in for the night, the story replays in my mind. I've heard ones like it countless times before, but never in as much detail or in such a way.

Leto hinted that our history inspired the trials, but I don't feel much more enlightened about what I'll be facing when we arrive at the court.

I suppose tomorrow will tell.

FOURTEEN

NOTHING COULD HAVE PREPARED me for Vilea.

The songs I've heard, the books I've read, the paintings I've pored over—all pale in comparison to the view before me now.

As our caravan crested the last hill, Leto called us all to a halt, giving those of us who hadn't journeyed here before the opportunity to view the capital from afar, to take in the city and palace in all their glory.

And they are glorious.

I stand at the peak of the hill alone, allowing myself a moment to be unguarded as I gaze out over one of the cities I have dreamed of visiting for years.

Built into the side of the smaller mountains within the Rithean Range, the Palace of Eretria is a wonder of smooth marble, standing tall and proud.

A polished jewel within a natural crown.

White columns and towers shimmer in the fading light of the sun as it peeks through the cloud cover, while every golden-trimmed window glitters with its glimpses of lingering warmth.

Tall oak trees climb up the slope, leaves of red and gold drifting in the wind, making the mountainside look like it's been set aflame. A winding pathway cuts through the towering trees, like the twisting body of a serpent, toward the sprawling city at the base of the mountain. Too many stairs to count are carved in marble, providing a singular pathway from the city to the palace that presides over it all.

Fortunately, that's not the only means to reach the court.

I watch in awe as carriages suspended on cables travel between the palace and the city below, making slow journeys through the air. They are a wonder I've heard about many times before, one of the many reasons Kal and I dreamed of visiting Vilea.

Sky-carriages.

A clever invention that allows the high society of the royal court to travel to and from the palace with ease.

My heart skips a beat as I watch one carriage glide toward the palace. The reality of what I'm about to do is sinking like a stone to the bottom of my stomach. A sense of foreboding washes over me. A cool draught of air penetrates my cloak, chilling me to the bone as the clouds above shift, hiding the sun behind their shroud once again. In the absence of its warmth and light, the city dims before my eyes.

There will be no turning back from here.

Not that there was ever a chance for that to begin with.

The stakes of this mission are too high, and any misstep could mean disastrous consequences for the world as we know it.

Something shifts within me—that same sensation that has been tightening like a coil and filling my limbs with tension for the past few days. I pause, trying to reach out to it, while reaching *in*. I sense a whisper of something at my fingertips. So incredibly soft—

"Well, Princess, did I do it any justice?" Pan's words jolt me from my trance, and the sensation dissipates. I turn to find the smiling man and his silver-haired companion, Eleni, at my side. At an earlier rest stop, Pan regaled me with tales of the city, much to the amusement of his older brother, who watched on in silence.

"To be honest, I'm not sure anyone could truly capture this place."

"You're probably right," he says with a chuckle. "Leto took all the storytelling talent for himself."

"So, what's your talent, then?"

"You mean, aside from spouting bullshit?" Eleni asks, an evil grin taking over her delicate features.

Pan holds a hand to his heart as though her words have mortally wounded him. But he very quickly recovers, grabbing her hand and pulling her toward him. He guides Eleni into a spin and she effortlessly pirouettes.

"I'm a dancer," he says, like it's obvious, "and I play the lute."

Eleni rolls her eyes, giving me a look that seems to ask if I'm buying said bullshit. I grin back at her.

"We actually came to tell you we need to get back on the

road," she interjects before Pan can continue with what I'm sure is a long list of self-acclaimed talents. "You'll want to make it to the palace before the light is completely gone."

"I imagine so." My words are distracted as I scan the group waiting by the caravans, looking for Raven. The steady beating of my heart speeds up when I spot him, already watching me with a small smile lifting the corner of his mouth. He tilts his head toward the city, questioning whether I'm ready to move on. Warmth pools within me, knowing he allowed this brief delay for me.

"Don't be a stranger in the court, Princess," Pan says, walking backwards as Eleni drags him to their wagons. "I'll put on an extra-special show for you."

I shake my head at his antics, looking down at my feet to hide the smile blooming across my face as I head toward my carriage. Climbing the steps, I pull the door shut behind me and take my seat.

Myna is already waiting inside, her nose buried in her book as though she hadn't moved from her spot.

I've just settled in when the carriage door slams open.

"Sorry," Nyssa exclaims, jumping up the steps and into her seat. "I got distracted by the view."

I arch a brow at my friend, taking in the slight pallor in her cheeks and the way she fidgets with the fabric of her gown.

Reaching over, I take her hand and give it a squeeze as the carriage jolts forward, starting its descent toward the sprawling city.

The moment my foot lands on the smooth marble of the palace courtyard, the tension in my body eases slightly.

Our group and *Thíasos ton Theíon* went our separate ways at the sky-carriage station in the heart of Vilea. Apparently, they must take the service carriages to the palace, which are at a separate station docked on the eastern outskirts of the city. The other Aviary members who traveled with us are staying below in one of the guard quarters at the foot of the mountain. I was nervous about traveling with so many of them, but it's a relief knowing they are close if we need reinforcements.

The ride in the sky-carriage was exhilarating. Terrifying, but thrilling. They were like the regular carriages we traveled in from Corinth, lined in red velvet on the inside with beautifully painted white-and-gold exteriors. Only, where those had wheels, these were suspended by a pulley system on thick, steel-infused cables. The clear glass windows gave us a perfect view of the expansive city and autumn treetops below as we climbed toward the palace, bobbing and swaying in the breeze.

I feel like I've been in a constant state of awe on this journey so far. Every sight and experience are more jaw-dropping than the last, and the palace that pierces the clouds before me is no different. As the others unload our luggage from the carriages, my eyes travel over the smooth marble courtyard, noting the only points of entry are the sky-carriages behind us, the treacherous stairs leading down the mountain, and the arched oak doors leading into the palace. No fewer than twenty guards line the courtyard walls, blending with the stone in their pristine white uniforms. I tuck those bits of information into the back of my mind, like I'm sure the rest of the Flight is also doing behind me.

The palace doors creak open, the sound echoing through the space, pulling my gaze away from the guards and toward a group of tycheroi approaching. A tall man leads them, his skin a warm olive shade and his hair a dark auburn. He looks to be in his late thirties, but his sepia eyes are framed with faint lines, hinting at an age greater than his appearance.

The group comes to a stop a few paces from ours, and they all bow at the waist.

"Princess Aella, welcome to Vilea," the auburn-haired man says, rising from his gentle bow and gesturing a young woman forward. "I am Lord Hestion, and this is my daughter, Titaia."

The two bear a strong resemblance, so I'm not surprised when he introduces her as his daughter. Titaia has the same olive skin, although her hair is such a deep shade it's almost black. Her eyes—the same intense red-brown as her father's—watch me closely with a mix of curiosity and mischief, matching perfectly with the slanted smile curving her lips.

"It's an honor to meet you both," I say with a smile of my own, taking in every detail of the pair. "Thank you for welcoming me to your court."

Lord Hestion is the younger brother of King Daedalus, making Titaia the cousin of the prince. From the information Raven provided on the royal family of Eretria, while there is no open animosity between siblings and cousins, there are no unbreakable family bonds either. I wouldn't go so far as to consider them potential allies, but it's a weakness that could be exploited. My eyes linger on Titaia's smirking face with the thought, but they're drawn back to Lord Hestion as he speaks.

"Allow us to escort you to the throne room. The royal family is waiting to receive you there," he says, gesturing to the silent group behind him. "Our servants will assist yours with taking your belongings to your rooms."

I take in the group as they hurry to collect trunks and luggage. My jaw clenches at the signs of age apparent amongst all of them: withering skin, graying hair, and stiff movements, despite their otherwise youthful looks.

Goiteían.

Servants employed by wealthier tycheroi to conduct the use of magic and *goiteía* marks for them. A sacrifice of another's soul magic to selfishly save their own.

Disgust burns in the pit of my stomach, but I smother it, turning back to Lord Hestion with a forged smile. "I appreciate it."

I fall into step beside the two as they turn toward the palace doors. A subtle glance over my shoulder shows Raven, Nyssa, and Myna close behind me. The rest of the Flight remains to handle our belongings.

The entry hall inside the palace is just as impressive as the exterior. A grand staircase leads to the floors above; banisters painted with liquid gold circle each floor and provide a barrier for the central void that rises as far as the eye can see.

I frown at the sight of small glass orbs filled with light that are suspended from the walls in golden brackets. When I glance around, I see them everywhere, illuminating masterfully crafted tapestries and paintings.

Apart from a few guards standing sentry, the space is devoid of life, our footsteps the only sound as we're led toward the staircase. As we climb, a murmur of noise becomes more apparent, humming from behind the heavy oak doors on the landing ahead.

As we approach, Titaia leans toward me. "Brace yourself, Princess."

Her warning barely registers before her father pushes the doors open and hundreds of murmuring voices slam into me like a solid wall. The owners of those voices all turn to face us, and I suck in a sharp breath as I suddenly find myself the target of their pointed stares.

Mentally checking for cracks in my facade, I steel my spine, lift my chin with an imperious tilt, and follow Lord Hestion into the crowded hall.

I keep my eyes forward, fixed to the back of Titaia's head, watching the way the glass lights cast a gleaming circlet of gold on her dark auburn hair. In my peripheral vision. I note row after row of finely crafted pews, each filled with immaculately dressed tycheroi who stare as we pass.

Whispers spread through the hall like wildfire.

I wonder what stories and rumors they have heard of me here. What they think they know of me. Do they repeat rumors of a daughter outcast to the Isle of Winds? Or do they wonder if I am as magicless as people say?

We reach the end of the hall and both Lord Hestion and Titaia step to the side, bringing me face-to-face with the royal family. On a raised dais overlooking the assembled guests, they sit in thrones of gold.

A picture of regal beauty.

King Daedalus' face is as hard as the stone this hall is carved from, giving away nothing of his emotions or thoughts. He looks so like his brother, though his build is larger, and his rich red-brown eyes show malice coiling in their depths.

A shiver crawls up my spine and I turn my gaze away, looking instead toward the woman on his right. Dressed in a pleated gown of shimmering gray, Queen Atalana sits still as a statue, her figure looking as though it's carved from marble. Long dark hair falls in carefully placed curls around her slim shoulders. Her expression is softer than the king's, but her eyes are distant and her complexion pallid, even as she smiles down at me from her throne.

Awareness prickles the back of my neck and I finally let my eyes drift to the last figure on the dais.

I've seen portraits of Prince Keres before but seeing him in person has the air hitching in my throat. His features are a striking combination of his mother and father. Keres' eyes are more red than brown, and mahogany hair streaked with shades of auburn falls in soft waves around a face that looks crafted by the gods themselves. His build is leaner than that of his father, but still well-muscled, his jacket hugging his broad shoulders and tapering to his waist.

He's beautiful.

The rakish smile on his face tells me he knows it too.

But there's a cruelty to the cut of his cheekbones, venom in the curl of his lips, and a coldness in his aura that belies the warmth of his skin.

Beneath the glimmer of interest in his eyes, something flashes in their depths. There and gone too quickly for me to fully understand.

"Princess Aella Sotiría of the Sorrows." King Daedalus' voice drags my attention from the prince. "It is an honor to have our friends from across the Solorai Sea in our home, and a delight to have you join the trials."

"The honor is all mine, Your Majesty," I say humbly, dipping into a curtsy. My hair falls over my shoulder—an ashen veil shielding me from the judging eyes and heavy stares.

When I rise, my face is a mask, as smooth as the polished stone around me.

"My queen, Atalana." The king gestures to his wife. "And my son, Prince Keres, who I am sure you are well aware of."

"A pleasure, Your Majesty." I bow my head to the queen, and she offers a small smile in return.

I look back to the prince, holding his red gaze. That same expression flashes through his eyes, and I recognize it for what it is.

Predatory.

A cat with a canary in its sight, waiting for the right moment to pounce.

Little does he know; this songbird's talons are sharp.

Calliope's lessons echo through my mind, a spectral voice guiding me in this moment.

Some men relish the hunt. But first, you must convince them you're worth the chase.

I let a slow smile unfurl across my lips, looking up at him from beneath my lashes. I drop my voice to a husky tone as I greet him. "Prince."

His reaction is barely perceptible, but I watch him closely enough to notice the slight flare of his nostrils. He inclines his head ever so slightly as he responds in kind. "Princess."

As we hold each other's gaze—neither of us willing to relent first—I notice silence has infiltrated the hall, the gathered tycheroi holding their breath as though they're waiting for their prince to pass judgment.

King Daedalus claps his hands, shattering my staring contest and the silence with a single gesture. "As part of the trials, each competitor will have a mentor from our family to guide them through life in our court. Lady Titaia shall attend to you, and will escort you to your rooms so you may settle in. The opening ceremony will be in three nights' time, so rest while you can."

At the clear dismissal in his words, I give a final curtsy to the royals. My eyes seek our guide as I rise. I don't have to look far as she steps up to my side, tilting her head toward the same doors we entered through.

Turning to the others, I gesture for Raven, Myna, and Nyssa to follow. They waited quietly during the entire exchange, and their faces remain impassive, though I can see tension riding Raven's shoulders as he drags his stare away from Prince Keres.

We make our way out of the hall, walking swiftly down the aisle, once again ignoring the lingering stares that track our every move. Once we pass through the arched doors, I can finally take a deep breath. I hold on to my composure as Titaia takes my hand and slips it through her arm, gently pulling me down the hall.

"That was a marvelous performance, Princess," she says with a sly smile.

"Performance?" I ask, drawing her to a stop so I can face her. I force my body to remain relaxed, though her words stir anxiety deep in my gut. With my arm in hers, she would surely notice if I tensed up, and I can't risk raising suspicion so early in the game.

"Yes," she nods, her sharp eyes wandering over my face. "I haven't seen anyone look Keres in the eye for so long."

Worry sparks, flaming the anxiety to a roar. I nervously bite my lip as I replay my actions in my head, examining each moment to see if I did anything that could be taken as a slight. "Did I offend him?"

"On the contrary, I think you have thoroughly captured his attention." Titaia flashes me a reassuring smile and tugs me forward. "Now come along. I'm sure you're tired from your long journey across the sea."

It's not until she says it that a wave of exhaustion rolls over me. The excitement from the past couple of weeks ebbs out of my body, leaving my limbs heavy.

With a small sigh of relief, I let her lead us on.

The board has been set, the players are in motion, and now all the pieces just need to fall into place.

FIFTEEN

I WANDER INTO ONE of the many courtyards of the palace, Lady Titaia at my side, Nyssa and Myna trailing behind us like twin shadows.

For the past two days, I have been mapping out as much as I can of the court. A challenge, considering everything here looks the same. Cold polished marble, gilded window frames, and golden oak form every inch of the palace.

Above, the sky is a canvas of brooding clouds, wrapping around the mountain peaks and shrouding the tallest towers in a thick veil. Weak sunlight filters through them, and I can feel it trying to warm my skin. But the crisp mountain air, carrying the scent of mildew, chases it away.

As we enter, the scattered groups of tycheroi pause their discussions, only for the whispers to start up again when my gaze passes over them. My shoulders want to tighten under their attention, but I force myself to relax. The purpose of my outing is purely to be seen.

A distraction.

I just hadn't realized how efficiently my mere presence would work in this place.

"Can you show us the library next?" I ask the lady beside me. "I've heard it's impressive."

"I could," she drags out the word, flashing me a pitiful look. "But I'd rather not. It up six flights of stairs, and you've already dragged me through half the gods-damned palace."

Her eyes widen slightly as they flash to mine, but she relaxes when I laugh it off.

"Fair enough," I say. "Another time."

My feet carry me toward the marble railing bordering the courtyard. Lady Titaia follows, and we lean against the cool stone. To my right, the city spreads out from the base of the mountain below. The buildings and trees appear small enough to fit in the palm of my hand. My eyes snag on a lone structure amidst the canopy of red and gold, about a mile out from the outskirts of the city. Thick cables lead from it and disappear around the back of the palace. It must be the servants' sky-carriage station.

"The view from here is lovely," I say, turning to where Nyssa and Myna stand behind me. "Come take a look."

They both step up on either side of me, taking in the view.

"*Lovely*," Nyssa says, and, knowing her as well as I do, I don't miss the boredom lining her voice. I force down the urge to elbow her and catch Myna's eye before looking pointedly out at the station. She follows my gaze, and a barely perceptible stillness takes over her body.

"It's beautiful, Princess." Myna's words would sound like a comment on the view to any prying ears, but I see the way her eyes take in the carriage station. Taking note of its location and the trajectory of the cables leading to the back of the palace.

I'm about to respond, but another beats me to it. The deep voice slides over my skin and constricts my throat.

"I'm glad my kingdom is held in such high regard by three beautiful ladies."

Prince Keres.

I glance toward his cousin, frowning as she shifts uncomfortably beside me, and then turn to find the prince standing a few paces away. His eerie red eyes examine us before settling on me with an intensity that makes the fine hairs on my body rise. I take a deep breath and force myself to stand up straighter.

"Prince Keres." I incline my head in greeting, and he tracks the movement.

"Princess Aella," he acknowledges, returning the gesture, before he looks dismissively at his cousin. "I had heard you were burdened with the disappointment of the family. But due to your station, it's protocol for you to have a higher-ranking lady, and my mother thought it would be a good match."

Fury bubbles within me, both at his words and the way Lady Titaia flinches. The spirited woman is nowhere to be seen as she remains silent beside me.

I force a pleasant smile as I turn back to him, somehow managing to keep my voice sweet as I ask, "How can I help you, Prince?"

"Walk with me." It's a demand, not a question.

"Of course." I glance at Nyssa and Myna, and they both drop into curtsies, drawing Lady Titaia along as they leave me alone with the prince. My eyes linger on them as they retreat to the center of the courtyard, where they make a good show of a light-hearted conversation between handmaidens. Yet Myna's piercing gaze never leaves me.

I smile prettily as I take the arm Keres offers, keeping my body relaxed as he places my hand in the crook of his elbow and leads me through the courtyard. The steady thrum of whispers fills the air once more, but I ignore it, making a show of admiring the deciduous wisteria trees as I wait for him to talk.

"How are you finding Eretria so far?" he finally asks.

"It's beautiful," I say honestly. "Not just the court and capital, but everything I've seen so far."

My response seems to please him, if his self-satisfied smirk is anything to go by. Like my words were a direct compliment to him.

"I would imagine it's very different to what you're accustomed to in the Sorrows."

We pass under another wisteria branch, and I draw to a stop, my eyes falling on the tall statue ahead. The air stalls in my lungs and a feeling akin to pins and needles prickles down my spine. Prince Keres notices my attention and his eyes light up as he leads me closer.

"Marvelous, isn't it?" he asks.

Despite the unease churning within me, I nod, struck

speechless by the statue. The body of a woman has been carved by a masterful hand, the artist somehow capturing the sheer quality of the material that drapes over her curves. In one hand, she holds the hilt of a shattered sword, the broken shards fallen on the base of the podium at her feet. Beautiful wings flare from her back, each feather captured with meticulous detail. But what fills me with a creeping feeling of dread is the fact that she has no head.

It's not that the statue is unfinished.

She's decapitated.

The artist clearly spent an inordinate amount of time carving the details of her severed ligaments and spinal cord, capturing her life's blood dripping from the wound. The statue is so realistic it looks like a winged corpse sealed in stone.

"She's called *The Fallen*." Keres reaches out, stroking a finger down the broken tip of her sword before turning back to me. "Have you heard of the Harpaurai before?"

I frown at the familiar name, recalling the bedtime stories our nursemaid, Melita, would tell Kal and me whenever we were restless and fighting sleep.

The Harpaurai are a mythical race—winged beings like the Anemoi. In the stories Melita told us, Boreas, the God of the North Wind and Winter, crafted the two original Harpaurai from the feathers of his wings. He made them like the tycheroi, with long life, enhanced hearing, and eyesight, and remarkable physical abilities. But the extra gifts he gave them are what made them truly special.

Feathered wings, and *theïkós* with the unique ability to control elements of the skies and wind.

171

I was so obsessed with tales of the legendary race that Kal once made me a pair of wings out of parchment feathers. I wore them for a full day, pretending to be one of the Harpaurai. Until my father saw. He was so furious he ripped the wings off my back and burned them in a fireplace.

I watched the parchment feathers burn until there was nothing left but ash.

That same night, Melita never arrived to tell us bedtime stories. Kal and I never saw her again.

A sharp pain slashes through my chest at the assault of memories, and air hisses through my clenched teeth. I twist the ring on my finger and avert my eyes from Keres' curious stare. "My nursemaid told my brother and I some stories long ago."

"The legends say the Harpaurai lived deep within the Thalkans. Boreas himself carved vast palaces and strongholds into the northern mountain range for them as their population grew," Keres muses, his gaze drifting back toward the statue. "That is, until the God War, when their true nature was revealed. They were a vicious and bloodthirsty race, carving up the battlefield."

"You speak as though you believe they were real," I say, a frown creasing my forehead.

"Don't all stories start with truth, Princess?" Keres looks at me, his red gaze piercing. "We have a vast private library here, documenting the God War. Many of the texts recount battles with the Harpaurai."

"Then why do most consider them bedtime stories?" I ask, choosing not to acknowledge his question.

"A question I have asked many times before. The texts we have state that Eurus himself held them back. This statue here immortalizes the moment he took the head of their leader in the ultimate battle." Keres runs a thoughtful finger back up the broken blade as he speaks, seemingly lost to questions that have remained unanswered. "After they were destroyed in the God War, they all but disappeared from our histories. Any scriptures or texts on their race vanished, like even the books couldn't bear to maintain the memories of them."

"Aside from yours."

"When my great-grandfather heard of the texts going missing, he hid my family's away. He would read them to me when he was still alive." He steps toward me. The same finger that stroked the broken blade runs along my jaw, tilting my chin until I'm forced to tear my gaze from the statue and look up at him. "You look quite sad, Princess. What's troubling you?"

"It seems like such a waste of life."

Keres cocks his head, his red eyes flashing in the light. The movement reminds me of the watchful eagles in the port back home, scoping out the morning haul.

Calculating. *Predatory.*

"You have such a sweet heart, Princess."

The way he says it doesn't sound like a compliment. Regardless, I smile like he's offered me one. It doesn't matter at this moment if it's the cool breeze, or the story, or the cruel gaze of the prince that sends a chill down my spine. All that matters is the need to bring back a hint of the earlier warmth I witnessed in his eyes.

He drops his finger from my chin and clasps his hands behind his back. The shadow of a smile hovers at the edge of his mouth. "I was hoping you would join me for dinner tonight."

"Won't we already be dining together?" I ask. "With the other contestants, I mean."

"I was thinking of something more private."

I glance away, granting myself a moment of respite from his penetrating gaze. Unable to force a blush, I settle for coyness and peer back up at him through my lashes. "I would love to, Prince Keres."

"I thought you might. We'll have dinner served in my chambers. Bring a chaperone if you must—I know the Sorrows have customs you must follow." He flashes me a wanton grin. "Until then, I hope you enjoy the court."

The sun has long since slipped below the horizon, leaving the sky a blanket of darkness, neither the moon nor a single star breaching the heavy night. Below, the city glimmers with thousands of flickering lights that cascade down the mountainside and sprawl across the land, making me wonder if the world has been turned upside down.

Aside from the crackle of the fireplace, my rooms are silent. The others are all out searching every inch of the palace. Since our arrival, they've turned up nothing. Not a hint or whisper of where the weapon may be hidden.

Despite the Flight's earlier work and preparations, we're no closer to success. Lark and Lory scoured the dungeons last night, while Raven, Dove, and Heron searched the royal quarters. With the opening celebration of the trials taking place tomorrow night, and the fact that we are no closer to having the weapon in our grasp, we'll have to keep up this charade longer than we all hoped.

Which means I will need to play my part well.

A soft knock at the door pulls my gaze away from the window as Raven slips inside, freezing in place when he sees me.

My breath hitches at the way his muscles go taut, bunching beneath the fabric of his guard uniform. His eyes spark with heat as he performs a slow perusal of my body, his gaze so intense I feel it like a physical caress against my skin. My body reacts as though it is, my skin breaking out in goosebumps and my nipples hardening to the point where I'm sure they can be seen through the fabric of my dress.

That thought is confirmed when Raven's eyes drop to them. His jaw clenches and throat bobs, as though he had to bite back words that attempted to spring free and swallow them whole.

I crave those words. I want to hear them, taste them, know them intimately.

Our kiss in Corinth has played on my mind more times than I can count. Despite knowing better—knowing that nothing will ever come from it—all I want to do is kiss him again.

Raven clears his throat, drawing my gaze up to his face.

Though his expression is locked down, Raven's deep voice, rich like honey, drips over me. "Are you ready?"

"Yes," I say, and—because I can't resist—I run my palms over the wine-colored fabric where it flares over my hips. "Do you think he'll like it?"

His eyes darken and he moves toward me. Each breath stalls in my lungs, matching the drawn-out pace of his steps.

"He will love it," Raven growls as he reaches me, backing me up against the window. His hands clench at his sides, like he's forcefully holding himself back from touching me. "And it will be perfect for what I'm about to ask of you."

The breath catches in my throat as my heart rate picks up, but his words pierce through the painful awareness of our proximity.

"And what's that, *Commander*?"

He stiffens, taking a step back. Although it makes it easier to breathe, I miss the warmth of his body being so close to mine.

"I'll be your chaperone while the others are out searching," Raven says. "But there is a locked door in his rooms that we've been unable to access. Heron says it's carved with *goiteía* he isn't familiar with. I need you to…distract the prince so I can take a closer look."

"Distract him how?"

"You know what I mean, Starling."

"I want to be clear," I say, stepping closer and gazing up at him through lowered lashes. "Should I look at him like this?"

The honeyed streaks in his eyes turn to flint. "You could."

"Perhaps a gentle touch here," I drag my fingertips along

the back of his hand, watching as it flexes, and then bring them up to where his chest rises and falls rapidly. "Or here."

"The prince sent word," Raven grits out, "he is ready for you now."

It takes a moment for his words to penetrate the haze of desire now clouding my mind, but when they do, frustration whips through me with the force of a hurricane. "And you're just telling me this now?"

"Apologies, *princess*," he says, without a shred of sincerity in his voice. "I seem to have gotten distracted."

Narrowing my eyes, I huff with irritation and push past him to head out the door. I shiver as the fabric of my dress grazes over my sensitive nipples and curse him out under my breath. When I glance back, Raven looks smug as he falls into step behind me.

Bastard.

The only way to describe the dining room in Prince Keres' chambers is *romantic*. Instead of the glass lights—which Titaia told me are called auras—I've seen all over the court, dozens of candles fill the space, their flickering flames reflecting off the polished walls and illuminating everything around me. A large oak table takes up the center of the room, set for two at one end with various dishes spread out, each looking more delicious than the last.

But my focus isn't on the food.

The prince lounges in his chair, the angles of his face cast in light and shadow by the glow of the candles.

"Prince Keres," I greet him, dipping my head as I take a seat.

"Come now," he says. "I think we can do away with titles between us."

I watch him closely for a moment, taking in the sly smile, the predatory gleam in his eyes, contemplating the best way to play out this scenario. I know if I make a mistake tonight, it could jeopardize the mission, but the only cues I have to go by are the ones he is obviously sending my way.

Taking a leap of faith, I meet his gaze with a saccharine smile. "And what would you call me, then?"

His eyes flash with heat and I know I made the right choice when he leans in closer, the faint brush of his breath fanning across my face.

"I can think of a few things I'd like to call you." His voice is low and husky, thick with suggestion I want to cringe away from, but I hold myself still. "But I think, Aella will be sufficient. At least, *for now.*"

Raven's gaze is a dagger piercing my skin, so I lean forward, reaching for my glass of wine and making the space between Keres and myself even smaller. I smile at him over the rim, taking a small sip. I make a show of licking the wine from my bottom lip before replying, noting the way his eyes hungrily track the movement.

"Then I suppose I'll return the favor."

Keres smiles at me like he's won something, and I can't help but smile back. Not a smirk with the intention to seduce, but a genuine smile. Because he may think he's winning, but the reality is that I'm playing an entirely different game.

I lean back, flicking my eyes toward Raven. "Leave us," I say dismissively, as though he means nothing to me at all.

Raven bows to us both, before disappearing through the door, and I turn my attention back to Keres.

"So, tell me then, what does a prince search for in his future bride?" I ask, swirling the cup of wine. "I'm sure you know what you're hoping to see through the trials."

"You mean aside from all the things my father expects of me?" His expression turns thoughtful, and he leans across the table, plucking a rose from the vase at its center. He holds it between two fingers, twisting it back and forth as he examines it, and—I assume—my question. Before my eyes, the rose withers. Keres leaches it of life, until nothing but a lackluster husk remains.

I'd once read the magic of the Anemoi gifted to the royal bloodlines was stolen. Ripped from the land they came from before they found the Empyrieos. At first, they'd claimed it for themselves. But after the God War, they had passed it on to the families who would rule in their stead.

The *theïkós* of Eretria was the exact opposite of its western neighbor, Reveza. Where they harnessed the power of spring and growth in the west, here they controlled the power of autumn.

The power to wither.

To *decay*.

Keres hands me the rose, and I accept it, suppressing a shudder as our fingers brush.

"I need a bride who is strong. Resilient," he says. "Someone who can be my match in every way."

It's an effort not to roll my eyes at the way his words roll off his tongue. As though he's practiced them in the mirror countless times before.

I let another slow smile unfurl across my lips, and Keres' eyes lock on them again. My heart falters when I think he's going to close that final gap between us. Fortunately, a knock pounds on the door, saving me from the moment.

The heat in Keres' gaze swiftly burns from desire to anger. His jaw clenches and he leans back in his chair, placing a more appropriate distance between us.

I place the brittle rose on the table, surreptitiously wiping my finger on the skirt of my gown.

"Enter," Keres commands, thinly veiled fury lining the word.

A guard steps inside, Raven right behind him. The former briefly takes in the scene before bowing at the waist.

"What is it, Jorah?" Keres demands.

"Forgive me, my prince," the guard says, "but something requires your attention."

I watch in silence as a series of emotions pass rapidly over Keres' face. He takes a deep breath through his nose and an impassive mask settles across his features, his previously warm eyes now stone-cold. Gone is the rakish prince I was to dine with this evening. In his place is a cold, cruel man.

Witnessing the shift sends a shiver up my spine.

Keres stands and I stand with him.

"My sincerest apologies for the interruption, Aella, but our dinner will need to be cut short."

"There's no need, Keres," I say, stepping closer and placing my hand on his arm. "Besides, there will be plenty more opportunities for us to spend time together during the trials."

The prince looks down at my hand before taking it in his own. Raising it to his lips, he places a lingering kiss on the inside of my wrist.

His eyes sear an unspoken promise into mine, and I silently pray to the gods that I'll never see it fulfilled.

SIXTEEN

As WE TURN THE corner, I push Raven into a shadowed alcove, placing a finger over his lips to silence the questions I see burning in his eyes. The reverberation of Keres' footsteps gradually dissipate, echoing through the distance as they collide with the marble walls. I wait until the sound has completely disappeared before cautiously emerging from our hiding spot. With a gentle tug, I guide Raven back toward the prince's room.

"What are you up to, Starling?" Raven's voice gently brushes against my ear, a blend of caution and motivation.

"You said you needed to look at that lock." The urgency of the situation has me moving quickly, my mind already racing with possibilities and potential consequences. We have limited time, but we can't miss this opportunity. "There's no time like the present, Raven."

My hand tightens around his as we approach the door. I test

the handle, and when I find it locked, carefully pull a long pin from my hair. Bending down to get a better line of sight, I insert it into the lock, using precise movements to manipulate the tumblers until I hear the satisfying click.

"Impressive," Raven murmurs as I push the door open. I throw a smug grin over my shoulder as we slip inside, silently closing the door behind us. Darkness envelops the room, with only a faint glimmer of light emanating from a solitary aura atop the desk positioned at the heart of the room. The soft glow casting ominous shadows across the now sealed doors to the adjoining dining room we were in a moment ago.

"Which door is it?"

Raven doesn't waste time answering and makes a beeline for the door on the right. "Grab me that aura?"

I do as he asks, the coolness of the glass orb in my palm is a stark contrast to the burning light emanating from within. With a sense of anticipation, I bring the aura closer, lowering myself to a kneeling position as I direct its aura's glow toward the door handle. As the light glimmers off the polished metal, my eyebrows instinctively rise in surprise. Intricate *goiteía* is carved onto every spare bit of space. There are the ones I know for seal, lock, and silence. But others are strangely unknown, and yet...oddly familiar.

"Have you seen these before?" I ask, eyes darting to him.

The set of his jaw is tense, the muscles visibly straining as he contemplates the symbols before him. When he gives a small shake of his head, a fleeting expression of disappointment crosses his face, causing my heart to plummet. The weight of uncertainty hangs in the air, casting a shadow of doubt over us. But I refuse to surrender to defeat so easily. Because if this door has been so thoroughly secured, we may have found what we've been searching for.

My heart beats harder in my chest, like a drum heralding the beginning of the end. I offer him the aura and he absently accepts it, his focus unyielding, while I quickly make my way back to the cluttered desk. I snatch up a scrap of parchment, a quill, and ink pot, returning to the spot where Raven remains fixated on the intricate handle. It's as if he believes that by sheer force of will and unwavering attention, he can unlock the hidden meanings that lie within the markings.

I keep my mind blank and my hand steady as I copy the marking onto the parchment, taking care with each stroke. The true magic of *goiteía* comes from the conscious thought of imbuing them with power. You need to visualize your intent as you take a little thread of the power from your soul and stitch it into the mark. Simply tracing them as I am now won't have any effect.

"There," I say, finishing the last mark and returning the inkpot and quill to the desk. "Now we can figure these out without needing to break into a prince's rooms every other day."

"Have I ever told you how brilliant you are?" Raven asks with a smirk.

I open my mouth, but slam it shut when I hear a sound.

Voices in the hall.

Fuck.

Raven must hear it at the same time as me, jumping to his feet as we both scan the room. My eyes land on a tall wooden cupboard in the room's corner. "Closet?" I ask.

"Closet," he agrees, before darting toward it and opening the door. He holds it open, and I squeeze in, pushing aside the hanging garments and pressing my back into the worn wood. Raven follows, pulling the door closed behind him as the one in the main room bursts open.

A shrill giggle pierces through the wood, followed by a masculine chuckle, and my jaw drops.

Did that arrogant ass really leave our dinner for sex?

As though Raven can sense my thoughts, a warm hand seals over my mouth, reminding me to stay quiet. I breathe deeply through my nose, drawing in the scent of woodsmoke, cinnamon, and a tantalizing hint of honey. The smell of him makes me all too aware of the situation—pressed so close, the heat coming off his body soaks into my skin.

"You know," he whispers in my ear, "if you wanted to get this close to me, princess, all you had to do was ask."

Outside the cupboard the teasing laughter turns to moans and soft gasps. The sounds combined with the press of Raven's body ignites a heat low in my belly and my thighs clench together, either to encourage the sensation or stifle it. With one hand still pressed against my mouth, Raven caresses the exposed skin along my ribs with the other. His fingertips dance over flesh leaving a trail of fire burning in their wake.

Reckless. Reckless. Reckless.

The word becomes a chant in my mind. Yet I can't bring myself to care. Not as the sounds of the woman's passionate cries reach their peak. Not as Raven presses his hips into mine. Not as I grab onto his shirt and pull him even closer.

Another shrill cry sounds, followed by a crash, and both Raven and I freeze. I tilt my head, listening intently as the sound of laughter and running footsteps lead farther away before another door slams.

Cautiously, Raven inches the cupboard door open, peering out through the crack. The room must be clear, because his hand drops from my mouth, capturing my own. He tugs me from our hiding spot and back into the reality of our situation.

Our mission.

Our purpose.

But unlike the last time in Corinth, reason doesn't have the desired effect.

Raven and I walk back to my rooms in silence, the tension so thick between us, it's almost a tangible thing. As though if I look hard enough, I'll be able to see it woven into the air like the threads of a tapestry.

When we finally reach my door, a tremor runs through me, and I grip my key tightly to suppress the slight tremor in my hand as I turn it in the lock. As I push open the door, the tension spikes—threads pulling tight—and my breathing speeds up in time with the beat of my heart.

I've barely made it a few steps into the room before he seizes me around the waist, pulling me back so that my body is flush with his.

"Did you enjoy that? Taunting me." His words are a deep

rasp, brushing against my ear. "Torturing me."

"*I* was torturing *you*?" I say, frozen in place, painfully aware of every inch of his body where it's pressed up against mine. His heat seeps through the layers of clothing, his need for me hard against my lower back.

Raven chuckles at my reply, the sound warm and rich and decadent. It melts into my skin, pooling low in my abdomen.

"Oh, you know exactly what I mean." He drops his head toward the base of my neck and slowly trails a path of fervent kisses back up, nipping at the corner of my jawline when he reaches it. "Tell me to stop."

I say nothing, my hands tangle in the skirts of my gown, clutching at the fabric as he nips at my ear.

"Tell me to stop, princess," he tries again, "and I'll take you at your word."

And I should. I know I should. There is no possible way we could work together—no foreseeable future with a happily ever after like the books I would read late into the night.

He was going to find the weapon we were searching for, and I was going to win these trials. In a few short weeks, he would head home, and I would stay. I may never see him again. And yet...

Fuck it.

I jerk out of his grip and spin to face him. My heart thunders in my chest while I watch him closely, noting the feathering of the muscles in his jaw, the tightness of his posture as he holds himself back. Reaching behind my back, I untie the straps of my gown and slowly drag the sleeves from my shoulders and arms. With nothing to hold it up, the silk easily slips free, gliding down my body to pool at my feet.

I stand before him, completely bare.

But my eyes never leave his—wanting him to see the truth of my words within them. "I will never tell you to stop again."

The darkening of his gaze is the only warning I get before he lunges for me, that fragile hold finally snapping.

One arm folds around my waist while his other hand grips my ass and lifts me. I wrap my legs around his hips and bury my hands in his hair as his lips claim mine. His tongue caresses the seam of my mouth, begging for permission, and I give it. Raw hunger awakens at the sweet taste of him, dragging a deep moan from the depths of my chest. His heat and his hardness are driving me to the edge of sanity, and before I know it, we're devouring each other.

I'm so consumed by him; I don't realize he's moved us to the bedroom until my back collides with the soft mattress. We come apart for a moment and I gasp for breath. Raven kneels to pull off his shirt, and then he settles his body between my thighs, grinding his hips into mine.

We become a heated tangle of ravenous kisses and roaming hands. I map out every inch of his broad shoulders and the flexing muscles of his back, while his heated palms set fire to the sensitive skin of my stomach and breasts. He rolls the peak of one hard nipple between his rough fingers, and I moan, writhing with need beneath him at the fluttering sensation that ignites deep in my core.

"Raven," I say with a desperate gasp.

"Gods, Aella."

The sound of my true name falling from his lips drives me

wild.

I want to hear it again.

I want him to say it a thousand times more—to never call me by another. I want to hear him chanting it like a prayer to the gods while he's buried deep inside me.

"Please," I pant out, my hands pushing at the waistband of the pants he still wears. "I need you."

Raven pulls back at my words, hovering over me as he pushes his pants down over muscled thighs. Desire burns through me as I finally see him in all his glory. Hair tousled from my wandering hands, broad chest rising and falling with short breaths, defined abdominal muscles leading down to the thick, hard length of his arousal.

His heated gaze burns a path over my skin, completing a study of my body. Like he, too, is committing every detail to memory.

"So fucking beautiful," he rasps.

The sound of his voice, so full of want, is my undoing. I grip his wrist and pull him toward me. With my other hand, I grip his thick cock and line it up at my entrance as he pushes forward, entering me in one hard thrust.

I cry out, but his lips slam down on mine, smothering the sound. My body clamps around him, like it wants to keep him there, savoring the feeling of being full of him. But I'm desperate for him to *move*.

When my body adjusts to him, he finally does, pulling back slightly before plunging in deep again. We both moan with the sensation.

Raven tears his mouth away, leaning his forehead against

mine as he continues to thrust in and out. "You feel like paradise, Aella."

I bite my lip and clutch him closer. The only response I'm capable of as he angles his hips and strokes against a sensitive part inside me. Raven kisses down my neck and chest, taking my left nipple into his mouth and watching me as he flicks his tongue over the peak. I cry out when he bites it lightly before making his way to the other. The hot and cold sensations wreak havoc on my mind as he relentlessly thrusts into me, and I drop my head back to the mattress.

Raven starts to move harder, deeper, murmuring my name in my ear, like it's a benediction. Everywhere he touches aches, burns. A sweet pressure builds up beneath my skin and deep in my core. He moves one hand between us, finding the tight bundle of nerves at my center and rubbing in small, torturous circles. I groan and arch up into his touch, demanding more, and he obliges.

"Come for me," he commands. "Let me feel you."

And I obey.

Pleasure bursts through me, filling my veins with liquid fire. I cry out, closing my eyes as stars flash in my vision and I shudder around him. Raven keeps thrusting, dragging out my ecstasy with each stroke. When my body finally stops trembling, he pushes himself up, lifting my legs over his shoulders. I whimper as the position allows him deeper, clutching at the silk sheets as euphoria starts to build once more.

My desire burns white-hot as I watch him, his muscles tensing and flexing. He drops one hand back to my center and starts circling the pad of his thumb over the sensitive nub as his pace quickens. Raven's fingers bite into my thigh and he tips his head back with a deep moan. The sight and sound combined pushes me over the edge once more and I clamp down around him, pulling him over with me. His hips stutter and he shudders, a strained curse falling from his lips as he fills me with his release.

When the pleasure finally relinquishes us both, Raven collapses on top of me. I wrap my arms around him, welcoming the weight of his body on mine.

We lie together, cradled in each other's arms, until our ragged breathing slows, and silence fills the room. Raven leans up, his eyes finding mine, and I swear I could happily drown in the warm depths of them forever. His fingers brush the damp hair from my face before he leans in with a soft, lingering kiss.

"What are you frowning at?" he asks, his thumb stroking the space between my eyebrows.

"This feels surreal," I sigh, rolling onto my side to face him as he settles beside me and arches a brow in question. "What if we wake up tomorrow and realize this was just a dream?"

Raven leans forward, pressing a kiss to my lips.

"Then it will be the best dream I've ever had."

SEVENTEEN

IT'S NO WONDER *Thíasos ton Theíon* is renowned throughout the kingdoms. The sight before me is truly spellbinding. Magnificent, just like their namesake—Troupe of the Divine—suggests.

After days of wandering through endless marble halls, I find the northern courtyard where we first arrived entirely unrecognizable. Brightly colored lanterns adorn the marble columns and hang from the boughs of blossom trees, creating a beautiful spectrum of light that shines against the velveteen night sky. Circus tents are scattered throughout the open space, adorned with flags of every color imaginable.

Music and laughter fill the air as the people of the court flock to each tent, eager to explore the mysteries inside, their eyes sparkling with anticipation of the wonders that await them. Servers weave through the crowd, carrying platters of sweet cakes with spun-sugar decorations and trays filled with steaming goblets.

A central stage surrounded by rows of seating has been installed for performances, and beyond it is a raised dais with a table for the royal family to preside over it all.

It's almost enough to sweep me away, but as my eyes land on the bored expression of the king and the vacant eyes of his queen beside him, the fantasy all but dissipates like the morning fog over the sea.

I turn to Nyssa and Myna behind me. They both look around with wide eyes, just like I did a moment ago. Myna's gaze drifts beyond my shoulder, her expression becoming guarded before she drops into a slight curtsy. Beside her, Nyssa does the same, so I fix a small smile on my face and turn to greet the newcomer.

"Lady Titaia," I say, my smile blooming into one much more genuine.

"Oh, please, Princess," the auburn-haired beauty replies with a mischievous smile. "I'm as much a lady as I am a milkmaid. Titaia is fine."

"Only if you return the favor."

"We'll see," she replies, her eyes sparkling as she loops my arm through hers and walks me into the fray. "I was hoping I would find you. I need to point out the competition."

"Competition?"

"Perhaps that's a generous term." Titaia snorts an unladylike laugh that has me warming even more toward her as she beckons to a server.

The young man hurries over, blushing slightly and keeping his eyes downcast as we both take a goblet from the tray he carries. I don't miss the fine lines marking his otherwise youthful face or the silvering hair at his temples, but I hold my tongue, focusing instead on the fact that the engraved silver chalice is warm in my hand, heated by the liquid inside, steam curling off its deep red surface.

I frown as I raise it and breathe in the scents of spice and citrus. "What is this?"

"Mulled wine," Titaia says, taking a deep drink of her own. "It's perfect for cooler nights, a bit stronger than *calda*. Try it."

I take a tentative sip. The moment the warm flavors of orange, cinnamon, and honey blended with full-bodied wine hit my tongue, I can't contain a small moan of appreciation.

"It's good, yes?"

"Delicious," I say, taking a deeper drink, the warmth heating me from within.

"Good. Now, onto more important matters—not that wine isn't important. Do you see that lady over there? The one in the red gown?"

I follow the direction of Titaia's gaze and find the lady in question. The flowing red gown drapes over the curves of her body, leaving the golden skin of her arms and back bare. Her hair falls in silky mahogany curls to her waist as she tilts her head back and gives a bell-like laugh.

"That's Lady Lydia," Titaia goes on. "She was born and raised in this court, and her parents groomed her to be the future princess. She's a nasty piece of work and one to watch out for. The brunette on her right is Lady Helen of Pyrene—the capital of Reveza, and on the other side with black hair is Lady Zina of Corinth."

I take in the other two ladies. They both wear pleated gowns in shades of gold; a fact that obviously displeases them by the way they keep scowling at each other.

"And they're all competing in the trials?" I ask.

"Yes, much to their dismay. The three of them have been friends since they were young," Titaia says, smirking like she finds their predicament amusing. "They'll stick together until they find themselves up against one another."

"Are there any others?"

"Lady Dehlia from Lienz, a small town south of here." Titaia tilts her chin toward another brunette woman, this one with bronze skin that glows against the soft white of her gown, before her eyes shift to another. "And the last is Lady Cynna from Arkhadia."

I blink in shock at the last lady. Her hair is like my own, ashen and wavy, though maybe a shade lighter. Eyes of icy blue—matching perfectly with the gown that drapes over her lithe form—flick toward me, narrowing at my scrutiny before they slide to Titaia and stay there.

I suppose I shouldn't be too surprised at the likenesses between us. My mother was from Arkhadia, after all. However, the similarities end there. Her skin is the palest I've ever seen, as if she's never seen a day of sunlight in her life.

Pulling my gaze away from Lady Cynna, I take in the others.

Five competitors. Six, if I include myself.

My eyes roam over each of them, noting the graceful way they hold themselves, the fluttering of their eyelashes, the tinkling sounds of their laughter filling the air. I twist the ring on my finger, trying to tamp down the flutter of nerves in my stomach.

Titaia heaves a sigh beside me, drawing my gaze as she pulls my arm from hers. "Duty calls," she says with a wry smile. "Enjoy the festivities, Aella. I'll see if I can find you after."

"Thank you, Titaia."

She bows her head and throws a smile at Nyssa and Myna, who have been our silent shadows throughout our conversation. I watch as she sashays her way through the crowd, taking a seat at her father's side on the royal dais.

The back of my neck prickles with awareness and my eyes flick toward Keres, finding his gaze locked on me. He's once again sprawled in his seat, a goblet held casually in his hand as a finger dances lazily across the rim. My shoulders start to rise at the intensity of his stare, but I force aside the instinct. Instead, I bite my lip and drop my gaze, a private smile curling the corner of my mouth. When I glance up again, it's to five additional sets of eyes watching me with equal measures of curiosity and venom.

Fortunately, the observation doesn't last long. A tall man steps onto the stage, his dark hair tied back from his smooth face and his body draped in regal attire. He raises his hands to the guests, the single motion enough to silence the courtyard and draw the attention of the gathered tycheroi.

"Welcome!" the man's voice reverberates in the now-silent night, a broad smile on his face. "For those of you who are not residents of the court, I am Cyril, the Master of Ceremonies. Tonight, we mark the official opening of the Eretrian Royal Trials, a tradition that has been an important part of the

Selmonious reign since the beginning of the monarchy.

"These trials will see ladies from all over the Empyrieos compete in a series of three tasks to determine the best candidate for our prince's bride and your future queen. In keeping with tradition, the only trial we can tell you of in advance is the third. This will be an opportunity for the candidates to truly shine by displaying a talent before the court, something they think will please our prince. The first trial will take place in three days' time. Until then, enjoy all our court has to offer."

I jolt at the sound of cannons that accompany the final flourish of the Master of Ceremonies' hands. My jaw drops at the flares of colored light that spark and dance across the night sky. Red, blue, green, yellow, purple—they all swirl together, creating a kaleidoscope of vibrant hues. Each burst illuminates in a brief moment of beauty before fading away into darkness, and when the final burst showers down upon us, the sparks of light solidify and scatter across the marble floor as tiny gemstones. I kneel and pick up a ruby-red stone, rolling it between my fingers and watching as it crumbles to dust, leaving nothing but a powdery residue behind.

I stand as music strikes up from somewhere and a crowd of lords and ladies descend. Throughout the countless conversations, I continue casting glances in the prince's direction, forcing flirtatious smiles. And once again, Calliope's spectral voice drifts through my mind.

Always wait for him to come to you. Temptation is a trap, lay it well.

When the tycheroi of the court grow bored of the foreign princess in their midst, Nyssa, Myna and I finally manage to steal a quiet moment for ourselves.

"I don't suppose you've been harboring any secret talents over the past seven years, have you?" Nyssa asks.

"I think I might have something," I say, standing on the tips of my toes as my eyes land on two familiar faces in the crowd. An idea looms in my mind, a finely crafted image that just requires the right threads to add the finishing touches to the design.

"I'm not sure the royal family will appreciate how accurately you can throw a dagger."

"I don't know," Myna muses. "I think that's something Prince Keres may find intriguing."

Nyssa laughs, but Myna's words barely register as I track my targets across the courtyard, watching as they slip into a tent.

"Come with me." I barely get the words out before I start to move, weaving through the revelers and throwing gracious smiles at any who bow as I pass.

When we reach the tent, I pause to listen before pushing aside the flap and slipping inside, Nyssa and Myna entering behind me.

"Well, if it isn't the Princess of the Sorrows herself," Pan says, smiling at me from amongst a pile of cushions. Beside him, Eleni sits at a low wooden table, a collection of crystals scattered across its surface and scented smoke curling from embers in a shallow dish. The two of them look whimsical, dripping in jewelry and gauzy fabrics while reclining amongst the décor.

"Care to join us?" Eleni asks, waving a hand to the cushions on the ground, setting off a tinkling chorus as the bracelets lining her arm clink together.

"What is it we're joining exactly?" I ask as I settle into the cushions across from the two nymphai and eye the table decorations with no small amount of skepticism. A quick glance over my shoulder reveals Nyssa and Myna sitting down behind me, both still performing the roles of dutiful hand-maidens.

"*Parémvasi tou theíou*," Pan replies with a flourish of his hand. "Intervention of the divine."

I send a questioning look toward Eleni. She smiles at me indulgently before translating, "we're playing at being oracles. Would you like a fortune foretold?"

I forge a smile as I struggle to suppress a shiver, recalling the last time someone predicted my future.

Nothing good, my sweet anemone. Nothing good.

Calliope's words haunt me. The woman's ability to bury herself within the deepest recesses of my mind is uncanny.

"Is 'playing at being oracles' something you do often?"

Eleni shrugs lightly, rubbing at the corner of her kohl-lined eye. "Master Leto thinks it adds to the mystery of the troupe."

I cast my gaze around the tent, taking in the scented smoke as it dances under the twinkling lights strung from the canopy, before looking back to where Eleni watches me expectantly.

"I think I'll pass on the fortune for tonight," I say. "I wanted to speak with you about something."

Pan perks up, a mischievous smile curling his lips. "What made you seek out the likes of us?"

"How long will the troupe be in residence at the court?"

"King Daedalus has booked us for the duration of the trials," Eleni says. "We'll be providing entertainment for most of the events."

I nod as my mind slowly turns over that information, and Pan's eyes light up with interest.

"Why do you ask?"

As I weave another thread into place in my tapestry, a sly smile spreads across my face.

EIGHTEEN

A SCREAM PIERCES THE silent night, cut off by a loud crack.

Shattered planks of a boat…bubbles floating to the surface of a dark, hungry canal…a too-small hand reaching—

A knock pounds on the door, jolting me awake. Each strike of the fist ignites an answering blow inside my skull.

"Ugh," I groan, nestling further into my blankets. "Anemoi strike me down. What do I need to sacrifice for a good night's sleep?"

"Not even the Gods can get you out of this, Starling."

I lower the covers and glance toward the door. Raven leans against the frame, mouth turned up at the corners. I narrow my eyes and glare at him, but that only makes his grin grow wider.

"Come on. Everyone else is waiting on you." His eyes flick to the other side of my bed. "That goes for you too, Sparrow."

A muffled groan comes from the pile of blankets next to

me, and Nyssa's head emerges. "I agree with Starling. I offer myself up to the mercy of the Anemoi."

"If I have to deal with these assholes, then so do you two!" Myna calls from the common room, sending up a chorus of chuckles.

Raven raises an expectant brow at us, and I reluctantly drag myself out of bed. Nyssa grumbles and kicks back the blankets, shooting me a miserable pout. Amusement trickles through me once again when I realize she fell asleep in the dress she wore last night. It's quickly replaced with chagrin as I glance down and remember I did the same. The smell of smoke and wine clings to the fabric and my hair, stirring the queasy feeling in my stomach.

"Give us a minute to change?" I say to Raven, my eyes pleading for a slight moment of mercy. He rolls his eyes, but relents, pulling the door closed behind him.

As quickly as possible, Nyssa and I strip out of last night's clothing, dressing in flowing linen pants and shirts. I quickly splash my face with water in the bathing chamber and tie my hair back into a loose braid.

When we join the rest of the Flight in the common room, they're all similar shades of wretched and bleary-eyed, nursing cups like they hold a miracle in their depths. I suppose sleuthing around a palace day and night for almost a week will have that effect. The corner of my mouth tilts up into a smile when I spot the vessel of *calda* on the low table between the lounges. I pour two cups, passing one to Nyssa as we drop into our seats.

"So, what's the update, boss?" Lory's voice has lost its usual luster. Now he sounds tired, deflated.

I know they thought they had narrowed down the potential locations of the weapon. That finding it would be the simple part of this mission. I can only imagine how they must feel to have only found dead ends and a seemingly unlockable door so far. Frustration rears its ugly head inside me. I hate that I'm unable to help with the search. Instead, I'm stuck playing a game of cat-and-canary with a potentially unhinged prince.

Raven unfolds a series of parchment sheets and lays them down on the table. I frown at each one before registering that he's sketched a detailed floor plan of almost the entire palace. In some places, the design fades off or falters where he is yet to explore. In others, it's clear he's come up against a locked door he failed to pick.

"Between us, we've mapped out most of the palace," he says. "The shaded areas are ones we've already eliminated from the list."

"So, we're not really any closer than when we arrived," Heron says, a frown creasing his brow. His silky, chestnut hair is tied away from his face, highlighting the way his jaw tenses as he flicks his eyes toward me. Something like sympathy lurks within his gaze.

"We have no choice but to continue as we are. Sparrow and Myna will continue acting as handmaidens. The rest of us need to search every shadow and crevice of this court." Raven's eyes drill into each of us, the intensity of his stare driving home exactly what we have to lose if we can't pull this off. "We have until the last trial to find the weapon. Any later and we risk not being able to make it out on the night of the ball."

A heavy silence steals its way through the room, settling like a weight over my shoulders.

"How did it go last night?" Raven asks me. "Any updates on the royal family?"

"None of them deigned to leave their table," I say with a shrug. I'd spent most of the night casting lingering glances the prince's way and—while he had barely taken his eyes from me—the entire royal family didn't move an inch from their positions overlooking the revelry. "Although they announced that the final trial will essentially be some ridiculous talent show."

"That seems a bit anticlimactic," Lark muses, "and not entirely the prince's style."

"Making a group of women parade around for him and compete for his attention?" Myna snorts. "It's *exactly* his style."

"Focus," Raven snaps, and everyone immediately jolts back to attention. He turns his piercing amber gaze on me. "Do you have something in mind?"

"Yes," I pause as I take a sip of *calda*. I'd spent the late hours of the night discussing my idea with Pan and Eleni, and I was confident we could pull it off. "I'll be dancing, but I'm more concerned about the first two trials. Do we have any idea what they are?"

"Not that we've been able to uncover. The royal family guards the information closely to prevent any unfair advantages amongst the competitors," Myna muses, tracing the faint scar on her lip with the tip of a finger. "Every time is different depending on the prince or princess. When King Daedalus held his trials, they were...bloody. During his mother's, there was more of an emphasis on strength and bravery. With Keres' reputation, we can assume he will follow the lead of his father. Still, the real trial will be having to *marry* the bastard when you win."

A heavy silence settles over us as Myna's words sink in. We may be a Flight working together on this mission, but in this I am truly on my own. Anxiety tries to creep in, but I swat it aside. I have no time to be nervous. No time to worry about what my life may be like after.

I need to win these trials, so the Eagle has no reason to follow through on his threats.

My eyes slide toward Nyssa beside me, and I let the sight of her harden my resolve.

"Starling—" Raven starts.

"You all need to focus on finding this weapon," I say, standing abruptly. I can feel the intensity of his stare on my face, but I refuse to meet his gaze now. "I have a trial to win."

The other contestants and I gather in one of the lower halls, tension heavy in the air amongst us. I take comfort in having Titaia at my side; she's a welcome respite from the glares of Lydia and her ladies. Master Cyril and his scribe are here, as well as two guards manning the doors before us.

I shift in place as I watch the Master of Ceremonies speaking quietly to his scribe, the young man frantically noting everything down. The nervousness in my limbs calms slightly at the familiar sensation of my sheathed dagger pressing into my thigh. I dressed in a dove-gray gown for the evening, the loose layers and pleats of the fabric make it easy enough to hide a slit where I can access my dagger underneath.

Movement to my left precedes the soft voice that travels to my ear. Despite the hushed tone, I don't miss the steel lining the words.

"Princess Aella, the North was unaware that the Sorrows desire to align themselves with Eretria."

I turn, my eyes locking onto frosty blue ones. Hers seem to peer right into my soul, and I feel something within me shift at the intensity that gaze.

"Lady Cynna," I say, taking in the fair beauty beside me. It's so rare for me to see someone with features like my own that I'm almost transfixed by the way her pale hair glimmers under the light of the auras. There is something ethereal about her, an almost nymph-like quality that has me wondering if her bloodline is mixed. "I wasn't aware Arkhadia was looking to do the same."

It's a lie, but she doesn't need to know otherwise. Our Flight had long since discovered a noble lady from Arkhadia had entered the trials. I was shocked when Raven told me. The relations between the northern and eastern kingdoms remain strained after the God War. A history stained with blood and loss that has never come clean.

Cynna's eyes turn even frostier at my words, but before she can respond, a throat clears at the front of the hall, drawing our attention.

"Welcome to the first trial," Master Cyril says, spreading his arms wide. "For the prosperity of Eretria, it is vital that our prince's future bride possesses astute knowledge and a sharp wit. Tonight, you will be tested on both. One by one, each of you will enter the room behind me, wherein you will be asked a single riddle. You will each have half an hour to answer the riddle and, if you are correct, only then will you be able to go through the door on the other side, where Prince Keres and the court will be waiting for you."

"What happens if we get the answer wrong?" Dehlia's soft voice rises above the whispers that break out amongst the competitors.

"I strongly suggest you don't," Master Cyril says, a wicked smile slowly spreading across his face.

"Doesn't seem so bad," I murmur to Titaia, but when I glance at her beside me, tension lines her face.

"Keep your wits about you," she whispers. "Don't rush into giving an answer out of fear."

"Princess Aella, you will be first."

My heart stutters in my chest, Titaia's warning echoing through my mind. I glance up to see Lydia sneering in my direction. I grit my teeth and move forward, approaching the doors with controlled steps.

The guards on either side wrench them open, and the doors swing wide with an ominous creak. I can see nothing but darkness within, but the hair prickling at the nape of my neck tells me darkness isn't the only thing lurking in the space.

I release a slow, steadying breath and step across the threshold.

The doors are closed behind me, stealing away the light from the hall, and I go still. My ears strain as I wait for my eyesight to adjust. Slowly, the faint outline of a door comes into view on the other side, and I take a few tentative steps toward it.

The sound of something sharp scraping across the marble floor makes me pause, and then an unnatural sense of dread creeps up my spine, freezing me in place.

"What have we here?"

The disembodied voice echoes throughout the chamber, but even without the acoustics of this room, it would have been enough to justify the dread currently pooling in my stomach. A single feminine voice that sounds like a hundred speaking at once.

Whispering, hissing, singing.

Glancing down at the goosebumps crawling up my arms, I embrace the strange dread pushing against my skin, welcoming it as I curl my shoulders forward and glance around the darkened chamber with wide eyes. Cautiously, I slip one hand through the slit in my dress, hiding it from view as I grip the hilt of my dagger. I force my words to tremble as I respond, "I am Princess Aella of the Sorrows."

"A title, a name," the voice says in its cacophonous cry. "But that's not *what* you are."

"And who do I have the pleasure of speaking with?"

Laughter that sounds like twinkling bells and shattering glass fills the dark room. Something wet and rough brushes along my shoulder, making me shudder as I spin to face my foe. But the room behind me is empty.

"Such manners," the voice says, seeming to come from everywhere and nowhere at once. "I am the holder of histories and worlds long forgotten. I am the keeper of secrets, and answers, and doors. But you may call me Sphinx."

The words scratch the surface of a memory in the back of my mind. I shake my head, conscious of the time I'm currently wasting, the seconds draining away like fine sand slipping through my fingers.

"I'm here to answer a riddle."

"And I am here to speak it."

A flash of movement draws my attention and I turn, only to once more find nothing at all.

"What is it, then?" I fight to keep my voice free from the irritation blooming in my chest. So far all this woman has spoken sounds like an Anemoi-cursed riddle.

"She tastes like wind, and fury, and mortality."

"Is that the riddle?" I ask with a frown, my eyes darting between the darkest shadows.

"No."

I bite my lip to hold back a frustrated curse, but then realization dawns on me. My eyes widen as I try to suppress the shudder that rolls through my body.

"Did you just…lick me?"

The laughter sounds again, and out of the shadows I was studying, a creature stalks toward me.

I was *somewhat* correct in my assumption that she was a woman. Cat-like eyes narrow at me from a sharp, angled face. A mane of black hair tumbles in wild curls around her shoulders, concealing the nakedness of her breasts. But that's as far as her resemblance to tycheroi extends. She prowls forward on strong but feminine arms, her otherwise elegant hands tipped with sharp claws. Below her chest, tawny skin fades into the golden coat of a huge feline body. The muscles of her powerful legs ripple, lethal clawed paws scraping across the smooth floor with each step. Two wings are folded over her back, the same color as her fur at their base, darkening to the midnight shade of her hair at the tips.

The sight of her brings the memory of Leto's story roaring to the surface, tearing words from my throat. "You're real…"

Sphinx sits back on her haunches and cocks her head at me, her tail flicking behind her like I've seen the irritated alley cats do so often back in the Sorrows. "You have heard of me?"

"I heard a story."

"Don't all stories start with the truth?" she returns with a smile sharp enough to cut stone. My throat constricts and I tighten my grip around the hilt of my dagger. But she speaks again.

"Neither seen nor felt, its touch is naught,
Yet in your heart, a chill is brought.
It comes before, trailing in the wake,
A cloak of gloom, a path it makes.
It hides the truths that fear unveils,
In silence, it triumphs as courage fails."

Her golden eyes bore into mine as she finishes the riddle, a predatory smile curling her lips. "What is it?"

I release my dagger and turn away from her, pacing as I rein in my breaths. Probably a mistake, but I can hardly think straight beneath her penetrating gaze. I repeat the riddle over and over in my mind, considering answers before just as quickly pushing them aside.

Sphinx laughs again behind me.

Glass shattering.

Bells ringing.

The unnatural dread in the chamber seeps into my skin and a bead of sweat drips down my spine. I squeeze my eyes shut, trying to block her out—but it's no use. I run a hand frantically through my hair, opening my eyes again to stare into the suffocating darkness surrounding me—

My hand freezes in motion, breath hitching in my throat.

"Darkness." The word passes my lips in barely a whisper, but the silence that follows is telling. I spin around and face her again, repeating my answer with conviction, "Darkness."

The silence drags out as I await her judgement, and I run through the riddle over and over in my mind, until Sphinx finally responds.

"Correct," she says in that uncanny voice, a more genuine smile spreading across her face.

My breath comes out in a rush, draining most of the tension from my body. As it does, the sense of malice bleeds from the air as well.

I did it. I can leave.

But I can't move.

I'm rooted to the spot, caught in this magnificent creature's golden gaze. I know I should leave, but curiosity has always been one of my biggest flaws—and Sphinx had that very curiosity *raging* within me.

"Would it be rude of me to ask what you are?"

"It would depend on the manner in which you ask."

I don't speak, even though the question burns behind my lips. Instead, I watch her for a moment longer, taking in her lethal claws and lean, muscular body. She tilts her head and watches me back, her wild hair shifting with the movement.

After a long moment of mutual observation, Sphinx answers my unasked question. "I just am."

I barely hear her words, because—as she speaks them—I notice the collar at her neck, made from a dark gray metal that I don't recognize. But I recognize the marks engraved on its surface.

Goiteía.

Beneath the collar, her golden skin is chafed raw. I track a line of blood that drips between her breasts and grit my teeth. Any urgency I felt earlier is completely burned away by the heat of my anger as it flares.

"What have they done to you?" The words slip from my mouth unbidden, my voice dangerously low.

An unexpected, manic grin takes over her strangely beautiful face, sharp white teeth flashing in the dark.

"The prince awaits you," Sphinx states, leaving my question unanswered. But the bitterness of her tone tells me all I need to know.

I clench my jaw, knowing that she's right and my time is running out. But the thought of leaving her shackled like this has my stomach turning over violently in protest.

The mission. I need to remember my purpose here.

Relinquishing the handle of my dagger, I force my feet to move toward the door. Her sharp gaze burns a hole between my shoulder blades, and as my fingers grip the door handle, Sphinx speaks again. Hundreds of voices whispering and screaming and singing.

"We'll meet again soon, Daughter of the Tempest."

The door closes behind me before I can even consider what her words might mean, and the thunderous applause that greets me pushes them from my mind.

"Congratulations, Aella," Keres says as he sweeps forward, and I force a triumphant smile to my face as he takes my hands, placing a kiss on them. "I was hoping you would make it through."

No matter how genuine his words may sound, I don't trust them in the slightest. Even so, I beam at him like I do.

"Thank you, Keres," I say, struggling to keep the venom burning in my chest from leaching into my words. "Although, for a moment, I wasn't sure I would."

Keres flashes a sharp grin as steps back, and a crowd of lords and ladies surge forward, smiles and accolades dripping from their lips.

But I don't miss the flashes of disappointment on some of their faces.

I *especially* don't miss the glimpses of gold changing hands.

NINETEEN

THE AIR WHOOSHES OUT of my lungs as I step into the library the next day. Veins of gold crawl up the marble walls, blending seamlessly into the cavernous ceiling above.

Morning light streams in through the tall, gilded windows that line the circular walls, reflecting off the polished floor and filling the space with a soft glow. In the middle of the library, a ring-shaped counter sits atop a low dais, a group of elder tycheroi absorbed in their various tasks at its center.

Rows of white oak bookshelves stretch in perfect symmetry throughout the space, radiating out from the dais like sunbeams. Each shelf is overflowing with a collection of aging scrolls, gilded books, and ancient tomes. Tables, chairs, and small arrangements of lounges and armchairs fill the spaces between, scholars decorating each with stacks of books beside them.

A golden spiral staircase on the far side leads to a mezzanine level that curls around the walls. More bookcases and small, private alcoves crowd the space, a few tycheroi scattered amongst the nooks and strolling through the aisles.

Despite the sheer beauty of it, there's a coldness to the library—the same chill permeates the rest of the palace. It seeps through the marble floors and walls. A relentless cold that creeps into your bones.

"Well, there you have it," Titaia says, pausing beside me with a bored look on her face. "Books. Lots and lots of dusty books and old people."

"I take it you don't have any reading recommendations for me," I say, a small smile itching the side of my mouth.

It's just the two of us today. When Titaia showed up at my rooms, I put on a show of giving Nyssa and Myna the day off from their handmaiden duties. After our Flight's meeting yesterday, it's becoming clear they need to focus more energy into finding the weapon.

"Come along then, Princess." Titaia leads me through the tall shelves, mumbling under her breath as she starts to pull down books and pass them to me.

When our arms are heavy with our collection, we head to one of the smaller tables. I carefully place my stack, stretching out my arms and breathing a sigh of relief.

It quickly dries up when I count over twenty books piled high on the desk.

"This is a lot of books for someone who apparently doesn't enjoy reading." I flash Titaia a skeptical look, but she waves it aside, dropping into one of the chairs.

"You asked, I delivered. Think of it as a crash course in all things Eretrian history." She pauses, a slight frown marring her forehead. "Did you learn about that with the Acolytes?"

I open my mouth to respond, but a new voice cuts in.

"Princess Aella," a familiar man exclaims, rushing over. He bows deeply as he takes my hand and chastely kisses my knuckles.

"Lord Yiannis," I say, offering a smile. "What a pleasant surprise."

"The pleasure is all mine, of course." He turns to Titaia and his smile dims as he bows his head in her direction. "My lady."

"My lord," she replies with dry amusement. "I take it you've had the honor of meeting the lovely Aella on your travels. Tell me, how much did you offer the King of the Sorrows to convince him to send his daughter here?"

My jaw drops and I watch as Lord Yiannis goes red, blustering over his words. He turns to me and says, "I assure you, Princess. I did nothing of the ki—"

"We are quite busy, Yiannis," Titaia says.

"Of course, my lady." He nods again before bowing in my direction. "Best of luck, Princess. Not that you'll need it, I'm sure."

I watch in amusement as he scurries away between the shelves.

Titaia grins as she leans toward me. "He's so deep in my cousin's pocket, I'm shocked we even saw him here."

I bite my lip, holding in my laughter. Not that I needed to bother. It dries up in my throat as my eyes land on a servant returning books to their shelves. Despite the youthful structure of her face and body, her skin is withered and hair

216

hangs in limp, faded clumps around her face.

"Are there lots of *Goiteían* here?" I ask.

Titaia's shoulders tense as she follows my line of sight. "Yes, but not all of them look that way because of it."

"What do you mean?"

"Has Keres given you a rose yet?" She must read the confirmation on my face because she rolls her eyes so hard I worry she'll go blind. "I've heard half the ladies in this castle bragging about getting one at some point."

My nose wrinkles with distaste, but I smother the reaction before she looks back to me.

"The *theïkós* that runs through the royal bloodline of Eretria is unique—as they all are. We can make leaves fall, manipulate harvest and the autumnal elements, wither plants. But at its core, there is a decaying touch. Unlike the season of autumn, it does not strictly apply to plant life."

Stillness seizes my body and my breath stutters. "Are you telling me those people have been *decayed*?"

"Decayed, withered." Titaia shudders. "It's my dear cousin's favourite punishment for those who displease him."

This information is entirely new to me, and I highly doubt the order does not know. Resentment coils in my gut at the thought, and my gaze returns to the withered woman.

Is it possible I've found a place I despise more than the Aviary itself?

I jolt as a flash of lightning arcs through the sky; seconds later, the deep rumble of thunder follows as sheets of rain pummel against the windows. A chill rolls through me and I rub my hands up and down my arms.

"You probably miss the warmth of the Sorrows," Titaia says, drawing my eyes back to her.

"Yes, but I've always loved storms."

"Does it storm often in the south?"

"Not often enough, but whenever it does, I find the tallest building just to feel the world rage around me."

"Does a princess have a lot of pent-up anger to unleash?"

"I think everyone is angry." I shrug, flicking over another page even though my brain stopped absorbing the words a while ago. "Anger is often disappointed hope."

"I can't argue with you about that. Here."

She passes me a pale blue book. It's much thinner than the others on the pile, but large and square. Frowning, I open the cover to the first page.

It's a storybook. For children.

Slowly, I look up to find a now-familiar glimmer of mischief in Titaia's eyes.

"It's good to go over the basics."

I roll my eyes at her, but flick through the pages. It's a basic story of the Anemoi and the discovery of the Empyrieos, nothing I haven't read before.

I settle back into my chair and focus on the drawings, my eyes narrowing when I notice the same images from Leto's shadows painted on the page. I freeze when I turn the page and find a picture of a creature. My fingers trace over the feminine face, feline body, and feathered wings.

"This creature," I say, turning the book toward Titaia and pointing at the image. "You warned me to be careful before the first trial. Did you know of her?"

Her eyes lock on mine, no trace of the earlier humor in their red-brown depths. "Yes."

"Does she normally reside in that chamber from the trial?"

"Sphinx does not *reside* here," Titaia grinds the words out. She glances around nervously, before tilting toward me. "She's a prisoner."

I lean back and watch her; a frown creases her brow as her eyes flick between my face and the book. I can see the thoughts racing through her mind, though they're too quick for me to glean any understanding. She glances out the window, biting her lip nervously as the storm builds. Another roll of thunder sounds overhead.

"Why would you show me this?" I ask, trepidation twining through my mind.

"I may have only known you for a short time, Aella." She looks me in the eye as she says the words. In them I see a song of pain that harmonizes with my own. "But I have known my cousin all my life. I trust your intentions are kinder."

"What are you trying to ask, Titaia?"

"I want you to help me free her."

Aside from before the trial, I've never seen Titaia act any other way than cynical or mischievous. Now, her body radiates tension, her features solemn. The change in her usual demeanor—the seriousness of it—plucks at the strings of my heart, unleashing a bittersweet melody.

I need to remember my mission.

But it's easier said than done when the memory of Sphinx is burned into my mind. Blood dripping from scarred flesh beneath the collar at her throat, the tortured voice singing, whispering, *screaming*.

Words tumble from my lips before I can give them a second thought.

"Take me to her."

The tunnel is a yawning black abyss that stretches before us like the throat of a great beast.

My skin pebbles, either from the dampness in the air, or the faint scent of copper and decay. The only light comes from the small aura in Titaia's palm, but the warm glow doesn't reach far, barely illuminating the surrounding space.

My heart races as I follow her, beating a staccato rhythm that surges with each looming shadow. We must have been following this tunnel for at least an hour now. Every step takes an eternity as we venture deeper into the mountain's belly.

The walls are jagged and uneven down here, with small trickles of water running down them like sweat on a feverish face. Our footsteps echo in the darkness, along with the occasional drip from somewhere up above.

It's hard to tell how deep we have gone, even now my eyesight has adjusted to the dark. All I know is that every turn brings us further and further away from any sign of life or civilization. While that should probably put me on edge, there is something about Titaia that tells me I can trust her. Raven would surely tell me I'm foolish for believing so, but it's not like I'm about to tell her I'm a foreign spy here to steal a weapon. I simply don't think she's about to bludgeon me in the head and lock me in a cell.

We pause when the tunnel splits in two. Titaia points to the left. "This way leads to Keres' *workrooms.*"

The disgust coloring her voice leaves no doubt in my mind that whatever takes place down here repulses her. "And the other?"

"A tunnel that lets out at the eastern base of the mountain."

I keep my face impassive as I store the knowledge away.

Titaia turns to face me, slipping a second aura from the pocket of her gown into my hand. "Are you sure you want to do this, Aella?"

"I think you already know the answer to that question."

She nods grimly. "I can't go in there with you."

"Why not?"

"She asks all those who try to walk past her a riddle—exactly like your first trial." A frown lines her forehead and she hesitates before she speaks. "If you get it wrong, you die."

My heartbeat stutters. "What do you mean?"

"It's not her fault. It's part of her binding."

"The collar," I guess, disgust rippling through me. It was fortunate all the ladies from the trials had passed Sphinx's riddle, or else I imagine they would have faced a gruesome death.

Titaia nods. "I don't know what Keres and my uncle have her guarding, but it can't be good."

My heart rate picks up at the word *guarding.* I cast my mind back, trying to recall the maps Raven laid out in my chambers. Have they found these tunnels before? Surely not, since they didn't mention meeting Sphinx. She's difficult to miss, and impossible to forget.

"You don't have to wait for me." I grip her hands in mine, giving them a slight squeeze. "I have a feeling it wouldn't end well for you. I'll find my way back and if I bump into anyone, I can just say I got lost."

She hesitates, looking torn between doing as she says or damning the consequences and following me anyway. The former wins. "Be careful, Princess. It will be rather dull around here if you die on me."

"Well, I wouldn't want you to get bored."

Titaia flashes me a reluctant smile and takes a few steps backwards.

"Go," I encourage. "I'll let you know if I can figure out a way to help her."

She gives me a grateful smile and starts down the tunnel. I watch the glow of her aura disappear with the sound of her fading footsteps before I finally turn. Pushing my shoulders back and steeling my spine, I head into the darkness.

I've barely taken a hundred paces before the light from my aura illuminates a heavy wooden door. I test the handle, but of course, it's locked. Kneeling, I place the aura on the rough stone floor and push aside the skirt of my dress, flicking open the lockpick satchel strapped to my thigh holster. I pull out two of the picks and slide them into the keyhole. It doesn't take long before I'm rewarded with the sound of a sharp click, the lock snapping open.

Returning my picks, I swipe up the aura, stand, and push the door open. The same unease I felt during my first trial creeps up my spine as I step into the room. My senses warning me of a predator lying in wait.

"Sphinx?" The whispered word echoes in the space, followed by the scrape of a claw on stone.

"Daughter of the Tempest." Her voice comes before she appears from the shadows. "I did say we would meet again. Although this is sooner than even I foresaw."

I step further into the room as my eyes lock onto the collar at her neck. "You are not here of your own will."

"I am rarely anywhere of my own will."

My gaze flicks back up to hers, the golden cat-like eyes luminous in the dark. "I was hoping we could help one another."

"And what is it you seek?"

"What is it you guard?" I fire back.

A slow, predatory smile curls her lips.

"To some I bring death; to others I bring safety.
If it weren't for me, many would die,
But because of me, many will.
Tell me, Daughter, what am I?"

An answering smile blooms across my face. "A weapon."

Sphinx purrs, her eyes glimmering with approval.

"If I can remove the collar, will you be free?"

"As free as any of us can be," she replies, her layered voice echoing through the chamber.

"And if you are freed, will you stand in the way of any looking to pass through the door behind you?"

"I do not willingly stand in the way of fate."

I frown at the words, but approach her and slowly reach toward her throat. Sphinx hisses as I carefully spin the collar, committing the *goiteía* marks to memory. As I step back, a clawed hand flies toward me. I suck in a choked breath at the sting of pain, looking down to see an unfamiliar mark carved into my skin. Blood spills, dripping between my breasts.

I watch with a mixture of shock and awe as the wound heals, the mark fading into my skin until it disappears entirely. As though the magic was absorbed into my body itself.

"A bargain is struck," Sphinx says, her ominous tone igniting shivers along my skin. "You must go now."

Burning questions rise to my lips, but I hold them back in favor of one. "What did you mean when you called me Daughter of the Tempest?"

I hold my breath as she watches me, golden eyes flaring at the words. Disappointment blooms within me when it becomes clear she will not answer.

Not hesitating a moment longer, I leave Sphinx and her guarded secrets behind.

With my mind running frantically over everything I've learned, I don't hear the angry voices until I step back into the main tunnel. My heart leaps to my throat and I quickly dart to the right, retreating into the shadows of the exit passage Titaia showed me earlier. I press my body into the curve of the wall, shoving the aura deep inside the folds of my gown to smother the glow. As my eyes adjust to the dark, I press my mouth into the crook of my arm, muffling the telltale sound of my breath in the otherwise silent space.

"What do you mean 'it failed'?" A familiar voice carries to my hiding spot, the fury in the words making the hairs on the back of my neck stand up.

Keres. I know his voice well enough by now, but I've never heard him so angry.

"The subject died, my prince." The new voice is unfamiliar. A deep, raspy hiss, like the owner has been screaming for too long and shredded their vocal cords. "He was not a strong enough vessel to hold the power."

A growl of frustration echoes down the tunnel.

"You will try again," Keres demands. "I don't care how many *vessels* you have to go through."

"Of course, Your Highness."

I remain frozen in place as the footsteps and voices fade, and a door slams in the distance.

Once I'm sure enough time has passed, I creep out of the opening. I glance to my right, cocking my head to listen for any signs of movement in the tunnel.

An icy breeze claws its way out of the dark, like a cold hand sliding against the surface of my skin, causing the ever-present warmth of my soul magic to shiver within my chest.

And with deep certainty, I know.

I've found what we've been searching for.

TWENTY

I SCREAM AND THE sail snaps open. Too much—too hard—and the boat flies through the water, crashing into a dock on the other side of the canal.

A sob rips from my throat as her hand disappears beneath the bubbling surface last, as though she's reaching for me—begging me to save her.

A cold grip tightens around my throat—

A door slams in the outer room of my chambers and I bolt upright in bed, my heart racing as I blink away the remnants of my nightmare. They've been much too frequent since I stopped taking the somniseed.

The sound of raised voices and heavy footsteps gets closer, and I scramble toward my nightstand, grabbing my dagger and ripping it from the sheath as the door explodes open.

"Fucking Notos!" I shout, relief washing over me at the sight of Nyssa and Raven. "You almost gave me a heart attack."

I throw the dagger onto the bed and rub my hands over my face, flinging myself back down amongst the pillows. An expectant silence fills the room and I peer through my fingers to find two furious faces watching me.

"What?" I ask, dropping my hands.

"What?" Nyssa repeats, her voice dangerously calm.

"You can't ask what. I asked it first."

"What the fuck, Starling?" Raven thunders, storming further into the room. "Where were you last night?"

Realization dawns on me as his question penetrates the morning fog of my mind. The memories of last night's journey with Titaia through the tunnels crash through my thoughts. I bolt upright again, an unrestrained smile taking over my face. It only gets broader when I notice the way Raven's eye twitches with barely controlled anger.

"I found it."

"What do you mean?" Raven crosses his arms over his broad chest as he continues to glare at me. "You found what?"

"The weapon," I say with a casual shrug.

Nyssa's jaw drops and Raven's eyes sharpen on me, the muscles in his jaw flexing as he clenches his teeth.

I slip out of bed, stretching my arms above my head and saunter over to the closet. I grab the first gown I see and slowly dress, feeling their gazes burning my skin the whole time.

When I turn back, neither of them has moved an inch. While both still look incredulous and furious, I see the heat banking in Raven's eyes. He narrows them on me before turning sharply and stalking off.

"Meeting," he barks. "Now!"

Nyssa shakes her head at me. "You are in so much trouble."

I wince. "How bad is it?"

"I would fully expect spankings and angry make-up sex."

"I don't know what you mean," I say with a straight face. She snickers as we head into the sitting room.

I freeze when every pair of eyes turns toward me. Anger and irritation radiate from each of the Nightwings, making the atmosphere stifling.

"Uhhh, good morning?" I say hesitantly, folding my hands in front of my body as I shuffle on the spot.

Heron scoffs, shaking his head and looking around at the others with frustration written clearly on his face. "What did you all expect, taking Fledglings on a mission like this?"

"Songbirds," I correct, collapsing into the sofa.

"Enough, Starling!" Raven snaps, pinching the bridge of his nose as he squeezes his eyes shut. "Why don't you enlighten us all about your revelation this morning?"

I narrow my eyes and sit up straighter at his tone, irritation coiling through me. "First, let me preface this by saying I tried to find someone last night. But this is an enormous palace to search for trained spies and assassins."

Raven's jaw tenses, but he nods. "Go on."

"I believe I found the location of the weapon."

"You *believe*," he presses, "or you know?"

"I know." I say the words firmly, holding his gaze. We stare at each other, unblinking, neither of us willing to back down.

A throat clears.

"How did you find it?" Lory asks, and I tear my eyes away

228

from Raven to study the frowning faces of my Flight around me.

I take a deep breath, settling myself more comfortably on the couch as I mentally prepare myself for a long morning.

By the time I've finished relaying my story of Sphinx, the secret tunnels, and Titaia's wish to free the poor creature, my head pounds and I sigh in relief as I slip back into my bedroom. The others spent hours drilling me with questions and sketching floorplans of the passageways and tunnels that lead to Keres' workrooms.

As I predicted he would, Raven almost lost it when he heard how I followed Titaia. But his ire was nothing compared to the furious silence I received when I told them of my bargain with Sphinx.

I sketched out the *goiteía* from her collar, and Heron devised the best sequence of marks to nullify them. If those didn't work, he would need to damage the carvings enough to break through the binding effect. Afterwards, I'd watched in silence as the others made plans and Raven gave everyone orders to start preparing.

I'd hoped he would stay afterwards, but he stormed out before I even had a chance to ask. Sorrow and irritation war within me as I recall his refusal to even look me in the eye as he left. It's not that I don't understand what I did was reckless—*I do*. But taking a chance on Titaia and making the bargain with Sphinx is also the reason our mission may be a success.

A soft scuff sounds behind me, and I glance over my shoulder to find Lark watching me cautiously from the doorway, a more serious expression than I have ever seen on his face.

"What?" I grumble.

"I know you won't want to hear this," he sighs, running a hand through his hair. "But be careful with Raven."

"You're right." I glare back at him. "I don't want to hear it. Besides, there's nothing I need to be careful of. I'll be staying here, and he will be returning to the Sorrows."

"I only say it because you're like family to me, Starling…" he hesitates before continuing, "the Aviary is everything to him. Something worth bearing in mind, this life will always be his first love. It will always have his loyalty."

Lark turns and leaves, gently closing the door behind him.

I grind my jaw in irritation, but it slowly bleeds out of me. It doesn't matter because I know exactly where Raven and I stand.

Soon, it will be in two separate kingdoms.

Exhaustion settles in after my late-night adventure. Since Raven didn't leave me with any instruction for the day, I crawl back into my bed and curl up under the sheets.

It doesn't take long for sleep to claim me, and when it does, images of endless stone corridors and haunted golden eyes follow me into my dreams.

I wake as the bed dips beside me, the smell of woodsmoke and cinnamon heavy in the air. With my eyes closed, I lie still as fingertips ghost over my bottom lip, trailing down my neck and chest before tracing the spot on my sternum where the bargain mark hides beneath my skin.

"I know you're awake," Raven rumbles. "Keeping your eyes closed won't fool me."

Sighing, I peek up to find him smiling softly down at me. There's still a hardness in his gaze, but nothing like the burning fury I witnessed earlier.

"You're still mad?" I ask, biting my lip.

"Furious," he growls. His hand lands on my hip, and he tugs me closer to his body. I shiver at the feel of his hard muscles pressing into my curves. "But only because I was terrified. I couldn't find you, Starling."

"I'm sorry," I whisper, sliding my fingers through the dark waves of his hair and pulling his forehead down to mine. "I had a feeling and followed it. I didn't mean to worry you."

"I'm not sure *worry* effectively describes how I felt."

"But it paid off, right?" I ask, my eyes searching his for confirmation I didn't realize I needed.

"Yes," he says with a sigh. "We found the tunnels and the creature you spoke of."

"Sphinx."

"Never in all my years have I encountered something like her." A shudder rolls through him. "Heron and I both had to answer her riddles just so we could inspect her collar and the cells."

"She's not so bad after the first time," I say with a small smirk, but it dies a swift death on my lips when the implications of his words sink in. "So, you found it?"

"We did. *You* did." Raven's fingers start to stroke my hip. "We just need you to keep the court distracted and get through the last two trials. I need to make sure everything else falls into place."

My smile is forced this time. "I'm sure you can manage, Commander."

Raven grins wickedly back at me and my breath hitches as his hand gathers the fabric of my gown. The moment it slips beneath the fabric—calloused fingers dragging along my ribs—I arch into him. The heat coursing through me drives every other thought from my mind.

"Raven," I gasp. Fire dances along my skin, following the path of his teasing fingers, leaving me hot and wanting. I need him to do more than touch me. I need him to—fuck, I just *need* him.

Desperation charges my body as I push him on his back and straddle him, grinding down on the hard length I feel through his pants. Raven's hands land on my hips with a groan, encouraging my movement with demanding strokes. I grip the bunched-up edges of my gown and tear it off, the cool air and his heated gaze pebbling my skin and turning my nipples hard.

He sits up, one arm wrapping around my waist, the other hand tangling in my hair as he kisses me deeply, holding me close. But not close enough.

I groan in frustration, tugging at his shirt. "Why are you still wearing clothes?"

A sensual chuckle tickles the crook of my neck, teeth scraping the sensitive skin. "Apologies, Princess. Allow me to remedy that."

I gasp in surprise as he spins me, my back hitting the bed,

and watch hungrily as he tugs his shirt off over his head. His pants come off next, and then he's back on me, kissing and nipping every inch of my skin within reach.

He grinds against me, and my hips thrust upwards in response, liquid fire shooting through my core at the low groan that escapes him. I cry out as he enters me with a single powerful thrust, lifting one of my legs and wrapping it around his waist.

"Fuck," I moan as another wave of desire floods through my body. "Damn it, Raven. *Move.*"

He laughs again, slowly dragging himself out before he thrusts back into me, hard.

"Thank the gods," I gasp when he does it again.

"I don't think it's the gods you should be thanking, Starling," he growls, slamming into me again. "They're not the ones fucking you."

Reaching up, I curl a hand around his neck and pull his lips onto mine. I feel his moan deep in my soul as he finally picks up the pace. This time, he doesn't stop. He gives me no reprieve as he relentlessly drives into me, over and over again, each stroke pushing me closer to bliss.

My legs wrap around his waist and he angles deeper. He reaches between us, his fingers finding the sensitive bundle of nerves, and as he strokes me, I cry out. Pleasure explodes along every one of my nerve endings. I clamp down around him and he moans as we both careen over the edge into ecstasy.

Raven falls back onto the bed beside me, breathing hard as he pulls me into his side. He leans over and gives my ear a playful nip. But it's his whispered words that ignite a bittersweet ache in my chest. "We're not done."

"Never," I lie, pulling his lips to mine.

TWENTY-ONE

TIME HAS SLIPPED BY in the blink of an eye since my discovery, and the second trial is upon us. Like walking through a memory, I follow Titaia through another tunnel. Our footsteps echo against the raw marble walls, like they did a week ago when she led me to Sphinx.

At some point I notice the walls becoming more natural and less refined, the windows disappearing. The auras along the ceiling are now the only source of light. After what could be minutes or an hour later, we reach a single oak door.

Looking at the door itself would be enough to set me on edge if I wasn't already.

The wooden surface is carved with gruesome battle scenes and omens. However, the image that fills me with dread is of four winged men running through a twisting maze of wrong turns and dead ends. The way before them is barred, and even from my perspective, I can't seem to find a clear path to freedom.

"Ready, Aella?" Titaia says, turning over her shoulder to give me an encouraging smile that lights up her face.

I'd given her a brief cover story earlier in the week, so she now believes some of my guards are working on a plan to release the mythical creature. She's barely left my side since, feeding me any court gossip or information she thinks can be useful.

Despite the necessity of my deception, guilt still gnaws at me. I bury it deep and smile back at her. "As I'll ever be."

Titaia pulls open the door and I'm almost blinded by the bright, white light on the other side. My vision clears as I step out onto the side of the stage, but the sight before me only makes my already racing heart beat painfully in my chest.

Heavy gray clouds hover above an amphitheater, pale light glaring off the carved marble surfaces. The air is thick with anticipation, hundreds of whispers coalescing into a steady thrum of noise. Rows upon rows of seats, carved from the same white stone, circle around the sandy arena in front of the stage, hundreds of tycheroi filling them. The stage is a marvel, every surface adorned with intricate carvings and murals like the ones on the door we entered through.

Master Cyril and his scribe stand in the center, waiting for the royal family to arrive. The other girls are already here, distrust and discomfort clear in every angle of their bodies as Titaia and I approach. Not that I can blame them for it—each of them wears a gown more suited to a banquet than the stage of an amphitheater. Only Cynna looks at me with guarded curiosity in her icy blue eyes.

Heeding Titaia's veiled advice, I dressed in a light gray pleated wrap top that cinches at my waist. The sleeves are long and loose, barely offering protection from the chill in the air. The pants match perfectly, with concealed pockets that allow me to reach the dagger. Since I wasn't sure what to expect, I also brought my lockpicks and secured two small throwing knives in the straps of my sandals, hiding them beneath the flowing material of my pants. The outfit is like others I've worn at court and—paired with my hair falling in loose waves down my back—it still appears elegant while being more practical than a gown.

After so many years of remaining in the shadows and consciously avoiding notice, standing on a stage in front of a teeming crowd has my stomach clenching with anxiety. I feel exposed, as if they are displaying me for all of them to judge and pick apart like vultures.

"You're looking a bit pale there, Princess," Titaia whispers beside me.

"I'm not accustomed to being the center of this much attention."

"No, I don't imagine the Acolytes on the Isle of the Winds would have made much of a fuss over you."

I open my mouth to make some kind of excuse, but the arrival of the royal family saves me from the need, providing a distraction from Titaia's musings.

Keres enters from a similar door to the one I did on the opposite side of the stage, looking every bit the prince in shades of crimson that make his eyes all the more vivid, trimmed with a golden brocade to match the circlet resting over his brow.

The king and queen, adorned in their royal regalia, stand at the entrance, handing over center stage to their son for the oversight of the trials.

The presence of all three is enough to silence the crowd without a single word. A hush descends over the amphitheater, like all the guests are collectively holding their breath.

Keres' gaze runs over the contestants, lingering on my body in a way that makes my skin crawl. I stand still under his perusal, willing my face into a mask of nervous excitement. His eyes meet mine and I bite my lip, looking up at him through my lashes as he turns to the audience with the shadow of a smile on his face. Titaia scoffs quietly beside me, and I resist the temptation to glance her way as Master Cyril addresses the amphitheater.

"Welcome, loyal members of the court, to the second of the Royal Trials." He pauses dramatically as the crowd applauds. "In the beginning, our great gods, the Anemoi, were held captive, and to escape, they faced many a trial. Today, the ladies who stand before you will undertake one such trial, testing their resilience in the face of adversity and uncertainty. They will enter through the doors you see behind me and must emerge through the doors on the balcony above."

As Master Cyril talks, his scribe approaches each of us, passing out small auras. I take mine with a grateful smile, gripping it in my fist, as I play the master's words over again in my mind.

Pan and Eleni had made a joke about the troupe embellishing their gifts for prophecy to incite a sense of mystery. But the correlations between the story Leto told us on the journey to Vilea and the trials are far too obvious for it to be a mere coincidence.

I'm going to have to hunt down some nymphal when I'm finished here.

"No one knows what will meet them beyond the doors, but if they do not emerge within two hours, they will be disqualified."

His words send a tremor through my body as adrenaline seeps into my veins. The winged men carved into the surface of the door Titaia and I entered through earlier flash to the front of my mind. My eyes dart toward the back of the stage where six burly tycheroi— each dressed in the supple leather armor of the Royal Guard and armed with a crossbow—stand beside doors with similar carvings.

Trepidation creeps through me at the sight of quivers stuffed with wicked bolts.

"Ladies." Master Cyril's voice breaks through my thoughts. "If you would each select a door."

"Good luck," Titaia whispers behind me.

I nod in silent thanks, making my footsteps appear hesitant as I cross the stage with the others to stand before a door. I watch the guard by my door warily, taking his measure as he continues to stare stoically out into the amphitheater. He's of medium height, but still a head above me, with a stocky build that makes it hard to imagine him being stealthy.

If he pursues me like I suspect, I should be able to keep ahead of him without it appearing too easy.

"Let the trial begin!"

At Master Cyril's command, my guard opens the door,

revealing a gloomy tunnel beyond. I waver, and then plunge into the shadows. The door closes behind me, sealing me in. My heart skips a beat at the sudden darkness and silence, the only light coming from the soft glow of the aura in my hand.

I close my eyes, breathing deep as I cast my mind back to the campsite on the side of the road between here and Corinth, recalling Leto's story.

As they raced through the labyrinth, the Anemoi used an age-old trick, keeping their palms on the left wall to ensure they didn't get lost.

My eyesight takes a moment to adjust when I reopen them, but when it does, I can make out the tunnel walls as I scan the surrounding shadows. Breathing deep, I place my left hand against the wall and settle into a steady jog. The twists and turns are disorienting, and it doesn't take long before I find myself at a dead end.

"Gods damn it," I curse under my breath, following the wall. "I never want to see another tunnel after this."

As my hand glides along, the stone abruptly disappears beneath my palm. I freeze, blinking at the wall next to me. Tentatively, I reach out again, and a bitter smirk twists my lips as my hand disappears through the stone.

I take a step back and raise the aura, casting light higher on the tunnel walls. A thrill runs though me as I spot the *goiteía* mark for concealment carved into the rock face, but it's quickly chased away by resentment.

What a trivial waste of someone's life.

Pushing the thought aside, I take a breath and walk through the false stone.

The passage I step into is nowhere near as wide as the first one. I set a slower pace as the tunnel weaves and curls through the mountain, dashing away any sense of direction or time the longer I follow it. Anxiety creeps in, clawed fingers wrapping around my lungs as I start to wonder whether I've taken a wrong turn. But as a cold sweat breaks out on the nape of my neck, relief floods me as the tunnel curves once again and opens into a larger—

A gasp rips from my throat as the ground disappears beneath me. I twist and scramble for the ledge, pain stinging through my palms as the rocky floor scrapes them raw. Air hisses through my teeth as I pull myself up, collapsing back onto solid ground. I groan as I reach for my aura, having dropped it when I fell. Fortunately, it didn't go down the hole, but the light seeps from a large crack in its surface. It won't be long until I'm trapped in the dark.

My breath comes in small pants and I run my fingers through my hair, nails scraping against my scalp. The shadows stretch toward me, ready to claim my defeat.

My grip on the aura tightens as I shine the light over the hole beside me. It takes up the full width of the tunnel, a dark, looming pit with no end in sight. My stomach turns as I realize just how close I came to death, but a small ledge across the left wall catches my eye. Standing on shaky legs, I carefully skirt the hole. I'm plunged into darkness as I carefully tuck the aura into my pocket, so I run my hands across the rough wall until I find the ledge again.

My palms sting as I grip the stone, but I grit my teeth with determination as I slowly let my arms take my weight.

I bite my lip harder with each slight adjustment of my hands, gradually making my way across the ledge. I breath out a relieved sigh as I drop down on the other side. Pulling the aura out of my pocket, I inspect my palms, wrinkling my nose as I pull sharp bit of grit from the cuts.

In the distance, the scuff of a boot against stone sounds, and I freeze, tilting my head as I strain my ears. With a glance over my shoulder, I study the darkness of the tunnel I emerged from. Another scrape echoes down the passageway; the sharp metallic grind of steel against stone. As though the guard is purposefully making the noise to frighten me.

I bite back a grin.

Let the show begin.

Wasting no more time, I place my left palm on the wall and set off at a slightly faster pace, letting my footsteps land louder than before. The ground beneath me inclines, steadily leading me upward. The sounds of my pursuer grow louder and my heart beats harder against my ribcage with each echoing footfall.

Louder.

Closer.

I let a whimper escape me, and a dark chuckle answers.

And that's when I feel it.

A faint breeze coming from up ahead, so subtle, like the soft caress of a feather against my soul. I angle my face toward it and the light brush of wind strokes my left cheek.

It's the only encouragement I need to push myself harder.

A growl sounds behind me, reverberating against the cold stone walls. I don't bother looking back, keeping my eyes fixed firmly on the end of the tunnel as it appears before me, determination driving me forward. The door looms and I don't even consider slowing down as I slam into it, the force of my body sending it flying open as I stumble through.

Just like when I stepped onto the stage earlier, the white light is blinding, the roar of the crowd wrapping around my senses. I don't fall as I expect to. Instead, powerful arms wrap around me, holding me upright.

I blink to clear my eyes and peer up into Keres' face as he smirks down at me.

"Congratulations, Princess."

"I made it?" I pant out, widening my eyes.

"And you didn't even come last."

He intends his tone to be playful. Flirtatious. But it just makes me want to punch him in his beautiful face.

I smile at him instead.

But then his words register in my mind. I pull away from his lingering embrace, glancing around at the others standing on the victors' balcony. Lydia glares at me so hard I wish I had a *goiteía* charm to protect me from the evil eye. Her dress covered in dust, sweat sticking her usually perfect curls to her forehead. Zina stands at her side in a similar state, her eyes narrowed at where Keres' hand still lingers on my waist. Cynna stands off to the side, amusement on her face, barely looking like she's broken a sweat.

Two of the doors are still closed, so Helen and Dehlia must still be in the tunnels.

"If they went the wrong way, will the tunnels eventually lead to a way out?" I ask Keres.

"Perhaps. I've never been in the labyrinth myself."

The dismissive tone of his response makes me bristle, anger flaring white-hot in my chest. I bite my tongue, forcing back the vitriol that threatens to spill from my lips.

Minutes pass like years as we wait for the two final ladies to emerge. The hush has fallen over the crowd once again, everyone watching with bated breath.

"Time is up!" Master Cyril's voice booms through the amphitheater.

Finally, a door slams open. Dehlia rushes through and all but collapses on the ground, sobs shaking her body and a bloody hand clutching at her shoulder.

No cheers greet her arrival. Instead, the audience hisses their disapproval. The eerie sound of it echoing through the space sends a chill down my spine.

I fall to my knees beside her, pulling her hand away to inspect her arm. A crossbow bolt is still embedded in her shoulder, stuck in the bone. Blood oozes from the wound, staining Dehlia's clothing and my hands with sticky crimson.

"She needs a healer!" I shout, turning to the others on the balcony. Venom crawls up the back of my throat at the bored expression on Keres' face, but he nods, and Dehlia's mentor rushes forward, helping the sobbing girl from the ground and rushing her away.

"Titaia, take Princess Aella to get cleaned up," Keres orders, cutting off my thoughts. "Her sweet heart is bleeding on the marble."

Lydia titters like he said something highly amusing, and I bite my tongue harder. The taste of copper fills my mouth.

No doubt I'll have permanent scars on my tongue once this farce is over.

Standing, I glance at Titaia. She tilts her head toward the same door Dehlia was ushered through. I force my resentment down and fix a smile to my face as I turn toward Keres, blood-stained hands folded in front of my body in a grotesque vision of demureness.

"Thank you for the kindness, Prince Keres."

Without waiting for a response, I follow Titaia out of the amphitheater.

The more time I spend here, the more the twisted truth of the Vilea's court reveals itself. The jeweled and gleaming facade shedding, giving way to the foul reality beneath. One by one, my naive fantasies of the world have slowly withered and died before my eyes. A nightmare taking the place of daydreams.

I may have been a winner in today's trial, but as I leave the victors' balcony behind, I can't fight the feeling that I lost something too.

TWENTY-TWO

"READY?" NYSSA ASKS, LEANING against my bedroom door. She looks flawless in a pale blue gown, the fabric draping over her curves. Her dark cinnamon curls are pinned into the style they favor in Eretria, half up and half down.

It's been a week since the second trial, and I have had to endure visits with Prince Keres nearly every day. Sometimes it's no more than a stroll through the courtyard, where I pretend to hang on to his every word as he tells me tales of Eretria. Sometimes, it's a private dinner in his chambers, tensions running high between us for entirely different reasons. And other times, it's evenings spent amongst the other ladies competing in the trials, each of us vying for his attention.

Tonight will be such a night.

After the trial in the labyrinth, only four of us remain: Lydia, Zina, Cynna, and me. Despite making it through the treacherous maze within the mountain, Dehlia didn't escape in time and was eliminated from the trials. I haven't seen Helen since the moment she went through her door. A shudder rolls down my spine as I consider what that might mean, recalling the moment I would have plummeted to my death if not for the quick reflexes I developed at the Aviary.

My eyes flick back to my reflection in the mirror, taking in the woman's image who manages to look like me and a stranger all at once. Pinned in the same style as Nyssa's, my ashen hair falls in perfect curls against my glowing, tawny skin. My pleated gown falls to the floor with slits up both legs, while the top crosses over my chest before draping over my shoulders like a cape. The steely blue fabric is the perfect match for my eyes, making their color even more prominent. An intricate belt cinches in my waist, the design like a creeping laurel branch dipped in gold.

I look like a princess.

I want to tear the gown off and curl up under the covers of my bed.

"Let's get this over with, then," I say to Nyssa, stifling a groan.

We leave our chambers and stalk through the palace, passing by endless walls of white marble. With each step, I slowly add a piece of my armor: my shoulders pushing back, a sway taking over my hips, an excited smile blooming on my face. When we finally step into the dining hall, I'm sure I look like an entirely different person.

The room is much smaller than the formal dining hall, a space for the royal family's more intimate dinners. A large fireplace takes the chill from the air and auras flicker in sconces along the walls, casting shadows across the marble floor. The other contestants are already seated at a large oak table in the center, but with Keres still absent, the tension in the room is thick enough to cut with a knife.

Cynna sits to the right of Keres' vacant throne, smirking at Lydia and Zina on the opposite side of the table. I almost laugh at the matching scowls etched on their faces, but quickly bite it back. I slide into the spare seat next to Cynna as Nyssa stands off to the side of the room behind me.

"Has anyone heard from Helen?" I ask when the silence becomes stifling.

Lydia's glare flicks to me, her eyes narrowing impossibly further. "Why would we care to hear from her?"

I blink slowly at her words, shocked by the obvious dismissal of someone who has been her friend since childhood. I can't imagine simply forgetting about Nyssa like that. If it had been her that hadn't made it out of the maze, I would be right there trying to find her.

Cynna scoffs beside me. "Oh, I don't know. Perhaps because you are supposedly friends?"

"If she couldn't pass the last trial, then it's no concern of mine," Lydia sneers. "I don't even know why she bothered entering at all—it was a waste of her time. Everyone knows Prince Keres and I were made for each other."

My shoulders tense up at her words, and I'm not the only one. Beside Lydia, Zina's throat bobs as she swallows, her eyes narrowing on her friend.

I lean forward on the table, propping my chin on my hand. "Do *you* know that, Zina?"

The black-haired beauty looks at me, a frown marring her otherwise flawless face. "Do I know what?"

"That you're wasting your time?" I ask, widening my eyes sympathetically.

Cynna makes a choking sound beside me, covering what I can only assume is a burst of laughter with a cough.

I smile pleasantly, even as Zina's face turns thunderous.

"I'm not the one wasting my time, *Princess*," she hisses. "Everyone knows it will come down to a decision between me and Lydia. And it's as likely to be me as it is her."

Lydia's gaze whips around, glaring daggers at the side of Zina's head. She opens her mouth and promptly closes it, both ladies shooting to their feet as Keres enters the room.

Cynna leans in as we both stand. Her eyes dance with amusement as she whispers conspiratorially, "I wasn't sure who was going to be stabbed first, you or Zina."

"We'll have to place bets for next time."

"A gold *drachma* says it's you."

"That's exactly what my lady's maid said," I say with mock hurt, holding a hand over my heart, and Cynna snickers. I glance over my shoulder at Nyssa. She's gazing up at the ceiling, her lips pressed into a thin line as her body trembles with barely repressed laughter.

"Ladies," Keres says, settling into his throne at the head of the table. "I'm honored to find myself in such beautiful company once again."

I resist the urge to roll my eyes when the others drop into elegant curtsies. As I sit back down in my seat, Keres' gaze lingers on me, and I only release my breath when Lydia predictably draws his attention away.

"Are you looking forward to seeing my *talent* tomorrow, my prince?" The innuendo in her voice is so thick, I have the urge to avert my eyes.

Keres leans back in his throne, his thumb running across his lower lip while he stares back at her. "I am, Lady Lydia. In fact, I'm looking forward to seeing what *all* of you have to show me." His red eyes heat as they devour each of us in turn, like we're his own personal buffet.

As if on cue, servants flood the room, carrying large dishes of food and jugs of wine. My mouth waters as the aroma of spiced meats drifts over me, and I press a hand firmly into my stomach to tame the growl it threatens to let loose.

I needn't have bothered.

My appetite abruptly curdles as a young serving girl leans past me to fill my goblet with wine. A graying lock of her hair falls forward, bled of the rich brown shade amongst the rest of her curls. She can't be more than sixteen years of age, and already her magic has been so abused that she's being sapped of life.

Either that, or she's a victim of Keres' decaying touch.

Bile climbs up my throat when she places my goblet before me and her hand trembles, drawing my eyes toward the papery skin crawling up her fingers.

My gaze sweeps around the room, and I can feel the blood draining from my face at the clear signs of magic abuse amongst the servants: graying hair, dull eyes, aging skin that clashes with their otherwise youthful appearances.

I push away from the table. The sound of my chair scraping

across the marble cuts above the conversation. The other ladies look up in surprise, and Keres frowns when my eyes finally land on him.

"Thank you for dinner, Prince Keres." My voice comes out strained as I struggle to keep my disgust locked away. "I'm afraid I'm not feeling well."

"I'll walk you to your chambers," he says, starting to rise.

Lydia's furious eyes turn to me, and she opens her mouth to protest, but I quickly respond. "That won't be necessary. Stay, enjoy your evening with the ladies."

Keres freezes, irritation flashing across his face before he lowers back down. His expression settles into something un-readable, but I don't miss the bite in his next words. "Of course, Princess. I hope you are well before the trial tomorrow night."

I incline my head toward him and pivot on my heel. Nyssa rushes to my side, her usually tanned skin drained of color and a grim set to her mouth.

I manage to hold my tongue and composure until the door to our chambers closes firmly behind us.

And then I let it go.

"Do it again, darling. This time with more gusto!" Pan cheers. He's sprawled on the sofa, a small pipe hanging from his lips. Eleni and Nyssa both add shouts of encouragement between bouts of laughter from where they lounge amongst the scattered cushions on the floor.

Pan and Eleni turned up not long after Nyssa and I returned from the disaster of a dinner. They were coming to help me prepare for my last trial, but I was still fuming when they knocked on the door. They had quickly left, only to return carrying a large vessel of wine between them. I brushed aside the small voice in my mind that warned me to think rationally and welcomed them in.

After they listened to me rant about Eretria's prince and the kingdom's abusive customs, we went through almost half the jug of wine. It was then that Pan had the idea to steal the gilded portrait of Keres that now leans against my sitting room wall. The artfully captured rendition is now pockmarked with small throwing daggers.

Feeling emboldened, I swipe up another three knives from the low table. Balancing my wine goblet and two knives in one hand, I take aim with the other.

"He's a narcissistic—"

The blade flies, stabbing into the portrait.

"Abusive—"

The second strikes between the prince's eyes.

"Waste of life."

The final knife buries itself into his groin.

I sweep into a bow, promptly emptying my wine all over the floor. "Oh, fuck."

Pan claps his hands, the pipe falling from his lips as the three of them howl with laughter—

The door swings open.

My smile slides off my face as Raven steps into the room,

Myna and Lark behind him. As they still in the doorway, I freeze, watching in horror as Raven's gaze slowly shifts from me to the knife-studded portrait. A part of my mind is aware of my friends dissolving into hysterics as Pan falls from the couch and onto the floor. But my attention is locked on the ire building in Raven's eyes. I swallow roughly as they flick around the room, taking in the empty jug of wine, the pipe, and the two performers rolling amongst the cushions.

"Princess," Raven grinds out, his jaw flexing with barely repressed anger. "I think it's time for your company to take their leave."

My heart sinks as Eleni and Nyssa's laughter dies. Pan struggles to rein his in, and Eleni slams a hand firmly over his mouth.

"Oh! Would you look at the time," she exclaims dramatically, making me wince. Lucky she's a dancer and not an actress. "We need to leave. Performances to prepare for, courtiers to entertain, and all that."

The slight nymphai stands, dragging Pan along with her as he snatches the dew pipe from the table and raises it toward me. "Until next time, darling."

The door closes loudly behind them.

Raven pinches the bridge of his nose, squeezing his eyes shut.

Nyssa scoots to my side and we watch as he breathes deeply, waiting for the tirade that is no doubt about to be unleashed.

I expect him to shout, but his words are spoken with a menacing calm.

"Explain to me," he says, "what made the two of you think

this was a good idea?"

"We were just blowing off some steam," I say with a shrug.

"We're here on a mission, Starling!" Raven yells. "And instead of you distracting the prince at dinner, as you're supposed to, I find you here, intoxicated and hurling knives at a portrait of that very prince."

"In all honesty, I think it's an improvement," Lark chimes in, nudging the golden frame with his boot. Beside me, Nyssa makes a choking sound and I bite my lip hard.

"Not now, Lark," Raven barks. He runs his hands through his hair and paces. Pausing in front of the portrait, he lets out a string of curses that has my brows steadily inching higher on my forehead.

After further tense moments of silence, Raven pulls the blades from the painting. I flinch as each dagger drops to the floor. When he looks back to Myna and Lark, his words are clipped.

"Return this to where it belongs. With any luck, no one will notice before we are gone. If they do, I'm sure our *princess* will be low on the list of suspects."

The two of them spring into action at his command, carrying the portrait out of the room and disappearing into the hall without a backward glance. Raven turns back to us, and I watch him with a guarded expression.

"If you two were anyone else, I would send you home and request that you be exiled from the Aviary," he says, his voice purely that of our Flight Commander—no trace of the man who has held me in his arms late at night. "We spent months and months on this mission, before the two of you were even

Named, and you could have jeopardized it in one reckless night. Now two of our Nightwings are having to clean up your mess when their focus should be elsewhere. I will not tolerate any more of this behavior. Am I clear?"

My mouth goes dry and shame twists violently in my gut. "Yes, Commander," Nyssa and I say in unison.

Raven watches us, his eyes tracking over our features, ensuring the message has been driven home. With a terse nod, he turns to leave. As he opens the door, he looks back, his eyes searing me as he delivers his last words.

"I expected more of you."

TWENTY-THREE

I STAND IN THE shadows at the back of the grand hall. The vast space is shrouded in darkness, the only light coming from the strings of auras hanging above the stage directly ahead of me. Confusion marring the ever-present masks of superiority they typically wear, the gathered members of the court glance around.

Wondering. Waiting.

At the side of the stage, Pan raises his head, his eyes lock with mine, elegant fingers poised over the strings of the lute cradled in his lap. I steel my spine and lift my chin, watching a wicked grin take over his face as he begins to play.

The first note rings with the clarity of a bell, sounding through the hall and silencing the murmurs of the crowd. As the song builds, I step in time with its melody, letting the music soak into my skin and guide me.

When I'm almost to the stage, Keres turns in his seat, his

eyes piercing me like an arrow, and I can't help but feel a sense of apprehension.

A moment of self-doubt.

I'm not afraid to admit to myself that watching the others perform and show off their chosen talents set me on edge. As it turns out, I begrudgingly must concede that Lydia has the voice of a goddess, and Cynna plays the harp beautifully. Fortunately, Zina also sang as her chosen talent, and her performance left much to be desired. I watched as many in the audience blocked their ears against her shrill notes.

I know the performance I'm about to give is a risk, but I needed something that would make me stand out. Joining the Aviary at a young age hadn't meant the skills I was developing under royal tutelage fell by the wayside. I can sing and play musical instruments as well as the next court lady. Those skills are as important as spycraft for a Songbird.

However, in a trial where those talents would already be on display by other competitors. I needed to work with my other strengths.

The past seven years have given me exceptional balance, agility, and control over my body. My masters also allowed me to continue my dance lessons, and muscle memory and awareness went a long way in my private lessons with Eleni and Pan.

Thoughts flash through my mind like shooting stars as I continue to float through the audience, keeping my gaze on the stage ahead, even as more faces turn at my approach.

The fabric of my inky black gown hisses against the marble floor, parting with each step to reveal my legs. The dress is a southern style, something people at home wouldn't blink an eye at, but here it will be considered a bit more risqué. But I had managed to add a subtle touch of modesty by borrowing what Eleni called *stay-ups* from her. My legs are covered in the sheer glittering fabric, studded with tiny gems, which grows opaque as it climbs up my thighs.

I take a fortifying breath as I finally reach the stage and climb the steps, the glossy wood cool and smooth beneath my bare feet. I make my way to the draping layers of silk waiting for me. The fabric gleams in the dim light, shifting from pale gold to deep bronze, calling to me like a siren's song.

When I first approached Eleni and Pan, I hadn't thought I would enjoy it so much. But once I was in the air during our practice sessions, something simply fell into place.

A feeling of rightness. Of home.

As Pan's song reaches my cue, I wrap my hands around the fabric, feeling the strength of the silk beneath my fingertips. With a flick of my wrist, I launch myself into the air, my body spinning and twirling as I climb higher and higher.

Silk and air wrap around me like a second skin, sliding effortlessly over my arms and legs as I move through my routine. The gasps from below become part of the performance's melody, a discordant yet thrilling undercurrent to the symphony I enact above. And for a fleeting span, within the confines of the silk, the audience below fades as the music swells, and I fall into the now-familiar rhythm. I let it flow through my veins, spilling out of me as I lose myself to the thrill. Letting go of all thoughts and worries.

For a moment, I am *free*.

Free from the weight of my responsibilities.

Free from the expectations placed on me.

In this moment, there are only the silks and the music, guiding me through graceful loops and spins. The Empyrieos fades away, replaced by a world of my own creation.

The silk, my partner in this aerial dance, cascades from the high ceiling, a waterfall of shimmering fabric that entwines with my form. Each climb, each twist and suspended pirouette is a silent conversation between body and silken thread. Golden strands encircle my wrists, drawing patterns in the air as I spin, the world below blurring into an indistinct palette of colors and faces. I am both puppeteer and puppet within these wraps, commanding and at the same time yielding to the dance's whims.

All too soon, the music slows, and I match its pace, feeling the melody gently guiding my movements as my body twists and glides toward its graceful descent. My chest rises and falls with controlled breaths as my feet alight on the stage and the final note rings out, humming through the otherwise silent hall.

I raise my head, my eyes immediately finding Keres.

He watches me, unblinking, leaning forward in his seat. His face is an unreadable mask, but the heat in his gaze is unmistakable.

An air of anticipation fills the grand hall, as if time itself has been momentarily frozen, and I wait, holding my breath along with the rest of the gathered court. The flickering aura-light casts dancing shadows on the ornate tapestries adorning the walls, while the indistinct murmur of hushed conversations creates an atmosphere of tense energy that infiltrates my body. Everyone is waiting for someone else to break the ice that holds the crowd suspended in a frozen state, their eyes darting around in search of the first sign of movement or sound to shatter the stillness.

I blink in surprise when it comes from the person I am least expecting.

Queen Atalana rises from her seat and claps, a delighted smile on her face. The sound echoes through the hall, a catalyst of an avalanche, as the entire audience stands with a roar.

A rush of pride courses through me, although this is all for show. A pretty distraction to disguise perfidious intent. My eyes drop to the floor as I dip into a short curtsy. When I rise, the applause fades into murmurs as Master Cyril steps onto the stage.

"I think we can all agree that we have seen some exceptional talent tonight. However, not all of these ladies can proceed." He pauses, the crowd hanging on to his every word. "The ladies proceeding to the final stage of the trials are Lady Lydia, Lady Cynna, and Princess Aella. The prince will announce his decision after the upcoming masked ball."

The audience once again breaks into applause, and I use the moment to escape, heading to where Nyssa, Titaia, Pan, and Eleni all watch me with huge smiles.

I sashay toward them, a matching grin lighting up my face. "So, what do you think? Will Leto offer me a place in the troupe if I lose the trials?"

"Darling," Pan says as he takes my hand, "after that performance, if neither of them takes you, the three of *us* will run off into the sunset to start our own troupe."

"You mean the four of us," Nyssa corrects. "She wouldn't survive a day in these lands without me."

I can't hold back my laugh, still floating on the high from the dance. "Well, at least I have a back-up plan for my back-up plan. I'm glad I managed to pull it off."

"*I'm glad* the queen enjoyed it. If she hadn't broken the silence and knocked the crowd out of their trance, that could have been painfully awkward for us both," Titaia drawls as she rolls her eyes, but beneath the nonchalance I can sense she's just as pleased as the rest of us.

"Both?" I raise a questioning brow at her.

"Well, of course. I'm your mentor. Everything you do reflects on me."

Guilt stabs at me with her words, but I hide it with a smile.

"Oh, no need to worry. This was the best performance of the night, and that's all thanks to me," Pan says, mock bowing before standing with a flourish.

Eleni opens her mouth to argue, but a throat clears behind us, cutting through our moment of levity. Turning, I find Keres a few paces away, watching our group with thinly veiled curiosity. His eyes zero in on me.

"Princess Aella, I was hoping I could have a moment of your time?" His words are phrased like a question, but they ring with demand. Less asking, more telling.

"Of course." I incline my head in acquiescence, while a secret part of me growls in denial.

From the corner of my eye, I watch my friends melt into the shadows. Keres offers me an arm and I take it, allowing him to lead me away from the still-crowded hall and out to an adjoining courtyard.

The sky is a blanket of darkness, no sign of the stars between the thick canopy of angry clouds. Cold air bites at the exposed skin of my arms, and I let it, hesitant to use my magic in Keres' presence. The two of us walk in silence, an unspoken battle of wills, waiting to see who will be the first to relent.

We come to a stop beneath a wilting wisteria tree, lavender petals, and orange leaves scattered across the marble ground. Keres finally turns to face me.

"I must admit, I couldn't have predicted the Princess of the Sorrows performing like that," he begins, but I can already see his lips pulling into a smirk. "It was…unconventional."

"Unconventional? That's the best you can come up with, Prince?"

"What would you like to hear, Princess? It was enthralling. Intoxicating."

"Something like that," I say coyly.

His eyes light up with interest, and I let a slow smile curl my lips.

"It was," he agrees, his voice deepening as he takes a step toward me, "all of those things and more."

I force my body not to lock up as he slides a hand around my waist, drawing me even closer to him.

"You would make a beautiful queen, Aella," he murmurs. The brush of his lips along the shell of my ear sends a shudder up my spine. I bite my lip, hoping he mistakes it for desire. "If it weren't for the rules of the trials, I would have already asked for your hand the moment you set foot in my court."

I stare up at him, my eyes roaming over the planes of his face, like I'm trying to find the truth of his words written there. Internally, I struggle to rein myself in, trying to find a response that doesn't involve telling him to remove his hands from my body.

Fortunately, I don't have to.

"Princess?" Nyssa's voice cuts through the air.

Keres pulls away swiftly, his jaw tensing at the intrusion. I turn to face my friend. My eyes land heavily on hers, silently conveying gratitude.

"Yes?" My voice sounds convincingly breathless.

"A raven has arrived with a letter from your father." She hesitates before continuing. "Shall I take it to your rooms?"

The relief is as sweet as a southern summer storm.

"No, I had better read it now," I sigh, turning to peer up at Keres through my lashes. "Thank you for the walk, Keres."

Smugly, he inclines his head. "Any time, sweetheart."

Nyssa and I race back to our rooms, clinging to the shadows to avoid any members of the court still lingering in the halls. By the time we make it back, the high I felt earlier has well and truly faded.

"I could kiss you right now," I say as I collapse on my bed.

Nyssa's tone is smug. "I know."

"I genuinely thought you weren't going to get there in time, and I would have to kiss him."

She flops onto the bed next to me, an all-too-familiar evil grin taking over her face as she rolls toward me. "The thought did cross my mind."

My mouth falls open, and I stare at her in shock. "You were watching the whole time?"

"Well, 'you would make a beautiful queen, Aella.'" Her voice deepens into a mimicry of the prince as her eyes smolder at me.

"You bitch!" I grab a pillow and promptly smack her in the face with it.

Nyssa falls back onto the bed and bursts into a fit of laughter.

"You should have seen it," she says between gasping breaths. "I thought you were going to punch him in the throat when he pulled you closer."

I groan, dragging my hands down my face. "If I win these trials, I suppose I'll have to face it someday soon."

"Well, there's only so many times I can rescue you from it."

I huff a half-hearted laugh. "Are you staying in tonight?"

"Ugh," she groans, dragging herself off the bed with a pout. "Raven has me scouting that tunnel you found with Myna. I should probably go meet with her."

"Serves you right," I say smugly, reclining amongst the plush pillows and blankets while she heads for the door.

Nyssa throws her middle finger up over her shoulder, not even bothering to look back. My laughter chases her as the door slams behind her.

With a sigh, I drag myself off the bed and head toward the dresser. But before I've taken so much as three steps, a firm arm wraps around my waist, pulling me flush against a hard body.

"Quite the show, princess."

The husky tone of Raven's voice melts over my senses, sending a flood of liquid heat straight to my core. He tightens his arm around me, drawing me closer until I can detect the evidence of his arousal digging into my lower back.

"Why am I not surprised that you were spying from the shadows?" I ask, my breath hitching in my throat as he runs his nose up the column of my neck. I arch my body to give him better access, grinding back against him.

"I can't seem to stay away from you, Starling."

He kisses his way along my jaw as he pushes away the straps of my gown. The fabric slips from my body, pooling on the marble floor at my feet.

Raven groans, sliding his hands down the curve of my waist and back up again to cup my breasts. My nipples harden at his touch and I lean back into him, craving more.

"Did you enjoy my dance?"

He spins me around so I'm facing him, molten eyes burning a pathway across my bare skin as they devour me.

"Enough to know I need a private viewing."

He pulls several strips of golden silk from his pocket. The raw edges make it clear they've been cut from the same lengths I used in tonight's trial.

"On the bed, Starling."

The command and desire in his voice sends an answering pulse of arousal throbbing through me, and I don't hesitate to comply. I lay on my back in the middle of my bed, and watch him stalk closer.

Raven takes both my hands in his, binding them together with a butter-soft length of silk before tying them to the headboard. He leans in close, lips brushing against mine as he speaks.

"Trust me?"

A whispered *yes* leaves my lips seconds before he claims them. His tongue teases my lower lip and I open my mouth for him, deepening the kiss. As my eyes drift closed and shivers erupt over my body, he breaks the kiss, pulling away.

"Raven," I plead, my eyes snapping open.

The corners of his lips tug upward, but his chest is rising and falling with rapid breaths, his tanned skin flushed, and his pupils so dilated I can only make out a small strip of honey-brown at the edges.

"Patience, princess," is all he says as he slips the last strip of silk over my eyes, stealing away the image of his heartbreaking face and plunging me into darkness.

The soft rustle of clothes falling to the floor is my only warning before the bed dips under his weight. Strong, warm palms slide up the lengths of my legs until his fingers grip the sheer leggings where they start at my waist, dragging them down slowly, along with my underwear.

My breath hitches in my throat, my heart pounding in tandem with the throbbing pulse between my legs. I clench my thighs together, desperately chasing the pleasure, but with a low growl he grips my knees and pushes them apart.

I've never felt so exposed.

So vulnerable.

He starts from my ankles, painstakingly lavishing every inch of my skin with his lips and tongue. I feel every touch a thousand times over, every stroke a caress against the deepest parts of me. Pure heat scorches through my bloodstream.

When his mouth reaches the apex of my thighs, he holds back, the warmth of his breath teasing against my flesh.

Taunting.

Testing my resolve.

My wrists pull against the silk restraints. The last strands of my self-control fray at the edges.

"Please," I beg, arching my back, trying to close that final space between us.

"Tell me who you belong to, Starling. Even if it's a lie."

"Raven…" his name comes out as both a warning and a plea. The way he's holding back is maddening, but intoxicating.

"Say the words, and I'll give you what you want."

"Yours," I pant. "I'm yours."

The words have barely left my lips before he strikes.

Devours me.

Consumes me.

I moan as he pushes his fingers into me, the firm strokes working in tandem with his tongue. I'm burning with a need hot enough to rival a wildfire. Lust sears the blood in my veins as the sweetest pressure builds low in my stomach.

It doesn't take long at all before I shatter with my release. Shards of intense pleasure ricocheting through me, white light flashing behind my eyelids.

Without waiting for me to recover, his lips slam into mine

at the same moment he enters me with a single thrust. I cry out and he greedily swallows the sound, the evidence of my release mingling with the taste of him as our tongues tangle.

I wrap my legs around his waist, drawing him closer, needing him deeper. My arms strain against their bindings, wanting to touch him, to feel his muscles tensing and run my fingers through his hair. The frustration only adds to the heat building within me again.

"Not yet." His tone leaves me with no choice but to obey.

I hold on to the last remnants of my restraint. But each movement, each roll of his hips, has tension coiling. My moans sound louder, my breathing becomes ragged, and I reach the point where I can no longer hold on.

"Come for me, princess."

And I do.

My body shudders from the intensity of the pleasure ripping through me, and I'm torn between the sensations of falling and flying.

Raven silences my cry with his mouth over mine as he continues to thrust, dragging out my climax with each stroke. He tenses and lets out a guttural moan, biting down on the curve of my neck to smother the sound.

His arms give out and the weight of his body presses me further into the bed. I lie there, cocooned in his warmth and floating on a cloud of pure bliss. Our ragged breaths are the only sound amidst the silence.

He shifts, and a moment later, the silk slides from my wrists. I reach up and pull the blindfold away, my eyes immediately searching for his.

Raven is watching me with a tenderness that makes my heart skip a beat, and any words I planned to speak instantly dry up in my throat.

He pushes up, hovering above me as the tips of his fingers trace along the line of my jaw, tilting my face up to his. His eyes seem to take in every minute detail of my features, like he wants to commit each part of this moment to memory. When he's done, he falls to the bed beside me, pulling me over and wrapping me in his arms. I snuggle in closer, my head resting on his shoulder, as he idly traces his fingertips along my spine.

"Raven, what's your real name?"

I feel him tense beneath me. It's only slight, but with our bodies pressed so close, it's hard to miss.

"Why do you ask?"

"I want to know more about you. Who you were before."

Before the Aviary. Before his Naming.

Before he rose through the ranks to become who he is today.

"Raven is the only name that matters to me now."

At his reply, Lark's earlier words of warning push their way to the front of my mind.

The Aviary is everything to him. Something worth bearing in mind: this life will always be his first love. It will always have his loyalty.

He takes my hand, bringing it to his lips and kissing the tips of my fingers. I melt at the tenderness, until he strokes his thumb across the ring on my finger.

"You're always wearing this," he says.

"Kal gave it to me." I pull my hand away, hiding it and the

simple gold band beneath the sheets. "It makes me feel like I always have a piece of him with me."

Raven raises himself to an elbow and leans over me, trailing his other hand through my hair. "Perhaps I'll have to get you something to remember me by."

I smile up at him, trying to pretend my heart isn't breaking. But I see the same pain reflected in his honeyed eyes.

Raven lowers himself again and we start a slow dance of teasing tongues and lazy touches, each caress and breathless moan stirring the embers of our desire. I give in to it, succumbing to the fire, letting myself be consumed by the flames.

TWENTY-FOUR

THE DRESS SHINES LIKE the sun itself. The fabric caresses my curves and cascades from my knees to pool in a delicate puddle. It's a vision of gold and citrine, a masterpiece of light and dark, like I am wrapped in a veil of sunlight that disappears behind the clouds. An intricate floral pattern, woven with fragments of yellow quartz, glints in the soft glow of the auras around my waist. The gathered fabric crosses over my breasts before tying in a halter around my neck, leaving my shoulders and arms bare, aside from the decorative golden cuffs that clasp around my upper arms.

My ashy hair falls to the lower arch of my back in silken waves, and fine strings of gold dangle through the tresses from the circlet resting upon my head. The mask I wear is a work of art. Crafted from the same glimmering shards of quartz and little bits of broken mirror, it covers my eyes, leaving the rest of my face on display.

Never have I looked more like a princess than I do at this moment.

My chest tightens in response to the thought, and I release a tenuous breath.

I've been stuck here staring at my reflection for gods only know how long after Nyssa and Myna proclaimed their work was done and left. Finally, I work up the courage to head into the sitting room, my sunbeam gown whispering against the floor as it trails behind me.

The members of our Flight gather around the room. Aside from Nyssa, who wears a midnight-blue gown and will attend the ball with me, they're all dressed in black. Silence hangs heavy amongst them, tension carving the silhouettes of their bodies. They glance up as I walk in, varying reactions taking over their expressions.

Heron's reaction is the most subtle, his eyes widening a fraction, in complete contrast with the way Lory's jaw drops. Myna and Nyssa both wear smug expressions, like they deserve accolades for their efforts.

But it's Raven I'm focused on as he straightens from his position leaning against the fireplace. His eyes wander a slow path down and then up my body, devouring every inch of me. When they finally return to my face, they're molten. Heated with an intensity that curls around my heart and pools low in my stomach.

That warm, liquid heat turns to frigid ice when Lark opens his mouth.

"Nope," he says, standing and shaking his head profusely. "This is a terrible idea. Awful."

Tension creeps into my body. Nyssa crosses her arms and glares at him from across the room.

"What do you mean? Of course it will work."

"Uh, are you blind? Do you see her?" His face scrunches up as he gestures at me. "Do you see all of *that*?"

"Explain, Lark," Raven demands, steel lining his voice.

Lark turns to him, arms flapping at his sides and exasperation written all over his face. "The prince is going to take one look at her and want to eat her alive."

I wrinkle my nose, stomach twisting with disgust at the image his words paint.

"That's the point, Lark," Heron says with a roll of his eyes. "Are you done with the theatrics now? We have an assignment to complete. I'm sure Starling can handle herself from here."

The room immediately sobers at his words.

Raven clears his throat and my heart clenches as I turn to him. The light casts a halo across the tousled dark hair that curls around his face and catches on the bronze angles of his cheekbones. A small frown creases his brow, a muscle ticking in his cheek as though he's clenching his jaw.

My breath stalls as I commit every detail to memory. This is the last I'll see of him. And with the others around, I can't even say goodbye.

"Heron is right. The two of you should leave now," he says. "Remain at the ball and ensure the royal family is preoccupied until you receive my signal."

"What's the signal?" I ask, hating the slight tremor in my voice and praying the others didn't notice.

His honeyed eyes watch me intently, gleaming in the light. "You'll know it when you see it."

"Are you ready to go in?" Nyssa whispers, sympathy shining in her eyes as she adjusts my mask.

"We'd better not put it off any longer." My words are strong, but my smile trembles the the corners of my mouth.

With a deep breath, I center myself and give a final nod to the footman who waits for us. I bite my lip nervously as he inhales deeply and booms my name.

"Princess Aella Sotiría of the Sorrows!"

The projection of his voice obliterates any last chance I had to run and hide. With an imperial tilt to my chin, I step through the grand doors of the ballroom and walk out onto the balcony.

The sight takes my breath away, freezing my feet in place like I'm one of the many marble statues that adorn the halls of the palace.

On either side of me, staircases curve down toward the revelry below, their steps lined with lords and ladies in elegant attire, each one looking more beautiful than the last. The music of a hundred instruments swells to fill the room, reverberating through me like a thousand prayers whispered in unison.

Chandeliers of glimmering auras twinkle above a crowded dancefloor, setting the golden veins in the white marble walls alight, like rivers of molten flame.

The guests below are all masked and garbed in elaborate gowns of embroidered taffeta and silk, adorned with sparkling jewels and feathers, dancing along to the hauntingly beautiful music that echoes throughout the hall.

Despite the grandeur of the scene before me, I don't miss the vipers in the nest.

This is a poisoned court, full of poisonous people.

Sly eyes beneath elaborate masks watch, cruel and calculating, as I make my way down the stairs.

Faux smiles and greetings are thrown out as I pass.

I return them with my own.

They may be serpents in this court, but I am not just a songbird.

I'm a bird of prey.

When I reach the ballroom floor, the crowd parts before me, masked figures curling away as a man approaches me. His muscular torso is wrapped in a jacket that looks like it's been crafted from fine threads of pure gold. It hugs his muscular arms, trimmed in silver embroidery with ornate silver buttons trailing down the middle. His pants are made from the same fabric, molding to his leanly muscled thighs. Sepia eyes stare at me from behind an elaborate mask, embroidered with golden thread and yellow diamonds. His hands are heavy with stacks of rings and golden hoops glimmer along the arches of his ears.

Even with a mask, he's easy to recognize. Only the Prince of Eretria is arrogant enough to be dripping in this much gold. And me, of course. But I had a team of spies conspiring to make us match.

I do my best not to roll my eyes at the thought as he comes to a stop in front of me.

"Princess," he purrs.

"Prince," I respond with a coy smile.

"May I have this dance?"

He holds a gold-laden hand toward me, and I eye it for a moment before placing my hand in his.

"You may."

I fucking hate court politics.

I throw a quick glance over my shoulder at Nyssa. She returns it with a slight nod and melts into the crowd as Keres guides me onto the dancefloor. Tonight, she'll be keeping an eye on the royal family, while I watch the prince.

With my hand still clasped in his, Keres wraps his other arm around my waist, pressing his palm into the small of my back. His eyes capture mine as the music swells around us with the beginnings of a new song, and we sway to its melody in perfect time.

"So how am I faring in this last test?"

The smile that unfurls across his lips is slow. It's devastating. Like a snake spreading its coiled body in preparation to strike. "No one ever said this was a test."

"No," I say coyly, "but I can only imagine it is, since they will make the announcement of your decision *after* tonight."

He goes silent while we continue to sway across the dance-floor, and the contemplation in his eyes makes me nervous. "We match," he finally replies.

I almost breathe out a sigh of relief. "I'll take that as a good sign."

Keres continues to watch me closely, a glimmer of something in his eyes—there and gone too quick for me to make sense of—before he moves the conversation along.

"Do you like it here, Aella?"

"It's like nothing I've seen before," I say with a small, dreamy sigh. "Although, I haven't managed to visit the city since I first arrived."

His hand tightens on my waist, pulling me closer as we drift across the dancefloor. "What if I asked you to stay?"

His question catches me off guard and I miss a step. Keres recovers for me, and we continue to dance as though it never happened.

"Stay?"

"There would be plenty of opportunities to see the city if you were to remain here."

My heart is beating so loudly that I know for certain he can hear it. His eyes flick down to my chest, and I pray to the gods he believes it's from excitement.

As the song comes to a close and we pause on the edge of the dancefloor, he continues speaking before I have a chance to form a reply.

"Consider it, Princess?" He bows and places a lingering kiss on the back of my hand before heading off into the gathered crowd.

I'm speechless as I watch him vanish, but once he does, panic starts to seep into my veins. I blindly grab a cup of wine from a server passing by and throw it back, hoping it will settle my fraying nerves.

This was the plan. I should be glad the pieces are falling into place as we intended. But a part of me must have been harboring some small, selfish hope that I would lose the trials and be sent home. Keres' parting words clip the wings of that hope, trapping it within the cage of despair.

My breaths become thin as the realization settles like a heavy weight on my chest. Fortunately, nobody pays me any notice, their attention captured by a forceful gust of wind rattles against the ballroom windows, causing some of the gathered tycheroi to gasp in alarm.

I twist my ring as I search for Nyssa in the crowd, hoping the familiarity of her face will calm me—remind me of why I need to see this through.

"My cousin is definitely enamored with you," a voice says from behind me, and I latch onto the sound.

I turn, forcing a smile on my face. "It's the gown. It has that effect," I say, swishing my hips so the precious stones sparkle, scattering tiny shards of light across the marble floor.

Titaia laughs as she approaches me. The blood-red pleats of her gown cling to her figure in all the right places, the fabric dripping down her arms. Her dark auburn hair is scooped back from her face with two ruby-encrusted combs. An attached strip of the sheer red fabric covers her eyes like a veil, tiny garnets woven into its fine thread.

She loops her arm through mine, and I clench my hands together to still their faint trembling as she leads me from the dancefloor. Others greet us and smile as we weave past them, until she pulls us to a stop in a shadowy corner of the room.

"Would a belated word of advice be welcome, Aella?"

Titaia says. Her face never loses the pleasant smile as she looks over the masquerade before us.

"From you? Always." I keep my eyes trained on the room, following her lead.

"The bloom of belladonna may smell sweet. A siren may entrance you. But they're both deadly all the same."

I turn to her as she does the same. "Feel free to speak plainly with me."

"Don't take Keres at face value. Objectively, it's a pretty face, but beauty only runs skin-deep."

"That wasn't any less cryptic, Titaia." I deadpan.

"Well, I can't say it too plainly. I'd disappear in the middle of the night, and then you'd be bored without me."

We both fall silent at the meaning hidden beneath her words and watch each other.

I imagine she's watching me to determine if she's made a mistake by voicing her concerns. I'm watching her for a crack in her mask. The one beneath the brilliant lace and garnet creation. The one they all wear in this place, pretty lies to shield ugly truths.

I can't find one.

A sudden sadness fills me, tinged with regret. I may have found a true friend in Titaia. At every turn, she has met me with unwarranted trust and honesty.

All the while, I've been the one wearing a mask.

"Thank you," I say, putting everything I can't voice into those two simple words. "Rest assured, what you have told me will not be repeated."

She visibly relaxes at that, shoulders slightly lowering as her smile turns more sincere. "I better not hover in the shadows. They'll think I'm planning a coup and have me thrown in the dungeons."

She gives my arm a parting squeeze before heading toward a group of courtiers. I watch her as she goes, her words spinning around my mind with the force of a whirlwind.

With a sigh, I head back into the fray. By the time I leave the dancefloor again, my feet and lower back are aching from the ceaseless dancing. The masked faces of my partners eventually blurred together, time passing painfully slowly.

I still haven't received any signal from Raven. Worry is eating away at my mind, nausea swirling in my gut. I glance around for Nyssa, but the crowd is too thick. An impossible number of bodies crammed into the immense hall.

Air. I need air.

I need to breathe.

I push my way through the gathered tycheroi, almost gasping with relief as I step through the glass door and out into the cold embrace of the night. The balcony is deserted, all the revelers choosing to stay in the warmth of the ballroom. The wind wraps itself around me, a soothing lullaby whispered in its current.

Despite the slight relief, anxiety claws at me from the inside, sharp talons making my breath ragged. It's almost midnight and there has still been no signal.

Worry poisons my mind, conjuring visions of the Flight being captured by the royal guard and thrown into cells.

Or worse.

I pace frantically, torn between the need to go in search of them, to make sure they're okay, and the orders that bind me to this ridiculous charade.

"Some might think you have very little faith in me."

I spin, my glittering dress billowing around my ankles.

Raven leans casually against the outer marble wall, dressed in a tailored suit the color of midnight, an elegant black mask covering the upper half of his face.

I find myself conflicted once again. Only this time between the desire to either rip his clothes off or rip into him.

I choose the latter.

"What took you so gods-damned long?" I hiss, marching up to him.

"Why, Starling..." he says with a slow curl of his lips. "Were you worried about me?"

I slap him in the chest with the back of my hand. "Can you be serious? What happened?"

"We have the weapon. The others are transporting it through the tunnel now."

"And Sphinx?"

"She all but disappeared the moment the collar was nullified."

"Then why are you here? You need to leave—"

He pulls me into the shadows and kisses me. It's messy, and desperate—like kissing me is the only thing that will keep his heart beating. When he pulls away, all I want is for him to come back.

"I needed to see you." His whisper caresses my ear, sending a shiver of pleasure down my spine. "I needed to feel you tremble beneath my fingers. I needed to taste you on my tongue. But most of all, I needed a reminder of why I'm doing all this."

"You're a fool," I say. But if he's a fool, then so am I.

I tear off my mask, letting it clatter to the marble floor before I reach up and remove his. I drag his face back to mine again and kiss him softly. Slow and sweet, like we have all the time in the world, like this moment isn't the last time we see one another.

Like my heart isn't crumbling to dust.

We stay there until I finally pull away, leaving us both breathless.

He clenches his jaw before reaching into his pocket. I suck in my breath at the sight of the small heart-shaped pendant hanging from a long silver chain, engraved with a swirling pattern.

"May I?"

I nod wordlessly, spinning and lifting my hair while he clasps it around my neck. The pendant settles against my chest and I tuck it underneath my dress, keeping it hidden from sight. When I turn back, I frown at his grim expression.

"As much as I would like this to be a romantic gesture, the pendant contains a deadly dose of nightshade."

I go still at his words.

"Stay safe for me, princess. Only use it if you have no other option." He hesitates, like he's about to say something else. I hold my breath as his eyes search mine, but he simply presses his lips to the top of my head. "I'll dream of you."

I watch him fade into the shadows, my heart beating frantically against my ribs.

Closing my eyes, I exhale a shaky breath, my hands clench-ing in the fabric of my gown as a struggle against the torrent of emotion trying to drown me.

I am strong enough for this.

TWENTY-FIVE

GRAY LIGHT FILTERS THROUGH the tall windows of my room, mist curling against the glass and casting the room in an eerie glow. I twist my ring as I stare out at the coiling haze, hoping it will clear and finally let me see the city and lands beyond.

It's been two days since the ball.

Two days since Raven departed with half of our Flight, and it's as though he took my heart along with them.

There has been no word from Keres since that night. Both the prince and king have been absent, and the queen more withdrawn than usual. The air in the court is thick with tension. Everywhere I turn, courtiers whisper to each other in hushed tones, exchanging meaningful glances and furrowed brows. It's almost eerie how silent everyone has been; even the musicians of *Thíasos ton Theíon* have ceased their playing, as though sensing something isn't quite right.

I suppose the court was expecting an announcement by

now. Perhaps they think their prince is displeased with the selection, and that's the reason for the delay. The not-so-subtle glances they throw toward the other competitors and I certainly imply as much.

But I know the real reason.

The royals know the weapon has been stolen.

The *goiteía* mark Sphinx carved on my skin reappeared and then faded the night of the ball. I can only assume that means they were able to free Sphinx when they reached the tunnels, and now the bargain is complete. But since I last saw Raven on the balcony, there's been no way for us to stay in contact.

All I can do is hope they made it away safely.

I've been praying to every god that will listen that the others made it as far away as possible. I know the prince was at the ball until the early hours of the morning, so Raven and the others should have had a decent head start. And if they covered their tracks, Keres and the king wouldn't have been able to follow.

Despite my rationalizing, a seed of doubt still lingers in my heart.

It buds and blooms—

Glass shatters behind me and my hand flies to where my heart is now beating in my throat, my breath coming in sharp pants.

"Notos' balls, Nyssa!" I hiss, turning to find her with a sheepish grimace on her face.

"It was an accident." She eyes the vase where it lies in broken shards on the floor. "Besides, it was ugly."

Her words shock a laugh out of me, easing some of the tension I'm holding in my body. It's just the two of us here—Myna and Heron both having gone out to see if they can gain any information on the royals—and I'm grateful for not needing to keep up any pretenses.

The relief doesn't last.

A loud knock sounds on the door.

My shoulders stiffen and my mouth goes dry. Nyssa and I lock eyes across the room, and I see the same apprehension coursing through me reflected in her hazel gaze.

Nothing good, my sweet anemone. Nothing good.

A wave of anxiety passes over me as Calliope's warning echoes through my mind.

"Hide," I tell Nyssa, my voice barely a whisper.

Her lips press into a hard line, but she does as I ask, darting into her adjoining room on silent feet.

I walk toward the door, schooling my expression as I pull it open. Jorah, Keres' guard, is standing on the other side. His icy blue eyes sting as they track over my face.

"Jorah," I say with a tone of pleasant surprise, in stark contrast to the bitter taste in my mouth. "Do you need something?"

"Your presence is required, Princess."

"By whom?"

"Prince Keres, of course."

I offer him a sad smile. "Let me change into something more suitable." I turn to close the door, but he slams a palm on the golden surface.

"That won't be necessary, Princess. He asked for me to bring you to him at once."

"Of course."

The one time I don't have my dagger on me.

The smile on my face feels brittle as I step from the room, pulling the door closed loudly behind me. Hopefully, Nyssa could hear the entire exchange from wherever she was hiding.

"Are your ladies with you?" Jorah asks.

"No, I sent them to run some last-minute errands."

He says nothing further as he heads down the hallway. I follow. The halls are empty, not even a single servant in sight, and our footsteps echo off the walls. Each heartbeat assaults me like the strike of an executioner's blade, resonating through my chest. I breathe deep, willing myself to calm.

When we reach the outer doors of Keres' study, I've finally managed to rein in the fear, drawing it out from where it's been steadily poisoning my body like the venom of a viper. Jorah raps his knuckle sharply on the door, and I hold my breath as we wait for a reply.

"Enter."

Jorah opens the door and ushers me inside. He doesn't stay, instead pulling the door shut behind me and leaving me alone.

Keres stands behind his desk, his back toward me as he stares out of the bank of tall windows that lines the far wall. The same heavy gray mist dances beyond the glass, shrouding the view of Eretria normally visible below.

He doesn't turn at my entrance, so I take a moment to observe him in the silence. His shoulders are tense under his white-and-gold tunic, one hand braced on the window frame while the other cradles a glass of amber liquid. His usually meticulously styled hair is ruffled, like he's been running his hands through it, upsetting the glossy curls. His broad shoulders rise and fall with deep, controlled breaths.

Seconds drag into a minute, and with each passing moment, fear creeps back in, slithering through my veins and poisoning my mind again.

"You sent for me, Keres?"

Finally, he turns.

Furious red eyes clash with mine.

I am unequivocally fucked.

I stand my ground, a smile plastered on my face, as he rounds the desk and walks toward me. I track every move he makes, the way his eyes run over every inch of my body before once again settling on my face.

"I've heard stories of the Princess of the Sorrows. They say she was never accepted by her father. Instead of claiming her and giving her the title, he cast her out, sent her away to the Isle of the Winds. The stories end there, until you conveniently returned when I announced the trials."

A cold sweat breaks out over my body and I have to force my hands not to curl into fists at my sides as the intense need for fight or flight tries to take over my body.

"Those are stories, Keres. As you can see, I stand here before you." I hold my hands out to emphasize the point. "Royal title and all."

"Hmm..." He takes a sip of the amber liquid as he comes to a stop in front of me. "I think I've asked you this before, *Princess*, but don't all stories start with the truth?"

Before I can respond, the glass shatters against the ground and Keres' hand wraps around my throat. The air is driven from my lungs as he slams me against the door. I hear the soft click of something closing around my neck at the same time as a white-hot agony tears through my body.

"What the fuck, Keres!"

My facade splinters, but I snatch at its edges, hauling it close. Doubt may be the only thing that gets me out of this alive.

"Not quite the docile princess you pretend to be. I thought that might be the case."

"Take this off me right now." I force the words through gritted teeth. Horror inches its way up my spine as my fingers grip the collar, mapping out the *goiteía* carved into the metal. It's like the one they forced Sphinx into, designed to cause weakness. Exhaustion. Burning pain.

Designed to bend a being's will.

He presses in close, crowding me against the back of the door and slipping a leg between my thighs. It takes all my self-restraint not to show him how far from a docile princess I truly am by ripping his throat out with my teeth.

"I heard another story, too. Although, this one is more like…" he frowns thoughtfully, like he's struggling to find the right words, before a malicious smile twists his face into something ugly. "A song."

Icy dread grips my heart.

"I have no idea what you're talking about. This is insanity."

"Well then, let me enlighten you. Half of your cohort has gone missing, along with something *very* valuable of mine."

"I know nothing about that," I say as calmly as possible. "And since I thought I was safe here, my guards have been enjoying some time off in the city."

"Do not lie to me!"

"I'm not lying," I whisper, despising how my words tremble, since it's not entirely forced this time.

"Oh, Aella." He says my name affectionately, stroking a hand over my cheek. "I don't believe you."

Like the collar, I don't see the hit coming until it lands, knocking me to the ground. Shock clouds my thoughts and for a moment I wonder what hurt more: the strike or the fall. But those thoughts scatter as Keres grips my hair and I choke on a pained gasp.

He pulls me up and I stumble after him, my body incapable of fighting back as he drags me through another door.

The door Raven and I couldn't unlock.

The room is sparse, with windowless stone walls, the only light coming from the soft glow of an aura hanging from the ceiling. When I see the bed in the center, my stomach drops, and a new fear takes hold. I try to break the prince's grip, but with the *goiteía* collar around my throat, the fight leaves my body.

He shoves me to the ground at the foot of the bed and attaches a chain, which I didn't see in my earlier panic, to the back of the collar. The momentary relief I feel when he doesn't throw me on the bed is swiftly burned away by fury. I lunge toward him, but the chain snaps taut, choking me.

"I wouldn't bother. Not even your resolve is strong enough to break steel."

"The Sorrows will come for you when they hear of this," I spit the words at him, knowing they're not true, but they're the only defense I have, no matter how weak.

"I'm not concerned about that. Do you want to know why?" He continues before I can tell him exactly where he can shove his thoughts. "Of course you do. it's because you're expendable. *Disposable*. They sent you here, knowing the risks, and they *did not care*."

His poisonous words wrap around my chest. They constrict until I struggle to pull in a full breath of air.

It's not the lie in those words that pierce me.

It's the truth in them.

Expendable. Disposable. Outcast. *Songbird*.

"I'm afraid you're mine now, sweetheart," he speaks with genuine amusement, crouching down in front of me so that we're eye to eye. "My little pet princess. If I must torture the information out of you, I will, and I can't promise I won't enjoy it."

My lips curl back in a snarl. "You're a sick bastard."

"Many of my companions love that about me. You'll learn to love it too." With that, he turns to walk away.

"Keres, you can't leave me here like this."

He pauses in the doorway and glances over. A cruel smile mars his lips as he eyes me lasciviously. "Don't worry, I won't leave you alone for long."

The door closes behind him, the snap of the lock resounding through the room like the toll of a death knell.

I collapse against the end of the bed, flinching as the pressure causes the collar to dig deeper into my sensitive skin. My eyes start to burn with oncoming tears and I rub at them furiously.

I will *not* cry.

This was always a risk when the decision was made for some of our Flight to stay behind. It was a risk I accepted and planned for. But hope can be as toxic as fear, and I had foolishly thought we would get away with this.

Now that hope has burned away, replaced by bitter disappointment that tastes like ashes in my mouth.

Poison on my tongue.

The necklace Raven gave me hangs heavy where it's hidden beneath my gown. The deadly dose of nightshade seems to heat within the delicate capsule, reminding me I have a different method of escape.

But I'm not willing to consider that option yet.

I'm not ready to give up.

Cold fury seeps into my veins, burning through my fear and strengthening my resolve.

The gods themselves will have to rip my soul from my body before I'm done.

And they haven't been seen for centuries.

TWENTY-SIX

"Why did you come to Eretria?"

Jorah's sharp voice grates against my fractured mind. Each clipped note sends another stab to my already pounding head.

"To compete in the trials," I answer.

A blade drags across my already bloodied thigh. Achingly slowly, drawing out the pain.

"What are your friends planning with the weapon?"

"I know nothing about a weapon, and I'm getting really sick of your pointless questions," I grit out.

The blade slices again.

"Where have they gone?"

"I don't know."

Another cut. Deeper this time.

I clench my jaw, but a sob escapes me, tearing free from the depths of my tattered soul and clawing its way up my throat.

I have no idea how long I've been trapped here. Chained to

the end of this bed with this gods-damned collar at my throat.

If I had to guess, based on how many times Keres and Jorah have graced me with their company, I'd say three days.

Three days of questions.

Three days of biting my tongue.

Three days of more pain than I have ever experienced in my life.

They had found Raven's necklace earlier today—not that I would have used it, but the discovery solidified their suspicions and Jorah had redoubled his efforts.

At least the others are safe. Nyssa, Myna, and Heron—they would have escaped by now.

The thought isn't as uplifting as I'd hoped it would be.

My throat is raw, the skin of my neck sticky with blood where the collar has chafed away my flesh. The skirt of my gown is shredded, revealing my thighs covered in cuts and blood. Every inch of my body is beaten and bruised.

Except for my face.

After Jorah struck me the first time and split my lip, Keres insisted he didn't want to wreck something so pretty.

Especially since he still apparently planned on taking me as his bride.

Over my dead fucking body.

The memory of spitting blood in his face ignites a sick joy in me and I have to smother the smile that threatens to twist my lips.

"Give us the room, Jorah," Keres says from where he leans against his usual spot leaning against the wall.

He's always present.

He likes to watch.

Jorah stands and leaves without a word.

I slump against the footboard at my back, relieved to have a momentary respite from pain. My eyes lock onto Keres as he kicks off the wall and walks toward me.

Burning hatred simmers within me, heating my blood to boiling point.

Jorah may wield the blades, but Keres will always be the bigger threat in the room.

He's the reason the blades cut.

I flatten myself against the end of the bed as he crouches down before me, obviously not caring that he kneels in my blood where it pools between my thighs. I try to close them to keep him back, but between the *goiteía* collar and the blood loss, my body has no strength.

Keres takes my knees in a rough grip and pushes them further apart. He slides his hands over my sliced-up thighs, drawing out my breath in a hiss.

"Sweetheart, this would be so much easier if you tell me what I want to hear."

"How many times do I have to tell you I know nothing before you believe me?"

He tuts—like I'm a child he's disappointed in—and tilts his head to the side. The heat in his eyes as he looks down on my battered body has bile stinging the back of my throat.

"Maybe I'm not offering the right motivation."

He doesn't give me a chance for those words to sink in before he grips the backs of my thighs and pulls me toward him, knocking the breath from my body as my back hits the cold marble floor.

Before I so much as get a chance to inhale, he clamps a hand around my jaw and slams his mouth on mine. Keres grinds against me, the hardness of his arousal against my pubic bone making my stomach twist in disgust.

Fear and fury swirl together in my gut as I struggle against him to no avail. But when his other hand slips beneath my dress and roughly brushes against my core, the fury takes over.

I bite his lip, hard. The metallic taste of copper seeps across my tongue.

Keres rears back, laughing maniacally as one hand flies to his bleeding mouth. He looks at the blood coating his fingers for a moment before licking them clean, humming softly under his breath.

When he leans forward again, he grips my jaw and pours a bittersweet liquid down my throat. My panic rises and I try to cough it up, but he clamps his hand over my mouth and nose, forcing me to swallow when my lungs scream for air.

"A parting gift. Only the sweetest nectar for you. I call it mad honey, but you wouldn't have heard of it. I made it myself, and it was the only thing that would work on the last bird I caught here. Perhaps it will help you be more forthcoming."

The last bird.

My mind ricochets back to the Eagle's office when Nyssa and I had been told of the mission and given our first assignments.

After that first missive, we lost contact with our Songbird and can only assume he was caught.

My heart cracks a little further, a new wound added for a stranger and the fate they must have endured.

The Aviary was foolish to send us here when they already suspected there was a risk. The Eagle's pride made him reckless.

I look up and find Keres watching me from the doorway. He flashes a satisfied smile—as if he can see the connections being made—and as he repeats the words he spoke to me at the ball, they land like physical blows.

"Consider it, Princess."

I hold my breath until his footsteps fade into the distance. Waiting until I know for certain he won't be coming back. It's only when my lungs are burning and the edges of my vision is laced with tendrils of darkness that I let it go.

And then I scream.

The sound is guttural and broken. But it still contains enough fury and fire to burn as it tears through my throat to echo around the room.

When it dissipates, the only sound left is my labored breathing as I struggle to sit back up.

I look down at my bloodied thighs, counting the cuts and watching as my life's blood seeps from the wounds. I tally each scarlet bead, and let them fuel the simmering fury within me.

I'm going to watch as life slips from Keres' eyes.

Even if it's the last thing I do.

The thought barely crosses my mind before my body begins to tremble. My vision blurs at the edges, casting a halo of shadow within my sight.

Then the convulsions start.

TWENTY-SEVEN

"I HAVE THE WEAPON." Nyssa's voice is a frantic whisper. Her eyes dart around the shadowy room.

"Where is it?"

"It's safe. You can't let them know."

"I won't. I promise."

"No one can know, Aella." Her voice and face turn vicious. "Not even you."

Silver flashes before she lunges.

I scream.

And I bleed out on the floor.

TWENTY-EIGHT

ROUGH FINGERS GENTLY TRAIL up my inner thighs, pushing aside my underwear and drawing forth a soft moan from my lips. Raven's body presses into mine, and I grind my hips against his hardness. I groan against his mouth, and he bites down hard on my lip, transforming it into a gasp. The bitter taste of copper coats my tongue as he fills me with a long, hard thrust.

"You take me so well, Princess." His husky voice fills my mind, body, and soul, driving me further toward the edge. "Are you going to come for me?"

"Yes." My hands grip him, pulling him closer. His thrusts grow harder, faster, deeper; the pleasure building deep in my core.

"Oh gods," I cry as the feeling crests. I close my eyes as stars begin to dance in my vision.

"Look at me."

I open my eyes as the orgasm splinters through me. But Raven's honey-brown irises flash red.

Horror fills me, and I scream, fracturing the image into shards of glass.

I turn my head to the side and vomit.

When I turn back, the room is empty.

I close my eyes again.

TWENTY-NINE

TREMORS WRACK MY BODY and hazy voices pierce my mind.

"Any luck so far?"

"No, my prince. Nothing but mumbled nonsense."

A frustrated growl rips through the space, followed by an echoing crash.

"Muzzle her until she makes sense. And then *try harder.*"

Hands clutch at my head. Something cold and rough covers my face.

I try to rip it off, but it tightens. And I—

I can't breathe.

I can't breathe.

I can't

breathe.

THIRTY

I WAKE TO AN impenetrable darkness, a muffled gasp tearing
from my tortured throat. My body itches and burns, dried
blood and cuts covering me. Any sense of time and place
evades me. All I know is this room, with its frigid stone walls.

The hard wood of the bed pressing against my back.

Cold metal at my throat.

Something firm across—

My hands fly to my face, clawing at the strange leather
mask.

I can't breathe.

"Starling," a soft voice murmurs in the darkness, and I
freeze.

My vision clears enough for me to make out the concerned
features of Myna as she kneels before me. I flinch at the flash
of silver, but then take a shuddering lungful of air as the mask
falls free. It's both sharp and sweet; a first breath taken after

almost drowning.

Am I hallucinating again?

"Hallucinating?" Myna asks.

It's the mad honey. Bittersweet, terrible aftertaste. But I think the hallucinations might be the worst. Either those or the convulsions.

My imaginary Myna curses and I smile faintly. I can imagine her reacting like that.

None of this is real.

"I'm very real, Starling."

Then how do you know what I'm thinking?

"Because you're thinking out loud."

"Oh…" I stare at her a moment longer. She stares back.

Slowly, reality seeps in, like the first rays of morning light, forcing the veil of fog to lift slightly from my mind. I inhale a long, shuddering breath. Reveling in the sheer relief that cascades through me.

Myna's eyes darken as they take in my tortured body. "I'm sorry we didn't find you sooner."

"You stayed." My words are broken as they leave me, giving voice to the hopelessness I've fallen into. "I told Nyssa I wanted you all to get away from here."

"We couldn't leave without you."

"It's what you're supposed to do if someone is compromised."

Myna's eyes connect with mine, resolute and determined. "Not this time."

I offer her a small smile but turn away as tears threaten to spill over. With each passing second, delirium fades further and my grasp on reality strengthens.

I almost wish it wouldn't.

"I can pick the lock on the chain, but the collar will need to wait. Sparrow is standing watch in the hall. Heron went ahead to prepare the mounts below."

"Where's Keres?"

"Neck-deep in wine and women."

"Thank the fucking gods."

Myna shifts closer, examining the collar and chain at my throat. "This might hurt a little."

She goes quiet as she focuses on the lock, but instead of feeling comforting, the silence presses in on me. My breathing starts coming quicker and my shoulders inch up as my mind spirals. Maybe this isn't real. Maybe it *is* another hallucination—

"Is Nyssa okay?" I ask, my voice too loud in the quiet.

Myna winces but continues her examination of the lock. "She will be once we get you out of here. Now, hold still. We're going to lose some of this jewelry."

I offer her a small smile, knowing she's attempting to lighten the mood. "The prince really does have garish taste."

Myna hums in agreement as she gets to work on the lock. I hold my breath through the pain as the metal scrapes against my raw skin. Silence fills the room again, interrupted by the occasional rattle of the chain.

"What's your real name, Myna?"

The words barely pass my lips before the lock clicks, and the chain falls free, leaving only the collar in place. Myna gently places the chain on the ground beside me, as soundlessly as possible, watching me the whole time. I can see the question circling behind her shadowy eyes.

We sit in silence, both of us hovering on the edge of indecision, and I think she's not going to answer.

"Melantha."

Another tiny smile curves across my lips. I fold her name up like a secret scribed on parchment and store it in the shallows of my soul. "Thank you, Melantha."

She frowns slightly, and I wonder how long it's been since someone last called her by her name. "Can you stand?"

I grit my teeth and push myself to my feet. When I sway slightly, she loops a hand around my waist.

"Lean on me as much as you need. Now, should we get out of this gods-damned palace?"

"I thought you'd never ask."

Slowly, we make our way through the dark rooms and into the empty hall beyond. Hardening my resolve, I push through the pain.

It's nighttime. The world beyond the windows is dark, and the halls are lit only by the faint glow of auras lining the walls.

When we make it to the next hall, a shadow darts forward from an alcove, moving too fast for me to react in my weakened state. Still, I lift my arm and pull it back, ready to swing. Myna captures my wrist as the shadow collides with me. Every part of my body burns from the impact, and I gasp in pain.

"Aella." My name is a small, private whisper in my ear—dripping with fear and relief. But the sound of Nyssa's voice is the sweetest one I've ever heard.

I wrap my arms around her, returning the embrace. Even as it burns my skin to do so. Even as it makes my chest constrict.

The feeling lessens when she pulls back, cupping the sides of my face. Her eyes darken when she takes in the bloodied mess of my body.

"I'll kill that fucking prince." The violence in her voice has my throat tightening.

"I think you'll have to get in line," another voice says, and my blood turns to ice in my veins as Titaia steps from the shadows.

"It's okay," Myna says beside me when she senses my body tensing. "She's the one who helped us get you out. The door to the room was marked to only allow those of Keres' blood through."

My eyes dart back to Titaia's face, noting the pallor of her usually glowing skin and grief pooling in her eyes. "I sought them out as soon as I realized you were missing and had not taken ill like Keres was leading the court to believe."

Something in my chest warms at the realization that I've found a genuine friend in her. A beautiful bloom, standing tall in a field of rotting weeds. But then the usual panic sets in, my breath coming faster.

"What about you?" I ask. "Keres will realize someone from his family helped us escape."

"I'm going north," she hesitates before adding, "with a friend. But you don't need to worry about that. You need to get out of here."

I reach out, grasping her hand and giving it a squeeze. A slight gesture, but it's all I can manage right now. "Thank you," I say, holding her gaze so she can see how deeply I mean those words.

"We will meet again, Aella." Titaia squeezes my hand back, before spinning on her heel and hurrying down a shadowed corridor. I watch the darkness swallow her, praying to the gods she is right.

"What's the plan?" I whisper as Myna and Nyssa lead me down the hall.

"Most of the court is asleep or at the prince's party," Myna replies. "We'll head through the kitchens and take the servants' sky-carriage down the mountain."

I nod. "And where is Heron?"

"Heron left the palace a few hours ago to secure some mounts," Nyssa says.

We continue the rest of the way in silence, picking up the pace once we reach the kitchens. The door leading to the sky-carriages looms before us. Freedom calls to me like a siren song, urging my feet to move faster despite the pain. Myna pulls the door open—and we all freeze.

A young servant stands similarly frozen in front of us, arm outstretched and eyes wide with shock.

Despite the signs of being a *Goiteían*—or being on the receiving end of Keres' withering touch—she's still so young. An innocent bystander in the wrong place at the wrong time.

Indecision wars in my gut, panic creeping in.

Tension rolls off Myna at my side, and I turn, catching her eye. "Incapacitate only," I plead.

Myna hesitates, but something in my expression must convince her, and the reluctance vanishes. With a sharp nod, she lets go of my waist.

The servant blanches, her sweet face turning ashen as she

backs up.

"I'm sorry," I say sincerely, as Nyssa drags us past her.

There's a sharp intake of breath, a blur of movement in the corner of my eye as Myna strikes.

I wince at the dull thump of a body hitting the ground.

She joins us again as we round the corner, my heart rate picking up at the sight of the single sky-carriage swaying gently in the wind. I scan the deck, and relief blooms in my chest when I see no other guards or servants.

Nyssa and I pile into the simple wooden carriage, nowhere near as elegant as the ones used by the rest of the court. I turn back to Myna, waiting for her to join us.

She doesn't.

"Quickly," I urge. "We're running out of time."

She makes no move to enter, instead closing the half-door and taking a step away.

"Someone needs to pull the lever, Aella," Nyssa says softly.

"What?" I turn to her as the horror of those words rattle inside my head.

I lunge for the door. My mind screams with terror as my body screams in protest, but I'm too late. Too *weak*.

The carriage jolts as the lever is pulled, and then begins to make its descent.

"What the fu—" I shout, but the rest of my words fail me as I watch Myna with wide eyes. She moves away from the ledge before sprinting toward it. I can't hear past the roaring of my blood in my ears, the pounding of my heart, as she kicks off from the marble.

Myna's body slams into the carriage. The force of the impact makes it rock precariously. It's only when she's climbing over the half-door that I collapse into a seat and take my next breath.

Nyssa flops down beside me, scrubbing her hands over her face. "I think my heart stopped beating."

"*Never*," I say, glaring at Myna, "scare me like that again."

She gives me a weak smile, slumping into a seat on the opposite side of the carriage. "I'm glad to know you care so much."

I almost wish I didn't.

The three of us sit in silence for the rest of the ride, the cabin jostling in the wind as it gusts around us.

When we arrive at the bottom of the mountain, Heron is waiting for us in the shadows of the stable, two stable hands unconscious on the ground beside him and four horses saddled and ready to ride. His grim eyes track over our faces as we approach him.

Myna helps me mount, careful not to touch the tops of my damaged thighs, and then Nyssa climbs up and settles behind me.

"Here," she says, reaching around and pressing something into my hands. Tears sting my eyes as I stare down at my mother's dagger. "I know it's the only thing you have of hers, so I kept it safe."

"Thank you." The words are barely a whisper, but they shake from the weight of the emotion they carry.

With the blade clutched tightly between my hands, I close my eyes, and let the numbing embrace of darkness reclaim me.

THIRTY-ONE

IT TAKES THREE DAYS to reach the forest.

We sit astride our horses at the top of a hill, looking down at the sprawling canopy of treetops that stretches out below. Autumnal leaves spanning as far as the eye can see.

Eretria is so...*red*.

Blood staining marble. Cruel red eyes flashing—

The images are there one minute, gone the next. But it's enough to have saliva pooling in my mouth and bile creeping up the back of my throat.

Breathe.

I draw in a rattling breath, choke on it, and try again. In a distant corner of my mind, a memory emerges of Nyssa asking me what a forest looks like. The answer finally lies before me, but I struggle to really take in the natural beauty of it all. The wonder of discovering this new land has lost its hold on me.

The stormy clouds that hung over Vilea during our time

there followed us, casting the forest in their gloomy shadow, turning the ancient trees menacing. The wind causes the branches and leaves to sway, and the movement makes the forest look like a great beast, waiting to swallow us whole.

I draw in another shaky breath, wrinkling my nose at the scent of damp grass and rot. I have never yearned for the tang of salt in the air like I do now.

On the second day following our escape from the court, we found a blacksmith in a small town. I didn't want to stop, too concerned we were being pursued. But Myna insisted I couldn't go much longer wearing the collar. We paid the blacksmith handsomely to carve away the *goiteía* marks, cut it from my neck, and ask no questions.

The relief was indescribable.

Overwhelming.

That night, I quietly cried to myself, praying to the gods that the others didn't notice. If they did, they must have taken pity on me and chosen not to question it.

I feel like I'm slowly fading. Like a slow-acting poison is still running through my veins. I have no idea what was real or not during those days, every moment fusing together into a single feverish nightmare.

I don't want to confront it. I prefer not knowing.

The blacksmith ended up referring us to a healer in the same town who helped with my wounds and the lingering effects of the mad honey.

She did her best but couldn't remove the damage completely. The collar left me with a silver scar that circles the base of my throat, and dozens of faint scars now trace an artless map of trauma across my thighs.

The healer said they may very well fade with time, and I'm trying to convince myself I'm not bothered. Flawless skin isn't important in the grand scheme of things.

But I hate them.

I hate each scar with the heat of the burning sun.

A permanent reminder of those torturous days—trapped and at Keres' mercy—to haunt me.

I now wear a shirt laced all the way up and a cloak tied firmly around my neck. The less I see my scars, the better, and I certainly don't want others noticing them and asking questions.

"Do you think they're still here?" Nyssa says behind me. We have shared a horse for the entire journey, despite my protests that I'm fine and can ride on my own. She simply ignored me or told me I needed to reserve my strength.

"It's not likely, the plan was for the others to remain at the safe house for only a day or so." Myna says. "But let's pray to the Anemoi they are."

"Let's not get our hopes up," Heron says, flicking his reins to encourage his horse forward. "Raven wouldn't linger unless something went wrong on their end."

Myna nods in agreement, and my heart curls up inside my chest, trying to protect itself from the truth lining Heron's words.

It's a brief ride down the slope of the hillside, and soon the forest looms before us, it's ancient trees stretching well overhead.

The air changes as we pass the tree line—a faint, cool brush against my skin carrying a scent that manages to be rotten and fresh at the same time.

A heavy silence hovers over our group as we navigate between the towering trees. The only sounds are the occasional bird calling its mate home to nest and the crackle of dry leaves as they're crushed beneath steel-capped hooves.

It doesn't take long for the light to fade, taking any remnants of warmth in the air with it, the shadows unfurling the deeper we travel. Eventually, it's so dark that if it weren't for our enhanced eyesight, we wouldn't be able to see at all.

Pinpricks of light appear in the darkness ahead, like the luminous, watchful eyes of nocturnal creatures. They continue to grow as we approach, and the trees thin, a wooded veil parting to reveal a neglected farmstead, forgotten and falling to decay amidst the overgrown grass of a small clearing. A barn in a similar state of disrepair is next to the house, the entire structure on a lean, somehow fighting against the pressure to collapse. Its doors hang ajar, darkness looming within.

We draw our mounts to a stop a short distance from the homestead, our eyes glued to the sight before us. The light shining from within the house could be a beacon from the gods themselves. It beckons us closer, invites us in. Gives life to hope where we had previously believed there was none to be found.

I tighten my hands on the pommel of the saddle in a vain attempt to control their trembling.

"They're here." Myna's quiet voice is thick with a relief that mirrors my own.

A tremor runs through my body. Tears sting my eyes, but I brutally blink them away.

"Nyssa!" A shadow darts from the barn, and soon an ashen-faced Lark stands before us. In the blink of an eye, Nyssa jumps from her horse and throws herself into her brother's waiting arms. He wraps her in a fierce hug, and then he looks up.

"Starling." Lark says my name as though I'm a ghost. Like he's questioning his reality and sanity. It's like a summons, because a heartbeat later the homestead door slams open and my world stands still as Raven rushes toward us.

I'm so lost in the sight of him—lost in the angles of the face I thought I wouldn't see again—that I don't notice Lark's approach until he's reaching for me. I flinch away from the touch.

"Back up, Lark," Myna snaps at him, and my face burns with embarrassment and guilt at the confused expression on his face.

I glance away from the questions I can see building, closing my eyes as a lump forms in my throat.

"What happened?" another voice asks, and I freeze in place. Because I know that voice more intimately than I know my own. I dreamed of it in my lowest moments, held onto its tenor during my darkest nights. Prayed to any god that would listen so I could hear it again.

I turn slowly until my eyes finally land on Raven. But instead of the relief I thought I'd find in the familiar planes of his face; I see something different. He runs a frustrated hand through his hair, eyes pinning me in place while he waits for an answer.

"There was a complication," Myna says, jumping down from her horse. "We were compromised."

I jump down from my mount, hissing as the impact makes my thighs throb. They all fall silent, and I shift under the weight of building tension.

"Inside. There's leftover stew if you're hungry," Raven eventually says, his words strained. "And a stream not far behind the homestead if you want to bathe."

We follow them into the house, and I stand back as my Flight members all greet one another, exchanging hugs and relieved words. I fiddle with the ties of my cloak, watching the others remove theirs and make a beeline for the pot of stew. My stomach grumbles, but as hungry as I am, a few moments of privacy and a clean body are more tempting.

I quietly slip outside and head toward the trees at the back of the house. The hem of my cloak whispers against the tall grass, masking the sound of my rapid breaths. I don't have to walk for long before I find the stream Raven mentioned, and by the time I do, I've reclaimed a semblance of calm.

The stream looks like a spill of black ink across the floor of the forest, trickling slowly between the ferns and moss-covered rocks that border its banks. A few fireflies drift aimlessly across the surface of the water, adding their soft light to the eerie glow that peeks through the canopy.

I remove my cloak, folding it up and setting it down on one of the rocks before untying the laces at the neckline of my shirt. The chill in the air bites the scarred skin at my exposed throat, pebbling my flesh and sending a shiver through my body.

A twig snaps behind me and I spin, my dagger already unsheathed. My heart pounds against my ribcage like a wild beast trying to break free.

"It's me," Raven says as he steps out from the shadows. The pale blue light falls across his face, deepening the furrow on his brow.

"Raven." His name escapes me in a shuddering breath and my shoulders slump as I lower my blade.

Faster than a strike of lightning, he stands in front of me, warm hands cradling my face as he tilts it up to his. But as he leans in to kiss me, dread rises so swiftly—so *violently*—I flinch, taking a step back.

Raven tenses and drops his hands. The muscles in his jaw bunch and his eyes track me. Neither of us move, both simply watching the other. I tentatively take a step closer, relishing the warmth emanating from his body, but he doesn't touch me again.

"We didn't think you would still be here," the words rasp from my too-tight throat.

"Neither did I."

I look away from his amber gaze, his words momentarily stunning me. Of course, I understand that we shouldn't have found them still here. "What happened?"

"I couldn't leave without you."

Warmth blooms in my chest, so intensely it steals the air from my lungs.

"What happened, Starling? The others have told me all they know, but no one else knows exactly what happened while

Keres had you locked in that room."

The blood in my veins turns to ice, snatching away any warmth I was feeling. I step away, turning my back to him and approaching the stream. "Nothing that matters."

"I need to know what we're dealing with here."

"We should probably leave before first light."

"Why?"

"Raven, I'm not talking about this now. I need a moment alone."

Silence follows.

"This isn't over, Starling."

I remain still until his footsteps fade into the night. Only then do I finish undressing and dip myself into the stream. It's not deep, and the icy water chills me down to the bones, but it cools my burning skin as I scour away the sweat and dirt that clings to me. I scrub until my limbs are raw. Despite that, I still don't feel clean. The taint runs bone-deep, staining my very soul.

When I finally emerge, it's like I have shed a layer of my skin, but patches of the old one still cling to me, a snake caught in shedding scales. I quickly dry myself and dress, lacing the collar of my shirt high to hide my ugly truths beneath.

Lark is leaning by the front door of the homestead when I return, his eyes tracking me as I approach.

"You're on the first watch, then?" I ask, forcing a fragile smile.

"Sure am. Head in and get some rest. You can take my spot next to Nyssa."

"Thank you. You can wake me when you end your shift." I

hesitate a moment before adding, "It's really good to see you, Lark."

His eyes soften, and I note the way he keeps his arms tucked firmly at his sides. "You too, Starling."

I swallow roughly as I pull away and head into the house. The fire still crackles in the hearth, casting dancing shadows across the walls. On the far side of the room, Nyssa is fast asleep in a makeshift bed of blankets. My eyes drift toward Raven to the right, where he watches as I softly step through the slumbering bodies and settle in behind Nyssa's back.

She sighs softly, rolling over, so she's facing me and carefully taking one of my hands between hers. The heat of her skin sinks into my chilled fingers, and it's only then that I realize how cold I am. My body is shaking with small tremors.

"Are you okay?" Nyssa whispers to me, concern etched into every angle of her face. Her hazel eyes search my own, and I fight the urge to close them.

"I don't know," I say just as quietly.

I don't know.

I don't know.

Those three words echo through my skull. Relentless, raging waves crashing against stony cliffs. And I know, like the stone, the waves will eventually wear me down. They'll carve me up with enough time and force.

Changing me.

Eroding the person I am, until years from now I become unrecognizable.

"We'll get through this. Soon we'll be back in the Sorrows, and we can leave this all behind."

I close my eyes and squeeze her hand, the only response I'm able to muster right now. Nyssa shuffles closer and I lie still as she tucks my blankets more tightly around me.

As the warmth from the fire and her body slowly settles into my bones, I give in to the pull of unconsciousness, welcoming the darkness as it drags me under.

THIRTY-TWO

THE BLADE DRAGS ACROSS my thigh again.

And again.

And again.

A sob pours out of me, pooling alongside the puddle of my tears and blood, crimson smeared across the white marble floor.

Cold, wet hands grip the backs of my knees, pulling me closer.

I struggle against the chain, pulling desperately against the collar at my throat that chokes and burns.

I kick, and I scream, and I beg.

The hands relent—only to wrap around my throat.

"Look at me."

I wake in a cold sweat, choking on a ragged scream. My heart is pounding so hard I feel it in my throat. In my entire being.

My hands fly to my neck, clawing at the skin. It's only when I notice the sharp sting of pain and the warm trickle of blood that I realize there's no collar there.

It was a nightmare. I'm safe now.

No matter how many times I repeat the words in my mind, my panic doesn't subside.

The fire has died, and the darkness that I welcomed earlier is now oppressive and disorienting as it wraps around me. Reality and memory collide, and I can't drag myself from my windowless prison in my mind into the night-painted present.

I kick away the blanket tangled around my legs and push myself up. Barely waiting for my eyes to adjust to the dim light, I frantically dodge the sleeping shapes of the others, tearing my way toward the front door.

I'm vaguely aware of the cold night air slamming into me as my knees hit the dirt. Tremors wrack my body as I bend forward and vomit, my stomach spasming violently as it works to purge its contents.

When my body has nothing left to give, I collapse against the decrepit homestead, tipping my head back against the rotting wood and squeezing my eyes shut. I try to control my shaky breaths as I fight off the fear that clings to me like thick spiderwebs. I focus on inhaling slowly, holding, and releasing on the count of three.

When my breathing finally stabilizes and the tremors subside, I open my eyes.

Moonlight leaks through the canopy of clouds above, illuminating the tall grass swaying in the wind. The icy air freezes the tears as they track down my face. I let them fall, digging my fingers into the dirt beneath me, relishing the sting of the cold and the grit beneath my fingernails.

This is real. I made it out. I survived.

Barely, a distant part of my brain whispers.

I gag as bile rises in my throat again and I double over.

When my stomach finally ceases its protest, I lean back against the wall, a shuddering sigh falling from my lips. The wind steals it as another tear carves its way down my face.

I don't have time to sort through the chaos raging in my mind. Because just as the wind snatched my sigh, it sends something back.

I tilt my head and listen intently to the sounds carried to me, like the gods themselves are whispering in my ear.

Footsteps. Dried leaves crushed under careful heels.

And they're heading straight for us.

I scan the clearing, noticing for the first time there's nobody on watch, and scramble to my feet. I fly through the door quicker than I can even organize my thoughts—the fear from my nightmare still grips me like the skeletal fingers of a specter, making my panic surge wildly.

"Wake up," I say, my voice somewhere between a whisper and a shout. Raven bolts upright, like he wasn't asleep in the first place, and I start grabbing the others by their shoulders, shaking them from sleep. "People are approaching from the woods."

My words spread through them like wildfire, any lingering fatigue burning to ash in their wake. I rush to Nyssa's side, taking in her grim expression and the twin daggers already in her hands.

"Who was on watch?" Myna hisses.

Lark turns from the window and glances over his shoulder.

"Lory took over from me."

"Not important right now. Lark and Myna, you're with me. We'll face them off and draw them toward the house." Raven's deep voice is steady, not a shred of fear or uncertainty to be heard. "Heron, Sparrow, and Starling, go out the back. Head into the woods and come up behind them."

He doesn't wait for them to answer before he stands and grabs his blades, the others following quickly. Heron heads toward the back door without hesitation, Nyssa stalking after him.

I can't move.

My feet are rooted to the ground while my stare is fixed on Raven's back. He stops and turns. My heart clenches at the sight of his face, illuminated by the silver light shining through the broken shards of a windowpane.

"Go", he mouths, and then he's gone.

My body snaps back into action, feet finally carrying me out the back door. I crouch down in the shadows where the others are waiting for me, giving Heron a small nod to let him know I'm okay.

I'm not okay. But he doesn't need to know that.

"I'm sorry, Starling, but I have nothing else," he says, gently taking my wrist and drawing the *goiteía* for concealment on my skin with his own blood. I sense the moment the magic settles over me, a feeling like silky threads of cobwebs draping over my head as I disappear. He turns to Nyssa and repeats the mark before drawing his own, and I watch them both fade away. "They won't be able to see us, but we'll have to move quietly. Don't smudge the mark. Now move."

I stand and creep across the clearing, watching for the impressions of the other feet in the grass. A chorus of muffled shouts reaches us from the other side of the cottage. We need to make it into the trees—it's not only our lives that are at stake here, but our kingdom as well.

We've almost made it when a blood-curdling scream pierces the night, cutting through the clash of steel on steel.

My blood chills.

But I manage to hold myself back from charging forward. My whole body is trembling from the restraint by the time we step into the shadows of the trees. Adrenaline courses through my veins, pumping through my body with each pounding beat of my heart.

"Get to the other side." Heron's disembodied voice whispers beside me. "Keep the concealment on but stick to the trees."

When we reach the others, I choke on the overwhelming smell of blood. The metallic tang fills the air, drenching the grass. Bodies lie on the ground, unmoving, but relief hits me when I see our Flight still standing, facing off against the remaining soldiers.

I watch as three of them corner Raven, and my earlier dread is burned away by the fury that takes its place. Wasting no more time, we fly out from the tree line. I head straight for the soldiers trying to box Raven in.

I don't hesitate as I lift my dagger and sink it into the first soldier's throat. It slices through muscle and arteries, spraying my face with warm blood. I pull the blade free, and the man falls, his lifeless eyes stare unseeing toward the stars.

Another soldier swears, whirling when he sees his comrade crumple to the ground. He looks up, and…stares straight at me.

Fuck.

I glance down at my arm, silently cursing myself. The *goiteía* Heron had drawn is no more than a smear of blood, mingling with that of the dead soldier.

The other man advances, raising his sword.

The moonlight reflects off his blade and time seems to slow. I feint right and he follows, and slip under his guard, punching my dagger into his stomach. He lurches back and stumbles, one hand pressed to his stomach to staunch the bleeding as he slumps against the side of the homestead.

The soldier looks up at me, eyes wide with terror. "Please—"

I leap at him, slamming my dagger into his chest. It doesn't go all the way, and I snarl as the blade gets stuck. I throw my weight against the dagger, forcing it through to his heart.

My stomach clenches as the light fades from his eyes. Not from my actions, but from the fact that they don't sicken me. Something deep within my soul writhes in satisfaction at the bloodshed, urging on a need to take vengeance for what I endured.

"Starling!"

The shout cuts above the sounds of clashing steel, wrenching my body around. I roll out of the way as a sword slashes through the space I was in a moment ago. I wrinkle my nose as the new soldier's sword pierces the corpse of his fallen comrade. But I'm on my feet with my next breath, backing up as the man snarls and wrenches his weapon free.

My eyes dart toward the body, my dagger still embedded in the man's chest.

The other soldier follows my line of sight and smirks. "I think I'll take you back to the court, Princess. I may even get a promotion. Maybe my prince will be so grateful he'll let me take a turn with you as well."

"No." The word escapes me on a terrified gasp, and a malicious smile cuts across his face as he steps toward me.

I will not go back there.

The thought has barely finished forming in my mind before I'm reaching for my ring and slipping it off my finger.

I let it fall.

And the world holds its breath.

THIRTY-THREE

"QUICKLY, EL," HALI SAYS, panic sharpening her voice. "We need to get the sail down."

I don't know what I'm doing, but I rush to help her with the boat sail. Her father was a fisherman, so she knows better than I do. I fumble with the ropes, my hands trembling, but finally the sail falls.

A smile tugs at my lips, but the triumph doesn't last long.

"This was a mistake, Aella," The cold voice freezes me in place, and my eyes widen with terror as they land on the man standing at the dock's edge, two cloaked figures hovering behind him.

The Eagle.

"Grab her," he says, "kill the other. There is no room for disloyalty in the Aviary."

Hali whimpers beside me, gripping tightly to my arm.

Fear clutches at my heart, a sharper pain than Hali's fingernails biting into my skin. I shove her back and charge toward the cloaked men before they can board. I slam into one, knocking him into the *other, and we fall to the dock.*

"Go, Hali!" I scream at my friend.

One man grabs me, and I struggle against him as the other stands and makes for the boat.

"I can't," Hali says, snatching an oar and pushing off from the dock. "There's no wind! Please, Notos."

Don't let her die. Please don't let her die.

Something wild rises within me. Something chaotic. Destructive. It's too much—

I scream and the wind screams with me.

The sail snaps open. Too much—too hard—and the boat careens through the water, crashing into a dock on the other side of the canal. It shatters and Hali cries as her body is thrown, the sound cutting off as her head smashes into a wooden post, and she falls into the water.

A sob rips from my throat as her hand disappears beneath the bubbling surface last, as though she's reaching for me—begging me to save her.

A cold grip tightens around my throat.

"Such a shame."

I blink away the remnants of the memory, but my unleashed *theïkós* latches onto the lingering pain.

The moment I'd taken the ring off, it roared to life, rising from that hidden place within the depths of my soul.

The place it had been slumbering.

Suppressed.

Suddenly the world is sharper, the air crisper. And rather than hearing the wind like a whisper, I hear it like a *scream*.

Fear forgotten, I breathe in deep, relishing the way the

air dances through my fingers. I clench my hands into fists and pull—drawing the element toward me—watching with a mixture of horror and fascination as the soldier's eyes go wide. He drops his sword and both hands fly toward his throat as he falls to his knees, his face turning blue as he struggles to draw his next breath.

"Not...possible," the soldier chokes out.

"It shouldn't be," I agree. Because he's right.

The Anemoi had never gifted control of the wind and skies. That power belonged to the gods and mythical beings in bedtime stories. The very idea of anyone else possessing it would be considered blasphemous.

Dangerous.

Cautiously, I step forward, picking his sword up off the ground.

"More...will come," he gasps, "he will..."

I straighten and hold the blade to his neck. My eyes connect with his as they beg me for air.

"Let him try," I say, drawing the blade across his throat.

With a shuddering breath, I turn and walk back a few paces until I spot the ring, nestled amongst the blood-stained grass where I dropped it. I kneel and pick it up, the moonlight shining across the small *goiteía* carved on its inner surface. The ones that kept my *theïkós* hidden for so long

The wind keens—a broken sound— and whips the loose hair around my face.

I ignore it, slipping the ring back on my finger.

My eyes close with relief as the world fades around me. But the relief morphs into dread when I open them again and find

Myna in front of me.

Her face is impassive, but her gaze bores into mine. I hold it without blinking, even though I'm screaming on the inside.

There is no doubt she saw.

"Myna." Her name comes out choked. I have no idea what I'm going to say. Panicked thoughts clamor in my mind, each fighting to take precedence. I clear my throat and start again. "Myna, what you saw—"

"I saw nothing," she says firmly. Her resolute stare has the half-formed explanations dying in my throat.

"Thank you." The words travel from my lips on a sigh as relief rushes through me. A lifetime of keeping this secret, and my efforts almost crumbled away in the blink of an eye. It's not that it would have been strange for me to have *theïkós*, I just shouldn't be able to harness the power of the wind. To many, the idea would be sacrilegious.

My panic may have made me vulnerable, but my fury left me completely exposed. I can't let it happen again. I need to regain control, to tame the maelstrom that rages within me.

"Aella!"

Nyssa runs at me, throwing her arms around my neck. Over her shoulder, Myna frowns. The air stutters out of my lungs when her lips firm, but she shakes her head and turns away.

I pull back from Nyssa, cupping her face as I examine every inch of her. The tension in my shoulders shifts a fraction when I see she's mostly free of blood.

"Are you okay?" I ask anyway, needing to hear the words from her lips.

"Yes. And you?"

"I'm fine." I lean in closer, until my nose brushes the arch of her ear, and whisper, "Don't forget to call me Starling."

Her eyes widen and she nods.

Raven approaches us, the others in tow. They're all painted in gore from head to toe. Lark moves to Nyssa's side, carefully draping an arm across her shoulders and drawing her in. Uncaring or oblivious to the filth that covers him, she nestles in closer.

The remaining tension drains from my body as my eyes track over Raven. Even though blood drips from his skin, none of it appears to be his own. His gaze is cold as it wanders my body, but when his eyes meet mine, the iciness retreats, relief returning some of their usual warmth.

My heart clenches with the need to go to him, to touch him and talk to him, and reassure myself that he is okay. But my muscles lock up, my feet growing roots and making me immobile.

He must see a hint of my internal struggle written on my face, because a small frown creases between his brows before he turns to Lory. "How the fuck did they catch us unaware? If it weren't for Starling waking us, we would all be dead right now."

Lory winces, showing no trace of the typical jokester I've come to know. "I was checking on the weapon to make sure it was still secure. I'm sorry, Commander. They must have been too far out at that point—I didn't hear them approaching."

Raven's jaw clenches before he nods tersely. His eyes flick back to mine, but he doesn't question me. If he was already awake when I went back to wake the Flight, then no doubt he witnessed my nightmares chasing me from the homestead. Gods, the walls are so worn down he could have heard me falling apart outside.

"It's no longer safe to stay here until morning," he says. "The soldiers must have tracked you when you left the court, and we don't know if they've communicated with Keres or not."

"More will come," I say, the soldier's dying words as he struggled for breath flashing through my mind. I clear my throat when all eyes turn to me. "The last soldier I…he said more will come."

A heavy silence falls across the clearing. Even the creatures of the night make no sound, as if they're too fearful to draw our attention.

Quiet and solitude never used to bother me. In fact, I craved it, loving the moments where I could escape the world around me. But now, the silence is suffocating. It gives space to memories I would rather forget, inviting nightmares to fester and wreak havoc on my mind. The skin along my spine starts to itch and pain pulses in my upper thighs.

When Raven finally speaks again, I almost sob with relief.

"Take a moment to get as clean as you can and gather your belongings," he says. "We leave within the hour."

True to his word, Raven has barely allowed us to stop since

we left the homestead behind. We exited the forest earlier this morning. It continues to crawl alongside us, but to the left, rolling hills of rust-colored grass stretch out as far as the eye can see.

Behind the heavy veil of storm clouds shadowing our journey, the sun wanes in the dusky sky, casting an eerie light over the countryside. The air is heavy with the scent of decaying leaves. Each breath I take is accompanied by the taste of damp earth and the lingering tang of impending winter that will never touch these lands.

Exhaustion crawls through every inch of my aching body and my joints are stiff from constantly being in the saddle. I have no doubt everyone is feeling the same bone-deep fatigue as I am, but our Flight has pushed on in resolute silence.

Beneath me, my stolen horse, whom I have decided to call Grace, moves with anything but her namesake. The dappled gray of her coat shimmers in the fading light as her hooves crush fallen leaves like brittle bones, the sound echoing through the stillness of the land. Her inky mane, tangled and wild, dances in a gust of wind, and I close my eyes, relishing the sensation of spectral fingers sliding against my skin.

It's always softer with my ring on. More playful and significantly less chaotic.

Easier to control.

When I open my eyes again, they land on the large tarp-covered crate hitched to two horses that Lory leads along. I've barely been able to tear my attention from it since I watched Lory and Lark drag it from the decrepit barn the night we left the homestead. It's always covered, the tarp tied tightly in place, only the rhythmic clinking of chains coming from within.

The sound has been slowly driving me insane. Each metallic clink sends shivers coursing over my skin. Unable to stand the feeling much longer, I finally give in. "So, what is it?"

"What?" Raven responds from beside me, his eyes fixed ahead, as if he's refusing to glance in my direction.

I shift in my saddle as my heart clenches uncomfortably in my chest. The tension between us has only continued to grow since the first night by the stream, and being constantly surrounded by others has meant we haven't had a chance to clear the air. Not that I'm even sure how we could. Raven made it clear our conversation wasn't over, but the thought of telling him what happened makes me want to be violently ill.

"You know exactly what," I say dryly. "The weapon."

Lark shifts in his saddle on the other side of Raven, and the movement draws my attention. His shoulders are stiff, his mouth set in a firm line. It could very well be from fatigue, or the constant threat of another attack. But I know Lark better than that. He's been acting this way ever since we showed up at the homestead. There isn't much that can dampen his typically blithe demeanor—it's how he copes with everything life throws at him. To be seeing this side of him means he's dealing with something he can't quite comprehend. The way his eyes slide to me before nervously darting away only confirms my suspicions.

"Don't ask questions you don't want the answers to," Raven says shortly.

I bristle at his response, eyes narrowing on his profile. "Don't tell me what I want."

"It's need-to-know, Starling," he says with a weary sigh. "As a Songbird, you don't need to know this."

I stay silent, even as words burn up my throat like acid. I swallow them down and cling to that feeling, to the bitter burn of anger. I let it wash over me until I drown in it, so I can ignore the hurt that tries to bubble to the surface. *That* emotion, I push down. I push it as deep as I possibly can, until it sinks to the deepest recesses of my soul.

His jaw flexes. "Don't be like that."

"Don't be like what, Raven?" My frustration flares. It's been like this from the very beginning. From the first moment Nyssa and I were brought into Lord Malis' study, we've been given the bare minimum. Half-truths and carefully selected pieces of information designed to keep us in line and in the dark. And I get it—we've only recently been made Songbirds. But the understanding doesn't ease my resentment.

"I'm following orders."

"And those orders explicitly say I'm not to know?"

"Yes," Raven growls with frustration, running a hand through his hair. Finally, he tears his gaze away from the horizon and turns to me. "Don't use this as a reason to push me away."

"That's not what I'm doing," I force out.

"What would you call it, then?"

I fix my stare back on the covered crate, flinching as it jolts over a shallow hole in the road, the sound of chinking metal coming from within. "I'm so sick of being left in the dark,

Raven."

"I'm sorry." The words are strained, a mix of resignation and sincerity filling them.

"But there's nothing you can do about it."

His silence is answer enough.

THIRTY-FOUR

By the time night fell, I could barely hold myself upright. My eyelids were drooping, and I had to slap my cheeks to keep them open. It wasn't just our Flight that was exhausted. Our horses strained, their breaths coming in heavy pants and perspiration dotting their necks.

Fortunately, with no sign of pursuit and none of the soldiers who had attacked us getting away, Raven thought it was safe enough to get a few hours rest. We set up a makeshift camp just beyond the tree line of the forest, hidden behind the low-hanging branches.

Despite my sheer exhaustion, sleep evades me.

Or rather, *I* evade *it*.

Every time I close my eyes, unwanted memories rush to the surface. They cling to my conscience like a festering wound, seeping poison into my veins. Sleep has always felt like my enemy. But now it is a tormentor that grants no respite, no solace from the things that haunt me. It's as though the depths of my mind have become a labyrinth of darkness and despair, not unlike the maze in the mountain that lies beneath the Palace of Eretria. Every night has been the same. I give in to the pull of sleep, but as soon as it drags me under, I find myself on yet another journey through the twisted corridors of my subconscious.

The bitterness of bile in my mouth.

A blade slicing deep.

Echoing screams.

Honey-brown eyes brightening to the color of freshly spilled blood.

Fear grips me, its icy tendrils coiling around my heart, squeezing the breath from my lungs. My vision blurs, and I frantically kick the tangle of blankets from my body, digging my nails into my palms until they break the skin.

The cold night air and bite of pain manages to ground me, drawing a line between memory and reality. I force myself to breathe deeply, and after a few painful moments, a steady rhythm returns as the panic bleeds from my body and mind.

The sound of my sleeping Flight presses in around me while I stare sightlessly up at the leafy canopy. Restlessness itches its way through my limbs and my scattered thoughts chase each other until I finally relent, quietly slipping out from my place amidst the slumbering bodies.

The cold eats its way into my skin, spreading goosebumps in its path as I put further distance between myself and the circle of bodyheat the others provided.

My gaze drifts toward the wagon and the shrouded crate

atop it. Myna leans against a nearby tree, looking out toward the road.

I should be relieved to see her alert and keeping watch, but frustration fills me. The incessant restlessness tugs at my being again, like silk sliding beneath my skin, tiny sparks of energy making me shiver. It tries to pull me forward—but Myna is standing in my way.

My steps are light as I stalk deeper into the forest, taking extra care not to step on the dried leaves littering the forest floor as I skirt around the campsite. When I reach the road, I kneel and pick up a small rock. Standing, I throw it as far as I can into the distance, and then slink back to the shadow of the trees.

Myna pulls out two daggers, and prowls toward the sound. When she's far enough away, I dart from the shadows, crouching by the wagon. As I work on the ties, a metallic sound comes from inside and I freeze, waiting for the moment I'm caught out.

For Myna to return and catch me in the act, or for Raven to appear behind me.

Time stretches out, the moment dragging by.

But nothing happens.

I take a steadying breath, palming my dagger, and then, in a single smooth motion, I throw back the heavy sheet covering the crate.

The air seizes in my lungs.

Not a crate.

A cage.

Behind thick iron bars, a man stares back at me.

All I can see of his face are quicksilver eyes lined with thick, dark lashes, currently glaring at me with the fury of a thousand storms. The rest is concealed behind some kind of barbaric leather muzzle. Limp silver hair hangs in clumps past his broad shoulders, in stark contrast to his dark, frowning brows. His clothes appear no better than rags, his shirt shredded, revealing ancient-looking markings on every visible inch of his muscled torso. Even crowded into the cage as he is, I can tell he has to be taller than six feet.

A metal collar and cuffs chained to the bottom of the crate circle his bloodied neck and wrists, carved with *goiteía* that are sickeningly familiar. But it's the leather muzzle covering his face that has my stomach revolting.

My hand lifts and I thoughtlessly graze my fingertips across my mouth. The memory of the suffocating sensation makes me flinch.

He can't breathe.

A muffled growl rumbles from the man's chest, jolting me from my horrified stupor.

"What have they done to you?"

My words are barely a whisper, each one choked like it had to claw its way out of my throat and into reality.

The man cocks his head at that, the movement more animal than tycheroi. It looks like his mouth moves beneath the muzzle, but whatever his reply might be gets trapped behind the thick leather. A growl rumbles in his chest and he shakes his head in frustration.

I stare at the leather, a small seed of fury taking root in my chest. It grows and flourishes, taking over my shock and disgust.

The vile thing encases the whole lower part of his face and is secured by thick straps around the back of his skull—

The hard wood of the bed pressing against my back.

Cold metal at my throat.

Something firm across—

I blink the memory away, panting raggedly, and look down at the dagger in my palm. My eyes flick up to see the man's gaze narrowed in on the blade.

"I don't expect you to trust me," I say, watching as his quicksilver eyes finally drag from the dagger to meet mine. "But there is one thing I could do if you're willing to try."

His shoulders stiffen as I glance pointedly at the muzzle. After what could be seconds, or minutes, or hours, he finally shifts forward, holding his shackled arms close to muffle any sound from the chains. Finally, he kneels before me, and we are face-to-face, only the iron bars separating us.

It's not until my lungs start to scream that I realize I'm holding my breath. I release it on a tenuous exhale, my eyes never leaving his as I slowly reach up, angling my hand between the bars to cradle his leather-lined jaw in my palm. I tilt his head to the side, gaining better access to slip the blade of my dagger beneath the leather. When my blade nicks his temple as it slices through the straps, I hiss softly, but he barely flinches.

His blood spills at the same time the muzzle falls, and I quickly retreat a few steps. My eyes widen as I take him in.

The strange markings disappear beneath a matted beard the same shade as his hair. Full lips set below a strong nose and sharp cheekbones complete the striking image of his face. Based on his appearance alone, I'd guess he's several years older than me. But with our kind, it's hard to tell.

I'm starting to understand why everyone called him a weapon. Despite the *goiteía* collar and shackles binding him, I can sense his power. It runs so deep; it seeps into every part of his being.

He stretches his mouth wide, flashing rows of white teeth and pointed canines that give me pause.

I've never seen sharp teeth on a tycheroi before.

The thought simmers in my mind as I silently watch him work his jaw like it's the first time he's been able to in months. It probably is.

He slumps back, his relief a palpable thing.

"Do you…" I start, but now that he has the ability to talk back, words fail me. A fact he clearly finds amusing when he flashes those strange, sharp teeth in an even sharper smile.

"Lost your song, little bird?" His voice has a low timbre, raspy from disuse.

"What are you?" I don't mean to ask, but the question escapes me anyway.

He gives a low, gravelly chuckle. Like the sound of rolling thunder in the distance, echoing over the open seas.

"Many things and nothing at all," he says, his tone self-deprecating, "but you can call me Xan."

"Xan," I say, testing the sound. Those three simple letters don't seem quite enough to name the man in front of me.

"And what shall I call you, little bird?"

"Starling." The name feels like sandpaper scraping over my

346

tongue. I barely hold back my wince, but I get the impression he sees it anyway.

"Ah," he says, "so it's to be like that, then?"

"I don't know what you mean."

Xan smirks knowingly but offers no reply. Instead, his silvery eyes drop toward the dagger still gripped tightly in my hand. An odd expression flashes across his face too quickly for me to discern. But it makes me nervous enough to slip the blade back into its holster and out of sight.

I'm about to offer him food and water, but as I open my mouth, he speaks first.

"Better go back to sleep, little bird. Your friends won't be too happy if they discover what you've done."

THIRTY-FIVE

MY EYES REMAIN fixed on the covered cage as it's loaded onto the deck of *The Nightingale*. The knowledge of what is hidden and trapped behind the tarp draws my eyes like the needle of a compass pointing toward true north.

If anyone has checked on Xan since we left our campsite, they haven't said a word about his muzzle being removed. I'm not sure if that makes me feel more relieved or anxious.

We arrived in Port Serre at mid-morning to find the coastal town a hive of activity.

Children run across cobblestone paths worn smooth by countless footsteps, the sound of their laughter clashing with the din of saws and hammers. The docks are under construction, crawling with tycheroi as they work tirelessly to build new piers alongside the three older ones.

The storm clouds have finally relinquished their firm hold upon the sky and the freshly oiled planks gleam under the morning sunlight.

Captain Nikolas and his crew were anxiously awaiting the Flight as planned, and if they were confused about the extra passengers, they didn't show it. I was happy to see the charming captain again, but the relief I thought I would have at the sight of the ocean didn't come. Instead, unease grips me, oily tentacles wrapping around my chest and squeezing tight.

When I drew back the tarp and saw those silver eyes staring back at me, it was like pulling back a curtain from my own. And now—with the removal of a veil I wasn't aware had been there in the first place—I can finally see my surroundings with clarity.

I haven't confronted any of the others about my discovery, preferring to keep my knowledge secret. As my great-grand-father said when he built the Aviary, *knowledge is power*. Instead, I've kept a close eye on each of them—watching and waiting—desperate to know who else is aware of what our *weapon* truly is. Obviously, Raven, Lark, and Lory all know, since they were on the team responsible for getting him out of Eretria. Based on Lark's behavior over the past few days, I would guess he's not particularly on board with this mission now either.

They've clearly kept Nyssa in the dark. If she found out, she would have told me straight away.

Guilt gnaws at me with that thought.

Heron has always been a bit of an enigma, so he's much harder to read, but I'm truly hoping Myna isn't aware of what she was searching for this whole time. I grew close to her during our time in Vilea. After the trust we've built, the thought of her hiding this knowledge twists something sharp and painful in my gut.

I exhale harshly as the cage is secured to the mainmast and Lory makes sure the tarp is firmly in place.

"Starling!" Raven shouts, and I tear my gaze away.

He and Nyssa are both waiting for me on the dock, watching me expectantly. The rest of the Flight must have already boarded the ship. The realization spurs me on, a sudden sense of urgency nipping at my heels.

"Sorry," I say when I reach them. "It's surreal to finally be going home."

Nyssa takes my hand and leads me up the gangplank, offering me a smile that doesn't quite reach her eyes. It's a small smile. One made of broken glass and fragile things—as if, despite not knowing what happened, she feels my pain viscerally anyway. We've always had that sort of friendship. The type where if one of us bleeds, the other's blood spills too.

When my boots hit the deck, emotions flood me. Too many for me to possibly sort through, so I swallow them down instead. Two of the crew members slip past us and haul up the plank. Once they've strapped it down securely, one of them looks to the helm and signals with his hand. I follow his line of sight up to the grinning captain who grips the wheel.

"Now that my favorite passengers are on board, let's head home!" he shouts.

The crew cheers in response, and part of me wants to smile with them, but when my eyes once again land on the covered cage, I can only manage to grimace instead.

"Thank the gods this trip won't take long," Nyssa mutters

under her breath.

The ship pushes away from the docks and we both stumble, but a hand lands on my hip to steady me. The heat of Raven's body burns at my back, and I know if it weren't for Nyssa standing right beside me, he'd be demanding answers. I hear his intake of breath as though he's about to speak, and my chest tightens painfully at the sound.

"I'm going to go check in with the captain," I say abruptly, setting off toward the helm before he has a chance to respond.

I throw a surreptitious glance over my shoulder as I climb the steps and see Raven and Nyssa with their heads bent close, exchanging sharp whispers. I grit my teeth but force a smile on my face as Nikolas comes into view.

"Should I be preparing myself for another of your wild rides, Captain?"

The look he throws my way is wicked and my mouth pops open in horror when I realize how my question could be construed. My cheeks heat and I start to backtrack, but he talks over the top of my attempt.

"Sweet Starling, I'm not sure you could ever be prepared enough for a *wild ride* with me."

A strangled laugh escapes me, and I slam a palm over my mouth, my eyes going wide like I'm not sure where the foreign sound could have possibly come from. Nikolas quirks a brow at me, his blue eyes glimmering like the ocean that spreads out before us.

I tear my hand away from my mouth to slap him on the arm instead. "You're appalling."

"I think you missed a vowel there. What you really meant

is *appealing*."

"Only in your dreams, Captain."

"And what wonderful dreams they are," he says wistfully.

I snort a laugh and roll my eyes, leaning against the railing as I watch the crew rush about the ship below as they make the final preparations. "How long will it take us to reach the Sorrows?"

"Didn't want to ask your *commander*?" His tone drips with insinuation. I turn a sharp glare his way, and he offers me a knowing look before his eyes dart toward the front of the ship.

I follow his gaze and see the rest of my companions standing at the prow. Lark tucks Nyssa beneath his arm and they lean against the railing, watching the others have what looks like a rather heated discussion. Raven's arms are crossed over his broad chest, a steely expression in his eyes as he listens to whatever Heron and Myna are arguing about. Like he can sense my attention, those eyes snap toward me, his mouth set in a firm line before he forces his gaze away.

There's a wry twist to my lips as I turn back to Nikolas. "Why would I do that when I have the ship's captain at my disposal?"

"Careful, my lady, or I may be inclined to have you walk the plank." There's a mischievous twinkle in Nikolas' eyes. "But to answer your question, we should arrive as the sun sets."

A companionable silence falls over us. Between it and the light-hearted banter, the tension in my chest shifts, loosening enough to make it easier to breathe. I close my eyes, relishing the feel of the wind tugging at my hair, the salty spray on my skin, and the sun on my face as it steadily grows warmer.

Neither of us speaks for a long time, content to watch the waves slip by as the ship cuts through the water. But when Nikolas does, he repeats words he said to me what now seems like an age ago.

"Tell me, Starling, did you feel the fear of the unknown? The rush of excitement flooding your body? The thrill of triumph?"

He's too perceptive, this captain. He asks the questions with the slightest hint of hesitancy. As though I'm an injured wild animal and he fears his approach may startle me enough to send me running.

I wait for the feeling to hit me. For the muscles in my limbs to bunch up, preparing to take flight; for the dread to wrap its icy fingers around my heart.

But it doesn't come.

I tilt my head as I consider that, and decide to offer an almost-stranger a small shard of my fractured self. The words spill from my mouth as easily as tears from a newborn.

"My fear was so great I don't know if I'm capable of dreaming anymore. Instead of adventure and dreams, I have poison in my blood and nightmares in my soul."

The heavy silence that follows presses in on me and I can sense the intensity of Nikolas' scrutiny burning the side of my face. The weight of his gaze settles upon my chest like a heavy stone, making each breath shallow and labored. A rapid drumbeat starts to echo in my ears, the sound growing louder and more chaotic with each passing moment.

"We don't get to choose the things that happen to us, Starling. Those decisions lie solely in fate," he finally replies, and the weight shatters as quickly as it appeared. "What we do get to choose is how we respond to them. Whether we stay the same or let them change us."

"A captain and a wise man," I say with a bitter chuckle. "Who would have thought?"

My eyes drift back to the covered cage on the deck as his words bury themselves deep within my mind. My gaze doesn't shift until the setting sun burns the sky, and the Sorrows loom on the horizon.

THIRTY-SIX

IT'S A SURREAL FEELING to see the world around you unchanged when you yourself are so completely and irrevocably different.

I perceive the hours passing. I witness the sun rise and fall as each day slips by. Yet everything here seems to have been frozen in a momentary pause, untouched by the relentless passage of time.

The Sorrows are exactly as I remember them. The isles and waterways are still bustling with life under the baking heat of the setting sun while the aroma of grilled octopus and crisp citrus lingers in the air. Whitewashed buildings with blooming bougainvillea spilling over balconies and grape vines crawling up trellis walls. At the center of it all, the Palace of Sorrows is cast in its usual golden glow, light catching and reflecting off the windows of the towers that rise above the other structures. The same white flags emblazoned with golden sea eagles flutter from the tops of the cerulean domes.

A group of Nightwings met us at the docks when we arrived, handling our *cargo* while we headed straight to our debrief with the Eagle.

We make our way through the Aviary halls in silence, avoiding the curious looks from other order members and the awestruck gazes of Fledglings. When we reach Lord Malis' study, he's already waiting for us.

The room is just as I remember it. Shelf-lined walls filled with old books and parchment scrolls, scattered candles casting flickering shadows, and the Eagle sitting at a heavy wooden desk.

"Take a seat," he drawls, and I'm immediately reminded of the last time I was here, receiving this very assignment. My lip curls at the memory as Malis waves his hand at the scattered chairs.

As we each take a seat, he leans forward, steepling his hands in front of him as he casts that dead gaze around the room.

"It appears we have a surplus of Flight members here."

I flinch as my heart cracks a little further. I wrap my fingers around the edge of my seat and squeeze. I will not let *him* see how deep my hurt goes.

"Eagle, the mission was compromised," Raven speaks up, the failure of this mission is clear in the thickness of his voice. He clears his throat before continuing. "We split into two teams as directed: one for extraction and one to remain with Starling once she won the trials. However, after we left with the weapon, it became clear Prince Keres is aware of the Aviary, and the Sorrows was his lead suspect."

The silence that falls over the room in the wake of his words is so complete that I can hear my pulse as it pushes blood through my veins. I stare at the floor, noticing a deep gouge mark on the otherwise smooth floorboards. The grains of wood have splintered and scratched.

"Start from the beginning," the Eagle commands.

Raven recounts the story from the moment we first set off on *The Nightingale*. When he finishes with the group arriving at the homestead, Myna takes over. She tactfully glosses over the details of my capture, providing enough information to hopefully not prompt further questions.

When she ends the report, we collectively hold our breath as the Eagle watches us. When his eyes sharpen on mine, I stare back with a deadened gaze of my own. I burrow deeper into my skin, shielding myself behind layers of tissue, muscle, and bone.

"I expected more of you, Starling," Lord Malis scowls, disdain curling his lip. "Not only were you captured, but by allowing the others to rescue you, it has put the order and the Sorrows at even greater risk. You may as well have sung your confession of guilt."

My jaw clenches, but I say nothing as the Eagle continues. "Despite that, your mission was a success, and the weapon is now in our hands. I will ensure that we use it effectively to keep the Sorrows and our people safe from whatever is to come."

His words set off alarm bells in my head.

My mind flashes back to a clearing in a forest, a crumbling homestead, the unfamiliar weight of a sword in my hand, and a man on his knees as he gasps for air.

More will come.

I know Keres well enough to know he will not rest until he has revenge for our actions. We infiltrated his court, led him astray, and stole from him. He will come for us, just as his soldier claimed with his dying breath.

"Commander, stay behind." The Eagle's voice pulls me from my spiraling thoughts. "The rest of you are dismissed."

My eyes flick toward Raven as I rise from my seat, but he stares stoically ahead. If he perceives my attention, he ignores it.

I follow the others from the room, moving slowly behind them, so I'm the last to leave. When I step into the hall and pull the door closed, the others are already out of sight. Only Nyssa and Lark linger. Both wear matching angry frowns.

"Go on without me, Nyssa," I say to my friend, casting my eyes between her and the door, giving her a meaningful look. "I need to speak with the Eagle."

She hesitates, exchanging a glance with Lark while he continues to frown at me from her side. "I can wait for you."

I shake my head before she even finishes speaking. "I'm not sure how long this will take, but I'll be fine on my own."

After further encouragement, the two of them finally leave. My eyes dart around the hall, searching every nook and shadow. When I'm satisfied there's no one else around, I crouch down by the door and lean in close to the keyhole.

"You retrieved the documents?" the Eagle asks.

"Yes." Raven pauses, the sound of rustling paper filling the silence. "The full procedure is outlined here. Based on what we learned from the last assignment, the power transference is relatively simple. The complications arise if the vessel isn't strong enough."

Their conversation scratches the surface of a memory in the back of my mind. Frowning, I lean in closer.

"I'm not concerned about that," Lord Malis snaps. I hear him take a deep breath and exhale slowly, reining his temper in. "We have everything we need to complete it?"

"Yes, my lord."

"Excellent." A pause. "How is our guest?"

"Certainly not grateful, but he's been inside a cell for well over a year now. It's not much different to where he was already." Raven hesitates before adding, "he was wearing a muzzle when we took him, but on our journey, it was removed."

My heart plummets at his words. I was foolish to believe that Raven wouldn't notice the muzzle. Then again, I hadn't been thinking at all; I'd simply acted.

The clink of glass precedes the sound of liquid being poured.

"You think one of your Flight removed it?" Lord Malis' voice is lethally soft.

"That remains to be seen. If they did, it was probably to give him food or water so he didn't die on the way, but I can investigate it."

"Don't bother. He'll be dead before long. No being can survive without their *theïkós*. Not even *him*."

"Of course."

"Leave the documents here. I'll take them to the Owls in

the morning. Dismissed."

"As you command, Eagle."

I scurry away from the door, darting across the hall on light feet and hiding in the shadows of an alcove. Raven slips into the hallway a moment later, pulling the door closed behind him before making his way down the hall.

I listen as his footsteps fade, until the only sound I hear is the pounding of my heart. I push deeper into the shadows, curling myself into the corner of the alcove, and wait.

It's not long before Lord Malis appears. The satisfied expression on his face makes my teeth grind and my hands ball into fists.

I remain in my hiding spot until his dark silhouette disappears. And then I wait even longer to be sure he has no intention of returning before I slip from the shadows.

I test the handle of the door, but I'm not surprised to find it locked. Kneeling, I slip the lockpick from my holster and angle it into the keyhole. As soon as I hear the satisfying sound of the latch bolt releasing, I'm on my feet and slipping inside.

Smoke curls from extinguished candles, the room lit only by the swiftly fading light shining through the windows.

In the quiet privacy of the room, I allow myself a smirk as I head straight to the desk and the stack of parchment that wasn't there during our debrief. Just as I expected, Lord Malis' arrogance and self-assured belief that no one would dare enter his study without invitation made him careless.

I lift the first page and angle it toward the window. When the lingering light pools on the surface, my heart stops.

The smirk slides from my face and I struggle to draw air

into my lungs.

It's a detailed sketch of two bodies lying side by side, a complicated series of *goiteía* drawn on both. While I can identify the markings for drain, transfer, and absorb, many of the symbols are ones I don't recognize.

But it isn't the *goiteía* that causes my reaction. It's the words written at the top of the page, their inked forms bleeding into he parchment like an ill omen.

An Instructional Guide for Theïkós Transference.

With a shaky hand, I place the parchment back on the desk and sift through the others. My heart climbs further up my throat with each line of text I scan. When I reach the last page, my eyes pause on the jagged handwriting scrawled off to the side.

> *Theïkós transference has proven to be a complex and mostly unsuccessful endeavor. I can only conclude that there are unknown factors which need to be discovered relating to the compatibility between the vessel and the theïkós they receive. In all attempts thus far, the mortality rate has been high, with only one successful case of transference. In all attempts, when the theïkós was completely drawn from the original bearer, the death of the vessel was immediate.*

I stare at the words, my own suppressed magic curling up

inside me.

To steal someone's *theïkós*...the very thought of it is abhorrent. But I know without a doubt that's exactly what Lord Malis is planning to do. Steal Xan's magic and no doubt claim it for his own.

My thoughts flash to the silver-haired man, and I see him as clearly as if he were right before me now, collared and bound behind the bars of a cage. My fingers drift toward the scar at my throat and I wince at the phantom pain that follows. What if this had been my fate? What if Keres had learned my secret somehow and decided he wanted to take it from me? Could I let that very thing happen to another?

As the frantic thoughts chase one another through my mind, I carefully tidy the parchments, ensuring they're left exactly how I found them.

Of one thing, I am certain.

If I want to save him, I need a plan *now*.

THIRTY-SEVEN

MY MIND IS NO less frantic by the time I make it back to my room, a whirlwind of conflicting thoughts and emotions. It feels as if there's a battle raging inside me, a war of ideas and anxieties that leaves me exhausted and confused.

I kick the door closed with the heel of my boot and lean against it with a sigh, closing my eyes while I try to force the chaos within into some semblance of order.

The things I've learned…

My great-grandfather may have valued knowledge above all else—it was why he founded the Aviary in the first place—but some things are best left unknown. The documents I left in Lord Malis' study are such a thing. For a moment, I wonder if I should have just burned them, but when the back of my neck tingles with awareness, the thought fades into the background.

I open my eyes and they immediately land on the dark

figure leaning on the edge of my desk. Soft light from the rising moon spills through the window behind him, casting his features in shadow. Despite it, his gaze is like a brand on my skin. My heart skips a beat before it sets off again at a frantic pace.

"Raven…" My voice trails off as I search for the right words to say. Guilt burrows under my skin and makes itself at home when I cast my mind back over the past weeks. He was right when he said I was pushing him away. Even now, I don't move from where I lean against the door.

But it's not just the guilt pressing down on me that holds me in place—it's the fact that even if I wanted to confide in him about all the things preying on my mind, I can't.

The Aviary will always be his first love.

"We need to talk, Starling." The warm cadence of his voice wraps around me soothingly, but the words make my shoulders stiffen.

"What do we have to talk about?" I ask casually. Restlessness seizes my limbs and I push off from the door. My hands move to take off my cloak, but I hesitate at the clasps, the image of the silver scar at my throat charging to the front of my mind. Cursing softly under my breath, I tear it off and throw it over the armchair in the corner of my room, putting my back to Raven in the process.

"Perhaps about what exactly happened after I left you in that gods-forsaken palace," he growls.

I sit down and unlace my boots, feigning intense concentration on the task. "You know what happened. Myna just spoke about it in the debrief."

"If something else happened to you, I—"

I don't let him finish. The tension that has been growing within me finally reaches breaking point, and I snap. Before I can even take my next breath, I'm standing before him. "You'll what, Raven? You'll ride back there? Take vengeance for me? Stop lying to me and stop lying to yourself."

"Star—"

"Stop calling me that!"

Even in the dim light, I see his bronze skin pale and his eyes go wide. "I just want to be able to help you. I can't stand seeing you like this."

A shattered laugh escapes me, shaking free from the charred depths of my soul. "You can't stand seeing it? I can't stand *being* it." The words are meant to be bitter, but they come out broken instead, my voice cracking over them as tears slip free from my eyes.

"Maybe talking about it will help…"

"What if I told you I don't know?"

"What do you mean?"

"I don't know what happened." My body shakes and my voice trembles as the words pour from the cracks in my heart. "I don't know how long he held me there, chained and collared. How many minutes, hours, days. I don't know what I told him. What truths and secrets passed my lips after he forced that poison down my throat. I don't know if he violated me, or if the fear and poison and pain just twisted my mind so much that it was truly broken by that point. I don't know what was real and what was not. So no, I can't tell you what happened."

He watches in helpless silence as I unlace the ties of my shirt. Slowly laying myself bare for him, even as it flays me alive.

"What I can tell you is how a collar with just the right *goiteía* burns through your flesh to your throat, until it hurts just to breathe. I can tell you which parts of the thigh are the most sensitive to the cut of a blade. I can tell you the thoughts that flash through your mind, just as you think you're about to die. But I don't *want* to tell you that."

My exposed scars glimmer under the silver light of the moon and I watch his throat bob as he takes note of each one. His eyes meet mine, and the anguish I find in them would break my heart all over again if there was anything substantial left of it.

"Then what do you want, Aella?"

His voice is a broken rasp, and I shudder as it caresses all the sharp and shattered parts of me.

"I want to forget. I want to feel *alive*."

He's on me barely seconds after the words leave my lips. Teeth clashing and tongues warring. I pull him closer as his hands grip me hard enough to bruise, and he hauls me up before carrying me to the bed. Raven quickly sheds his clothes and falls upon me. We come together in a collision of eager mouths and violent thrusts.

It's not loving and gentle.

It's desperate and messy and raw.

I want to live in this moment and just *feel*. But despite how much I want to give in and let go, I'm caught in the crossfire of my own thoughts. They hook into my mind like the sharp claws of wild beasts, trying to drag me back into reality.

After we both find release, we fall back to the covers, our breaths frantic and bodies trembling.

I stare up at the draping canopy above me, listening to the cadence of Raven's breathes as they deepen, and a desperate craving engulfs me. A familiar, relentless gnawing sensation deep within makes my mind wander to the small vials of somniseed lost beyond the sea. With a groan, I roll over, bury my face in the soft pillow, and will myself to fall into oblivion.

But when sleep does finally come, it haunts me with dreams of impossible choices and lightning-struck eyes.

Tap, tap, tap.

I groan and roll over, nestling deeper into my sheets and burying my face in my pillow. The movement ignites a series of aches throughout my body, bringing back the memory of Raven last night. My lips start to form a smile, but then the full scope of yesterday's events comes charging to the front of my mind, trampling all others under raging hooves. The almost-smile becomes a grimace as the bitter taste of bile stings the back of my throat.

Pushing up to my elbows, I focus on the other side of my bed. My heart clenching at the sight of it being empty, twisting further when I reach out and run my hand over the sheet, finding them cold to the touch.

Too many emotions to discern rise within me, a furious flood threatening to drag me under.

I drop back down to the mattress and scream into my pillow, muffling the anguished sound, but that doesn't stop it from shredding my throat.

Tap, tap, tap.

My body goes still as the incessant noise that pulled me from sleep sounds again. Sharper, more insistent, pecking at my mind.

I push up with a gasp. "Cinder!"

In a flurry of tangled sheets and limbs, I scramble from the bed. Not even caring about the fact that I'm naked as I launch myself at the window and throw it open.

In a flurry of soot-spotted white wings, my feathered friend flies into the room with a shrill cry. Tears prick my eyes and my vision blurs as I watch him swoop around the room before settling on the desk. I drop to my knees, my heart almost bursting at the familiar sight of him perched on the scratched wooden surface.

"I missed you so much," I breathe, reaching out a hand to stroke his feathers. But instead of feeling their silky texture, I yelp as a sharp pain pierces my fingers. I stare dumbly as blood drips from the puncture of Cinder's sharp beak before looking up at him incredulously. Cinder glares back, his beady black eyes narrowed with accusation.

"Are you mad at me?"

He indignantly ruffles his feathers, causing his sleek body to puff up, and then turns his head away. My jaw drops open in shock, but I promptly close it in case that response only annoys him further. Nursing my stinging hand at my chest, I shuffle closer.

"I'm sorry. I didn't have a choice about leaving."

When he continues to ignore me, I reach up and grab the small jar of dried fish flakes from my desk. Unscrewing the lid, I pour a generous pile in front of him. A peace offering I know my gluttonous little friend won't be able to refuse. I force back a smile as he cocks his head slightly toward it.

"How about this," I say. "From now on, I won't go anywhere without telling you first. Does that sound fair?"

His piercing gaze latches onto my face, like he's genuinely considering my words. After a moment, he lets out a shrill squawk and holds his leg toward me.

My breath hitches at the sight of the small scroll there.

As Cinder launches himself at the pile of fish, I carefully unwind it, smoothing out the parchment. Relief surges through me at the sight of the familiar curling script, and I fight back tears as I trace the quill-strokes.

East gardens. Half past noon.

Kal.

I couldn't wait to see him again, and thankfully I won't have to wait long.

My eyes drift toward the open window. From the angle of the shadows, it's still early morning, and I have at least a few hours before I need to leave.

Just enough time to set my plans in motion.

I rifle through my desk drawer until I find a graver sharp enough, and then grab a small jewelry box from my bookshelf.

Sitting on my bed, I open the box and remove a simple golden ear cuff. I close my eyes and focus on the warm glow within my chest—the soul magic the Anemoi gifted each tycheroi to carve *goiteía*.

The magic my mother gave me.

I've always pictured it like a golden ball of yarn, one that slowly unspools and shrinks the more you use it. With my mind's eye, I reach inside with spectral fingers and grab the end of the thread.

And, for the first time in years, I carve a mark.

THIRTY-EIGHT

DESPITE THE CONCEALING *GOITEíA* charm hanging from my neck, I hover in the dungeon stairwell, clinging to the shadow where the light from the antechamber doesn't quite reach.

In all my years with the order, this is my first time down here. The cells are off limits to Fledglings, and I was sent off to Eretria as soon as I was Named. Even if that weren't the case, I've no doubt I would have avoided coming here for as long as possible.

The dungeons are well below the Aviary; the entrance located just down the hall from the kitchens. It's always bothered me. The idea that someone thought it made sense to build such a desolate place so close to the most heart-warming one.

The atmosphere down here is cold and damp and heavy. Salt from the ocean has slowly seeped into the walls over the years, and I can see some places that have started to crumble and been patched up.

Misery and despair taint the air, and—despite the chatter amongst the Nightwings in the guardroom—an eerie silence presses on my mind.

I take a step down into the room, freezing when the grit on the floor crunches beneath my foot. My eyes drift over the four guards seated at a rickety table and joking amongst themselves as though they have no cares in the realm.

As though they aren't here guarding a man who is about to lose his life.

Disgust curls my lips, and I look past them, gaze landing on the one stoic Nightwing stationed by the heavy wooden door that presumably leads to the cells.

Myna.

I hold in the sigh of relief that wants to break free when she doesn't look my way. Instead, she huffs and shakes her head at the others before pulling a ring of keys from her pocket and slipping one into the door behind her.

Myna mumbles under her breath as she walks through, and a whisper thin sigh escapes me when she leaves the door ajar.

Fighting to keep my body relaxed and placing my feet as carefully as I can manage, I follow her, watching the other guards as I slip through the crack.

My eyes narrow as I take in the gloomy corridor. Empty cells line the walls, their doors hanging wide like the gaping maws of beasts waiting to lure victims in.

The faint snick of the door closing sounds behind me, and I whirl, watching Myna as her dark eyes scan the surrounding space. Even though I know she can't *see* me, I remain motionless, as if my very being is sculpted from marble. The only movement is the frantic pounding of my heart, a trapped bird desperately trying to break free from the cage of my chest.

"You have five seconds to show yourself, Starling," Myna says, her words shattering any lingering hope I had. "One..."

My eyes narrow on her, taking in the dark cloud of curls, the familiar scar that always pales slightly whenever her lips pull into a smile.

"Two..."

Do I...have to kill her?

I cringe away from the thought, shoving it aside as violently as it pushed into my mind.

"Three..."

Perhaps I could think more clearly if she would allow me a mo—

"Four..."

"Oh, stop with the fucking counting," I hiss, reaching up and pulling the necklace over my head. The telltale sensation of cobwebs sliding off my skin confirms I'm visible once more, so I send her a glare she can see this time. "How did you know?"

Myna crosses her arms and cocks a brow at me, entirely unfazed. "On the road to Port Serre, you didn't truly believe it would take me that long to scout the area and return to camp, did you?"

"You saw?"

"Yes."

Instead of the dread I expect to feel at her confirmation, a new feeling takes flight.

The hesitant flutter of something more dangerous.

Hope.

"And you didn't say anything?" I ask, trying to keep my words steady. To not let that tentative feeling creep into the cadence of my voice and betray me.

"Obviously not."

"Why?"

She shrugs, a subtle shift of her shoulders that manages to be both lethal and elegant at once. "Perhaps you're not the only one who is uncomfortable with the Eagle's plans."

"Then help me stop him," I plead, taking a cautious step toward her. "Please, Melantha."

"Oh, we're resorting to true names now," she says dryly, her eyes flashing in the dim light. "So, should I call you Aella? Or address you as Your Highness?"

She knows.

The realization hits me like a wave, cool and shocking, leaving me momentarily breathless. Suddenly, the ground beneath my feet seems less stable, the air around us charged with a new energy. All this time, I'd wrapped myself in a veil of anonymity, believing it shielded me from recognition, from the past I had been cast from. Yet here she stands, seemingly unaffected, casually tossing my true name between us like a weapon that she's decided, for now, to leave sheathed.

"When did you figure it out?" I finally ask, forcing the words past the tightening of my throat.

She laughs bitterly, running her hands through her midnight curls. "There were signs. So many, I feel foolish for not piecing it all together sooner. Your hair color never quite suited you. You handled court life and etiquette better than a Songbird fresh from the nest should have been able to. But then when I saw your *theïkós* and heard Sparrow calling you Aella after the attack, things started falling into place."

Myna falls quiet, and I search for something to say, but her revelation has stolen my ability to speak. Instead, we both stand in silence, eyes locked, each of us warily watching the other, cautiously waiting for the next move in this standoff.

"Does the Eagle have any idea you know?" Myna eventually asks, and I breathe a sigh of relief. It echoes faintly, the sound too foreign in a place like this.

"No," I say slowly, "and I'm *hoping* he won't find out."

Myna curses under her breath and starts pacing, the muscles bunching in her shoulders as she runs a hand through her hair again. When she turns back, I can see the conflict swirling in the dark depths of her eyes, gradually losing the battle to a glimmer of resolve.

"This is dangerous, Aella."

"No, Myna, this is *wrong*," I say firmly, latching onto her uncertainty and ignoring the way my heart lurches at the sound of my name falling from her lips. "You know that just as well as I do. What Lord Malis has planned…I can't stand by and let that happen. And after the time we spent together in Eretria, I don't think you can either."

Myna closes her eyes and draws in a deep breath. When she opens them again, they burn brighter and clearer than before.

"If I allow this—*if I help you*—we are going to do this my way."

A wave of relief washes over me, and I make no effort to conceal my smile.

"I can work with that."

"I was wondering if I might see your face again, little bird."

Xan sits slumped against the damp brick wall. His dirty silver hair brushed roughly to the side, as though he's been running his hand through it repeatedly.

"Is that so?" I ask, keeping my voice low, so it doesn't carry down the corridor.

"It's nice to look at something pretty before you die."

"I'm flattered," I deadpan, before I take a step closer, examining the *goiteía* carved into the iron bars. They're basic markings, mostly to infuse strength into the metal and cause pain to anyone who touches them. It's almost laughable how poorly guarded Xan is—particularly for someone planning deception from within the order.

Just another example of the Eagle's hubris at play.

Xan shifts, drawing my attention, and I take a moment to study him more closely. Fresh blood, weeping from half a dozen large cuts across his chest, stains his ripped shirt.

He averts his face from me, but I can still discern a split above his right eyebrow, blood dripping from it like garish face paint. He still wears the collar and cuffs, but at least no longer burdened by chains now that they think he's secure enough behind these bars.

"What happened to you?" The question is hollow and broken, leaving an acrid taste in my mouth.

His responding laugh is self-deprecating. The sound is like a knife twisting in my chest, tearing through nerves and tissue. "It would be much quicker for me to list all the things that *haven't* happened to me."

I unsheathe my dagger and carefully run my thumb along the flat of the feathered blade. The movement draws his eye, and he zeroes in on my weapon.

"Where did you get that?"

I frown, remembering how he'd appeared interested the first time he'd seen it when I removed his muzzle. At first, I'd thought he was simply interested in a weapon. But maybe it's something more. I shift the dagger slightly, watching the way he tracks it. "I'll trade my song for yours."

"Typical bird," he bites out, slumping back against the wall.

"I haven't survived this world by just giving my secrets away for nothing."

Xan tilts his head and considers me. Slowly, he pulls himself up from the floor and prowls toward the bars.

"And I haven't lived this long by trusting poisonous words that fall from pretty lips."

"Is that what you think this is?" I scoff. "A good-captor-bad-captor routine? I'm not here to spy on you, you daft bastard. I came here to help."

"And why would you want to do that?"

"I just do." I shrug like it's no big deal, forcing my hand not to drift toward my throat as the memory of my own collar burns through my mind.

Xan's quicksilver eyes flicker in the faint light and his lip curls, baring the sharp points of his canines.

I clear my throat and glance away. "So will you let me?"

"Let you what?"

"Help you."

He watches me wordlessly and I stare back. A drop of blood slowly beads at his brow and drips to his cheek, making me wince. Xan opens his mouth to reply, but before he can, a commotion sounds from the hall.

"Watch what you're doing, Nightwing." Lord Malis' icy voice cuts through the distance and wraps around my lungs.

"Apologies, Eagle."

Myna's voice is loud enough to echo in the space, and I take it for the warning it is. With a sharp glance at the caged man, I dart to the neighboring cell, slipping past the open door and crouching in the shadows. I slip the concealing necklace over my head and muffle my frantic breaths in the crook of my elbow, waiting in painful silence as footsteps pause just a short distance away.

"Lyxander," Lord Malis says, his voice dripping with disdain. "How the mighty have *fallen*."

"Amon." The name is a growl that resonates through the hall. The sheer animosity in the sound sends a shiver down my spine, and the fine hairs all over my body rise. "I should have known you were behind this. Pests tend to be quite resilient in the face of death."

The familiarity of their exchange snatches my attention and holds it tightly. They know each other. And they're not simply acquainted. There's an ugly history there, brewing beneath the bitter words and pointed barbs.

"Now, now. You should be thanking me. My Flight did

rescue you, after all."

"Of course," Xan drawls. "I'm so grateful to be taken from one cell to another."

"Well, you won't need to suffer much longer. We both know I'm aware of the reason Keres was holding you prisoner—what he was attempting deep in that mountain of his. I have a team working on the plans now, and very soon that power will be mine."

Xan barks a laugh, a broken, raspy sound that almost shocks a gasp out of me. "You think you'll be able to survive it? It will burn you alive from the inside out. Just like it did to every one of their *vessels*."

"I will succeed where that foolish prince failed."

With that last proclamation, the sound of Malis' footsteps fades into the distance. Still, I hold my breath in the silence that follows.

"What do you want?" Xan spits the words.

"See that he gets food and water, Myna." Raven's voice is like a bucket of ice water pouring over my head. It trickles down my spine, making me shiver. I dig my nails into my arms, the stinging pain barely distracting me from the burning in my lungs.

"I'll have Maria fetch something," Myna says. Her tone bland but unbothered. However, I know she must be teetering on the edge of panic, just like I am.

If Raven finds me here…

I don't allow myself to finish the thought, instead channeling my focus on controlling my breaths as their footsteps echo down the corridor.

I remain in my hiding place, frozen in the shadows, until I hear the door slam in the distance. Even then, I wait longer.

When I'm sure they won't return, I slip from my cell, pulling the pendant from my neck, and peering through the bars of Xan's. He paces back and forth in the cramped space, but abruptly stops, turning furious silver eyes on me.

"Alright, little bird. If you manage to get me out of here, I suppose I can play along with this plan of yours."

The door at the end of the corridor creaks open and I freeze, relaxing slightly when Myna appears.

"Out," she whisper-shouts. "*Now.*"

Knowing my time is well and truly up, I turn to leave, but I hesitate and glance back at Xan, wanting to extend an olive branch. A small offering for us to trust one another.

"The dagger belonged to my mother."

A strange expression crosses his face, but I don't have time to ponder it before Myna drags me from the cells.

I slink through the shadows of Santora, hiding in alleys and slipping past strangers. Even after the past couple of months, the cobbled streets and limestone facades are so familiar to me, this path etched into my memory from the countless times I've walked it.

The pristine white houses and manicured courtyards of the royal isle pass by me in a blur as my feet hurriedly carry me closer to the Palace of Sorrows. I'm not certain of what my standing is now that I have returned from my mission, particularly since I wasn't supposed to return at all. Am I still Princess Aella Sotiría, or was that title stripped once again? I'm sure the Eagle and his Owls are frantically trying to weave a believable tale over the mess this mission has made.

I'd carved myself a new *goiteía* earring when I'd made the concealment charm. But the familiar dark hue now tinting my hair doesn't feel the same as it once did. It doesn't feel like I'm keeping my identity a secret, but more like an attempt to hide from myself.

From everything that has happened.

I shake my head to clear the thoughts as the eastern gate-house comes into view. Crouching down in my usual hiding spot behind the old potted apricot tree, settling in as I wait for the guard to change over.

"What are we doing?" a voice whispers in my ear.

"Fuck!" The curse erupts from me before I can hold it back and I have to duck behind the pot when the guards' heads snap toward the sound.

I click my tongue and Cinder screeches, soaring overhead toward the palace. He'd been waiting for me in my room when I returned from the cells, and I was grateful to have him watching my back.

Even if he was doing a terrible job of it.

With my heart pounding in my chest, I carefully peer through the branches, sighing with relief as both the guards relax at the sight of the hawk.

Narrowing my eyes, I turn a glare on my shadow. A twinkling hazel gaze peers back at me.

"What are you doing, Nyssa?" I hiss.

"Following you, obviously." She shrugs casually and then looks at me expectantly.

I bite down hard on my lip to hold back the torrent of expletives that threaten to unleash. Closing my eyes, I breathe in deep. I only open them again when my heart is finally beating at a normal pace. "You scared the absolute shit out of me."

"I know," she says with a grin. "But back to my original question. Are we sneaking into the palace?"

"*I* am sneaking into the palace. *You* are going to turn around and head back to the Aviary."

A contemplative look crosses her face, and for a moment, I think she's going to listen to me. Clearly, I don't know my friend at all.

She shakes her head, sending her chestnut curls bouncing. "I think I'll tag along."

"You can't come with me, Nyssa. If you're caught, you'll end up chained to a wall in a cell."

I flinch at my own words, bracing myself for the memories to break free from the box I locked them in, but Nyssa's next words shock me enough to hold them at bay.

"Sounds erotic."

I huff out an irritated breath and rub the bridge of my nose. She watches me closely. Her eyes are still sparkling, but concern and resolve shadows them.

"Fine. Stay close."

When I peer through the tree again, the guard has changed. The previous pair replaced by the one wearing the cerulean himation and royal insignia, the same as the last time I snuck in.

"Let's go." The words have barely left my lips before I'm heading toward the gate, Nyssa shadowing my every move. I nod to the guard and slip through the gatehouse, barely sparing a glance at the palace before me, but I hear her suck in a breath at the sight. I carve my way across the paved pathways and through the sculptured gardens, picking up the pace as I draw closer to the green sculpture of King Cadmus.

My heart skips a beat and my steps stall when a figure moves out of the shadows. The sight of his rich brown curls and ochre eyes is like coming home. I would know them anywhere. I know them better than my own reflection.

"El," Kal's voice cracks with relief and the sound forces my feet to move once again. I launch myself at him and he catches me easily, pulling me into a hug tight enough to crack my ribs.

I'm not sure how long we stand in that embrace, but eventually a throat clears behind us. I push away, turning back to Nyssa.

"Are you going to introduce us, or…" her words trail off and she arches a brow at me.

"Nyssa, this is my brother, Kal." I gesture between them. "Kal, this is my friend, Nyssa."

I watch with confused amusement as Nyssa drops into a mock curtsy. "A pleasure to meet you, Prince."

Kal glares stonily back at her. "You're one of them?"

"You'll have to be more specific," she says with a coy smile, "one of what, exactly?"

"A Songbird." He spits the word.

"Kal, did you miss the part where I said she's a *friend*?" I step between the two of them, holding my hands up and hoping to defuse some of the hostility. "And Nyssa, play nice."

"I can't believe you're back. Things are bad, El." Kal says the words so quietly, I almost think he didn't mean to say them at all. When I look up, I see his tormented eyes, shadows dancing in their depths, turning them almost black. "Eretria has sent a demand."

His words freeze me, ice crawling through my veins, coating my lungs until it's hard to breathe. I know what he means. Of course I know. Keres is too proud, too arrogant, too cruel to let our actions go unanswered.

I force myself to ask anyway. "What do you mean?"

"They have made a demand for the return of their property," he hesitates before adding, "along with the prince's future bride."

The edges of my vision blur as panicked thoughts threaten to swallow me whole, my breaths coming faster with each passing second. The world around me shifts out of focus, and I—

"Breathe," Kal whispers, his voice slicing through the fog of panic clouding in my mind. I draw in a sharp breath, my focus returning with sharp clarity as I meet the concerned gazes of the two people before me. "You can talk to us. You don't have to shoulder this alone," he urges softly.

As I glance between the two of them—the two people I trust and love more than life itself—a sense of calm washes over me, dispelling the panic within.

And so, I do.
I tell them everything.
And then we plan.

THIRTY-NINE

"I MAY NOT BE able to see you, but I can feel the tension rolling off of you."

I huff out a breath as I follow Myna down the curving steps to the Aviary's dungeon, wrinkling my nose once again at the smell of copper and damp earth.

"Just stick to the plan," she whispers, adjusting the tray of food she carries as we round the last corner and step into the antechamber.

I almost groan when one of the Nightwings perk up at the sight of Myna. An antagonistic smile twists his lips—Cardinal, I think his name is—as he leans back in his chair, balancing it precariously on the two back legs while he throws a dagger in the air and catches it again.

"What are you doing here, Myna?" he sneers, and the other three guards at the table chuckle quietly beside him.

"I just left the kitchen and Maria asked me to bring this

down." She eyes the bowl of slop and stale lump of bread on the tray that looks nothing like the homely meals Mimi usually prepares. "I assume it's for the prisoner."

He plants the chair firmly back on all four legs and eyes the tray. With a dismissive grunt, he pulls the ring of keys from his pocket and tosses them at Myna. She barely manages to catch them before they land in the bowl of gruel. "You take it. I don't feel like dealing with the scum today."

Myna's jaw tenses, her eyes narrowing on Cardinal. But she ignores him, turning on her heel and heading to the heavy wooden door that leads to the cells. She balances the tray in one hand and unlocks the door with the other, and—after a brief glance in my general direction—she slips through, pulling the door firmly shut behind her.

I exhale—a low, shuddering breath—and steel myself. Because this next part of the plan depends solely on me.

And I cannot fuck it up.

Clenching my jaw in anticipation, I reach down and slip my ring from my finger. The ever-present *theïkós* slumbering under my skin surges the moment the metal slides free, and I thank the Anemoi that the air in here is thin and stagnant.

Still, my vision sharpens, the bitter tang of salt and mildew stings the back of my throat, and the temperature seems to drop even further. I wrangle my writhing *theïkós* under control and cast my mind back to the night in the clearing.

To the fear.

The fury.

The sluggish air starts to tangle around my fingers, and I coax it forward, gritting my teeth as I struggle to maintain my tentative hold on control. Slowly, I feel it move toward me, gradually picking up pace as I draw it further from the guards at the table.

"Did any of you feel that?" Cardinal asks, his voice tinged with uncertainty. He begins peering around the dimly lit chamber, his frown deepening, causing the brows above his keen eyes to pinch tightly together. The atmosphere in the room shifts, becoming charged with a sense of unease.

The question hangs in the air, unanswered, as his voice trails off into a tense silence. The other Nightwings pause their murmured conversation, glancing around the room, their expressions morphing into ones of curiosity mingled with concern.

Cardinal starts to rise from his seat, and my heart rate spikes. My *theïkós* responds to the panic instantly, pulling the air from the space around them so suddenly, they collectively gasp. As one, the four of them stagger, clutching at their throats as their eyes go wide.

It doesn't take long for the lack of air to take its toll. One by one, they collapse to the cold stone floor of the chamber, their bodies limp and unconscious.

Seizing the moment of quiet that follows, I slam the ring back on my finger, blinking at the sudden haze that drops over my vision.

Wasting no time, I dart to Cardinal's side and kneel next to his still body. Holding my hand over his mouth, I exhale sharply when I feel the faint whisper of breath against my skin. I quickly check the others, confirming they're all still breathing before I follow Myna through to the cells and head down the narrow corridor.

When I reach Xan's cell, I find Myna—the ring of keys hanging from her hand while she still holds the tray with the other—watching him with narrowed eyes. The man himself simply sits on the ground, head tilted back, and eyes closed. I pull the concealing pendant over my head, shivering as the magic falls away, just as Xan opens his eyes.

"Have you come to talk my ear off again? I think it might be more painful than the visits from your boy, Raven." He spits the name like it's poison on his tongue.

"Raven is not my anything." My heart splinters as I say the words, and I ignore the way Myna's eyes dart in my direction. "Besides, I'm not here to talk your ear off—kind of rude, by the way—I'm here to break you out."

"And how do you plan on doing that? If you hadn't noticed, I'm currently dripping in metal and locked behind bars." He lifts his wrists, displaying the cuffs still wrapped around his wrists.

Fortunately, they still haven't chained him to the wall.

"If you're going to be so pig-headed about it, maybe I should leave you here to rot," I say, glaring at him through the bars before I gesture toward the keys in Myna's hand. "If *you* hadn't noticed, we have the solution to your little problem."

Xan quirks an unimpressed eyebrow and regards us both skeptically.

"As fascinating as this all is," Myna says dryly, "must I really remind you both we're on a time limit here."

"Right." I take a steadying breath. "First things first—let's get you out of this cell and off these isles."

I hold out my hand and Myna wordlessly passes me the key for the cell. I step forward and push it into the lock, turning it with a resounding click. A pained hiss passes through my clenched teeth as I grab a *goiteía*-engraved bar to pull the gate open. From the corner of my eye, Xan lunges forward and my stomach drops.

Fuck.

I've made a mistake. Raven and Lord Malis both called him a weapon. A few brief conversations don't make someone less of a stranger, so I really have no idea how dangerous he is.

Xan snatches my wrist and pulls it away from the bar. His jaw clenches as he examines the patches of inflamed skin on my palm.

"You should have let me open it."

I roll my eyes and pull my arm away, feigning casualness as I struggle to breathe through the panic that has my heart racing and my magic roiling under my skin. "Save the chivalry for someone who needs it."

He laughs, a low and raw sound, more broken than amused. "Continue with your daring rescue, then, little bird."

The sound of pottery cracking pulls my attention from him, and I turn to Myna, eyes wide as she looks up expectantly from where she's dropped the tray. Broken bits of pottery and gruel splattered across the stone.

"You'll need to take me out too."

"I…" My heart pounds painfully against the cage of my ribs. The thought of harming her after everything she has done. The *risks* she has taken—

"May I?" Xan asks, brushing past me. I jolt from the contact, the thoughts eddying from my mind.

Myna goes still, a lethal glimmer lighting her eyes as they track him. He pauses in front of her, and I hold my breath as he seems to wait for her permission. Those dark eyes flick to me, a warning swirling in their depths before she inclines her head.

Xan extends a large, calloused hand, his fingers digging into the flesh when her neck slopes toward her shoulder. Myna inhales sharply, a sudden gasp escaping her lips, her eyes rolling back into her head as she succumbs to the pressure.

I rush forward, my arms outstretched, catching her just in time to ease her limp body to the ground. Rising from my crouched stance, I turn to face the man looming behind me. But with the gap between us bridged, my eyes catch on the finer details of torment that had eluded my earlier observation—the deep, ominous shadows beneath his eyes, the way he favors his left side, and the numerous scars that speak of suffering and resilience—and any frustration I felt withers away.

"Here," I say, passing him the pendant still clutched in my hand. "Put this on. It will conceal you from sight. Stay right behind me."

I wait for him to slip necklace over his head, blinking as the magic takes effect and his form fades from sight, and then lead him down the narrow corridor until we reach the guard room. When I see four Nightwings still passed out cold, I breathe a sigh of relief.

"Your handiwork?" Xan asks, and I shiver as his breath skitters across the shell of my ear.

"They're alive. But you'll hopefully be long gone before they come to."

I head up the stairs and—even though I can't see him, his feet as silent as mine on the rough stone—I can feel Xan's presence scorching my back. When we round the last bend and the door comes into view, I hold up my hand to get him to wait.

I open the door a fraction and peek out into the hallway, holding my breath as I scan the darkened corners where the light from the lamps doesn't quite reach. Satisfied that no one is lurking just out of sight, I dart down the hall.

As we near the kitchen door, I reach for the handle, but the sound of Raven's deep voice on the other side has my blood turning to ice in my veins.

"Fuck."

I spin and blindly grab what I think is the front of Xan's shirt, tearing it some more in the process as I drag him into a nearby supply closet, closing the door soundlessly and enveloping us in darkness. With his massive frame, the space is barely big enough for the two of us. Our bodies brush with each rapid inhale I take, and I inch away, pressing my back to the wooden shelves.

The warmth of Xan's breath tickles my ear again as he whispers, "How's the plan going so far?"

I scowl even though it's too dark for him to see, choosing not to respond. Pressing my ear to the wood of the door, I bite my lip when I hear a muffled shout and the pounding of running footsteps.

"Shit!" I hiss in frustration, running my fingers roughly

through my hair. "We left the door open."

"Then we should probably make a run for it."

"Stay close."

We abandon our hiding spot and rush back out to the hall. The door down to the dungeon is wide open, and I silently curse myself for being so careless.

I pause to listen at the kitchen door, knowing another wrong move could mean death for us both. When nothing but silence permeates the wood, I push through.

"Cursed Anemoi!" Maria shouts, her hand flying to her chest. "When will all you miscreants learn my kitchen is not a thoroughfare?"

"Sorry, Mimi." I flash her a smile, feigning a casualness I do not feel with the invisible presence hovering at my back and the threat of Raven's imminent discovery. "Ny—*Sparrow* said she left some things down here for me."

Maria grumbles some more under her breath, but waves a hand toward the door. I rush over when I spot the heavy bag leaning against the wall, hoisting it up as I pull open the door. I hold it open long enough until I'm sure Xan has slipped through and then call over my shoulder, "I'll see you for dinner."

Ignoring the way my heart beats in my throat, I step through the door, pulling it closed behind me as I scan the silent alley.

"Xan?" I whisper, worrying my bottom lip.

If he's left…

"Don't worry, little bird." His voice is a rough whisper at my side. "I said I'd play along."

"I wasn't *worried*." I lie. "Now let's get out of here."

I stalk through darkened alleyways, steering clear of popular paths in favor of lesser-traveled roads and bridges. By the time we make it onto Maricious, we haven't crossed paths with anyone, but I know this will be the hardest part.

As expected, the streets are crowded, tycheroi from all over the Sorrows drawn in by the seduction and revelry of what the isle has to offer. And all of them stand between us and our destination.

The Muse.

"Still with me, Chivalry?"

"Yes," Xan's disembodied voice growls.

"Good." I smirk, pointing to where The Muse stands at the end of the street, just as a chorus of boisterous laughs sounds from the group of tycheroi lining up by the doors. "We need to go there."

"This seems like one of the weaker parts of this plan."

"It's working out fine so far." I snark back.

"Debatable."

I roll my eyes, rise from my crouch, and set off at a casual pace, keeping my posture loose and plastering a smile on my face as we get closer. Just another person in search of a good time. But as we near the end of the lineup, a shadow darts from a side alley, snatching my arm and dragging me into the darkness.

My body reacts without thought. Heart pounding in my chest, I twist free from the hold and lunge at my shadowy assailant.

But Xan beats me to it.

With a rabid growl, the man is slammed into the wall—an invisible force pinning him against the stone. It's only then that the light hits the man's face, and the tension rushes out of me with a rough exhale.

"Kash, what in Notos' name are you doing?" I hiss, moving toward where Xan still has the promiscuous nymphai restrained.

"Darling," Kash drawls, although his voice is somewhat strained. "Care to put an end to…whatever the fuck is going on right now?"

A flicker of amusement flits through me and I make a show of considering his words, crossing my arms, and tapping a finger on my chin before relenting. "It's okay, Xan. He's a friend."

Xan must hesitate, because Kash remains pinned to the wall a heartbeat longer. But he visibly relaxes a moment later, straightening as his hand rubs at his throat, eyes darting around the empty space surrounding us. When his search comes up empty, his aqua gaze lands on me, sparkling with amusement. "I normally charge a small fortune for that kind of action."

"Add it to my tab," I say with a roll of my eyes.

"If only you actually had one," Kash sighs dramatically before his expression sobers. "Lark is here. I'm going to take you around the back."

I nod and follow him down the alley, arching a brow over my shoulder when the back of my neck prickles with awareness I assume is from the palpable tension rolling off Xan in waves.

We reach the back of the building just as Calliope slips through the door, a bundle of clothing in her arms. Like Kash did a moment ago, she scans the alley before turning back to me with a questioning look.

"Pendant," I say, holding out my hand in silent command.

The charmed necklace lands in my palm a moment later, and Xan reappears. In the darkness, his silver eyes shine like they're reflecting the light of the moon. His hair shimmers softly despite the buildup of dirt, and I thank the gods its full shine must be dimmed by its currently unkempt state.

"Can you control that?" I ask.

"Control what?" Confusion lines his hushed response.

I frown and wave my hand at him while my mind tries to puzzle it out. Can someone's magic truly be so powerful it's visible on the outside? Even when bound with a nulling collar?

"You're glowing."

He glances down at his hands, and we both watch as his shine dims. His gaze flicks back up to mine, but they no longer glow like they did a moment ago. "Better?"

I shrug, and he turns a narrowed gaze toward the others. Calliope passes the bundle of clothing in her arms to Xan after an assessing look. Without hesitation, he begins to strip out of his torn clothes.

I quickly avert my eyes, facing Calliope as she takes my hands in hers.

"It's best you don't waste any more time. Your chances are better if you head straight for the dock now. Kash will take you to where a friend of mine is waiting nearby. He'll be able to get you safely to the ship."

There's a strange distance to the tone of her voice that sets me on edge. "Have you seen something?"

"Many paths spread out before you, but I'm not sure which one you will follow. Even if I was, it's best not to interfere with what fate has planned."

I bite my lip and give her a quick nod. As much as her words unsettle me, my options are limited. I need to finish what I've started.

"Thank you, Calliope. I'll come see you soon."

"Good luck, my sweet anemone." She gives my hands one last squeeze, a small smile on her face. "May fate favor you."

The ferry Kash led us to drops us off at a lonely dock on the southernmost isle, Isola. The streets here are deathly silent; only the sound of the ocean permeates the air. The buildings are all asleep, their windows dark, the only light coming from the waning moon and flickering stars above.

A single vessel looms in the water, tethered to one of the dock posts and silhouetted against the slowly lightening sky. The ship isn't as big as *The Nightingale*, and I can't make out a name scribed on its hull. Most likely, it belongs to a privateer and not a merchant. Since they're here to assist in my rescue mission, that makes the most sense.

I watch as the crew works, barely making a sound to break the isle's silence. Like a choreographed dance, the tycheroi on board move in perfect harmony with one another. Their actions are so rehearsed and well-known they have no need for commands.

With a sigh that feels as though it comes from the depths of my soul, I finally turn from the ship and force myself to peer up at Xan. He's already watching me, silver eyes luminous in the moonlight.

"I suppose this is goodbye," I say with a small smile, ignoring the way my throat tightens at the thought. There is no rational reason I should feel anything other than relief at helping him escape the fate the Aviary had planned for him. Regardless, something close to jealousy sours my success.

"I don't suppose you'll finally tell me your name," Xan says, "or am I to forever say a little bird saved me?"

His words shock a laugh out of me.

"Ae—" I clear my throat, suddenly nervous. "It's Aella."

The same expression I saw the other day flickers across Xan's face before his features clear. "Thank you, Aella."

"You don't need to thank me. It was the right thing to do—the *only* thing to do."

"I don't think I'd have survived another day without you."

His words have a small blush of pride rising to my cheeks and, despite the dim light, I glance down to hide it. I sense Xan watching me, his eyes intense, as though he can see my thoughts as clearly as if they were a play taking place on stage. He takes a step closer, our bodies almost touching, and places a hand on my shoulder. I freeze as his thumb glides up the side of my throat until it hits my jaw and tilts my face up to his.

At his touch, a strange sensation pulses through me, like silk sliding beneath my skin. A thousand tiny bolts of lightning striking my nerve endings.

"And I truly am sorry."

I frown, confusion and concern sparking in my mind. I open my mouth to ask what he could possibly be sorry for, but a sharp pinch at the base of my neck snatches the words away along with my breath.

The edges of my vision darken, and I fight with every ounce of my strength to hold on to consciousness.

It's a losing battle.

I feel the vague sensation of being caught as my body goes limp, of words whispered in my ear.

The shadows close in, darkness embracing me like a long-lost lover, and those last words follow me into oblivion.

"You'll forgive me one day."

ENTHRALLED BY THE EMPYRIEOS?

AELLA'S STORY WILL CONTINUE IN 2025.

ACKNOWLEDGEMENTS

To be perfectly honest, I'm not entirely sure where to begin with these acknowledgements. This book would not have happened without the encouragement from a constellation of people whose support has been unwavering. My everlasting gratitude goes to:

My partner, Terence, for being the calm during the storm. For putting up with the late nights, the one-sided conversations, the endless sound of my typing, and for not binging the TV shows we agreed to watch together until I had the time.

Thank you to my sister, Shaynee, and my brother, Sheldon, for believing in me from the very beginning. To my parents, Kim, and Hermann, who taught me I can achieve anything if I set my mind to it. And to *all* of my family who have supported my dreams, no matter how unconventional they may seem. You have made writing and publishing this book possible.

To my editing team, Claire Bradshaw, Emma Hatton, and Rae Moody. Without the three of you, *Songbird of the Sorrows* would not have become the book it is now. Thank you all for your advice, your gentle guidance (excluding you, Rae), and your overall enthusiasm for this story.

To my incredible illustrator and cover designer, Catrina Barquist – I am so glad I found you. Deciding on a cover for my book was harder than writing the book itself, and the months before I stumbled across your art were stressful, to say the least. I cannot express my gratitude to you enough.

Thank you to my map illustrator, Virginia Allyn. I always knew it would be you. I would have waited an age to have you draw the map of the Empyrieos, and I am so grateful you made the time for me.

Thank you to Char, Jacqui, Jenna, Sarah, and Tayah for being brave enough to be to step into the world I created. To Cara, Jaz, Jess, and Mali for the constant support and endless encouragement. And to all of my street team, who have been a driving force behind spreading the word about this book.

Finally—because you're my reason for doing this—thank *you*, dear reader. Thank you for taking a chance on the unknown. Thank you for joining Aella on her journey. Thank you for sticking with her until the last pages. I cannot thank you enough.

Braidee Otto is an adult romantic fantasy author,
with her debut novel, *Songbird of the Sorrows*,
releasing in 2024.

As a self-described hopeless romantic, her writing style paints
vivid imagery, bringing to life lush landscapes, complex char-
acters, and intricate relationships to immerse readers in a
world where love, loss,
and redemption intertwine.

Braidee lives in Adelaide, South Australia, with her partner
and two dogs, and works full-time in the
events and arts industries. It has been her lifelong dream to
become a published author, and she's nothing
if not a dreamer.

To learn more about Braidee Otto's upcoming books or get in touch, visit www.braideeotto.com or scan the QR code below: